BROOMHANDLE

BROOMHANDLE

Hal Barwood

Casting a Spell on Drones
a paranormal adventure

Broomhandle

Copyright © 2014 Hal Barwood
All Rights Reserved
A Finite Arts Book
Published by Finite Arts LLC, Portland, Oregon
version 2.2

ISBN 978-0-9911566-3-4

This is a work of fiction. The California foothills, France, Pakistan, the U.S. Armed Forces, drones, spies, and people claiming to possess supernatural powers are real enough, but the political communities, government organizations, businesses, locations, and other settings depicted herein are either fictional in themselves or fictional in detail. All the characters in this fictional world are products of the author's imagination. No resemblance to any real person is intended.

Acknowledgements . . .

Many thanks to everyone who grappled with early versions of this story and offered suggestions and encouragement; especially Barbara Barwood, Jonathan Barwood, Tobias Barwood, Bob Bates, Betsy Blanchard, Curt Blanchard, Robert Dalva, Beverly Graves, Janet Robbins, Matthew Robbins, and Gordon Walton.

Thanks again to Officer Andy Litzius and Sergeant Dan Maciel of the Placerville Police Department for showing the author their city the way real cops view it.

And thanks as well to Google, Wikipedia, other World Wide Web sites too numerous to name, and radio station KQCB-FM for greatly enlarging the author's knowledge of the real world.

About the Author . . .

Hal Barwood is a veteran writer with multiple credits in multiple media. Find out more here . . .

www.finitearts.com

for

Jonathan & Tobias

boys and men

Table of Contents

Part ONE

1

"MARIANNE . . . are you a witch?"

"No, you moron, I am not."

Marianne Sarzeau, a Placerville, California, police officer for almost a year now, was sitting in her patrol vehicle backed into a steep driveway on Esparza Way, a fancy residential neighborhood clinging to the hillsides above the city's business district. Down below, bright lights traced the narrow valley confining Main Street and U.S. Route 50. On the heights, late on a spring evening, it was already dark.

"The rumors are out there. Magic powers, spells, carrying on with ghosts and such. True?"

"Jesus, Dez, I am not a witch. Got it? Just a cop, like you."

Marianne's questioner was Desmond Otis, another Placerville police officer. He was parked beside her, facing the opposite direction, bringing their driver's side windows together. He was thirty or so, a year older than Marianne. He had been on the force a year longer too, and he wasn't above using his superior position to needle her. She accepted his casual abuse in good humor, but this accusation was something new.

"Did you bring me some food? I can't quite conjure it up, in case you're wondering," she said.

He handed over a Subway chicken sandwich on Honey Oat bread and a Sierra Mist. "Here you go. Well? What have you got to say for yourself?"

"Just this — I've been camped here for two hours, and you're the only soul I've seen. This string of burglaries, this stakeout, Christ, we're wasting our time." She unwrapped her sandwich and took a bite. "As usual."

"The witch business? You're dodging me." He tapped her side mirror and lifted an eyebrow.

Marianne looked into his dark face, darker under the trees shielding them from view of the street. Otis was Placerville's only black officer. Still, even with his features shrouded, she thought she detected a twinkle in his eye and a sly smile.

"You sound like you swallowed the canary. What have you heard?"

"Yesterday I was out on a call to the Springs. Construction site, that new apartment complex? Shed broken open, lot of expensive tools gone. Well, one of the boys on the job there is also a policeman down in Applefield."

Marianne sipped her Sierra Mist and nodded. "Ricky Moss."

"That's the man. You know him?"

"Of course. Tri-Town. We served together for a year."

"Unh-huh. We got to talking about you."

"I'll bet you did."

"And he told me the story. A ghost, a dead cop, cheating the lottery, calling on the spirits to help you de-duce the perps and all."

"What a crock. Did he bother to mention what a terrible shot I am?"

"Yeah, that too. And your made-up name."

"Wait till the next time I see Rick."

Otis grinned. "He said you'd be mad as hell if I brought this up."

"Some people just can't stop the gossip. Okay, big guy, here's the deal. I like your ride, and I hate mine."

Otis was driving one of the department's new Ford Taurus Police Interceptors, while she was stuck with a tired Dodge Charger on its second engine and third set of brakes.

"I'll tell you my life story if you trade cars."

Otis chuckled and bit into his Meatball Marinara special. "Dream on, babe." He grew serious. "But you probably ought to get straight with the lieutenant." He let a meaningful pause hang in the air. "Unless you want me to do it?"

"Hey, Dez? How long did it take you to pick up a clue? There's a reason Kazmarek runs the operation and you don't — she asked me the same questions a year ago. And I told her the truth, laid it all out. She's up-to-date and, guess what? She does not give a damn."

"So, fill me in too. The truth. Your partner is all ears."

Marianne took a big swig of her drink, wiped her mouth, and stared out through her windshield into the deepening gloom.

"Okay, for what it's worth . . . why not? Maybe Rick told you how our boss got killed? Hector Ibañez, what a guy. Turns out he was my ghost, a weird type that only appears in mirrors and travels through time. The spook books call that a 'virtual visitor.' So he came back, pointed me at some clues I never would have found, handed me some winning lottery numbers — just the Fantasy Five, you understand, I'm no millionaire — and that's about it.

"My father changed his name on account of being embarrassed by *his* father, who was some kind of voodoo creep down in Louisiana, and I decided to change it back." She gave Otis a fierce look. "Satisfied?"

"This runs in the family?"

"Apparently so."

"Does your old man see ghosts?"

"I have no idea. I haven't seen him in fifteen years. He's a sergeant in the Army."

"They say you shot a cop."

"Well, I shot *at* one. A cop on the take. He hit his head on a tree branch, fell into Upper Bar Lake, and drowned. That unraveled a big drug operation — a cartel trying to move into the foothills here."

"No shit. Scout's honor, cross your heart?"

"I'm no scout, but yeah, that's the whole tomato and nothing but."

"No broomstick, no spells, no funky hat?"

"Sorry. No black cats either."

"All right, if you say so. Still see this ghost?"

"Not for months."

"Hmm. Can you call him for me? I'd like to have a look."

"No you wouldn't. Believe me, it's no fun."

Otis studied his young colleague. Not too tall, not too small. All of five-seven, maybe, in her cop shoes, cute on the plump side, friendly when she wanted to be, and, he judged, a tad sharper than your average twenty-something. But . . .

"You are one strange bird, lady."

Marianne was about to defend her reputation, but just then she got a glimpse of a figure hiking up the street toward their position. He was tall and lanky, dressed in black running gear, and he walked with the ease of an athlete. She punched Otis on the arm.

"Shut up, Dez. We've got company."

Otis cranked his head around to take in the scene. The two cops watched the man approach, then pause at a high concrete retaining wall. After a quick inspection, he leaped onto the wall and scrambled up, as swiftly and easily as a gecko. He rolled over the top and continued on into someone's back yard.

"Whoa. Did you see that?"

Marianne squeezed herself past her police laptop and riot gun, threw open her passenger door, and stumbled onto the pavement.

"Wait here!"

She took off up the street, around a bend, running to negate the advantage of the climber's shortcut. A block up the hill she was puffing and panting. Her quarry was nowhere in sight. She ran up another switchback, stopped for another look. Still no one. In another block she was on top of the hill. She loped along the crest, searching for the climber.

There! Down there, on a lot below, there he was, moving silently and stealthily toward a palatial McMansion. She started into the bushes above, trying to figure out a good way to descend, and wound up behind a high chain link fence separating the upper and lower properties.

Damn!

She struggled to lift herself over the barrier, then stopped to watch as the climber found a purchase on the McMansion's rough stucco exterior and climbed effortlessly to the second floor, where he pushed open an unlocked window and slipped inside.

"Holy crap!" she said aloud.

Her police attire, especially her shoes, did not encourage an ascent over the fence. Instead she worked her way to the corner of the lot and followed the fence line down the hill. Her traversal was filled with trees and underbrush, and she had to duck and weave to make any progress. Then she came to a precipice where the land abruptly fell away below her. A small rocky cliff, too high to jump down. Muttering and cursing, she worked her way along the edge until it merged with the hillside two lots away.

From there she crashed through a hedge, sprinted across a backyard, sidestepped a swimming pool, and rounded into a narrow driveway. She squeezed between a huge SUV and a tiny Prius and stopped on the front lawn. She was three houses away from the ongoing burglary.

A U-Haul truck drove up to the McMansion and parked. She watched the driver turn off the headlights. In less than a minute her climber emerged through the building's front door toting bags stuffed with stolen goods. He threw them into the U-Haul's cab and sprang in after. The U-Haul's lights came back on, and the truck pulled away. Marianne ran out into the street behind it, trying to pick off a license plate number.

"Stop, dammit!"

She was walking back down the steep roadway when Otis arrived in his Taurus.

"Did you see that truck, Dez? Get a plate?"

"No. What truck?"

"That U-Haul, that's our burglars. Their getaway car."

"I think it must have went down Frazer, and I missed it. You were a lot closer, did *you* make the tag?"

"No. Me neither. Shit, everything happened so fast. The guy we saw, he went right up the side of the house. I couldn't believe it."

Otis dropped Marianne off at her own vehicle.

"Night, Squeek. Hey, at least we saw some action. File a report, and next week we'll do this all over again."

"Or not. That U-Haul — it was distinctive. There was a big picture of a yellowish spider on the side. Maybe we'll spot it."

"Maybe. Except that sounds like luck — too good for cops."

"You're probably right." She slapped Otis' fender, and off he went.

She stood on the street, breathing in the soft spring air, pulling burrs out of her pants, re-thinking the evening's events. Whatever it was, whoever was doing it, she had just watched a slick operation.

She was turning toward her patrol car when she heard the whisper of a jet airplane approaching. She looked up. It was heading north, wingtips strobing red and green. Landing lights flared as it sailed overhead.

Something unusual about the sight kept her eyes glued. The craft was small, a business jet heading north instead of west, away from the ordinary course of commercial flights. And it was low. Military, she guessed. Heading where? Not Sacramento, out in the Big Valley. Beale Air Force Base up near Yuba City, probably. The wings and fuselage seemed to shimmer. She tracked it through the tree tops and watched it disappear over the horizon.

Long after the airplane was gone, she was still wondering about it. She wondered about the faint glow she had observed. A side effect of the northern lights, maybe? She wondered about sitting in the cockpit. Did the pilot see anything? She wondered about the passengers, if any. Who was relaxing in the cabin, contemplating some important mission? Most of all, she wondered why she was wondering about any of it. In her mind, for reasons she could not explain, the moment seemed otherworldly.

She shivered involuntarily.

2

"NORCAL, this is Easterly Sprite Five, coming out of the dark, over."

"Sprite Five, contact Beale tower on two eight four point seven five."

"Two eight four point seven five. Beale, Easterly Sprite Five."

"Beale Tower, hello, Sprite Five, eyes are open."

"Approaching you at three thousand five hundred, two five zero knots, one niner miles. Thanks for the welcome mat."

"Sprite Five, say type."

"Charlie-Two-One, rock star special delivery."

"Sprite Five, you are high and wide. Reduce and maintain speed one eight zero."

"One eight zero."

"Sprite Five, descend and maintain one thousand seven hundred."

"One thousand seven hundred."

"Sprite Five, turn right to three zero five."

"Turning to three zero five."

"Right approach runway three three."

"Runway three three."

"Sprite, you are wide."

"Uh, correcting."

"Tiptoe right to runway three three."

"Sliding right."

"Sprite Five, reduce speed to one six zero."

"One six zero."

"Note we have trace precip below one thousand. Visibility three miles."

"Trace . . ."

"Descend at pilot discretion."

"Descending . . ."

"Sprite Five you are still wide. Show you in the weeds."

"Correcting . . ."

"Sprite Five, hold that track, you are cleared to land."

"Descending . . ."

"Sprite Five, drifting wide again."

"Correcting . . ."

"Sprite Five, go around. I say, go around."

"Beale, did not copy."

"Sprite Five, abort. Go around. You are wide. Climb to three thousand six hundred via B-A-B Tacan, and hold."

"Wilco. Easterly Sprite Five aborting."

▼

The *Channel Four News* van blew its horn, causing a small crowd of umbrella-toting protesters to scurry out of the way, and motored slowly toward the Main Gate of Beale Air Force Base, a large and loose collection of low buildings out in flat country bordering the Sierra foothills. The hour was late, almost time for the eleven o'clock show.

The van pulled to the side of the road just outside the concrete K-Rail barriers. The driver hit a button, and a prominent microwave antenna atop the van began to unfold and telescope upward, reaching for an audience.

A young woman reporter in a plum-colored jacket stepped out of the passenger door. The driver, who was also the cameraman, held an umbrella over the reporter's head to ward off a light drizzle while he fluffed her blond hair, applied some lipstick, handed her a microphone. Then, working swiftly, he deployed a pair of baglights on tall stands, shouldered a huge video camera, and hit a switch. The lights flared, bathing the scene in artificial daylight.

"Glasses, no glasses?" asked the reporter.

"Glasses, for sure," said the cameraman. "This is serious. Don't smile."

"Okay, on me in three."

The reporter used her fingers to count from three down to *On The Air*.

"Mila Jansky here, in Marysville, just outside Beale Air Force Base." She adjusted her glasses and swept an arm around to draw attention to the crowd gathering behind her. "The protest vigil continues, and tonight they have something new to worry about. For the third time in less than a month, we've had a crash. Two drones, and now, just a couple of hours ago, a manned jet airplane.

"Details are scarce, but we do know the incident didn't involve Beale's famous U-2s. Not a surveillance mission gone wrong. Instead, we're told the aircraft in question is a C-21, the military version of a popular business jet, ferrying personnel from the east coast. Apparently it attempted to land on the taxiway, where it collided with several support vehicles. The cause?

Unknown at this time. Nobody I've talked to will confirm that the new arrivals are here to investigate previous accidents, but I believe we will find that to be the case.

"The good news — base information officers assure us there are no fatalities. Five people were aboard, and they are being treated in the Beale infirmary. None of the injuries appear to be life-threatening.

"For another perspective, let's hear a reaction from the protest group."

A thin little man stepped out of the crowd and joined the reporter. She turned her microphone his way.

"Hello, there. And who are you, please?"

"Nathan Harris, *Live And Let Live*."

"You've been here off and on for weeks, right? Objecting to the drones. Did you see the crash tonight?"

"We did. Heard it too. Pretty big bang, lot of smoke, flames."

"Does that trouble you, Mr. Harris?"

"No one likes to see lives in danger. My group has long opposed these murderous aircraft. Now we see how deadly they really are, when they threaten our own people, and not just some poor family in a tent halfway around the world. We demand that all flights into and out of the base be suspended in the interest of public safety, pending a firm conclusion to this rash of accidents. We cannot tolerate this sort of negligence in the name of a phony war on jihad —"

The cameraman twirled a finger over his head. The reporter jerked the microphone away.

"—thank you, Mr. Harris, you make some very good points. We'll stay with this story until we have all the facts. Meanwhile, this is Mila Jansky, *Channel Four News*, back to you, Bob."

The cameraman turned off the lights, and the crowd slowly dispersed. A few folks lingered to watch the news team pack up their equipment. Among them were an old man and three children. They were sitting on a section of K-Rail, holding hands. The old man pointed at the van's tall antenna, explaining how newsgathering worked with a series of expressive gestures. The kids nodded respectfully. At length the old man stood up, tugged at his young charges, and they strolled away.

3

PLACERVILLE was a tourist town. Ten thousand people, give or take, lived in the narrow valley slicing into the Sierra Nevada foothills, halfway between Sacramento and Lake Tahoe. Once upon a time it was an important mining center, known then as Hangtown for the rough justice used to tame its rowdy inhabitants. But as gold fever faded, so did the town itself. Now it was simply the El Dorado County seat. Many of the quaint old buildings remained, however; stone and ironwork alongside concrete and glass; history vying with the modern world.

Here, tucked in among wooded hills, local residents pursued their needs and desires as they would anywhere, with hard work. In spite of life's usual setbacks they were unusually fortunate, because the town's dominant theme was a second and continuing gold rush — the steady flow of travelers to and from vacations in the High Sierra. Businesses made a point of reminding visitors of the glamorous past with colorful names and nostalgic décor. Money changed hands. Prosperity followed.

Marianne parked her patrol car under the rickety old bell tower that defined Placerville's picturesque downtown and hiked east along Main Street. A light rain that developed overnight had dissipated, and the narrow street and its tourist attractions were sparkling in late morning sunshine.

She paused at a newspaper rack just outside the Smoke & Firewater convenience store to read a headline in the day's *Sacramento Bee:*

ANOTHER CRASH AT BEALE

She scanned the first paragraph of the story and learned that the downed aircraft was a small business jet. Wow. The one she spotted? She wondered about it, but not for very long, because urgent police business drew her onward to Gold Country Gifts, a fancy boutique offering arty trinkets to wealthy shoppers.

A sign on the door read, *Open Noon to Six.* She knocked and rang a little bell hanging by the doorknob. The sound brought a man out of the stock room. He acknowledged the intrusion by pointing to the sign.

"Not open yet, come back after lunch."

"Police business, sir."

He nodded, smiled when he realized the police uniform belonged to a pretty young woman, and opened wide.

Marianne stepped inside. The man positioned himself behind his little sales counter. She consulted her notebook.

"Mark Frey?"

"That's me."

He was thirty-five, probably, with regular features, dark hair, a trim goatee. He peered inquisitively at Marianne from behind a pair of steel-rimmed glasses. She thought he was rather handsome in a bookish sort of way.

"You own the store here?"

"Is that okay with the law?"

"Sure. It's just . . . I thought you'd be much older."

"My father opened the shop, years ago. He knew some artists over in Marin, liked their stuff, thought he could sell it, and he did. So he's the real owner, and definitely *much* older. But he retired. I also run our location on the lake in Tahoe City."

"Right. And, uh, do you reside at eleven-fifty Esparza Way?"

"Yup, when I'm in town. Is this about . . ."

". . . your house. The burglary."

"Oh boy. I was up in South Lake."

Marianne smiled. "Gambling the night away?"

"I guess. In both places, when you think about it. The house doesn't have an alarm system."

She looked around at the merchandise on display. Small paintings in little silver frames scattered here and there, greeting cards racked up near the window, ornate candlesticks, beaded necklaces, redwood wine stoppers, even a bronze prospector statue that looked like a small copy of the one she knew down in Applefield.

"Have you had a chance to check, see what's missing?"

"I gave it a once-over. Some jewelry, as you might guess. Pieces that I hadn't brought down to the store. My mother's pearl necklace, a diamond pin. There was a cookie jar full of household cash. Somehow, whoever broke in recognized it, and that's gone too."

"How much cash?"

"Enough to slow me down. Five hundred bucks, I suppose. An iPad. A bucketful of Lego. I kept most of my childhood memories here . . . so . . ."

He winced in embarrassment.

"Toys?"

"Yeah. A GI Joe, a Mattel Vertibird, my Stratego set. An original *Star Wars* poster commemorating a year in the theaters."

"You're kidding."

"The GI Joe is a Duke with Kung Fu Grip. You can't even buy a Vertibird on eBay anymore. And Stratego — 1961, first Jumbo edition from the Netherlands. Original box, all the instructions. I haven't had it appraised, but that's money to those who know."

Marianne, having little interest in boys' toys, was perplexed. "And a *Star Wars* poster, you said?" She was taking notes.

"Worth more than a thousand dollars."

"Geez, who knew? Who would want stuff like that? Any ideas? Aside from yourself, I mean."

"Not a clue, officer."

"Have you contacted your insurance agent?"

"Not yet, but I will."

"It helps to have photographs. Got some?"

"Not really. I should have been more careful." He gave her an appreciative look and smiled. "I may cry on your shoulder."

"Unh-huh, just don't sneeze into my radio mike."

"What are my chances, anyway?"

"We'll look into the matter, but valuables like these tend to disappear forever. I hope that doesn't come as a shock."

He held up a hand and grinned, clearly a lot more interested in the messenger than the message.

"That's not what I meant."

"Pardon?"

"I meant, what are my chances of taking you out to dinner? I know a great place just down the hill in Shingle Springs."

This abrupt proposition annoyed Marianne. She made a mental note to toughen up her police manner in the future.

"Uhhh ... really, that's very flattering," she said, being careful to maintain a breezy tone. "But this isn't a social call. I'll have to take a rain check on that."

"More bad luck. I was hoping for a silver lining here."

"Keep those doors and windows locked, Mr. Frey. Upstairs and down."

"You bet I will."

"We'll investigate, we'll be in touch."

"Looking forward to it."

▼

Back on the sidewalk, Marianne snapped her notebook shut and strolled down Main Street to The Golden Goose Omelette Shoppe and lunch with Lorraine Wagstaff, her motherly best friend.

Over lattes, sun-dried tomato scrambles, and hash browns, the two women played catch-up.

"How's biz at the Book Nook?"

"Dismal. Nobody reads anymore."

"Come on, Lorraine, Tom said you were sitting pretty."

"Tom doesn't do my accounts. It's all video games and texting now."

"Are you just bitching, or is the store in actual trouble?"

"I'm okay, I guess. For a while, anyway. There's a new e-reader, something called Kobo. I'm retailing it, just to keep an eye on the future. I've started a used book section, buying back at a discount, selling on some tiny margin. The wolf isn't exactly howling at my door. How about you?"

"I'm all right. Settling in. I've moved into an apartment. Almost as sleazy as my old trailer, but not quite. That's what a real paycheck will do for you."

"And Tom? How's that going?"

"Really well."

Tom Wagstaff was Marianne's steady boyfriend, and Lorraine was Tom's mother, making for a complicated three-way relationship. Something in the older woman's tone made Marianne frown.

"Why? Is there a problem?"

"No. But he's down in Tri-Town, and you're up here. Long distance romances, they make me nervous."

"Hey, it's twenty miles. Not that far."

"When was the last time you two got together?"

"Um, last week. No, wait, it's been almost two. I had a training session. How to catch drivers yakking on their cell phones."

Lorraine tilted her head to a skeptical angle. "Unh-huh. Not that far."

Marianne put down her fork. "What's biting you?"

Lorraine finished her scramble, dabbed at her mouth with a napkin. "The *Courier*, you know what a pain that newspaper is, you've watched him working on it."

"Yeah . . . ?"

"And you know how long it takes him to put it together every week."

"Hey, he's dedicated. I like that."

"Who doesn't? But now he has some help to ease the burden."

Marianne sat upright. Her eyebrows knotted in consternation.

"What are you trying to tell me?"

"Nothing, really."

"Out with it, woman."

Lorraine shifted around in her seat. She stirred her latte, sipped a bracing sip. "He's hired someone to organize the layout."

"Who is this person? Some babe, right?"

"It's only part time."

"Who?" Marianne's face was grim.

"Her name is Kari Hamilton. She's a web designer, also makes jewelry. Very successful. Lives in some big house over in Tarvolo. Inherited wealth, as I understand it."

"Jesus Christ."

Marianne stared at her unfinished lunch. She was turning pale.

"Don't be too concerned. I talked to Tom, and this is strictly professional."

"Oh sure. What does she look like?"

Lorraine thought about the question for a while before answering, then decided to deliver the blow. "She's beautiful. Classy. Kind of like, who's that old-time actress who became a princess?"

"Grace Kelly?"

"That's her."

"But with bigger boobs, I bet."

"Probably. I don't think they're artificial."

"Good God."

Lorraine leaned forward. "Talk to Tom. Don't sit around up here writing parking tickets. That's my tip o' the day."

Marianne took a deep breath. "I'm seeing him this afternoon. We're supposed to be buying a bed for my new digs, how's that?"

Lorraine looked relieved. She chuckled. "All right! Good. What I want to hear."

▼

After lunch, Marianne pointed her police car south on California State Route 49, and took off toward the Golden Hills Tri-Town Special District. She had spent her first year as a sworn police officer there, patrolling the tiny foothill villages of Applefield, Ragtown, and Tarvolo.

But when she crossed County Road 520 she turned west toward Jackson, the Amador County seat. On the outskirts of town she pulled into the wide parking lot of a new U-Haul Moving & Storage Center.

She worked her way through a forest of trailers toward the prefab office. A mustachioed man with prematurely greying hair stepped out onto the pavement to greet her.

They saluted each other.

"Marianne, looking good."

"How're they hanging, Wade?"

"I'm fine. Keeping up."

"This is yours?"

"Well, the bank owns some of it. And U-Haul floated the inventory."

"I'm impressed. You went and did it."

"So it seems, so it seems." Wade Gawley was a police officer in the Tri-Town department, a former colleague. His long-held dream was owning and operating a U-Haul franchise. Neither one of them really thought it would ever happen.

"What can I do for you? We heard you got an apartment. Need a truck?"

"No, not much to move. Jammed everything into my little Mini, did the job in four trips. Except the bed. Tom's going to help with that . . ."

"Oh, is he now?"

She blushed. "Yeah, you know the story."

He laughed and paused to look her over. "Very spiff, that uniform. You make it look good."

"Thanks. How's Tri-Town?"

"Quiet, a little too quiet, now that you left. Chief Fabriano, though, he's almost as tough as Ibañez."

"That's impossible."

"I suppose. I'm straddling now — here, there — but someday I'll put away the gun and the cuffs. This is me . . ." He opened his arms to embrace the trucks and trailers.

"Before you do that, I need some professional help. We're tracking a series of burglaries up in Placerville. Very slick operation. Not much to go on, but I did catch a glimpse of the getaway car. Get this, it was a U-Haul truck."

"Unh-huh."

"And it had a big picture of a yellow spider plastered all over the side."

"Unh-huh."

"I thought you might be able to identify it."

He crooked a finger and led her across the lot, where he pointed to a line of short-body trucks. Two of them sported huge pictures of yellow spiders on the cargo box sides. Incongruously, the spiders wore prominent smiley faces on their abdomens.

"You mean like this?"

"Oh, man . . ." Marianne walked over for a close-up. She read the caption below the illustration. "*Theridion grallator*, the Happy Face Spider."

"Looks intimidating, blown up like that, right?"

"Yeah."

"Gave me the willies too, so I looked it up. These things live in Hawaii, and they are about this long . . ." He measured out an eighth of an inch between thumb and forefinger.

"Are their pictures pasted on every third truck?"

"Quite a few. But we also have a squid, a snake, birds, motorcycles, mushrooms, cool things from the different states. It's the U-Haul SuperGraphics program, paying tribute to America."

"But the spider's not unique, like I hoped."

"Sorry, detective. Not much of a clue, I'm afraid."

"Shit."

Marianne scowled, walked around in a circle. Then she brightened. "How about this — got anything rented out in Placerville right now?"

"I dunno, could be. Let's take a look."

They moved into Gawley's little office, where he paged through recent transactions on his computer.

"Sorry, Marianne. My whole fleet is accounted for."

"I figured. Look, if something comes up, if someone turns in one of these spider trucks and you get a funny feeling, let me know, okay?"

"Will do."

"It's a long shot, I know." They clasped hands again. "Don't let the excitement up in Applefield give you a heart attack."

"I'm calm as a clam."

She headed for her patrol vehicle.

"And tell Rick I'm going to smack him upside the head when next we meet."

"Any particular reason?"

"Telling tales."

Gawley nodded. Marianne threw the car in drive and pulled away.

▼

Although she was still on duty and twenty miles outside her jurisdiction, Marianne felt her investigative session with Gawley gave her leave to do some investigating of her own. So instead of returning to Placerville she drove up the hill into Applefield.

Images of this charming village, her former territory, were a regular feature of postcards and travel magazines, affirming its status, over and over again, as the ideal foothill town. A hundred and fifty years ago a major gold strike, the Headwall Mine Bonanza, put it on the map. Now, as with most upcountry settlements, time had diluted its heritage with trendy gift shops, chain stores, and a hip coffee shop.

Marianne parked just off Main Street, under tall oaks sheltering the concrete block building that served as offices for the local newspaper, *The Amador County Courier*. She was intent on following up Lorraine's report on the paper's new hire, and she wanted to hear about it straight from Tom Wagstaff, the editor.

She stood at the main entrance trying to turn jealous thoughts aside when the door flew open and a stunning woman stepped out, sliding an arm into a light jacket. She was laughing over something she had just heard. She tossed a tangle of blond curls and called back inside.

"So you say. Just wait, tomorrow I'll fix everything, you'll see."

Then she turned to discover Marianne.

"Oh, hello," she said.

Awkward pause.

"The police are here. Where did we go wrong, officer?"

"Um, innocent until proven guilty, I guess."

Marianne regarded the woman through narrowed eyes. She was tall and slender, poised, clad in a fashionable blouse and slacks. About her age, or maybe a year or two older. High cheek bones, straight nose, full lips, bold breasts. The complete package.

Marianne forced a smile. "Unless you want to confess . . ."

"Oh my God." The woman brought a hand to her face in a mock slap. "Forgive me. You're Marianne. I've heard so much about you." She thrust out a hand. "I'm Kari."

Marianne stretched for a perfunctory handshake. "Nice to meet you."

Ms. Hamilton finished donning her jacket and pushed the office door back open. "Woo-hoo, Tom, someone to see you."

She winked at Marianne and crossed the street to an expensive black Audi.

Marianne watched her drive away, then climbed the steps to Wagstaff's office. He stood up as she crossed through his loft-like living area and approached his desk.

"What was *that?*" she asked, directing a thumb at the door.

Wagstaff ran a hand through his shaggy blond hair and tugged at his closely-cropped beard. "That, babe of mine, was the new *Courier* staff. She is a whiz."

"I'll bet."

Wagstaff cocked his head. "Hey now, do I detect a suspicious cop?"

"Mmm."

He wound her into his arms. He kissed her on the nose. "You will not believe how this woman has helped me get my damn paper under control."

She kissed him back. "I might, if you make the case. And it better be good, mister — you're the defense attorney."

"Ahem. I need help, and she's a designer. Went to art school back east. School of Design, Rizzdy, wherever that is. She's rich, so I can pay her pennies to keep herself busy, and she has the chops."

"She's also very good-looking."

"As I have noticed. I'm not blind."

"And I did not observe a ring on the third finger of her left hand."

"Nope, but I think she's seeing somebody."

Marianne considered the information.

"All right, testimony is believable, the jury will deliberate." Another kiss. "So . . . what about our date? I thought we were supposed to go buy a bed."

"Nope. No can do."

"Uh-oh, why not? Now you're scaring me."

"Oh stop it, you're a brave law enforcement pro."

He opened the back door and pointed outside. Marianne walked over. Wagstaff's big yellow FJ Cruiser SUV was parked there, and on top was a stack of wooden planks, lashed to the roof rack with tie down straps.

"What . . . ?"

"What do you think? Boards, long and narrow? Little slats all bundled up?"

"Oh my God, it's a bed. You built a bed! How? Where?"

"In my workshop on the Lodi campus, of course. The mattress will arrive at your new address later this afternoon. It's a Beautyrest from Sleepy Town with 'recharge technology.' Firm, that okay?"

She gave him a hug. "I'm on duty till six, and then . . . we'll find out."

4

U.S. ARMY Brigadier General Vernon Weaver, a solid man in his fifties, stood in a corridor of the Beale Air Force Base Clinic in conference with the 19th Medical Group doctor on duty. He was staring out the window at scattered oak trees on folded land rising into the foothills. All 12,000 feet of the base's only runway, built to accommodate SR-71 and U-2 spy planes, was miles away to the west and out of sight. Things had gone wrong on that runway, his right arm was in a sling, and his expression was grim.

"So what's the damage, aside from this?" He raised his bad arm.

"Luckily for the crew, when the plane's wing clipped that tow tractor, it spun around and skidded into an open hangar, where it hit another service vehicle. That was a pretty big piece of machinery — a fire truck, yet — and it stopped the show. So the pilot and copilot were on the far end of the crash — and you and the other passengers took the impact."

"I see the crew has been discharged. Anyone talk to them?"

"I think the pilot said he fell asleep."

"Fell asleep." Weaver shook his head in wonderment.

The doctor wrung his hands. "Sad, the damnedest thing. Maybe there's a future in crop dusting."

Weaver grimaced. "I'm sure the inquiry will sort it out."

They moved along the hall, looked in on a room with a man propped up in bed. His head was bandaged, he was laced into a back brace, and one arm was linked up to an IV drip. He was reading a book. He attempted a clumsy salute.

Weaver returned it. "How is he?"

"Major Bagwell will be fine. Laceration on his head there, nicely stitched by yours truly, a wrenched back, bruises. Nothing a lot of Advil can't take care of. I expect to discharge him tomorrow morning."

"And my asset?"

The doctor sighed and led the general around a corner to another room. There, medical equipment crowded the floor, and a jumble of long tubes and cables ran from the bedside carts, oxygen bottles, and IV packs to a figure lying on his back in the bed, eyes closed. The doctor beckoned, and Weaver stepped into the room.

"Emile? Sergeant Sarzo? Helluva landing, huh? How you doing?"

The figure did not answer.

The doctor pointed to the monitor beside the bed.

"See here — he's got a steady heartbeat. Breathing is normal. Brain waves look like anyone's when you're asleep. Blood chemistry is okay. We've had to catheterize him, but urine production is normal, no blood there."

"So what's the problem?"

"No external injuries, luckier than you in that, I guess." He spread his hands to show helpless ignorance. "He just won't wake up."

"That must change. He's here for a reason."

"We don't have an ICU at Beale. Want me to transfer him?"

"No, no. Improvise. Bring in whatever equipment you need. We're basing onsite for the duration."

5

THE GOLDEN NUGGET Apartments were a clapboard and stucco complex located in one of Placerville's woodsy side canyons, a few blocks away from the racial, economic, and social complexities of Little Mexico. It was by no means the most attractive spot in town. Not anyone's idea of luxury. But Marianne had been living in a rusty old trailer just outside the city limits, and during the winter a unit came up for rent. The prospect of a dwelling built on solid concrete with a full-size bathroom and kitchen, no matter how old and musty, made Marianne fool around with her personal budget and justify, in her mind, the idea of living there. Since moving in, she had been sleeping on a fold-out futon. She had yet to invite Tom Wagstaff for a visit, unsure how he would react to the genteel decrepitude of the place.

Now he was there with her, helping dispose of that same futon. Together they lowered the new bed parts from Tom's SUV and tied the futon onto the rack for later delivery to Dunnigan's used furniture store. Then they hauled the rails and slats up a flight of stairs to Marianne's rental and hammered them together in her only bedroom.

"It's a queen," she noticed. "Room for two. Mighty sure of yourself, bub."

He grinned. "I thought, plan ahead, who knows what the future holds?"

She screwed her mouth into a wry pucker. "You were probably just thinking about my cat, and realized I needed space for him to keep me company."

He picked up a U-shaped metal channel and snapped it between headboard and footboard. Together they laid the slats across.

"I've got a better idea about keeping you company, if your cat won't mind."

"I don't actually have a cat."

"In that case you can have me."

"Oh really? Aren't *you* easy." She swept a lock of hair off her forehead. "Seriously?"

"I've been meaning to tell you . . . I just landed a new job in Sacramento."

"What — ?"

"Long way from Applefield, and just down the highway from here."

"Doing what, may I ask?" She manufactured an exaggerated pout. "We did not consult."

"Teaching journalism at Sac State."

"Whoa, that's news. Put *that* in your paper!"

They raised fists and bumped.

"It's only part time, and it's an extension course. Spring term, then summer."

"But still, pretty great."

"Four-year college, and I think they've got their eye on me." He shrugged. "So, yeah, I'm stoked."

Marianne ran to the kitchen and yanked open the refrigerator.

"This calls for a celebration."

She was opening beers when the porch bell rang. Wagstaff beat her to the door.

Standing on the threshold was a large man holding one end of a mattress. Behind him, a burly teenager gripped the other end.

"Sleepy Town delivery. Unit 30?"

"That's us."

The two men walked the bulky package into the bedroom and stripped off the plastic wrapping. Wagstaff signed a receipt, tipped them twenty bucks, and sent them on their way. Then he and Marianne tilted the mattress down onto the bed slats. They eyed the thing, eyed each other.

"We should probably get a cover."

"And some queen-size sheets. All I've got are twins."

She sat on the edge and bounced, testing the springs. He joined her.

"Firm. Feels good."

She flopped backward, threw her arms over her head. He nestled beside her. She turned toward him. They kissed. He ran a hand over her breasts, started to undo buttons.

"Oh crap, I'm still wearing my world. Hang on while I get rid of this damned Glock."

She unlaced her duty belt and hung it over the footboard.

"Now then, where were we?"

Pretty soon their clothes were all over the floor, and the new bed was getting an important test drive.

▼

Next morning when Marianne woke up, light was blooming through the linen curtains on her window. Wagstaff was already in the shower. She tiptoed into the bathroom and joined him there.

"Morning, sir. Scrub your back?" He nodded. They traded soap and loofah.

She was still washing her hair when he finished dressing. He poked his head back through the shower curtain.

"Hey, M, gotta go. *Courier's* on the stands tomorrow, and the local ads are still a mess. I'll call you."

She blew him a kiss. "Keep your hands off the staff, Buster. Avoid those sexual harassment charges you should have read about."

"Promise."

She was humming to herself when she stepped out of the tub and stood before the washbasin. The mirror was all steamed-up, so she ran a hand over the glass to wipe it clean. There, that's better. She was inspecting her upper lip for stray hairs when she became aware of a blur in her image. She dragged her hand over the glass again, clearing the way for a close look at her eyelashes. Her image blurred again. A shadowy form rippled into view.

"Ahhh — !"

She jerked back as if scalded by boiling water. The shadowy shape twisted and writhed in the glass. It set her heart thumping. After a while she calmed down. She folded her arms and watched, hoping the apparition would fade away. But it didn't.

"Are you kidding me? After all these months? What are you doing here? I'm not even dressed." She grabbed a towel to cover herself.

The shape continued to gyrate. She tapped a foot. Then she reached out and angrily swiped her towel across the mirror.

"Hey! I've had enough! Go away!"

The shadow did not obey. It stabilized, sharpened into focus. Now she could see a definite head and torso. The outline of a man. Wispy hands appeared. A mouth opened and closed, trying to say something. Marianne resigned herself to an unusual conversation.

"What? Can't hear."

The shadow tried again, but Marianne couldn't begin to read the shadowy lips.

"I'm lost." She raised her arms in an Egyptian-style dance pose and swayed back and forth. "Charades used to work, remember? That is, if you are who I think you are."

The shadowy figure made a *stop* sign. Then he hooked thumbs together and flapped his hands.

"Okaaay . . . that's a bird . . . bird in flight, I guess, right?"

Now the shadow bent his hands back, flattened his palms, and made a duck-like walking motion.

"No, wrong, it's a walking bird."

The shadow emphatically waved her answer away and repeated the pantomime.

"Bird, flapping — feet, walking."

Another dismissive wave. This time the shadow locked hands and bent his fingers together; a bird folding its wings. Then he carved a *plus sign* in the air and flattened a hand into an imitation of some sort of foot.

"Bird, not flapping, not walking. Bird plus foot. Bird foot."

She pondered the display while the apparition repeated every detail. Suddenly she let out a little shriek. Her hand shot up and covered her mouth.

"It's not a thing, it's a name! Crow-foot."

The shadow nodded.

"Crowfoot — how's that for deduction? I am a winner!"

The shadow shook his head. He pointed a finger at her, thrust an arm to the side several times, and flicked his hand impatiently.

"Get a move on? What? Why? Where?"

The shadow pointed to his mouth, cupped an ear, brought fingers and thumbs together in a staccato pattern to indicate talking.

"Talk — ?"

The shadow alternately pointed at Marianne and himself several times. Then he vanished.

6

MARIANNE didn't understand everything her ghost was trying to tell her, but she was pretty sure she got his drift. Accordingly, she threw on a pair of well-worn jeans and, skipping her usual morning dose of coffee, roared away down Route 49 in her own car, a little blue Mini Cooper, heading south at high speed.

"Shit — Crowfoot! — that old bag! — I'm off today, with a million little errands waiting." She was talking to herself as she zoomed through the hills and corners, as she often did.

Sixty-five miles later she arrived in Angels Camp, a tiny community straddling the highway. She motored slowly past the clutter of roadside retail, continued into the historic old town, and turned onto Bush Street. She was there to pay a visit to Hannah Crowfoot, an unfriendly self-proclaimed spirit woman, who had caused her a lot of trouble in the recent past.

She pulled up to the old lady's house, a crumbling shack half-hidden behind flowers and shrubs. A sign on the door advertised *Readings & Spiritual Advice*. She knocked and waited. No one responded. She paused for a few seconds and knocked again. While she was cooling her heels a fat old cat slipped past her, nudged the door open, and padded inside. Marianne hesitated timidly, then steeled herself and followed.

She was in a little foyer, assaulted by strange and pungent odors. Cat urine, probably. Chicken broth as well. Something else oddly perfumy. A side table stood against the wall, with a brass bell sitting on it. A tented paper notice read, *Ring for Service.*

Marianne bit her lip and gave the bell a good *clang!*

Shuffling footsteps approached down a flight of narrow stairs. A wrinkled face peered around the corner. Cataract-filled eyes blinked at Marianne through thick lenses. The face jerked back out of sight, then slowly came into view again.

"Ha! So it's *you*. What do you want?"

Marianne regarded her with loathing. The woman's face was tense and pale, her expression fearful. But little more than a year ago she had set a trap, and Marianne had nearly been killed by it.

"It's Marianne Sarzeau."

"I know who you are. Stay back."

"I need your help."

"So you say." The old woman whinnied scornfully. "What sort of help could I ever offer to someone like you?"

Marianne was determined not to get in a fight. "What do you mean?"

"Someone with talent who can't be taught."

"You think I'm a know-it-all?"

"You act like one."

"I know nothing."

Ms. Crowfoot seemed to soften. She took a step forward, looked her young visitor up and down. "What's your problem?"

"Remember my ghost?"

"Oh yes. The reflection."

"I think he wants to talk to me. But I can't hear what he's saying. He sent me to you."

The old woman brushed long strands of grey hair out of her eyes.

"Time is money. I don't run a charity. It will cost you."

"Uh, okay, I don't mind. How much?"

"Fifty dollars for a consultation."

Marianne gulped. "Do you, um, take credit cards?"

"An old 'savage Indian' like me? Cash on the barrelhead, Miss Sarzeau."

Marianne's spirits sank. "Oh, gosh, I don't have anything like that on me."

Ms. Crowfoot started creaking back up the stairs. "Come back when you do."

"Okay, whew, got a phone number? I'll call you when I figure this out."

"Won't work, I'm out of minutes."

"Really." Marianne brooded about the problem. "Tell you what, I'll hit the bank downtown, I think I saw an ATM driving by. Be back in a flash."

Ms. Crowfoot paused in her laborious ascent. "I could use a good roast chicken. I don't get to the store as often as I used to."

Marianne planted her fists on her hips, tapped a foot, flicked a hand out in frustration, turned, and left.

▼

A half hour later she was back, lugging a big bag of groceries. She rang the bell several times, and after an irksome delay old lady Crowfoot reappeared. She folded her hands over the shapeless sack of a dress she was wearing.

"Yes?"

Marianne held out a small plastic card. "Four hundred minutes for your no-contract phone."

Ms. Crowfoot examined the card, raised an eyebrow. "AT&T — how did you know?"

Marianne smiled. "It's not an example of my superpowers, if that's what you're thinking. The woman behind the counter at the Save Mart knows you pretty well, I guess."

"Hmm."

"And here we have a loaf of whole wheat bread, some biscuit mix, a bottle of olive oil, a bottle of milk — two-percent, want to eat healthy. Oh, a cheap bottle of white wine — it's actually drinkable, or you can cook with it — and this, a roast chicken, hot off the rotisserie." Marianne pulled the items out of her bag one by one and set them down on the side table. Then she opened her wallet and offered a fifty dollar bill.

"Plus the cash."

Ms. Crowfoot stared at the food with evident appreciation. She took the fifty dollar bill, stepped toward a curtain veiling her consultation room, and motioned Marianne to follow.

When Marianne was seated, Ms. Crowfoot drew the blinds on her windows and lowered herself into a leather easy chair.

"Let's see now — you've got a ghost, and you want to hear what he says."

"Yes."

"What color am I?"

"Pardon me?"

"I need to know a little bit more about you, what your aptitudes are. What color?"

"How should I know? It's dark as a toilet tank in here."

"Come on, Miss Sarzeau, you know what I'm talking about."

Marianne stared across the table into the shadows where Ms. Crowfoot was lounging. She furrowed her brow, trying to imagine what the spirit woman meant. Then the hairs on her forearms rose up.

"Green. It's faint, but . . . green. Green, I think."

In Marianne's eyes, nothing showed. But somewhere in her mind, the shadowy bulk in front of her radiated a faintly greenish impression. She shuddered.

"Very good. And what does that mean?"

"I couldn't tell you. Is this some sort of Native lore?"

"It's an *aura*. Not all adepts can see them, but you do."

"Oh boy."

"Again, what does the color mean?"

"I have zero clue."

"No, I guess not. In case you're wondering, I too can detect auras. This morning, when you arrived, you were red. Now you're green too."

"And . . .?"

"Well, it's never really quite so simple, but think of it this way — red means 'enemy.' Trust not! Blue means 'friend.' Green — 'be wary'."

Marianne let out a nervous laugh. "I feel like I'm at the dentist. Maybe he'll turn out to be green too."

Suddenly a small fire blazed up on the table between the two women, fueled by a Sterno canister. Ms. Crowfoot blew out a match and peered intently at Marianne. She held up a plastic crystal dangling from a little suction cup, a "suncatcher" that probably spent most of its time stuck to one of her windows.

"What do you see?"

"Oh man, firelight coming through whatever you've got there."

"Look more closely. Relax, or focus."

"Which?"

"Whichever you're doing now, the opposite. My goodness, you really don't know diddly, do you?"

"Like I said — like you once warned me."

"All right, keep looking."

Marianne turned her face away. Out of the corner of her eye she thought she could spot a funny pattern.

"Crackles. Jagged lines, like little lightning strikes. They come and go."

"Anything else?"

Marianne continued to peer into the suncatcher. "Uhh, nothing definite. Every now and then the lines seem to converge."

"Yes, and then what?"

Marianne shook her head. "Nothing really . . . except . . . maybe . . ."

"Maybe what?"

"Maybe . . . a little face?"

The spirit woman nodded, put the crystal away. She dropped a pinch of salt onto the Sterno canister. Sparks erupted.

"Now look at the fire. What do you see?"

"A fire."

"Keep looking."

Marianne stared intently at the little blue flame until her eyes were crossing with fatigue. After a while she told herself that a pair of tiny eyes were staring back at her from within it.

"Okay, I'm probably making this up, but something is watching me."

Ms. Crowfoot brought a hand down and smothered the flame. Then she popped out of her chair, crossed the room in three steps, and whipped the curtains open. Marianne was startled. The old woman's face had gone grey.

"You . . . you've got something . . . some potential. It is possible you might be able to hear that ghost of yours, but you'll have to prepare yourself."

Ms. Crowfoot shuffled around the table and eased back into her chair. She held up three fingers.

"Three things."

Marianne nodded. "Three things."

"First — you need a *talisman*. Something to focus your attention."

"Like Father Eisen told me, like Catholics using relics to draw nearer to the Almighty."

"We're not talking about the Almighty here, but yes, that's the idea. Second — you need a *portal*. Somewhere you can summon the ghost."

"I've seen him in a lot of places. He's everywhere."

"Pick a good one for your first try. This isn't radio, but you need a good connection to talk."

Ms. Crowfoot leaned forward.

"Third — you need to *attune* yourself. You need . . . fudge, wait a minute, I never can remember the names." She picked herself up, lifted a well-thumbed volume from her bookcase, and slowly leafed through it.

"Here we are. You need a pine fritillary — that's a lily — *Fritillaria pinetorum.*" She showed Marianne a picture of a tiny flower. "Crush it and make a tea. Looks like a little lion face, don't you think?"

Marianne didn't know what to think.

"I had a talisman, a little calavera girl, but it flew to pieces right after Chief Ibañez got killed."

"Give it some thought. Pick something associated with him."

"Okay. And the flower, where — ?"

"It says here, blooming on the Sierra crest, May to September. The Carson Pass is mentioned."

"Can't I just hit a flower shop in Placerville or Folsom?"

Ms. Crowfoot snorted. "Don't be silly, this is a wildflower, very rare."

"Christ. The snow is ten feet deep up there right now."

"Yes, it's early in the season, but on a sunny slope, protected from the wind, you might find one."

Marianne groaned. She wondered if Ms. Crowfoot was deliberately trying to trick her. She stared at the old woman long and hard. Then she shook herself and stood up from the table, face hardening in resolve.

"Okay. I'll do it."

Ms. Crowfoot cocked her head. "Are you all right?"

"I'm fine. Just checking."

"Checking . . . ?" The spirit woman arched her bushy brows.

"You're turning blue. Not as green as you were."

▼

On her way back north, Marianne pulled into Applefield and parked at the Tri-Town Police Department, a former Victorian house adapted to office work. She pushed open the door to the dusty old station, and found Officer Ricky Moss sitting at a battered oak desk under high windows, doing paperwork.

"Rick, you bastard."

Moss stood up from his desk. He noticed her grumpy expression and blushed. She shook her fist.

"Uh-oh. Sorry, Marianne, don't hit me. You're a good story."

"If you tell any more stories on me, you pathetic jerk, I am going to cast a spell on you."

He recoiled in mock horror. "Please don't."

She relaxed. They slapped hands.

"So . . . how's it going up there on a real police force?"

Marianne shrugged. "Okay, I guess. You sure gave Dez Otis something to think about."

"Yeah. He would of bit on anything I told him."

"Embarrassed the shit out of me, thank you very much."

Moss grinned like a guilty schoolboy. "Hey — people you work with, they should know."

Marianne bobbed her head. "You're right, you're right. But it's a pain in the butt, let me tell you."

He looked her over. "If anyone's giving you a rough time up there, gotta say, it doesn't show. So . . . today, right now, what can I do you for?"

"Whatever happened to all the stuff in Chief Ibañez' office?"

"I think Wade bagged it up after the funeral and carted everything down to the warehouse. Why?"

"I need something. How do I get in?"

"Go see our mayor, I guess, the honorable Howard Turnbow."

"You don't have the keys?"

"Not a chance."

"Crap. Okay, stay out of trouble."

"You too."

Marianne got back in her Mini and motored along Applefield's Main Street. In spite of all the tourists swarming around, she found a parking spot within a block of the town's modest City Hall.

Inside the antique brick structure, a renovated nineteenth-century fire house, an empty counter greeted her. A button screwed into the Formica surface was labeled *Mayor's Office*. She pressed it, and after a leisurely interval a middle-aged woman appeared from somewhere down the hall.

"Is Howard, I mean Mayor Turnbow, here?"

The woman eyed Marianne with suspicion. "Who is it?"

"Marianne Sarzeau. He knows me, I used to work for him."

"Just a minute, please."

The woman stuck her head into an office concealed behind frosted glass. A few seconds later Howard Turnbow came barging out, arms raised in familiar greeting.

"Officer Sarzeau, the Golden Girl of the Golden Hills, how *are* you?"

Marianne managed a twisted smile. "Hello, Howard." She raised a warning finger. "You know, I'm not your Golden Girl anymore. Just a cop."

"Jesus, what the hell. It's been months. Too long. How are things in Hangtown?"

"I'm coping."

"And what brings you back to me, may I ask?" He grinned. "Looking for a better job?"

Marianne fidgeted with her handbag. "I need to find something of mine. I think it got mixed up with Chief Ibañez' stuff. Rick told me everything was all boxed up down in the warehouse."

Turnbow ran a hand through his curly grey hair. "Chief Ibañez . . ." He let a mournful thought drift.

"So my question is, can I have a key and go take a look?"

"I don't know, Marianne. It's a security protocol situation."

"Come on, I'm no thief."

He gazed at her. A mischievous idea formed. "I'll consider it," he decided, "provided — *provided,* that is — you'll sub for me down at the station now and then."

"Geez, Howard, you're twisting my arm. We went all through that."

"I know. But my staff has vacations coming up, and, truth be told, you're better than any of them. You could be full time if you wanted."

A year ago, Marianne had been the Sunday night disc jockey at Turnbow's rural radio station. She quit when she joined the Placerville department, and he had been after her on and off ever since. She gave him a dirty look.

"K-V-I-G, Golden Girl, huh?"

"You've still got that voice. Plenty of authority behind that mike."

"All right, give me the key, and I'll think about it."

He nodded assent and used one of his own keys to unlock a drawer under the counter. He rummaged around inside and held up a large key ring dangling from a little plastic pig.

"Do we have a deal?"

"Things are pretty formal up north. Twelve hour shifts, three days on, three off, then four on, four off. We're short-staffed, so I pull plenty of overtime too. Slot me in around all that, and yes, we have a now-and-then deal."

"Sunday night?"

She sighed. "I'm daytime this week, so it looks clear." She snatched the key ring out of his hand. "Sunday it is."

He regarded her warmly. "I knew you'd be back."

"Don't get smug, Your Honor."

▼

The Tri-Town Special District warehouse was a concrete tilt-up building on the edge of affluent Tarvolo, a hideous eyesore that prompted many a complaint from the gated enclave's wealthy residents.

Marianne parked her Mini in the adjacent maintenance yard and hiked past the road repair vehicles to a wide roll-up door. She looked it over, but there was no lock and no obvious way to crank it open, so she worked her way around the building, sidestepping gravel heaps, sacks of concrete, and backhoe parts until she located a narrow doorway on the far side. There she used Mayor Turnbow's keys to spring a padlock on the heavy steel latch barring the entrance.

Once inside she pushed past a small fleet of pickup trucks, vans, and a jungle of spare road signs to a pile of crates and boxes, stacked haphazardly in one corner of the cavernous structure.

"Now then, where oh where . . ."

It took her forever to find her former police chief's effects. They were stuffed into three cardboard boxes half-crushed beneath a wooden crate inexplicably full of mercury vapor lamps.

She tugged and pulled, pried the boxes open, aimed a little flashlight into their dark corners. After another hour she had what she came for.

"Well, hello there . . ."

It was a small picture frame holding a brass police badge from the Big City pinned to a velvet background. She worked the glass out to free the badge itself. She recognized it as a memento formerly displayed behind Chief Ibañez' desk. She buffed the thing on her jeans, saw it start to take on a shine. Did it fulfill old lady Crowfoot's idea of a talisman? She thought so. What kind of object could be more closely associated with the man than this?

▼

Marianne's next stop was downhill in neighboring Ragtown, a tiny hamlet not much more than a wide spot in the county road. The Book

Nook, Lorraine Wagstaff's little shop there, was the only important bookstore in the Tri-Town Area, and culture-hungry locals were happy to make the trip to sample her thoughtful collection and equally impressive pastries.

When Lorraine first opened the store, fifteen years previously, she had enough money to blow the front walls out of an old house, install inviting picture windows, and put up powerful ceiling lights that gave the otherwise homey interior a sparkling commercial appeal.

Marianne plunked herself down on a stool in the nature section to study wildflowers. She had sounded the alarm while still at the warehouse, and both Wagstaffs were on hand to help.

"I can't find it anywhere, not even in the *Sierra Nevada Natural History Guide,*" she announced.

Tom was studying Google maps.

"Well, if you ever do, I think I can get us to a sunny slope."

Meanwhile, Lorraine was roaming through botanical websites on another computer.

"What's the flower name again?"

"*Fritillaria pinetorum.* It's some kind of lily."

"Aha," sang Lorraine after a few minutes online. "Here it is, at the California Native Plant Society."

Marianne dropped her flower books and rushed over. "That's it! Print the picture."

Lorraine clicked on a button, and her printer whirred. Marianne seized the printout.

"Got you."

Wagstaff peered over her shoulder. "Doesn't look like much. We'll need our woolies for this, babe."

7

NEXT MORNING Marianne parked at the Grocery Outlet in Jackson, a block from the intersection of the Golden Chain Highway and State Route 88. She wandered through the unfamiliar store until she found the deli counter, and there ordered up sandwiches, chips, candy, and coffee. Then she returned to her little Mini to bask in the sun and wait for Wagstaff. Pretty soon his big yellow four-by-four came into view. He honked. She flagged him down and hopped aboard.

She stuffed their lunches into backpacks while he turned up 88 and aimed his truck toward the Carson Pass, one of few routes over the High Sierra kept open during the winter.

Marianne handed him a cup of coffee. "Sugar, nonfat milk, right?"

He nodded. "Weatherman says we'll be okay until late afternoon, and then we might see a snow flurry." He pointed out the window to the clear blue sky overhead. "Hard to believe, huh?"

"I'm more worried about snow on the ground," said Marianne. "I'm going to sink to my chin."

"Take it easy, I stopped at the Miners Market on the way up here and bought you some snowshoes."

"What do I owe you?"

"Nothing. It's spring, they're on sale, so you're a cheap date."

They sipped in silence for a few minutes. East of Pine Grove, the highway steepened. Roadside snowdrifts plowed up during the winter were still eight feet high, but sheets of water ran out from under them, soaking the road and bouncing morning sunlight into their eyes. Wagstaff donned a pair of sunglasses.

"It's thirty-five miles up to the pass, where the crest trail crosses. That's our best bet."

"I hope you like ham sandwiches. Or salami and cheese. One or the other, that's all they had."

"No turkey breast?"

"Not today. And no beer, we need to stay sharp."

"It's a grim life, right?" He leaned over and kissed her on the ear. The car swerved.

"Watch it, bub. Eyes front. I want to talk to my ghost on this side of eternity, thanks."

As they drove east, the land rose. Tall peaks closed in. Marianne fumbled around and cranked the car's heater up. "Where's that warm sunny slope, anyway?"

They passed Caples Lake at 7500 feet. Ice was still in evidence around the edges, but steady spring sunlight was causing clouds of steam to rise from open water in the middle.

Just before the actual pass, Wagstaff turned into a paved parking lot on the north side of the highway. In summer it offered access to the Pacific Crest Trail, a Mecca for hikers. Now it was plowed out to accommodate families with children looking for winter fun. A detached Caltrans road sander was sitting there on the asphalt ready to be hauled away for the season.

Wagstaff and Marianne stepped out of the car, saw their breath, and threw on winter jackets. Marianne tucked her hair into a knitted cap. Sunny it was, warm it was not. They were 8500 feet up.

Wagstaff pointed northeast to a weathered granite dome. "Snow's gone off that rock. Lots of little niches where plants might be growing."

He helped Marianne get her snowboarding boots into her new snowshoes, laced on his own, and they trudged up the slope.

It took them fifteen minutes to reach the granite face, and another hour poking around the rocks to be sure they hadn't missed any *Fritillaria* plants.

"Nothing but dead weeds," grumped Marianne. "Sorry I dragged us all the way up here."

She shed her backpack, broke out their sandwiches. Wagstaff opened cans of Sprite. They sat down on a stone slab facing south and tried to enjoy a chilly picnic.

"Look across the road there, behind that bump, see?"

Marianne squinted into the sunshine. "Yeah, what about it?"

"Frog Lake. Worth a shot."

"I guess." She snuggled over against Wagstaff. "I'm cold."

"Hey, let's go." He pointed skyward. Out west, a line of thin clouds could be seen. "Snow flurries coming, remember?"

"Mmm."

They drove a quarter of a mile onward to the pass itself, turned into the Information Center lot, also plowed out, and parked in front of the El Dorado National Forest sign.

The store was closed for the season, but the chemical toilets nearby were open. Marianne yelped when she sat down on the cold seat inside.

Then they laced up their snowshoes, crossed the road, climbed a towering drift, and hiked south to Red Vista Road, still covered with snow several feet deep. They followed it for a hundred yards under stunted fir trees, then turned aside and worked their way up a steep ravine carved out of solid granite. They were puffing and panting when they topped the ridge and looked down upon tiny Frog Lake. It was still covered with ice, but here and there holes had appeared. Patches of fog hovered above them.

"Here we go," said Wagstaff. He started to descend, skidding, hopping, moving quickly. "Let's see what we can see down along the shore there."

Marianne followed cautiously and without enthusiasm. Halfway down, she put her hand out to steady herself in a steep little gully and abruptly stopped. Wagstaff was already at the lake.

"Hey, Tom, I've got something. Have a look a this!"

A slender green shoot was poking out of a muddy rivulet nestled in between boulders. Three little brownish blossoms were nodding on long stems. A plant, but what the heck was it? She fumbled in her backpack and withdrew the printout Lorraine had made. As she opened it up, a gust of wind yanked it out of her cold fingers and blew it down the slope.

"Whoa!"

Wagstaff looked up, saw the sheet flying toward him like a paper airplane, and snagged it out of the air.

"Don't you wish the real thing was this easy?" he yelled triumphantly.

"Bring that up here! I think I've nailed our culprit, but we need to ID this bad boy."

Wagstaff struggled back up the slope. They looked at the printout, looked at the plant.

"Tah-dah!"

▼

Down in Applefield, in the offices of the *County Courier,* the kettle whistled on Wagstaff's stove. Marianne was busy crushing three little *Fritillaria pinetorum* blossoms in a blender. She interrupted herself to turn off the burner. When the flowers were well-shredded, she picked up a pair of kitchen scissors and cut a scrap of cloth out of an old T-shirt Wagstaff had donated to the cause.

From across the room, Wagstaff and Kari Hamilton stopped formatting newspaper articles and turned to watch Marianne empty the blender onto the fabric, then twist the combination into a little tea bag. She poured boiling water into a cup and held the bag aloft.

"Here we go. Want some?"

Her two onlookers shook their heads in horror.

"Okay, then."

She plunged the bag into her cup, making tea. She let it steep until the water turned brown.

"Are you really going to drink that?" asked Hamilton.

"How do you know the flowers aren't poisonous?" wondered Wagstaff, although he was resigned to Marianne's experiment.

"I don't."

She brought the cup to her mouth.

"Look, if I fall over and start having convulsions, call 9-1-1."

"What a good idea."

Marianne inhaled the brew's aroma and sipped an exploratory sip. She scrinched up her mouth, evaluating the flavor as if tasting a new wine.

"Uchh," she decided. "It's terrible."

She downed the rest of the cup in quick gulps.

Wagstaff and Hamilton stood up from their desks anticipating a medical emergency.

Marianne looked at them through hooded eyes. When she was a pre-teen child, she had suffered from occasional seizures. They subsided when she reached puberty, but last year, in the middle of the worst stress of her life, the problem recurred. Now she thought it might be happening again. Office objects were taking on a jagged look. Wagstaff and Hamilton seemed to have acquired neon outlines. The overhead lights pulsed in eerie rainbow hues. She staggered.

"Urrrrrf . . ." she said.

Wagstaff rushed to her side and held her upright. She grinned a sloppy grin. She was drooling.

"Whoa, M, want to lie down?"

"Nuhhh . . ." she replied. Color was draining from her face. She swayed back and forth, hiccupped, and bolted for the bathroom.

They heard her retching uncontrollably. Hamilton wiggled her eyebrows in alarm. Wagstaff moved to assist, then stopped when he heard the toilet flushing. He sat down on a chair beside the bathroom door to wait her out.

It took ten minutes for Marianne to emerge from her ordeal. When the bathroom door finally opened, she was cheerfully drying her face on a towel. She paused, reading the concern.

"What?"

Wagstaff and Hamilton exchanged puzzled glances.

"You okay, M?"

Marianne's color had returned. She seemed alert and well.

"Yeah, I'm good."

She picked up her jacket.

"Gotta go now, just in case the effects of whatever the hell I just went through wear off."

"Safe to drive?"

She shrugged. Wagstaff opened the office door. He tapped his forehead against hers. "You better call me."

She nodded, put on her jacket, and stepped outside.

▼

A late-season storm might be threatening the Sierra, but the sky in Applefield was clear. The afternoon sun was bright, the temperature balmy. Marianne decided to leave her car where it was and hike to the municipal park, a former apple orchard. She had once seen her ghost in the pool of water under the town's famous prospector statue and hoped to repeat the experience.

When she arrived, however, she saw that the park's trees were in full bloom, and tourists were likely to get in her way. Sure enough, someone was fussing with a tripod-mounted camera while her extended family congregated around the bronze gold miner, framed by a spectacular array of apple blossoms. The woman still hadn't accomplished a single shot when Marianne walked up and offered her assistance.

"Oh, would you? I can't seem to work the self timer on this thing."

The grateful woman joined her loved ones, and Marianne snapped several photos, one of which was probably destined for next year's

Christmas card. Then the group meandered away, studying their guidebooks for directions to the next foothill attraction.

Marianne watched them go. She was now alone in the park. She advanced to the statue, removed Ibañez' old police badge from a jacket pocket, gave it a quick polish on her sleeve, and clutched it tightly in her right hand.

"Okay, Mr. Ghost, here I am, come on out."

The pool of water stirred. Ripples appeared. A light breeze puffed up and tugged at Marianne's hair. But nothing uncanny darkened the basin's surface.

"It's always like this," she grumbled. She held the badge up high, gripped it tightly. Her knuckles turned white.

"Hey, you!" she called, resorting to the crude summons that had sometimes worked in the past.

All at once the ripples rearranged themselves into a wavering image. A face materialized. Eyes peered at her. Lips parted.

"Hello, Marianne," it said.

Marianne jumped back. "Whoa, did you speak?"

"You heard me."

"Well, no, I didn't. I don't think so." She shook her head, poked a finger in her ear to check for wax buildup.

"Inside your cabeza. In your mind, you did."

"Oh. I get it. Like seeing auras, it's all mental." She barked out a peal of nervous laughter. "Ha ha, *I'm* mental."

"No, you're not. You're perfectly sane."

"In that case . . ." She thought about how to proceed. "I guess Crowfoot had it figured. You wanted to talk to me, so talk."

The ghost started to say something, but Marianne held up the badge to interrupt.

"But first, now that we're going to be so chatty, I want to get something out of the way. You're Hector Ibañez — my old chief, who was killed by the cartel. You know that now, right?"

The ghostly image flickered. *"I can't talk about it."*

"Why not? What's the point, anyway? Why talk at all?"

"I have some news."

"Hold on, I want to know. Not everyone sees ghosts, so come on, give!

Otherwise, how can I trust you?"

"*I'll say this much — Hector Ibañez was a worthy avatar. He was part of me.*"

An unexpected revelation.

"Okaaay . . . that's very weird."

Marianne's skin prickled.

"So, um, why talk now? Why not last year, when things were tough?"

"*I was in your future then. Now I'm not. So listen up, Little Miss Golden Girl . . .*"

Halfway across the park, Tom Wagstaff stood under an apple tree, watching his girlfriend at the water feature angrily waving her arms and stomping back and forth. He sidled forward, hoping to hear both sides of whatever conversation was underway.

Suddenly Marianne threw up her hands. She leaned over the pool, searching for something. Then she sat down on the edge and tipped her head into her lap. Wagstaff guessed her little interview was over. He walked up beside her.

"M?"

His approach jolted Marianne. She sprang to her feet, pointed an accusatory finger. "Shit, you followed me."

He shrugged a guilty confession.

"Did you hear what he said?"

"No, not a word. It would help, you know . . ."

She leaped into his arms.

"Tom — oh my God! — my father is in a coma at Beale Air Force Base. He was in that plane crash we all read about."

8

THE WEEKLY PROTEST was well underway in front of Beale's main gate when Marianne drove up to the base. Cars and RVs everywhere. She was obliged to park in a dirt turnout fifty yards from the K-Rail barriers. There she stood, watching the demonstrators and the armed guards, trying to guess whether the evening was going to turn violent.

The *Channel Four News* truck was also on hand. The cameraman switched on his lights, hoisted his camera, and the ragged crowd burst out singing *We Shall Overcome*. They began to march, looping around an illegal bonfire that was already melting the asphalt, waving their signs:

STOP DRONE ATTACKS

DRONES MAKE ENEMIES

DRONES FLY CHILDREN DIE

Some good-hearted soul had set up a table with snacks and coffee. The sweet-faced older woman supervising the refreshments offered a cup to Marianne.

"Kill the drones, not the children," she said.

Marianne nodded, accepted the coffee, and declined a lemon square.

"Right on," she replied.

The crowd segued into a halting rendition of John Lennon's *Imagine*.

Marianne elbowed through the singers to the gate itself. She locked her fingers through the chain-link fence.

"Hey, there! I need to get in!" she shouted, waving her police ID for effect. "My father was badly injured in that plane crash! He's in the infirmary!"

One of the guards took a step toward her.

"Step away from the fence, ma'am," he said, brandishing his M-16.

"I called the infirmary and everyone in charge here, and they denied everything. He's in a coma! Let me in!"

"You! Away from the fence! Move back — right now!" commanded the guard. Two of his buddies came forward to assist. Marianne groaned and retreated into the crowd.

The reporter from Channel Four moved in front of the camera with a woman holding a *Drone Free Zone* placard.

Marianne edged over for a better view.

"Hello, Bob, Mila Jansky here at Beale, where memories of the recent plane crash are fresh, and opposition to U.S. drone surveillance is strong. I'm standing in front of the Schneider Gate with, um, tell us your name again, please?"

"Gladys Underwood."

"And what is your take on drone operations here?"

"They must be stopped. They're immoral."

"As you know, the Golden Hawks based here don't carry weapons, just sensors," noted the reporter.

"Yes, but they pave the way. What they see, others shoot."

"You've been coming out here for months now. Drone operations continue. Are you having any effect at all?"

"People are waking up. We're going to put an end to this."

"Oh sure you are," said a rabbity little fellow who had taken up a position beside Marianne.

She swiveled around to see who was talking. The man's arms were folded. His expression conveyed ironic contempt. When he realized he had her attention, he continued his critique.

"*Code Red.* A bunch of well-meaning old ladies. Whoopee."

Marianne rocked back. "You're in favor of the drones?"

"Good God, no. But our protests pack a lot more punch. It's getting so we have to reserve space here when we want to march, and these old hens keep on clucking and scratching."

"How do you know I'm not one of them?"

"You're much too young."

Marianne took notice of a long tapestry being carried around the fire. It was filled with children's primitive drawings of other children who were dead.

"So what's wrong with this? It's pretty dramatic. They've got Channel Four here. People will see this on the news tonight."

"Yes, they're on the air, taking up *my* slot with stupid slogans no one will remember. We need to *educate* Americans, not yell at them."

"You have a different group? You guys compete?"

"*Live And Let Live.* We are, how do you say, a lot more rational."

"Really."

"And a lot more *tactical*. No one is going to stop drones by dancing around a bonfire."

"Oh?"

"No."

Marianne was losing interest in this nutball. The TV interview was over. She surveyed the crowd, the guards, and the fences, wondering how on Earth she was ever going to get past them and find her father.

"What then?" she asked absently.

The man leaned over to let her in on a little secret. "Direct action."

"What could be more direct than this demo?"

"We're taking the fight inside. Civil disobedience. They'll catch us for trespassing, they'll have to prosecute, we'll be on trial, it will be a media circus."

Marianne snapped to attention. Her cop radar switched on.

"That sounds really great. Really, um, tactical. But first you have to get in there, right?" she asked with an innocent smile.

"Not that hard. Want to join us? Hi, I'm Nathan Harris." He stuck out a hand.

Marianne gripped it. "Marianne Sarzeau."

"Next week," he said. "You can be part of it."

"Have you actually been inside?"

Harris looked hurt. "Of course. Several times. Well, just beyond the fence. We'll do a full reconnaissance before the big event."

Marianne nodded. "What's wrong with tonight? I'm your girl."

"Hey, slow down, we're still gearing up."

"Listen, Mr. Harris. My father's in there. You heard about that plane crash, right?"

"I was right here when it happened," he avowed.

"Well, Dad was in that crash. He's in the infirmary, and they won't let me see him."

Harris was confused. "Why not?"

Marianne adopted a conspiratorial tone for his benefit. "He's a secret agent."

Harris' eyebrows shot upward. "You're pulling my leg."

"No, I'm not. Special forces. He's here on some kind of secret mission. Help me, maybe you'll have some grist for your mill."

▼

Miles away south, at Beale's Wheatland Gate, the evening was quiet. No crowd, no cars, no eager TV news crews. The lonely guard on duty felt safe enough to play his radio over loudspeakers. Tim McGraw's manly pursuit of love and respect wailed across the fields; country music laid over open country. The sum of the action was a bat chasing moths around the security lights.

But, as the sky darkened into night, an anonymous Chevy Malibu drove up, fresh from a rental counter somewhere. A lanky young man was sitting at the wheel. An adolescent girl was in the passenger seat beside him, and two younger kids flanked a bearded old man in the back.

The driver asked to enter the base and was denied. The guard demanded the man's driver's license and explained how to turn the car around.

"My license?" asked the driver, looking confused.

"Do a one-eighty around the K-Rail here" — the guard pointed — "and when you're facing the other way, I'll return it."

"I'm sorry, I left my wallet at home."

Mild suspicion flickered across the guard's face. He picked up a telephone handset and punched a number.

"Yasmin?" said the driver.

The adolescent girl leaned across his lap for a clear view of the guard. She thrust up her right hand and muttered something. Not in English.

The guard's jaw sagged open. His eyes rolled up in his head. Eyelids fluttered, and he slumped sideways against the frame of his kiosk window. He was out cold.

The driver snicked the Chevy Malibu into reverse and rolled backward for a hundred feet until clear of the gate's complicated barriers. There he performed a sedate U-turn and motored away south.

▼

It took forty-five minutes for Harris' old Nissan pickup truck to arrive at the jumping-off spot he had identified on the east side of the base. Marianne was prepared to navigate the circuitous northern route with Google maps, but Harris insisted that she turn her smartphone off.

"They could be tracking us through the cell towers," he said, with a paranoid glance at the empty countryside.

"Unh-huh," said Marianne. She sank down in the passenger seat. His mood was contagious, and she was starting to catch his disease.

They motored across the north end of Beale on the Hammonton-Smartville Road, then turned south at the eastern margin onto Chuck Yeager Road. Now they were in gentle hills. Oak trees were filling in the fields.

Harris veered left onto an unpaved backcountry byway.

"We're heading for Dry Creek at the Waldo bridge. Amazing as it is with all the security back there at the big show, there's a gap in the fence where the creek runs into the base."

Marianne was incredulous. "You just tootle right around it?"

"Worked for me."

They bumped along for a few more miles. Then they found themselves on a wide and unexpectedly substantial concrete bridge. Dry Creek was flowing beneath them, brimming with spring runoff water. Harris slowed and turned west onto the Spencerville Road, narrower, bumpier, barely a scrape in the spring grass.

"Okay, now, here's the deal. The Beale fence is less than a mile away. I'll get you a little closer, but I won't lie, it's going to be a long walk. What are your shoes like?"

Marianne raised a foot, showing off her Nike Airs.

"Good, you can hike."

Harris turned off his headlights. They followed the rough track for another quarter mile, guided by shadows and the faint skylight from California cities just beyond the horizon. Harris brought his truck to a halt under a canopy of oaks.

"This is it. Last chance to back out. When you cross the line, it's a federal offense."

Marianne opened her door. "Just an infraction unless aggravated. Dad's in there, no one is going to prosecute me. And anyway, I've gotta risk it." She stepped out of the truck and then leaned back in. "Aren't you worried I might spoil your plans?"

"Nah. They try, but the Air Force is a bureaucracy, and they just don't know how to react to a teensy-tiny threat like this. They'll need a hundred meetings and memos and directives to figure it out. We'll be fine. Just don't step in any cow pies, they're all over the place."

"Okay, thanks, Mr. Harris."

"It's Nate. Want me to stick around, just in case?"

"No, get out of here. I'm pretty sure someone will offer me a ride to my car" — she made a face — "one way or the other."

"Final instructions, then. Stay on the creek bed slopes as much as possible. Harder for cameras and night vision goggles to pick you up. Once you pass the fence, be aware of the road here, beside the stream. It runs right into the residential section of the base. Once you hit pavement, with houses around, no one will notice you."

"Got it."

"The medical command is up beyond the north end of town, on Warren Shingle Road. Two miles, max."

"I'm ready."

He fussed around behind his seat for a small silvery package. "These guys patrol, and they've got a lot of tricks. Might be using infrared. Wear this thing like a poncho, it will trap your heat signature."

Marianne took the package and tore it open. "A space blanket . . . ?"

"Yeah. Who knows?"

Marianne gave him a cynical look. "So I'm the guinea pig?"

He nodded sheepishly. "Let us know if it works."

She waved goodbye, and he backed his truck around.

She stood in place for a little while, watching him go, allowing her eyes to adjust. After a couple of minutes the landscape came into sharp relief. She struck off southwest, keeping the wheel marks of Spencerville Road to her left.

Harris, meanwhile, switched on his headlights on his way back to the Waldo bridge. He was surprised when the taillight reflectors of a late-model Chevy Malibu blazed up from concealment among a jumble of manzanita bushes. The car had been entirely invisible from the opposite direction. He puzzled over the meaning. Lovers' lane? A late-night fisherman? Another intruder? But the hour was late, he was hungry, and his mind was more intent on avoiding deer than anything else. Soon he was miles away.

Marianne hit the fence line as expected, a few yards from the road and well away from the bushes enclosing the creek. She turned north. In twenty paces the chain links came to an end where the land tilted down to the stream. She shook her head.

"I'll be damned. So much for security."

She rounded the end post with a little hop and continued onward, staying within the sheltering bowl of the creek bed.

Ten minutes later, she was checked by an especially dense creekside copse. Oaks, cottonwoods, laurels, and blackberries — every bit as good as a prison wall. She worked her way up the slope and around the thicket. There she paused.

The lights of Beale's residential community were now in view. She was almost there. She thought it prudent (or maybe just superstitiously correct) to wear the space blanket, so she wrapped it around her shoulders. It made her look like a silvery tent walking along under the stars.

She was approaching pavement when she sensed a reddish glow coming toward her. Bent on reaching the anonymity of homes and street lights, she failed to register the meaning of the faint glimmer.

Suddenly she became aware of five people standing in the shadows, right in front of her. Two men, one young, the other old, and three children. A Beale family, out for an evening stroll? She stopped dead, wondering how to fake her way past some real residents of the base.

"Hi, there," she said. "Nice night, huh?"

"Zohra, your turn, I think," said the old man, speaking to one of the children.

The youngest child, a little girl possibly nine years old, raised her hand toward Marianne, palm out. She muttered something in a foreign language.

Marianne's eyes rolled up in her head, her arms went slack, and she fell to the ground like a rag doll.

The middle child, a boy, pulled at the old man's sleeve.

"Dada. Automobile."

A Humvee was coming their way in a hurry, preceded by the whine of its engine. Headlights swept across the grass. Air Force security police had discovered the intruders by some means and were hot on their trail.

"You there! Stay where you are! Do not move!" commanded a harsh voice through tinny loudspeakers.

The two men herded the children in among the trees, leaving Marianne where she lay, a distracting lure for the security team.

The Humvee skidded to a stop beside her, and the occupants jumped out. The driver snapped on a powerful flashlight and played it over Marianne's crumpled form.

"Christ, Bill, what's this?" He tugged at the space blanket.

The second patrolman bent down and checked for a pulse.

"It's a woman. She's breathing. What the hell?"

He snapped on a pair of night vision goggles and scanned the area, but the rest of the intruders were already down along the creek, running away, well out of sight.

The first patrolman had Marianne's wallet open.

"Fuck me, she's a cop."

He sighed.

"What a night."

9

IN PLACERVILLE, a Chevy Malibu rental car drove slowly uphill under the streetlights of Cedar Ravine Road, past Rotary Park and the hospital. Just before the Church of Joy Everlasting it turned onto Billy Hill Drive and came to a stop at number 229, an anonymous clapboard house. There it parked in the street, because the shadowy driveway was already occupied by a U-Haul truck with a monstrous picture of a yellow spider faintly visible on the cargo box.

Inside, lights were on. Steaming bowls of lentil soup were waiting on the dining room table for two tired men and three bleary-eyed children.

"What's this, Darius?" marveled the younger man, inhaling the fragrant food odors with appreciation.

Before his companion could answer, an athletic woman of forty or so entered from the kitchen with a plate full of flat bread. The skin and eyes in her narrow face were brown. A silk scarf covered her head. The kids started yelling and ran over to hug her.

"Firoz! Firoz! Firoz!" they cried, dancing around and pulling on her apron strings. She rubbed their hair and gave them each a squeeze.

"Firoz, this is our host, Habib Rajput."

The woman nodded a greeting. The younger man nodded back.

Then the group sat down for a late-night supper.

Firoz took care to keep her eyes lowered. "Golay, sir, did you find success today?"

The old man shook his head. "No flights. We were hoping for another drone, but not so lucky."

"Will you go again tomorrow?"

"Ahh, that is the question. We ran into an interesting problem."

The boy piped up. "We met someone."

"Yes, we did," the old man confirmed. "What about her, Yasmin?"

"She is one of us," replied the adolescent girl. "We could feel her long before she appeared."

"But we got her! She was wearing a metal cloak to protect herself, but Zohra's spell burned right through it," said the young boy, puffing up with pride.

Firoz' head came up. "You saw an adept? A woman? She was American?"

The old man nodded.

"She could not have been there by accident," said Firoz.

"No, I suppose not. But why? What brought her there? That is what I do not know," said the old man.

"She's a policeman!" said Zohra. "She wasn't dressed right, but I could read her."

"She sees us. It must be so. Somehow, she knows what we are doing," said Firoz.

"I am not sure." The old man shook his head in confusion.

"We should kill her," insisted Firoz. Under her mild surface breathed a fierce spirit.

The old man put down his spoon. He stirred uncomfortably. "Firoz, the children are exhausted. It has been a very long day. Will you see them to bed, please? We must discuss our plans."

Firoz nodded, collected the children and ushered them toward the stairs and the bedrooms above. As she moved she made an audible clicking sound — *klik!* — *klik!* — *klik!*

Rajput was very curious about the woman. "Who is she? Where did she come from? And what in the world — what is that *clicking* sound?"

The old man smiled. "She is their nanny. She arrived today, while we were gone. We had some trouble with her passport. The first one did not withstand scrutiny."

Rajput stirred uneasily. "The clicking — ?"

"Ah, yes, that. Well, you see, Firoz is blind."

"Blind — !"

"From early years. She is not adept like the children, but she has other powers. She sees with her ears, like a bat."

"Echolocation?"

"Yes, exactly. It is not unknown."

"Wow."

"So, let us think. Suppose we were to kill that American woman," mused the old man, toying with a piece of bread. "How and by what means?"

"No idea."

"We must not let any deed poison our mission. Rajput, you're practically an American. Could we approach her, strangle her perhaps, place the body out of sight? If Zohra has guessed correctly, she is a police officer. Would she be missed? How soon?"

The old man raised an inquisitive eyebrow. Rajput remained silent.

"Or suppose we stabbed or shot her, would investigators blame local criminals? What do you recommend?"

Rajput drummed his fingers on the table. He pushed his chair back and stood up.

"Darius, you're talking about murder — not something I signed up for."

"It would not be murder, but a wartime necessity. Think of commandos, the Russian *Spetsnaz,* American special forces. What they do every day."

"I'm not going to kill anybody," insisted Rajput. "Don't ask."

"But, you do agree that the drones are an evil, a mockery of Pakistani sovereignty?"

"Yes, of course. Absolutely."

The old man pondered the matter. He seemed to change his mind. "Well, now I think about it, and I see you are right," he conceded. "A dead policewoman would arouse our enemies. Fellow officers would avenge her."

"Yeah, they would. Big trouble."

"Our presence must not become known. By anyone. To protect our mission, I believe we must move on to our next target. It is time."

"Next target?"

The old man smiled a chilly smile. "If I have caused distress, please be at ease. We are eternally grateful for your assistance, for your perfect discretion."

Rajput nodded and breathed a sigh of relief.

10

MARIANNE woke up in bed. Sunbeams were angling through the corridors outside her room in the Beale Air Force Base infirmary. A 19th Medical Group nurse, male, a young Asian dude, placed a tray on the roll-around stand at her bedside.

"Have some orange juice. Sugar Puffs if you want 'em, and I brought you an English muffin."

"I'm not hungry. Just hung over."

"You're a wreck. You need fuel. Eat."

Marianne struggled to sit up. The nurse leaned over and touched a button to tilt her bed up. She looked around. Her clothes were stuffed in a plastic bag on a chair in the corner. She herself was wearing a lavender examining gown, and the loose folds made her feel like a medical specimen.

"What time is it?" she asked, trying to get oriented.

"Ten or so," he replied.

She noticed the insignia on the breast pocket of his blouse.

"You're Air Force. I'm at Beale?"

"That's right. What happened? Security found you down near family housing. Unconscious. Lights, O-U-T, out."

"I don't remember very much," she murmured, hoping to conceal the basis of her questionable activities. "Just this — there was a little girl. She raised her hand, and . . . here I am."

The nurse nodded. "Interesting. No one mentioned anyone else."

"I guess she did something funny to knock me out, unless you found Taser burns or a tranquilizer dart stuck in my butt."

Marianne stared at the wall. She was slowly becoming aware of a faintly bluish glow somewhere beyond it. She closed her eyes, trying to pinpoint the source, remembering the color test old lady Crowfoot put her through. The sensation disappeared. But then, a few seconds later, it was dancing in her head again.

"You all right?" asked the nurse.

She sucked in her breath, gasped, and dramatically clutched her head in both hands.

"Whoa, there — !" he exclaimed.

Marianne moaned.

"Hey, hey, tell me what's wrong."

"Um . . . not sure. I've got this pinging in my head. First over here" — she pointed vaguely to her left temple — "then up here. It bounces around. I feel sick."

"I'll be right back, doc's going to want a look at this."

He rushed out of the room. Marianne waited until he was gone, working hard to suppress a smile. Then she peeled back the covers and tiptoed into the corridor. She closed her eyes, searching in her mind for the source of the glow she felt. It was vague, her sense was undeveloped, it was hard to pinpoint.

But wait — *there!* — down that way.

She padded along the corridor in her bare feet, rounded a corner, passed an empty nurse's station, rounded another corner. Now she was confronted by a T-junction. Which way? She closed her eyes again, emptying her thoughts. It seemed to take forever, but a tentative impression gradually built up. The glow, she realized, faint and intermittent as it was, emanated from a room at the end of the hallway to her right.

She quickstepped to the room and peered inside. A forest of medical gear surrounded a single bed. Tubes and wires ran from the equipment to a small man lying unconscious on his back.

In Marianne's mind, the man shimmered with a faint but discernible blue glow. She realized she had seen that same glow on the airplane that flew overhead a few nights ago in Placerville. The airplane that crashed, it seemed.

"Dad!" she exclaimed.

Before she could step inside the room a doctor and a security detail rushed to intercept.

"Stop! You can't go in there, ma'am," said the doctor as the security men grabbed and restrained her.

"Why not? This is my father!"

"Please, ma'am, come with me."

The doctor motioned with a finger, and the security men started to drag her away. She thrashed this way and that to resist. Her heels were squeaking on the polished floor.

"Sergeant Emile Sarzo, right? Special forces. I'm his daughter! *Let me go!*"

The doctor regarded the half-naked crazy woman with her wild hair and flapping gown and shook his head.

"We're not treating any patient by that name."

"That's a lie!"

The doctor hooked a thumb toward the exit.

"Get her out of here," he said.

▼

Later that day, having been delivered to the Schneider Gate in a security Humvee and unceremoniously thrown out of Beale, Marianne drove down to Ragtown to tell her bookselling friend all about her adventures.

"Are you sure it's your father?" asked Lorraine, nibbling an éclair.

"I'm sure."

They were sitting in the back of Lorraine's brightly-lit store, which was nicely outfitted as an internet café, with snacks on racks, a second-hand espresso machine as big as a piano, and a line of aging computers for surfing the web.

"You're all about a thin little guy in bed with tubes up his nose. How do you know who the heck it was?"

"It's hard to explain, but I could see his *aura.*" Marianne was savoring a macchiato. Lorraine made the best coffee in the county.

"First ghosts, now auras. Do you know how that sounds?"

"Crazy."

"Yes it does. Get a grip, kiddo."

"I don't actually see anything, if you want to know. But I can sense things as if they *were* colors."

"You have always been weird, and now you are the Queen of Weirdosity. How does Tom feel about these, ah — insights — of yours?"

"Uh-oh, sorry — *Mother* — guess what? I don't see Tom that way."

"But I thought —"

"— only other adepts. Tom is just my main squeeze. I know him like you know anyone. Like I know you."

"Is that supposed to be comforting?" huffed Lorraine.

"Look, Dad is up there at Beale, and he's there because he is what he is. So, what's going on? Is the CIA running some sort of geek show? He's a sergeant, but maybe he's not really in the Army, know what I mean?"

The puzzle aroused Lorraine's curiosity. She snapped her fingers and revved up one of her computers. "Let's see what we can see."

They googled every keyword they could think of, but a long half hour of mouse clicks and hundreds of hits failed to turn up any evidence of unusual government operations.

"Maybe your dad is just as weird as you are, and it's all a big coincidence," sighed Lorraine.

"Unless it's top secret crap. What about that kid who knocked me out? Something's up, Lorraine, and Dad is mixed up in it."

"What does your ghost have to say?"

"Hmm. I wonder."

▼

Marianne left the Book Nook and zipped up the hill to Applefield in no time, grooving her little Mini through the switchbacks with aggressive purpose.

In the town park she pulled out Ibañez' old police badge, held it high and tight, and called out her usual summons.

"Okay, here we go — *hey you!*"

The pool of water at the foot of the park's prospector statue rippled. A formless shadow appeared. It glided back and forth.

"That you, Mr. G?"

The shadow wobbled.

"Come on, show yourself, I need some help."

She stared into the pool for more than a minute, waiting for some change. She was all ready to give up when the shadow suddenly expanded and turned into the flickering silhouette of a human figure.

"Marianne. How are you?" said the apparition.

Marianne winced. She was still disturbed by the voice in her head.

"Hello, Chief, what took you so long?"

"I was far away."

"Unh-huh, whatever that means in Foreverville. Listen, I saw Dad up at Beale, but the Air Force threw me out. What's going on?"

"How should I know? I'm not a doctor."

"But you were in touch with him, you warned me."

"I could sense distress."

"He's comatose. Does that mean he's . . . um . . ."

She couldn't quite frame the thought.

". . . a vegetable? No, his mind is working."

Better news than she feared. She started to calm down. "Well, that's something. Could you tell why he's here? Did he come to see me?"

"Wouldn't that be warm and cuddly?" said the ghost.

"Laugh if you want. Is he going to wake up?"

"I don't know. If he wants to, he will. That's how it works."

The shadow lurched. The ghostly head swiveled back and forth. His attention seemed to be wandering. Marianne was quick to pick up the signs of impatience.

"Gotta go? Okay, okay, give me a sec. Let's try this . . . last time we talked — *talked!* I'm still amazed — you said Chief Ibañez was part of you. What part is that?"

"I could have said I was him — I am him — only . . . more."

"Unh-huh. So what is it like over there in Ghostland anyway? You fly around, check in on all the planets?"

"Look, Little Miss Mortal, it's complicated. If I don't understand it — and I don't — you'll never figure it out on your side of the fence, so stop obsessing."

"Oh great. No Dad, no ghost gossip, big help you are."

The ghost shrugged, and his shadow vanished.

Marianne reached into the pool, picked up a penny someone had thrown in, looked it over, idly tossed it back. The coin made a little *bloop* sound as it hit the water.

"I wish . . ." she said. ". . . I wish . . . damn, what *do* I wish?"

She watched the penny float down to the bottom, glinting brightly as it tilted back and forth.

Part TWO

11

THAT SAME AFTERNOON, in an austere office overlooking the
flight line at Beale, General Weaver stood up at a knock on the door to
welcome U.S. Army Major Raymond Bagwell, who entered without
saluting.

"Hello, Ray," said the general, pushing aside a pile of paperwork.
"How's the head? The back?"

"Soldiering on." Bagwell was a round balding man in his late forties. A
butterfly Band-Aid was taped to his forehead. He placed a fist on his pelvis
and tenderly arched his back. "And your arm?"

"Doc says, give it six weeks. The fracture was not displaced."

"We are a couple of sorry souls, Vern."

"Could be worse."

Bagwell nodded. "Mmm, Agent Scanner."

He stepped to the window and peered out at a Golden Hawk
surveillance drone glistening in bright sunlight on the taxiway. "Those
things are a lot bigger than I thought," he mused. Slowly he collected
himself and turned to the business at hand.

"You've read the report, yes?"

"Of course. So what? It's all preliminary."

"Both our pilot and copilot state — officially and for the record — that
they fell asleep at the controls."

"It's absurd. A ridiculous attempt to conceal some real human error."

Bagwell's attention was drawn to the runway, where a Chevrolet
Camaro was streaking north behind the wide wings of a descending U-2,
guiding the pilot down onto the concrete.

"What if it's true?"

"Did the ding on your head addle your brain? Pilots don't fall asleep."

"Milo — sorry, Agent Scanner — certainly did. He's still out."

"Severe concussion in the crash," said Weaver. "That's also in
the report."

"A report you just dismissed. Forget it. It's a form. Someone filled in a
blank. But I had a long talk with the doctor, checked the brain waves. You
saw those monitors too. He's not concussed. Just sleeping."

Weaver flexed his bad arm. "What are you talking about?"

"Three people on our airplane fall asleep just as we're landing. It's not a coincidence."

Weaver paced around his desk. "You think the air supply was sabotaged? We were gassed?"

Bagwell shook his head. "After a fire like that we can't be sure, but no, it wasn't something wrong with the AC."

"What, then? Christ, Ray."

"Sergeant Sarzo is an adept. As such, I have learned, he is particularly susceptible to other adepts."

"Others? What others? What are you suggesting?"

Bagwell turned away from the window. He jammed his hands in his pockets and adopted a what-if pose. "As you know, there were questions about pilot fatigue when the drones crashed here. Maybe those guys nodded off too."

Weaver stopped pacing. "Your conclusion?"

"We've got saboteurs, all right, as we both suspected when we took this case. But they're not using gas or bombs."

"What then?"

"How about curses and spells?"

"Jesus. Have you and Scanner ever encountered anything like this before? Any other adepts?"

"No, we have not. This is new."

Weaver resumed his seat, tilted the chair back, and stared at the ceiling. "Let's hope your pal Spooky wakes up soon, because without him our little operation won't solve any of this."

"There's something else," said Bagwell, arching his back again.

"Yes? Going to tell me?"

"Scanner's adult daughter was found on the perimeter last night, attempting to infiltrate the base. Now get this — she was unconscious, had to be treated in the clinic."

"How on Earth — ?"

"— Yeah, how did she know? I ran a check — she's a cop down in Placerville. My sources claim that she's also an adept."

"A chip off the Scanner block?"

"So it seems. A sleepy one."

12

MARIANNE was awakened at 4:30 AM by the tones on her smartphone. She jabbed frantically to turn it off before Tom Wagstaff, slumbering beside her with no early obligations, was jarred awake as well.

After a quick shower, a bagel, and a cup of instant coffee, she was on her way through Placerville. Rays of the rising sun reached into the narrow valley, lighting telephone poles and treetops. By 5:30 she was in the station gearing up. By 6:00 she was out the back door and trudging toward her patrol car. There she crossed paths with Desmond Otis, on his way home after a long night on the graveyard shift.

"Morning, Dez."

Otis nodded and kept on walking.

"Hey, grumpy. Wait a sec."

He raised a hand and gave her a tired wave. "Not now, Sarz. I'm beat. The Kings were battling the Lakers last night. I'm going to pop a top and watch the replay on my DVR."

"If you don't stop and talk to me," she said, "I'm going to tell you the score."

This brought Otis to a halt. "Don't you dare." He turned around. "You don't even know the score."

"Wanna bet?"

"Okay, okay, what's up, what do you want?"

"What do you know about Beale Air Force Base?"

"Uh, spy planes. Keeping an eye on the forces of evil. Why?"

"Nothing, really. Just curious. Lot of protests up there. I was just wondering if there was a criminal element involved."

"Doubt that. Do-gooders looking for a cause, you ask me," he said.

Marianne shrugged. For reasons she didn't quite understand, she was reluctant to tell her story. "What about our burglars? I miss anything?"

"Don't I wish."

"You didn't happen to run across our U-Haul last night, by any chance?"

"Believe it or not, I looked. Eyes wide. And I got nothing. But yesterday I called like fifteen U-Haul shops, and nobody has anything outstanding from a Placerville address."

"Shit. Looks like we're hosed."

Otis unstrapped his duty belt and continued toward the station.

"Yeah, hosed. Hope the Kings done better."

13

LATE ON SUNDAY afternoon Marianne arrived at the *County Courier* offices with a large pizza from Foo Long's Chinese Italian Kitchen and a six-pack of beer.

After a quick supper with Wagstaff, she got back in her Mini and drove a mile south on Copper King Road to KVIG, the local FM radio station. Three-foot-high call letters, outlined in orange neon, were the only ornamental touch on the grey cinder block studio. A red hazard light faded on and off atop a tall mast in the southwest corner of the property, a lonely entertainment beacon in the evening sky.

The Mini's tires crackled on the long gravel drive as she approached her old domain. A year and a half ago she had signed on as a weekend DJ when Howard Turnbow, the wealthy businessman who owned the station, decided that he liked her voice. After a while she was also subbing on weekdays, and pretty soon she had her own fan base. But mixing police work with show biz proved tiring, so she used her transfer to Placerville as an excuse to quit.

Now she was back. The wealthy businessman was now mayor of the Tri-Town Special District, and she found it impossible to refuse his blandishments.

She unlocked the little red door and stepped inside. The entire interior, except for a tiny bathroom, was a single room. It was dimly illuminated by little LEDs glowing on the racks of electronic equipment that filled every corner. The scene brought memories of her first impression — a night full of stars winking and blinking. She hung up her jacket and sat down. To get back in her DJ mood, she rolled her chair around the studio on its oversize casters, kicking the walls and bouncing off. After a final twirl she turned her attention to the controls.

Since her last session, the station had undergone some remodeling, and a spiffy mixing board and large flat computer monitor now dominated her desk. Cryptic lines of text were rising upward on the screen in little jumps. She checked to see what was playing. The top line of text, bracketed by a pair of arrows, registered a title: *Mine Would Be You*, Blake Shelton's country hit. Like a lot of the music that pulsed through the studio, she had never heard of the song.

KVIG was a Class-A station, spraying a piddling six thousand watts over the neighboring countryside. People in nearby Jackson had trouble tuning in, and down in Lodi, just thirty miles into the Big Valley, the signal disappeared altogether. Two secrets made the station successful. First was the internet — more people heard it on their computers and mobile devices than over the air. Second was Spin-O-Matic, Inc., the playlist service from Dallas that automatically generated the station's music most hours of the day. The service's hip selections of country and alternative rock tracks made it possible for someone as ignorant of pop culture as Marianne to hold down her job.

But Spin-O-Matic had its limits, which is why Marianne was in the station preparing for an evening of listener requests. Each song someone called in live twiddled the playlist, slowly and imperceptibly molding the station to its audience's tastes. All Marianne had to do was type some titles into the keyboard on the desk, read some local advertisements, and say the call letters now and then in accordance with FCC regulations.

Under normal circumstances she would be more than pleased to cooperate, but tonight her thoughts were elsewhere — on a bed in the Beale Air Force Base infirmary, where her father was taking a long involuntary nap.

To prepare herself and rev up to speed she recorded a couple of ads, first singing the praises of the tire selection at Abbott's Automotive, and then smacking her lips over the swill produced by a Diamond Springs brew pub she actually abhorred. She reminded herself that she was being paid well.

She checked the clock above her desk. Almost time. She hit a button, leaned into the mike, and made an introduction. Working swiftly, she uploaded the resulting file to Spin-O-Matic, and watched it slot itself into the playlist. At precisely 7:00 PM her intro jumped up between the arrows . . .

"This is The Golden Girl of the Golden Hills, coming to you from *The Vig* — K-V-I-G — in Applefield, California, at ninety-three-point-one on your FM dial. It's seven o'clock."

She rose from her chair as Robin Thicke's innocently raunchy *Blurred Lines* danced out over the local hills. She bopped around to the infectious beat as she made coffee on the little hotplate in the corner.

Her first request came in ten minutes later, while Daft Punk were doing their disco-best to *Get Lucky*.

"This is your Golden Girl. Whatever you say, we play. Got a request for me?"

"Uh, yeah, can I hear *Gone?*"

Marianne consulted Spin-O-Matic. A dozen songs were listed. She had no idea which was the right one.

"You mean the Kanye West song?"

"No, no, it's Robert Plant and what's her name? They did a country record together."

Marianne was flummoxed. What the hey? She typed in Plant's name as fast as her fingers could fly. Then, exuding authority, she advised:

"You mean, *Gone, Gone, Gone,* I think. Alison Krauss is the name you're looking for."

"Oh yeah, her, the fiddler chick."

Three seconds later heavy drums were beating, and the unlikely pair were slamming out the track from their Grammy-winning album.

Marianne tapped her foot in time to the drums. Like riding a bicycle, she decided. A small crisis already handled, and after a year rusting away, she still felt comfortable behind the microphone.

▼

Later that evening, while Kacey Musgraves was busy telling everyone to *Follow Your Arrow,* a black Cadillac Escalade SUV rolled slowly down the drive to the station with its headlights off. It turned onto the grass and parked near the building, out of sight of the door.

An overhead light came on inside, illuminating the driver, a pudgy man in a leather jacket. He reached under the passenger seat for a padded nylon pouch, unzipped it, and extracted an S&W .38 Special revolver, a 442 model with the internal hammer. He spun the cylinder to check the loads and laid it on the passenger seat. He removed a small bottle of some brownish liquid from the glove box, gave it a shake, and placed it in a cup holder. Then he turned on his radio and tuned to ninety-three-point-one on his FM dial, just in time to hear the Golden Girl of the Golden Hills sign off for the night.

Marianne was humming to herself as she cracked the door of the station building and stepped out into the spring air. Unpleasant previous experience had taught her to take a look around before heading home, and she did so. The survey was negative. Nothing out there, nothing moving.

She looked up at the sky. This far out of town, the stars blazed down in glory, barely obscured here and there by thin cloud wisps. Orion was setting in the west, and she noted a bright star just then rising over the eastern hilltops, briefly wondering if it had a name.

The night was warm, so she tucked her jacket under an arm, got her car key out, and started toward her little Mini. She was thinking about Tom, who was probably still in his office, frantically working up the latest edition of his little newspaper and, unfortunately for her, not likely to be very entertaining company. She unlocked her car door and was trying to decide whether to drive straight home when she heard footsteps crunching on the gravel behind her.

She turned around. A chubby man was standing there. She reached down to her ankle for the little Beretta she always carried and froze in mid-motion. The man was lazily pointing a gun in her direction. He wiggled the stubby barrel to direct her hands away. She slowly stood up, hands empty, heart racing, forcing herself to breathe.

"Marianne Sarzeau?" he inquired, just to be sure.

"Yeah . . ."

"Come with me, please."

▼

An hour after Tom Wagstaff heard her sign off, Marianne had still not appeared at his door, or call him to say why not.

He looked up from his layout tasks and began to wonder what was going on. He tapped her contact number on his smartphone. After four rings her breezy message played.

"Hi, this is Sarzeau, can't pick up. Say your say, call you back."

Wagstaff glared at the computer screen. He spent five minutes jiggling advertisements around the paper's back pages. He attempted to re-write his lead article on Tri-Town property taxes. Then he abruptly stood up, unable to continue.

"Where *are* you, M?"

He backed up his work on a flash drive, jumped into his truck, and motored down to KVIG to check on her.

As he turned down the gravel drive his headlights picked up Marianne's Mini, still sitting where she left it. He parked beside the car and got out to look inside. He put out a hand to try the driver's door and stopped himself with a sharp intake of breath.

"Jesus."

A smear of blood ran from the door handle down along the sheet metal. Wagstaff ran over to the station door. He gave it a yank, but it was locked, as it should be. He then dashed around the building, shouting as he went.

"Marianne! Marianne! Marianne!"

Back at the station door he stopped cold, paralyzed by something he should have already spotted. At about waist level, a nice round hole a half inch in diameter spoiled the door's red paint. He poked a finger into the cavity. A deformed bullet popped out and dropped onto the concrete step. He bent to pick it up and stumbled backward, horrified by a splash of fluid trailing from the concrete into the gravel. It was brownish red, a bloody puddle.

"Ohhhhh . . . God Almighty."

He pulled out his phone and dialed 9-1-1.

14

THE STORY, when it appeared, only made it to page three of the *Sacramento Bee*, and the alarming headline was set in small type:

POLICEWOMAN MISSING

Marianne Sarzeau, a Placerville police officer, failed to return home last night after signing off her duties as a substitute disc jockey at KVIG, rural Applefield's radio station. Blood and other marks of a struggle were found at the scene, including evidence of gunfire. Thomas Wagstaff, the editor and publisher of a local newspaper, and a professed "friend" of the missing woman, brought the disappearance to law enforcement officials. He is currently being questioned by the Amador County Sheriff's Department as a person of interest. Foul play is suspected.

Anyone with information on Ms. Sarzeau's whereabouts or other knowledge of this tragic event is asked to please call the Golden Hills Tri-Town Police Department, which is coordinating the investigation.

▼

A mournful group of Marianne's friends were gathered in the Book Nook for mutual consolation. Lorraine was serving espresso in all its forms, and everyone was trying to see the bright side of the situation. Mayor Turnbow slouched in to join them.

"Morning, morning. Anything new?"

Wade Gawley was there, representing local law enforcement. "Not a word. Rick and Chief Fabriano have been out since daybreak sweeping the countryside, just in case they spot something . . . well, you know."

"I just came from the radio station," said Turnbow. "Except for the bullet hole, everything's fine. But Marianne's car isn't there anymore."

Gawley nodded. "We towed it up to the station. It's in our lot for the time being. I got out our old kit and dusted for prints, but all I found match the ones we have on her."

This information didn't help anyone's mood.

"No news is good news," said a downcast Tom Wagstaff without much conviction.

"Mayor Turnbow — what can I offer you? A latte? A scone?" said Lorraine in her perkiest manner, hoping to dispel the gloom.

"A latte would be great, thanks. Just don't tell my baristas," Turnbow replied. The Pick & Shovel coffee shop in Applefield was one of his enterprises.

"Here you are, and your secret is safe with me," said Lorraine as she handed over the frothy drink.

Turnbow sipped doubtfully. Then his eyes lit up. "Say, that's pretty good. You can come to work for me any time you want. Give my girls an education."

Lorraine smiled.

Gawley's mobile phone rang. "Tri-Town Police, Gawley here, help you?"

The rest of the group stopped to listen. Inwardly they were all cringing, expecting bad news.

"Unh-huh. Yes, I will. Right. Placerville. Got it, Chief, I'll let them know." Gawley ended the call and found three pairs of eyes staring at him.

"What is it? Whatcha got?" asked Wagstaff.

Gawley raised a hand, palm out. "Nothing. Chief called Placerville, and an Officer Otis up there has been out searching for . . . whatever. Checking the hospitals, the obvious body dumps, and so on. We have pretty much covered the territory now, and we don't have a clue."

Wagstaff slumped into a chair.

"Well, I think that gives us something to hope for," said Lorraine. "I think she's alive, and she'll turn up."

"Either that, or we'll be getting a ransom note or a phone call. However the bad guys operate these days," added Turnbow.

"Anyone know of any family members?" asked Gawley.

They all shook their heads.

"If anyone gets a call, it's going to be the Tri-Town hotline or one of us, I think," said Lorraine.

"Oh, I forgot," said Gawley. "You're off the hook, Tom. Chief Fabriano heard from the Sheriff, and they're backing off the 'person-of-interest' bullshit."

"I should be grateful," sighed Wagstaff. "But this whole thing stinks."

15

AT BEALE Air Force Base, Sergeant Emile Sarzo was still fast asleep in his infirmary bed, maintained by the same snarl of wires and tubes that had nursed him since the crash. A bedside medical monitor displayed his heart and pulmonary rhythms.

To Major Bagwell and to General Weaver, standing beside him, the little green spikes were a frustrating mystery. They indicated a man lightly sleeping. Someone who might be awake, but somehow was not.

To Marianne Sarzeau, also standing nearby, they were signs of hope.

"The spikes — they're tall and regular. That's good, right?" she asked.

"Theoretically, yes. But he hasn't stirred since our plane hit the taxiway." Bagwell shrugged. "That's why you're here — we understand you share some of his . . . abilities . . . and we're hoping you can wake him up."

"You kidnapped me and dragged me up here because you think I'm what? Some kind of witch doctor?"

"No, but you are an adept." said Bagwell. "That much we know. Can you see him? Or feel him? In your head, I mean."

Marianne gently placed her hand on her sleeping father's forehead. She closed her eyes and did her best to quiet the evil thoughts that had been whirling through her mind ever since she was captured at gunpoint outside the KVIG studio. After a while she could discern a faint bluish luminescence emanating from him. It came and went in a slow rhythm. It seemed to carry with it a silent message — *hello . . . angel . . . hello . . . angel . . .*

Marianne shook herself.

"Here's what I see — and it's not much. He's my Dad all right, and I guess he knows I'm here. Sort of. Beyond that, I have no idea."

"We can't have our primary asset turning into Rip Van Winkle. What is causing this, this . . . damn siesta he's taking?" asked Weaver. He seemed to expect an expert opinion.

"Listen, guys, I'm just a cop. A few days ago I learned that sometimes I can detect an aura — just barely — if the person is also an adept, like now. But I don't really know what I'm doing. You understand that?"

"We know you're not trained. But you're all we've got now that your father is out of the picture."

"Me and a dollar will get you a cup of coffee. Now, how about you take me home, I'm about twenty-four hours overdue."

Bagwell and Weaver looked at each other.

"And leave your father sleeping here?" asked Bagwell, feigning naïveté.

Marianne leaned over and kissed her father lightly on the cheek.

"You're wrong about me — I don't have the faintest idea how to wake him up. You two keep me posted, and I'll come back. Meanwhile, I've already missed two shifts. Let's go."

Bagwell swore under his breath and turned to the general.

"Your, uh, anxiety is understandable, Ms. Sarzeau. But we can't really let you go, I'm afraid," said Weaver.

"What are you talking about?"

"We're volunteering you for military service."

"Oh, no, you're not. And anyway, for your information, I'd flunk the physical."

"Of course — your seizures . . ." said Bagwell.

Marianne glowered, beginning to realize that her captors had more of the picture than she did.

"How did you know? What the fuck is going on here?" she sputtered.

"Show her, Ray."

Bagwell produced the missing persons article from the *Bee*. Marianne skimmed it. Her face fell.

"Oh my God."

She read it over again. She turned pale.

"You bastards! Everybody will think I'm dead. Tom will think I'm dead. Lorraine . . ."

"That's the idea," affirmed Bagwell.

"The point is, the bad guys will also think you're dead," added the general.

"Bad guys . . . ?"

"The saboteurs, whoever put your father under. Probably the same ones who put you to sleep the other night. We think they put some of our pilots to sleep, too."

Marianne threw the *Bee* report on the floor and crossed her arms. "Look, I'm an American citizen. A free woman. Life, liberty, blah blah blah, and I do *not* volunteer for your war game."

"But you already did."

"Fuck you."

"Going forward, you are no longer a local police officer, you're a federal agent."

"Good God, this is ridiculous. I see the uniforms, but you're not really military. Who are you? CIA? NSA? Homeland? Who?"

Bagwell shrugged. "The *Full Spectrum Threat Assessment Program*, if that helps."

"Utilizing the special talents of your dad, here, we investigate . . . unusual security issues," Weaver explained.

"*FULTAP*," summarized Bagwell with evident pride.

"Wonderful," said Marianne.

Bagwell bent over the sleeping sergeant, brow furrowed with genuine concern. "You may be interested to know that your father is with us on this. He's done his time. He could have retired. But he's a patriot. He grasps the threat. We're hoping you will see it the same way. It will be so much easier for everyone."

"Shit. Dad . . ."

Weaver adopted a sterner tone. "FULTAP is a national intelligence operation. A special side branch that relies on the unique abilities of its staff. And guess what? Recruitment is almost impossible. People like your father — *like you!* — are very rare."

"That's why we put the grab on you, why you are vital to our business," said Bagwell, lightly touching Marianne's shoulder.

"I'm a zoo animal," said Marianne, shoulder and spirit slumping.

"With your help, we're going to revive your father, and we're going to stop these drone crashes," said Bagwell stoutly, showing some of his *esprit de corps*.

"Drones? When my friends find out I'm saving drones they'll never speak to me again. I don't know what to do. I need to talk to my ghost."

"We keep actual identities quiet," said Weaver. "We don't want to embarrass you or cause difficulties later. So here's your trade name. For those in the force, for those who read and respond to our reports, and just in case anything leaks, from now on you're simply *Agent Broomhandle.*"

16

"SO, WHOSE BLOOD was it you poured all over my radio station?"

Marianne leaned across the table toward Major Bagwell, who was chewing on a hamburger. They were sitting in a Denny's Diner, just off Highway 50 in Folsom.

"Some volunteer, I guess. Best not to know all the details, I've found."

"I'm sure it scared the living shit out of all my friends. You're turning me into the new Amelia Earhart. Vanished without a trace."

"Except for the blood," said Bagwell, delicately wiping his mouth on a napkin. "I sympathize." Dressed in civvies, in a rumpled suit, he looked like an overworked accountant.

Marianne took a bite of her Super Bird, put the sandwich back on its plate. "And the food . . . do you always eat at Denny's?"

Bagwell finished off his burger and turned to his coffee. "I travel a lot. This saves culinary anxiety, disappointment, depression. Nothing like consistent low expectations to get you through the day."

"That's no way to look at things."

Bagwell stared out the window.

"What's the problem? You don't like drones either?"

Bagwell registered the challenge with a cool indulgent smile. He spread his hands. "My feelings hardly matter. What would you have us do?"

"I dunno. Those things kill children."

"How many?"

"A lot."

"Well, if one considers the world to be at peace, then drones are terrible, a violation of international law, an affront to civilization."

"Yeah."

"On the other hand, if one considers the world, and especially our beloved country, to be at war, then the casualties are minimal by any standard."

"That's pretty cold-hearted."

"You think world affairs are conducted for sentimental reasons?"

"I have no idea how it all works."

"We are facing multiple threats. Believe it or not, they're real," said

Bagwell, being careful not to over-dramatize.

"We've been attacked. Our enemies are plotting to attack again. It could be worse than before. There is no obvious battlefield where we can *smash* them, no way we can haul them into court and *try* them. So, now and then, we intervene . . ."

"Intervene." Marianne twisted her lips into an expression of disgust.

Bagwell didn't seem to notice, but he changed the subject. "Forget about the drones. Think about the pilots who fly them, think about your father, and yes, yourself. None of you just *fell asleep*. Narcolepsy does not play a role here. Someone slinking around out there has powers like yours and is using them against us. I think you met them. Would you at least concede the danger?"

Marianne rolled her eyes, but inwardly she was recalling the odd moment when three children stood in front of her on Beale's eastern boundary.

"I guess."

"Aha, the righteous one discovers a shred of doubt. I call that progress." He nodded grim satisfaction and finished his coffee.

"Now, logistics. I was wondering about your fountain in, where is it, Applefield? Why can't we find a puddle somewhere nearby and contact your spiritual adviser with that?"

"For the longest time we communicated with gestures — charades. What a pain. But now — sometimes — I can talk to my ghost, and he talks to me."

Marianne eyed her dinner partner, trying to figure out how gullible he was under that professorial surface.

"The thing is, I need a good contact for speech. The pool in Applefield's town park is the only place I've actually been able to hear him."

"Unh-huh. He's not an ordinary ghost, he's a 'virtual visitor,' you said. Does he have a name?"

"He was the Golden Hills Tri-Town police chief, Hector Ibañez."

"What happened?"

Marianne felt her eyes clouding. "He was murdered by the cartel." She waved a hand with studied indifference. "Drugs, the usual shit you read about every day."

Bagwell gave her a searching look. "You admired him. You were a rookie, he was tough, but you liked him."

"I hated him. No, I didn't. You're right."

Marianne was wearing sleek black-framed glasses instead of her on-the-job contact lenses. She removed them and dabbed a napkin in the corner of an eye. Then she put her glasses back on and looked intently at the Army major. "But now, there's a twist."

Bagwell sat back. "Uh-oh. Better tell me."

"The problem is, I can't *summon* my ghost without special equipment. I need a relic, like Catholics use to tune in the Man Upstairs — you know, old bones and candles, that sort of thing."

"I'm not Catholic. What are we talking about, exactly?"

"I use Ibañez' old police badge from the Big City."

"So, use it."

"Right. It's in my car — wherever that is."

Bagwell held up a finger, stood up from the booth, tapped a number on his smartphone, and walked away toward the restrooms. She heard him say, "Broomhandle transport," before he moved out of earshot.

A few minutes later he slid back into his seat.

"Your car — a little blue Mini Cooper, right? — is sitting in the police station parking lot in Applefield."

Marianne was impressed. "You have powers too, it seems."

"Well-placed friends, anyway. Got a key?"

She showed it to him.

"Okay then, we better get going."

▼

They drove in silence down to Jackson and then uphill to Applefield in Bagwell's Cadillac SUV. There he cruised slowly under the streetlights along Main Street, looking for a parking spot. Out-of-towners flocking to the Apple Ranch restaurant already had most of them occupied.

"What would a cartel want with a little tourist town like this?" he wondered aloud.

"They had a farming operation on the local hillsides. Quality product made in America," said Marianne with a shrug.

"Where's the station?"

"Up ahead, five blocks."

Bagwell pulled in across the street. They could see Marianne's Mini sitting toward the rear of the parking lot, squeezed in between Tri-Town police vehicles. The station itself was dark.

"Local cops all go home after supper?"

Marianne shook her head. "Somebody's out on patrol, but there's no staff, so they lock up after dark."

Bagwell turned toward his passenger. "All right, go get your badge."

Marianne nodded and cracked open her door.

"I'm putting my trust in you, understand?"

She nodded again, held up her key, and crossed the street. Bagwell let her take a few steps, then got out and followed. He took up a defensive position in front of the little Mini, folded his arms, and watched her unlock the driver's door and search around inside.

After some grunting and cursing, she held up her hand. Bagwell could see a shiny metal object through the windshield. She stood up, re-locked the car, and brandished the badge.

"Okay, got it."

Bagwell cocked an elbow at his SUV. "Good. Now, the fountain."

"Right," she said. She pocketed the badge and then, quick as a deer, bounded away behind one of the Tri-Town patrol cars, dashed back along the other side, sprinted out of the parking lot, and ran away up Main Street.

Bagwell whirled around, waving and shouting.

"Sarzeau! Goddammit!"

He watched her go, then scrambled for the Cadillac, which was parked facing the wrong direction. He leaped aboard, executed a screaming one-point turnaround, and barreled up Main Street in hot pursuit.

Marianne ran the length of a block and, just before the Miners Market, turned east into Juniper Street. Behind the store she found an alley, jogged along past the dumpsters and trash barrels, and emerged on Digger Creek Road. She turned west to the intersection with Main Street and stopped there for a quick reconnaissance. Bagwell's SUV was bearing down on her. She melted into the recessed doorway of the Pick & Shovel as the car shot past.

She waited a second, then skipped across Main Street, ran another block down Digger Creek, found another alley, and ran north along that. One block, then two. She stopped to check — and there went Bagwell, briefly visible between buildings, zooming back the way he came. She was breathing hard, so she paused in the shadows, walking around in a little circle with her hands on her hips.

When her heart stopped racing, she hiked to the end of the alley and had another look around. Bagwell's SUV was nowhere to be seen, but the rear of the *County Courier* office was there before her, with Wagstaff's big yellow Toyota angled in near the loading dock.

She ran to the back door and hammered on it. No response. She hammered again. After an anxious eternity lights came on inside, but the door remained shut. She pounded and pounded. Finally, the door swung open, and Tom Wagstaff was staring at her, pale with shock.

"Marianne?"

She threw her arms around him, held him tight. "Oh my God, Tom!"

"You okay?"

She nodded. "Here's your headline: I'm alive, I'm unhurt."

"Where have you been? All that blood. What's going on?"

Before she could answer, the government-issue Cadillac came crawling along the alley. It nosed up beside Wagstaff's truck, and Bagwell got out. He didn't say anything, just leaned up against a fender. There was a gun in his hand, which he allowed to be seen.

"Jesus, who is that?" Wagstaff wanted to know. "You keep the strangest company, M!"

Marianne looked over at the Army man. "Major Raymond Bagwell. Works with Dad. He's CIA, or something like it."

"Is he going to shoot us?"

"No. It's just a warning. I ran off the reservation."

"Unh-huh."

Marianne gripped Wagstaff's arms and pushed to break their embrace.

"Look, I gotta go. Dad can't seem to wake up. Aside from him, I'm the next best thing to a real adept, and there are bad guys, so . . ."

She hesitated, searching for the right words.

"So . . . what?" prompted Wagstaff.

"So . . . I volunteered to help these guys."

"You didn't."

"I might be gone for a while. Don't tell anyone."

"You are being very mysterious."

"Now listen — the organization is super secret. But it's called FULTAP, and I have a new name."

He frowned scornful disapproval. She cranked up a girlish smile.

"Yeah, another one. I'm not even me anymore."

She made a clumsy little curtsy. "As far as they're concerned, it's Agent Broomhandle at your service."

"Broomhandle?"

"Can you believe?"

Bagwell stirred, brandished his little handgun. "Marianne . . . it's time."

She thrust a palm out to hold him off.

"When will I see you again?" asked Tom.

"When you see me."

She leaned forward and kissed him, long and hard. Then she whispered in his ear, "Remember, you don't know a thing. Forget everything I told you. And your mother . . . Lorraine must never hear of this." She gave his earlobe a contradictory nip, squeezed his hand, and headed back to the Escalade.

She walked past Bagwell and opened the passenger door. "Looking for me?" she asked.

Wagstaff watched the SUV pull away in glum silence. Then he ducked inside, grabbed a pencil, and scribbled *Bagwell, Fulltap,* and *Broomhandle* on a piece of scrap paper. After staring at the enigmatic words for a while, he picked up the telephone and dialed a number.

"Hi, Mom. Guess who just showed up at my back door."

▼

Following Marianne's directions, Bagwell drove to the Applefield town park. There she led him to the bronze prospector statue in the middle, posing beside its little water feature. Diminutive street lights on the park paths lighted their way, and the pool itself glowed from a waterproof lamp shining upward from the bottom.

"Where should I stand?" asked Bagwell, looking uncomfortable.

"Doesn't matter," Marianne replied. "You may or may not see anything, but I don't think the Chief gives a damn one way or the other."

She held Ibañez' police badge high overhead.

"Hello, there, Chief. Can you hear me? Your pal Marianne here, calling long distance to your area code. I need some advice."

She waited for the faint undulations on the pool surface to give way to a ghostly image.

"Well?" asked Bagwell, skeptically rubbing his chin.

"Sometimes it takes a while. And usually I have to insist." She held up the badge again, squeezed it as tight as she could, and shouted —

"Yo, Chief! *Hey you!*"

" 'Hey you' — that's quite a spell," said Bagwell, with an ironic grin.

"You're not the first to wonder about that," she replied.

Suddenly ripples formed on the pool surface. An image surged outward, and there was her visitor, looking up at her.

"And usually it works. He's here."

Bagwell advanced a step. He peered uncertainly into the pool. "I don't see anything. Waves, maybe."

"Hang on."

Shadowy lips moved, and an eerie voice spoke inside her head.

"Little Miss Hey Yourself, what now? You are one demanding cop."

"Hello, love you too, and thanks for the visit. My Dad is still in a coma. The boys in his outfit — something called FULTAP, by the way — think the coma was induced by adepts. Witches, yet! Is that possible? What does Dad think?"

"I looked in again on your father. I can't read thoughts, and he can't talk too well in his sleep. But I feel his distress, and yes, he's worried about others like himself."

"You mean, he knows why he can't wake up?"

"Not sure about that. But there are no wounds, so it's possible."

"Great. What should I do?"

"If the coma was caused by adepts, I guess you better have another chat with Madame Crowfoot."

"That weird old bag."

"Old bag or not, she knows what she's talking about. Better listen up."

"I guess. She's spookier than you are."

"If unfriendly adepts are lurking nearby, you need help. Don't screw around because you're a Nervous Nellie. I was hoping you'd get over the jitters after a year on the force."

"Damn, you know me well. Things are a mess over here in Reality Land, in case you're wondering. My life is totally out of control." She smiled a wan smile. "What about you, Chief, what's heaven like these days?"

The ghost dismissed the question with a wave.

"What makes you think I'm in heaven?"

His image rippled away. Marianne slapped her thighs in frustration.

"Is he gone? What did he say?" asked Bagwell, brimming with curiosity.

"You didn't see him, didn't hear anything?"

"Nope," he grumbled. He dipped a suspicious hand into the pool, let the possibly magical water drain through his fingers. "I'm just along for the ride."

17

IN PLACERVILLE, in the house at 229 Billy Hill Drive, old Darius Golay called his three young charges away from their toys for a breakfast meeting at the kitchen table.

"Yasmin showed me this. A newspaper. See the picture?"

The children looked at a grainy photo of Marianne on the front page of the *County Courier*. The accompanying story described her disappearance and appealed to readers for help.

"That's her — the woman in the silver tent!" said Rafiq.

"I put her to sleep," added Zohra proudly.

"Yes you did," said the old man with a nod of approval. "I notice that her name is 'Sarzeau,' spelled E-A-U. We have been warned that the Americans have a paramilitary unit that includes an adept. Inter-Services Intelligence has given me the name 'Sarzo,' spelled with an O. I wonder, are the names connected? Is this young woman related to the agent?"

"I don't understand the stupid spelling," said Yasmin.

They turned their heads as a series of *kliks* announced Firoz. She settled down at the table with the kids.

"Firoz, what is your opinion?"

"I heard the television news. They have broadcast an alert. They say blood was found. They are hopeful, but blood is bad, so she is dead."

Rafiq stood up. "She is not dead."

"How do you know this?" asked Golay.

"I could feel her. She is moving far away, but she is not dead."

Firoz sat back in her chair. "Then the blood . . ." She paused to think. ". . . this is an American trick! However the letters look, the names are the same."

"Then the American authorities are aware of us. We must be very cautious," said Golay.

Firoz shook her head. "We must do what the blood claims has already been done. What we have already discussed. We must find her and kill her."

18

BAGWELL AND MARIANNE spent the night in the Forty-Niner Motel in Jackson. Bagwell agreed to separate rooms after extracting a solemn pledge from Marianne that she wouldn't try any more tricks. He was surprised when she agreed.

In the morning, Marianne wandered down to the courtesy breakfast nook in the motel lobby and made a waffle in the waffle machine. She made another one for Bagwell when he showed up a few minutes later.

"You're still here," he observed between bites.

She shrugged.

"Big decision," he said.

She shrugged again. "Dad . . . gotta rev him up, save the drones and their pilots, nail the bad guys, right?"

"That's right." Bagwell opened up a free copy of *USA Today* and buried his head in the pages. "I know you don't approve of our operation, but we're going to help each other. If you let me, I can be a valuable ally."

"All right, Major, get me back home someday, and it's a deal."

"Major is for military formality. Call me Ray."

"Ray, then." Marianne forked up a bite of his waffle. "Someday, when this is over — and soon, I hope — I'm going to be a cop again. Instead of sitting here, I'm supposed to be out investigating a string of burglaries."

"Don't worry — your lieutenant knows you're alive. You won't get fired."

"Well, aren't you considerate? What I'm wondering — when I'm not thinking about Dad — is what to make of the only clues I've got."

Bagwell looked up from his newspaper. "And the clues are?"

"They're using a U-Haul van for the swag, and the inside guy can climb right up walls, like a spider."

This problem in police work seemed to intrigue Bagwell. He folded the paper. "Check the rentals on that U-Haul, might get a name."

"Done already. Struck out."

"And " — he pondered the matter — "your burglar, with skills like that, he might be a professional."

"Professional what?"

"He might work as a climber."

"How could he ever?"

"At a gym, maybe. As a coach. What about REI? Don't they have those climbing walls in every camping store?"

Marianne tapped her forehead. "Now that is an idea I need to follow up."

"But not now, Officer. We've got more urgent business."

They downed cups of weak coffee and focused on their next move.

"So this woman, Hannah Crowfoot, what's her story?" asked Bagwell.

"She's the real thing, a Native American spirit woman. Not very friendly, I must say, although I don't think she'll turn us into frogs."

"You've met her?"

"Oh, yes. She tried to get me killed last year, but her scheme backfired. The last time I saw her she was helpful, taught me how to hear my visitor. She's poor as a church mouse, so we need to bring offerings, or she won't cooperate."

▼

An hour later, Bagwell pulled into the Save Mart in Angels Camp, where Marianne bought a basket of assorted groceries with his credit card. Then they motored on to Bush Street and Hannah Crowfoot's ramshackle little home, festooned as always with vines and flowers.

Bagwell looked upon the place with distaste. "Sure this is her house?" he asked.

"I'm Sure."

"She does business here?"

"Come on, Ray. You work with an adept every day. She won't bite."

She led the way into Ms. Crowfoot's little foyer and rang the bell.

Bagwell's eyes were roving unhappily all over the interior. The unfamiliar ripe odors made his nose twitch. He tensed when shuffling feet approached and shivered involuntarily when the old woman threw a curtain aside and appeared. She pushed her glasses up on her nose and studied her visitors through thick lenses.

"Hello, young lady," she said.

"Ms. Crowfoot, meet my, uh, partner, Ray Bagwell."

The old woman held out a pudgy hand. Bagwell grasped it briefly.

"Why are you here? The fritillaria didn't work?"

Marianne smiled. "No, it did. Now my visitor talks, and I listen. He told me to come see you again."

"Really."

"And I brought some stuff. This time a roast ham, some frozen dinners, just in case you don't want to cook, another bottle of cheap wine, Franzia red, but it's okay, and some already chopped-up salad stuff in this package here — you really should eat your vegetables." She placed each item on Ms. Crowfoot's little table.

"Thank you, dear. What can I do for you? Why did your ghost send you?"

Bagwell cleared his throat. "Ms. Crowfoot, I work for the government. I'm in the national security business. We have reason to believe some foreign agents are here on American soil with — how to put it? — special powers."

"What in the world?" said Ms. Crowfoot, completely dumbfounded.

"They can put you to sleep," said Marianne.

"What?"

"They put my Dad to sleep — he works with Ray — and one of them put *me* to sleep."

Ms. Crowfoot's eyes narrowed. "You want my advice about this? All right. But a consultation is fifty dollars."

Marianne signaled with her hand, and Bagwell held out a fifty dollar bill. Ms. Crowfoot snatched it up and led them into her little consulting room.

She sank into her leather easy chair. "Sit, sit."

They sat down on hard wooden stools.

"You are describing magic spells," said Ms. Crowfoot. "Those who can cast them are very rare. It's a gift. I couldn't do it."

"These are children. At least the attack on Marianne was carried out by children. Nobody was seen in the other cases," said Bagwell, "but we think it's the same group."

"Spells are difficult, hard to defeat. There is no protection, except that offered by counter-spells, wielded by an opposing adept."

"Could kids do this?" Bagwell was having trouble coming to grips with the idea.

"Not unless they are very powerful," said Ms. Crowfoot. She touched her nose. "It does suggest something. Something in your favor."

"Yes? What?"

"Why kids? Prodigies? Certainly. But adults would be so much easier to work with . . . if any were available. Whoever is behind this must be desperate."

"We're desperate," said Marianne. "How can I wake up Dad, that's what I want to know."

"Does your father share your abilities? Spells can have a big impact on people like us."

"I don't really know. I suppose so." Marianne had never discussed the details with him.

"He senses people and their intentions," offered Bagwell. "He's part of our security operation. But he's in a coma, a casualty of the strange little war we're in."

"Caused by the children you mentioned?" asked Ms. Crowfoot, struggling to get a sense of the situation.

"Pretty sure."

The old woman looked closely at Marianne. "Well, we know something about *you*, what *you* can do. Talking to ghosts? Fine and dandy. But you're still rough as gravel. Give me your hand."

Marianne tentatively stuck out her right hand. Ms. Crowfoot took it in her soft little paw.

"Mmm. You could do it, you could cast a spell or two, if you only knew the first thing about anything."

Marianne winced. Ms. Crowfoot studied her.

"Tell me your dream," she commanded.

Marianne blushed crimson. She yanked her hand away. "How do you know about any damn dream?"

Ms. Crowfoot displayed her eerie smile and grasped Marianne's hand again. "I just know," she said. "Tell me . . ."

Marianne did her best to pull herself together. She squeezed Ms. Crowfoot's hand in hers.

"This is weird. Ever since Dad was hurt in that plane crash —"

"— Plane crash?"

"That's how it all started. Just about every night since then I've been dreaming about a *stone*."

Ms. Crowfoot nodded. "A stone."

Bagwell was eyeing Marianne with great curiosity.

"And I pick up the stone." Marianne hesitated, recalling the strangeness of her nighttime experience. "And it bursts into flames."

She paused. Her mind was replaying the memory, trying to find details that weren't there, trying to make sense of an emotional surge of longing, trying to overcome a feeling of unworthiness whose cause eluded her.

Ms. Crowfoot and Bagwell remained silent, waiting for a punch line. Marianne looked at them, understood their suspense, and obliged with a sardonic smile.

"Only it doesn't hurt me. My hand is on fire, but I'm okay."

Ms. Crowfoot leaned back in her chair, let Marianne's hand drop. Her face was grey. "A stone catches fire, but does no harm to the holder," she summarized. "God in Heaven, if there is one!"

"What does it mean?" asked Marianne, much relieved to have a troubling secret come out in the open.

Ms. Crowfoot leaned forward. "This is no ordinary dream. Dreams have shapes, and this dream was shaped by the mind of an adept. Your mind. Where is your stone? That is the question."

"You think the stone is real?" asked Marianne in amazement.

"Oh yes. Think! You must find the source. That is how you will advance."

Bagwell shifted doubtfully on his stool. "Now wait a minute. It's my business to know something about this sort of thing, and what you're talking about isn't in any book I've ever read. Dreams and stones, really!"

Ms. Crowfoot looked at Bagwell with ill-concealed disdain. "You haven't read Robinson's *Native Methodologies and Practice*, evidently. Volume two. It's all in there."

Marianne was hooked. "My grandfather was some kind of voodoo man down in Louisiana. Could be?"

Ms. Crowfoot shook her head. "Stones on the bayou? The ideas don't fit. A bayou dream would involve a different object. Snakes, perhaps."

"I saw a picture of good old Granddad holding one," said Marianne helpfully.

"No, no, Louisiana is merely a way station. Nothing originates here in America. All adepts trace their lineage back in time, across the oceans. We're all immigrants. Go back far enough, even us Natives."

"My family is from France. 'Sarzeau' is the name of a town in Brittany. Is that important?"

Ms. Crowfoot's cataract-glazed eyes lit up. She slapped the table. "Standing stones! Druids! Of course!"

"The *menhirs*, I've heard of them," said Marianne, nodding agreement.

Bagwell puffed out a silent obscenity.

"This is your heritage," Ms. Crowfoot declared. "You must go to France. There you will find what you need."

"Marianne, this is all unproven," warned the government operative. "Your father never made mention —"

"— If the trip wakes Dad up — wakes up your super agent! — it's worth it, no?" said the worried daughter.

Bagwell rubbed his balding scalp.

"Big if."

Part THREE

19

MAJOR BAGWELL led Marianne across the tiled floor of Sacramento International Airport to a private area. They were both pulling roll-around suitcases. Bagwell was wearing his Army uniform, with oak leaves on his epaulets. Marianne affected stylish grunge in jeans and a hoodie.

At the gate they were met by a tall and wide young man wearing an Army combat uniform and boonie hat.

Bagwell made introductions. "Marianne, this is Jeffrey Pike. General Weaver isn't too sure about our little foray, so he's given us a babysitter."

Marianne spotted silver bars in the uniform's camouflage pattern. "Nice to meet you, Captain."

"My young friend here is a police officer in Placerville. Her father is in my unit."

He nodded politely. "Ma'am."

They shook hands.

"We'll be on our way at fifteen-fifty hours," he said. He reached in a pocket and handed Marianne a U.S. Passport.

"This is you in Europe. Major said you didn't have one."

"I've never been out of the country before." She inspected the document suspiciously. "Mary Ann Sarnoff — ?"

Bagwell smiled. "Don't worry, it's an excellent forgery."

Captain Pike hefted his duffel. "First leg is to Travis. From there we're hitching a ride in a blimp, then a C-17, and that ain't Air France. Now's the time for coffee and doughnuts, and a good book if you can find one." He motioned toward the airport concourse.

Marianne shook her head and took a seat by the window. Bagwell and Pike sat down nearby. For five minutes she stared straight ahead. Neither of the men could guess the thoughts that were obviously passing through her mind.

Then she jumped up.

"Hey, guys, I need to find a bathroom."

Pike stood beside her. "I'll go with you."

Marianne pursed her lips. "Not really a great idea."

"Someone needs to keep an eye on you."

"In Sacramento?"

Bagwell put a hand on Pike's arm. "Take it easy, Captain. She'll be okay."

"Don't worry, back to the hive in five," said Marianne with a wave.

She walked quickly into the main hub of the airport, past the women's restroom, under the giant red jackrabbit art piece hanging from the rafters, and into the nearest book and news shop. There she purchased a pay-as-you-go mobile telephone.

She strolled out into the crowd, stepped aside into a niche with huge windows looking out onto the runway, and made a call.

"Officer Otis. Hello?"

"Dez, it's me."

"Whoaaaaa, there. Marianne? Officer Sarzo? You been seeing ghosts, shit, you're dead, and now I'm talking to one."

"I'm not a ghost, you dumbbell. And I'm not dead. I'm, uh, temporarily reassigned."

"Unh-huh, where to? Heaven? Hell? Which is it, bitch? The commander will want to know."

"Kazmarek has been told. So you — you keep your mouth shut. Gossip will put me in danger. Let's talk about our burglars."

"If we must. Whatcha got?"

"Nothing, really. You?"

"I'm writing parking tickets. Corralled a shoplifter yesterday. Life is good."

"Right. Okay, then. So . . . I got to thinking about Spider-Man. He made climbing look like walking. He was so good, maybe he's a professional. Climbs for a living."

"Oh why not? Are you kidding? How could anyone make a living like that, except up on Mount Everest?"

"Maybe he's a coach. Maybe he works in a mountaineering shop down in Yosemite. Listen, doesn't REI have a couple of stores in the Sacramento area?"

"I don't know. I'm not that outdoorsy myself."

"I think they all feature a climbing wall along with their bikes and kayaks."

"Yeah . . ."

"You should check 'em out while I'm gone."

"Shit, Sarz, you're handing me a wild goose chase."

"Probably. It's an unturned stone."

"All right, all right, I'll turn it, but I'm not driving all the way down to fucking Yosemite. Call you."

"That won't work. I'm on this cheap-o phone here, because my new friends don't want me chatting away, blowing my cover. I'll call you when I can."

"Cover? You sound like a spook, not a ghost. What's your cover?"

"Being dead, of course. All that blood at the radio station."

"I read about that. When you coming back?"

"Hard to tell."

"Ghosts, secret shit, all right then, go on with your bad self."

"You too."

She hung up and returned to her companions.

On her way through security she disguised the phone by placing it in a plastic bag with her hand sanitizer. Bagwell never noticed.

20

ON MAIN STREET in Placerville, late on a sunny afternoon, old Darius Golay allowed himself to be led to the Foothill Flavors Gelateria by his three young charges, where he bought ice cream for everyone.

"This is our last day. A final treat, and we say *Allah wahi* to California."

Golay and the girls settled down on a nearby bench, but Rafiq wandered away to gawk at the gold mining equipment in the window of the TrueValue hardware store. Suddenly he came running back.

"Dada! Yasmin! Zohra!"

"*Shh*, young man! What are you yelling about?" cautioned Golay.

"I have felt something new, Dada."

"Oh ho, and what is that?"

"A presence, Dada. A new one, not the same."

"Not the same? Who then?"

"The policewoman is gone. Now I feel another one."

Golay stood up and scanned the area. He seemed to expect an unknown adept to step out of a store front or emerge from between parked cars.

Yasmin stood up with him. She closed her eyes and held up her hands for silence. "I feel something too." She swayed back and forth for a minute or more gathering the hints of a faint emanation. Then her eyes popped open. "It is a woman. She is like us. But she is far away."

Golay took Yasmin's hand in his. "Tell me, girl. Why did you not feel her before?"

Yasmin bowed her head. "I think the policewoman's presence hid her from us, Dada."

Rafiq nodded agreement. "Yes, it must be so."

Zohra's mouth turned downward. She sniffled. "I can't feel anyone."

"Where is this woman?" demanded Golay.

Rafiq pointed a finger.

"South, eh? Come, children. Perhaps she knows where the policewoman has gone. We should question her."

21

MARIANNE, Bagwell, and Pike flew to Travis in a twin-engine turboprop. After a boring layover, a blimp, which Marianne discovered was in reality a C-130 Hercules, ferried them to Dover Air Force Base in Delaware via a stopover somewhere in Kansas. They endured another layover, then a long hop across the water to Ramstein Air Base in western Germany. They made the trip strapped into canvas seats facing the cargo in a C-17 Globemaster.

As soon as they stepped aboard, Bagwell rolled his jacket into a pillow and fell asleep. Marianne surveyed the freight.

"I see the vehicle" — she was looking at an armored personnel carrier — "but what's inside the shipping container?"

Pike stared at a big metal box lashed to the deck with wide nylon straps. "Notice those sockets on the surface there?"

"Yeah."

"That's to connect with some antennas. So it's not a load of ammo, it's a cockpit. Pilots fly drones inside. Bound for Afghanistan, probably."

"Well, what do you know? So that's how they do it. Can I get a tour?"

"Ha, not from me. When we land, maybe."

He opened his duffel and brought out a deck of cards.

"How good are you at gin rummy?"

"I've never played."

"Now you learn."

He dealt hands, knocked with two cards unmatched, and patiently explained the deadwood concept.

After a dozen games, Marianne actually won one. She pumped her fist.

Pike decided they'd had enough of that. They both unstrapped, found the heads, relieved themselves, and returned with bitter cups of stale coffee that had boiled a few hours earlier.

"Now you're ready for some Zombie Dice."

"Oh no," she said.

"See these thirteen little cubes? You roll three at a time, and stop when you think you've done pretty good. But if you turn up three shotgun blasts, you lose everything on that turn. First one to thirteen brains wins. So, go ahead, you start."

She rolled, saw footprints.

"Your victims escaped."

She rolled again, then again, and was feeling pretty chipper with three brains to her credit, when suddenly three blast icons were staring at her.

"Damn."

Pike rolled and rolled, and went over the winning total on his first turn.

"I can't shoot a gun very well either," said Marianne.

In this way they passed the time.

After four thousand miles and nine hours in the air they touched down in Germany. Bagwell did some talking, and Marianne got her tour of the portable drone cockpit.

Two pilot stations were set up inside the container, each one equipped with large video displays and "glass cockpit" screens showing vital aircraft status information. In front of the videogame-style controllers were two sumptuous leather chairs, the better to comfort pilots on long boring shifts.

"Inside all this steel, how could some kid's spell do any damage?" wondered Marianne.

"Metal may reduce the effects," said Bagwell, speculating without any real information, "but not completely, or our dedicated and well-trained pilots wouldn't be nodding off."

▼

From Ramstein, they boarded a high-speed *ICE* train for Paris. Bagwell fell asleep again in his first-class seat. Pike produced an iPad from his voluminous duffel, and he and Marianne watched *Toy Story 3* while speeding along at three hundred kilometers an hour.

In Paris, they changed over to a *Train à Grande Vitesse* and continued rolling west.

They shot through Le Mans, Rennes, Redon, and finally disembarked in Vannes. *Brittany at last!* There Bagwell hired a little Citroën automobile and drove them twenty-five kilometers around the Gulf of Morbihan to *SARZEAU,* Marianne's namesake city.

22

IN PLACERVILLE, Golay, Yasmin, Rafiq, Zohra, and Firoz left the house at 229 Billy Hill Drive, and piled into their rental car.

"You sit in front, Yasmin. I will drive, and you will guide us," ordered the old man.

Rafiq was upset. "I should guide, I felt her first, let me sit up front."

"No, you can be a double check, but Yasmin is oldest."

The car pulled away from the house. Zohra peered out the window at the empty driveway.

"Where is our truck? Why are you driving, Dada?"

"I am oldest of all. So I do it."

"But where is Habib? He is our real driver."

"Yes, Dada, where is he?" asked Rafiq. "I like him, he is a real crazy American."

"Rajput is not with us. He has other business. It is just our group now."

"Go that way," said Yasmin, pointing to an intersection looming ahead.

▼

After two hours and many wrong turnings, Golay and company rolled into Angels Camp, erratically closing in on the aura sensed by Yasmin and Rafiq. They both pointed madly at Bush Street as they drove through town. Golay braked hard and swerved to make the corner.

"Here she is! Here she is!" cried the children as they rolled slowly toward old lady Crowfoot's house.

Golay parked in front. "I will go in with Yasmin. Firoz, look after these two."

"I should be with you," said Firoz. "There might be trouble."

"I doubt it. If there is, Yasmin will work her magic."

Golay led Yasmin to the door. He knocked. After a minute fidgeting on the porch, he pushed the door open and stepped inside. Yasmin picked up the bell in the foyer and gave it a good *ring*.

Soon old lady Crowfoot shuffled into view. She stared at her visitors with curiosity and trepidation.

"Yes? I don't know you two. Are you looking for spiritual advice?"

"Yes," said Golay.

"How did you get my name?"

Golay looked at Yasmin. "We were referred," he said.

Crowfoot didn't seem convinced. Something was amiss, but she didn't know what.

"The child here has powers," she noted. "I see this very clearly. Is that why you have come? Confused by unusual abilities? Worried by strange feelings?"

Golay hesitated, and then decided to play along. "Yes, we're very confused."

"I can help. My consultation fee is fifty dollars."

"We don't have that much money."

Crowfoot had a short way with hagglers. "Sorry. Come back when you do." She turned to go.

"Yasmin?" Golay made a small gesture.

Yasmin raised a hand and muttered something. Crowfoot staggered backward. She put her hands to her throat and gasped for air.

"We will talk now!" said the girl. She extended her hand and Crowfoot found herself wobbling into her consultation room. Yasmin pointed, and Crowfoot collapsed into her easy chair.

Golay sat down on the stool across the table. Yasmin stood behind him, hand upraised.

"We believe it is possible you are acquainted with a young policewoman. A Miss Sarzeau."

"Yes, we've met," said Crowfoot, wheezing audibly.

"We want to know where she is."

Crowfoot started to protest, and stopped as Yasmin's hand rose up to warn her.

"I don't know where she is," she said.

Yasmin's hand twitched.

"But I did consult with her. I told her to go to France, where her family comes from."

"Where exactly?"

"Sarzeau."

Golay raised an eyebrow.

"Yes, *Sarzeau*. Marianne and the town share that name."

Golay stood up. "Thank you, Madame. Your spiritual advice is most helpful." He turned to the girl. "Yasmin?"

Yasmin thrust out her hand, muttered another incantation. Crowfoot tried to rise, then fell back in her chair. Her eyes rolled up, her head lolled to one side, her arms drooped.

"Is she asleep?" asked Firoz, appearing suddenly behind them.

Golay leaned over the old woman. "Oh yes. No one can defy Yasmin's spells."

Firoz was carrying a nylon cord with a small wooden ball held in the middle by knots — a tidy little garrotte. She took a step toward Crowfoot.

Yasmin moved in between. "No, no, no."

"We should make an end to this. The old one may call the police and cause trouble," insisted Firoz. She looked to Golay for confirmation, but the old man hesitated.

"Why not, Yasmin?" he said. "Firoz' words are wise."

"*Daadii* cannot hurt anyone. She is old, her powers are weak. It is stupid to kill her — it might affect us."

Golay and Firoz looked doubtful.

"I am casting a confusion spell. She will not remember us." Yasmin murmured strange words while twisting her hands in the air. Crowfoot's sleeping form quivered.

"How long will she sleep?" asked Golay.

"At least a day, maybe a whole week."

Golay nodded. "All right. Duty calls us. We must leave the area anyway. We will be merciful."

23

MARIANNE woke up early in Sarzeau, discombobulated by jet lag. She had been traveling for twenty-seven hours by her count, and she was still numb with fatigue. Bagwell had booked them all into the *Hotel Lesage*, a pile of old stone near the center of town with a very fancy ultra-modern interior. To her it seemed scandalously luxurious, considering that the government was paying her bills. She wanted to remain in bed, but the bells of the Church of Saint-Saturnin across the street jarred her into action.

She opened the windows on her fourth floor room, leaned out over the railing, and inhaled. The warm and humid spring air suggested seawater and diesel fumes. Puffy clouds rode above the horizon to the north. Looking past the church she glimpsed shops and cafés crowding narrow cobblestone streets.

Her first morning in another country. The novelty cleared away some of the cobwebs in her head, but the idea that this ancient little town was the home ground of her family was intoxicating. It made her feel giddy.

"Yo, sleepyhead!"

She looked down. Pike was waving. He and Bagwell were sitting in a little outdoor café in front of the hotel, having breakfast.

She threw on some clothes, a sweatshirt over her standard jeans, and joined them.

Bagwell sorted through his notes, laying out their day while Marianne munched on a chocolate brioche.

"The report I have says your family name is 'Pasquillou.' Ever hear that mentioned before?"

"No," said Marianne through a mouthful of food. "But hey, these rolls are delicious."

"Apparently, the family is still here in town. They run a bakery, *Boulangerie Pasquillou*. It's just a couple of blocks up the street. Who knows, maybe that's where the pastries come from."

He put down his notes and looked her over. "Feel anything? See anything?"

Marianne slowly turned her thoughts away from the excellent *petit déjeuner*. "You mean, inside? Adept stuff?"

"Of course."

"Well, no, nothing so far. But I can't concentrate while I'm eating. How'd you find the name, Pass-whatever?"

Bagwell grimaced. "Your dad and I have been working together for quite a while. We've talked about names. And, more to the point, the hotel has Wi-Fi. I did a search . . . using an encrypted connection, of course."

"Of course. You spies and your toys."

▼

What appeared to be idle tourists touring the principle boulevard of a French tourist town was actually a carefully planned assault on *Boulangerie Pasquillou*. Pike, in a button-down shirt and chinos, strolled past the shop and peered into the window of a nearby *tabac*. From there he had a commanding view of the store and anyone approaching. Bagwell, ever the professor, and now on sabbatical, rolled up his copy of *Le Monde* and ventured inside for a *baguette*. Marianne followed, making no attempt to disguise her American citizenship.

Three people were working the shop. A young man and a young woman, possibly married, were standing behind the counter, filling orders, pouring *café au lait*, and ringing up sales. An older man was sweeping the floor, arranging chairs at the miniscule side tables, refilling the coffee maker.

"Bonjour, madame," said Marianne, instantly exhausting her French. "I'm an American, over here trying to figure out my family background. I wonder . . ."

"Qu'est-ce que c'est?" said the woman.

The older man stopped sweeping the floor to listen to the *gauche* American.

Marianne looked at a little English-French phrase book Bagwell had given her. "Um, *je m'appelle* 'Marianne Sarzeau.' But I know that's just what my people were called in America, and I was told 'Pasquillou' is the original family name here in, um, *Bretagne*."

"Eh? Je ne comprends pas. Désolée."

"I was wondering if you are a long-lost relative. That would be so cool."

"Ah, mais non. Moment. Henri?"

She signaled to her husband, standing nearby. He sidled over, smacking flour off his hands. "Sorry, no English. Pastry? *Du café?*"

On cue, Bagwell moved to rescue the situation. "Excuse me, you're

American?"

Marianne nodded. "Yes."

"First time in France?"

Marianne nodded again. "I guess it shows."

"Well, let me help you, I speak French well enough."

"Thank God."

Bagwell proceeded to ask Marianne's questions all over again *en français*. Then he translated back into English for her benefit.

"No one named 'Pasquillou' here, *mademoiselle*. Once there was, long ago, but now it's just a brand name, like *Peugeot* or *Perrier*."

Marianne's face fell. "Shit."

"In French it's *merde,*" he advised.

"Merde," she said.

"There, doesn't that sound better?"

▼

The trio left the bakery in separate directions and regrouped in the hotel café.

"Let's try a little séance, shall we?" suggested Bagwell, "as long as you don't mind some company."

"Why not? It's never that entertaining, but you can watch the show."

"What do we need? A fountain?"

"Something reflective, that's all."

"There's a big mirror in my room," said Pike.

Pike led the way. His bathroom was a stunning collection of *moderne* porcelain fixtures on tiled walls and floor. A wide slab of mirror was hung over a pair of conical sinks. Marianne hauled out her police badge, gripped it tightly, and raised it above her head.

"Bonjour, Chief. Here I am in France, and I need a better guide than Rick Steves. Got a minute?"

The three faces in the mirror blurred. A tiny whirlpool of shadow appeared in the middle, flared outward, and Marianne's mentor was staring at her. His lips moved, and a virtual voice spoke to her.

"Marianne. Traveling, I see."

"Yeah, I'm over here looking for a stone. It's supposed to up my game, help me wake up Dad. But my French family isn't around anymore to explain where the stone might be."

"You expect me to know? I don't have any special insight. I'm just an ex-cop."

"Come on, Chief, you're on the inside now, right? I'm lost when it comes to stuff like this."

Pike took a step backward as the conversation unfolded. Without access to the other voice, Marianne's behavior seemed bizarre.

"You seeing a ghost?" He found it hard to believe.

"Oh yes. Right in front of you."

"Unh-huh, don't let him hang around in my room, okay?"

"Shh, he's talking!" warned Marianne.

"Think like a cop," said the shadow. *"Theoretically you are one, right? You didn't forget everything I taught you after moving up to Placerville, I hope. What are your clues?"*

"Well, I don't have any. What I really need is a *tip.*"

"France. Brittany. What's so special?"

"Ahh . . . stones. Lots of stones. The druids, and so on."

"There you go."

"Ray had me looking at a map. There are stones standing around everywhere you turn."

"So, pick a spot. Start with the obvious. When you see animals running through a field, think horses before zebras."

The image blurred and faded, leaving three puzzled faces staring at themselves.

"Well? What about it," said Bagwell, "What did he say?"

"Find some stones. Pick the obvious. Horses, not zebras. Sheesh."

Bagwell consulted a map. "That means Carnac. It's more than fifty kliks, we should roll."

24

OFFICER Desmond Otis had spent most of his morning in a campaign to nail drivers running the stop signs in downtown Placerville. Now and then, out of boredom, he cruised Benham Street, showing the force to rout drug addicts from their favorite haunt in the city park there.

Around noon his routine was interrupted by a call from the dispatcher, directing him to the Del Rio Apartments, a notorious complex filled with miserable low-wage workers and parolees. A dispute had arisen between residents over barking dogs, dogshit, kicked-over trash cans, and broken windows. It took him half an hour of questioning to understand the situation, and another twenty minutes to calm the parties, advise about future arrests, and get things back on an even keel without having to haul anyone into the station. He figured the truce would last for a day or two, no more than a week at most.

He decided to reward his civic-minded efforts with a milkshake. While he waited at the Coffee Depot, a little drive-through kiosk on the west side of town, he thought about Marianne's burglar. Spider-Man, she called him. So, while slurping away on a liquid lunch, he looked up the nearest REI address on his police laptop. Then he headed on down to Folsom.

▼

"Do you have a climber that works this here cliff, wall, whatever it is?" he asked of a nice young woman in the Folsom REI outdoor adventure store. He was gazing up at a rough pillar of grey concrete that towered from the ground to the third floor ceiling. It was covered with little colored knobs. Climbing ropes dangled from pulleys in the roof.

"I'm it," replied the nice young woman.

"What are you supposed to do? Grab those little things sticking out?"

"Pretty much."

"Whooo. Can you climb?"

"Makes me dizzy, to tell the truth. People love it, and we prevent accidents by strapping them into a harness with a rope attached. I know how to hold the rope and belay them so they can't fall, but I'm not a real climber. Want to try it?"

"Do I look crazy? And you, you've been at this how long?"

"About a year."

"Anyone else hired to do it?"

"One or two others know the ropes, ha ha, but they're not in the store today."

"Any serious climbers?"

"You mean, ready to scale El Capitan? No. They're both like me."

"Damn, I was hoping."

"We're not the only outdoor equipment store in the area, you know."

"My lucky day."

▼

Otis' next stop was the Mountain Madness sports shop in Jackson. It catered to the ski and boarding crowd, and was full of top-of-the-line equipment. Skis, snowboards, boots of every kind, expensive winter togs in electric hues. A rack of mountain bikes signaled the approaching summer season. Otis' idea of recreation didn't extend much beyond watching Sacramento Kings basketball games, and he felt edgy and out of place. A couple of long-haired white dudes were manning the establishment. One was a little older than the other. Hard to tell who might be in charge.

"Excuse me, gentlemen," he began, as he approached the sales counter, "either of you do any technical climbing? Grabbing little handholds on cliffs, that kind of thing?"

They looked at each other, looked at his uniform.

"Not me."

"Me neither."

"Freestyle skiing."

"Trail biking when the weather improves."

Otis nodded. "Got it. See, I'm looking for someone who can climb right up a wall. I thought, maybe, he might work at his hobby, know what I mean?"

"Not sure, man."

"Well, you ride bikes, and you also sell 'em," Otis explained.

"Oh yeah."

"So, you men don't climb for a living. Know anyone who does?"

"Not our thing, way too dangerous."

"Wait," said the older dude, "you want someone who gets paid to climb?"

"Just a hunch. You never know unless you ask around," said Otis.

"Well, there is that little carnival you see at the street fairs. There's always a portable climbing wall. Kids go nuts while their parents buy antiques."

Otis' police radar switched on. "What carnival is that?"

The younger dude fished around under the counter and brought out a business card. He handed it to Otis.

"This guy."

Otis looked at the card, which read:

> *Mr. Kite's Kolossal Kiddie Karnival*
> *3545 Coach Lane, Cameron Park*

He pantomimed stuffing the card in his shirt pocket. "May I?"

"It's yours, man."

Otis drove north on Route 49 to El Dorado, then turned west and weaved through a maze of back roads into Cameron Park. He drove along Coach Lane until the pavement failed. There, between a self-storage facility and a propane tank farm, he found Mr. Kite's enterprise. It was sharing space with a used recreational vehicle dealer. He parked his patrol car, stepped into the dirt lot, and maneuvered through the collection of rides toward the office, itself a dilapidated RV.

On the way he passed the *Puffy Panda* train, the *Astro Blasto* Ferris wheel, the *Ally Gator* roller coaster, and the *Strawberry Whirl* carousel, all of them disassembled, and some up on truck beds. Most of the whimsical machinery needed paint and repairs. Otis wondered about safety issues, like any guardian of the public welfare.

Mr. Kite turned out to be Mrs. Golda Katzenhof, a matronly lady in plaid shirt and bib overalls, as ready to wield a wrench as punch a ticket. She had taken over from Sid, her husband, after runaway prostate problems put him six feet under.

"In high season we tour. But it's still spring yet, and business is slow. Thank God Sid left me a little nest egg. While we wait, we paint, we maintain. These rides will sparkle come June."

"We? You have a staff?"

"Well, I hire out. Summer jobs for college kids mostly. I do a lot of the upkeep myself."

"I notice these rides — look at that alligator! — and I was wondering, where's your climbing wall? Those things are very popular, I'm told."

"Now that you mention it . . . one of my helpers, does some of the work here? He's got a portable wall he brings along. Kids love it, makes them feel like world champion daredevils."

Otis felt a little blip of adrenaline starting to flow.

"But I haven't seen him for a couple of weeks, and he's supposed to be getting Puffy into shape — that rusty train over there is scheduled to be thrilling little kids in El Dorado Hills this weekend."

"Unh-huh. Your helper — how do you deal with him, financially? He brings his own thing — his wall — do you rent it from him? . . . what?"

"He works for me. I pay him."

"Ahh . . . cash?"

"I haven't done a thing wrong in the eyes of the law, officer. And I doubt Hank has either. There's nothing under the table. I write a check and send it."

"Hank?"

"Hank Rogers. You should see him with the kids. He climbs up his wall like Spider-Man himself, and they all want to follow."

"Like *Spider-Man?*" Otis was tingling with anticipation.

"He climbed Aconcagua last year, down in South America."

"Got an address? I'd like to talk to him."

"Somewhere in Placerville, I think. Let me check my books."

▼

Otis roared east up U.S. 50 to the outskirts of Placerville, where he located Progressive Drive spurring off Missouri Flat Road. There he discovered an industrial motel catering to small businesses in need of warehouses and workshops. The sign on the driveway read:

Progressive Business Park

The suite he was looking for was wedged in between a muffler shop and a carpet-cleaning outfit. No identifying signage, just the number — *019* — painted above a corrugated steel garage door. A smaller office door with a tiny window stood beside it. Otis freed up his Maglite, directed the beam through the glass and panned it around the dimly-lit interior, which proved to be an open storage area.

Several large flat panel TV sets were lined up near one wall. DVD players and laptop computers were stacked nearby. Three exercise treadmills and a rowing machine were there as well. Plus three or four expensive-looking road bikes leaning against each other.

Otis whistled. Stolen goods waiting to be sold on eBay, he guessed.

In the rear he could just make out a long trailer balanced on four little wheels. What looked to him like a portable version of the climbing wall at REI was tilted down on top, ready to travel.

"Hell-o, wall."

Scattered on the floor just inside the office door was a pile of flyers, catalogs, magazines, and letters. If Hank Rogers used this address, he wasn't very diligent about picking up his mail.

Otis tried the door. Locked.

"Shit. Who owns this place? Who's got a key?"

25

MARIANNE arrived in Carnac with her military escorts in time for lunch at a little outdoor café. The food was simple, but so good that she found herself mentally downgrading her favorite eatery, the Golden Goose back in Placerville.

Bagwell parked the expedition's car in the lot at the *Musée de Préhistoire*. There he bought tickets for a guided tour of the world-famous standing stones, the only way to walk among them. Soon he, Marianne, and Captain Pike were trailing along behind a bevy of French school children, listening to the docent, a brusque middle-aged woman, deliver a lecture in French. Bagwell translated in telegraphic fashion.

"Les Alignements de Ménec . . . 1500 stones in eleven rows . . . some big, some little . . . local granite. They run a kilometer northeast from here . . . placed anywhere from 3000 to 4500 BC . . . by those druids we've all heard about. In modern times, thefts and vandalism . . . questions of proper management. French heritage, et cetera. That's why we're tagging along with these kids."

"They're beautiful," said Marianne, lightly touching one of the weather-beaten pillars. She was wearing a pair of stylish French sunglasses she had bought to ward off the glare of a warm afternoon. She swished her sneakered feet through the long grass. "Also creepy."

A couple hundred meters along the alignment they paused at *Le Géant*, a tall stone, vaguely suggestive of a human figure, that stood more than twice the height of Captain Pike.

"What's cooking? Got anything?" asked Bagwell.

Marianne looked at the cracked granite, ran her hand over the rough surface. "No. Afraid not."

"Aren't these things supposed to be talking to you?"

"I don't really know." She eyed the tall shape looming above her. "This one looks like it could."

"You *are* trying to sense something, right?"

"Sure. I'm tuning the radio, but it's all dead air."

Bagwell flapped his arms. "Keep trying." He ambled off to follow the tour. Captain Pike wandered over to another row, staying close enough to the group to avoid reprimands.

Marianne hung back. When the chattering children had moved some distance away, she did her best to empty her mind and receive whatever signals might emanate from five-thousand-year-old granite. Her expectations were low.

But gradually a greenish impression formed. It was coming from somewhere nearby, along the edge of the alignment. Warily, she craned her neck around *Le Géant* to get a visual. And, whoops, there stood an old man, just behind the rock wall that formed the park's border. She pulled her head back. Her heart started racing. She counted to ten, then looked again. He was gone. Where? Into the trees, probably.

"Marianne!" called Bagwell, up ahead. He was waving to her.

She jogged along the row of stones to catch up. Bagwell pointed to the ground at his feet, where a small fragment of granite was lodged in the dirt path.

"Look here. Small, like something you could pick up in a dream. Would this work?"

Marianne barely glanced at the rock chip.

"Listen, while I was back there, I started to sense an aura. A green one."

"One of the stones?"

"An old man. He was standing just outside the park here, along the wall, looking at me."

Bagwell scanned the wall. "Don't see anybody. Pike?"

Pike lifted a pair of dainty binoculars and examined the area. "Seems clean."

"Fine, but he's there. Let's just stroll along and see what happens next."

Ten meters up the row, the docent paused to discuss whether a particularly odd stone was naturally formed or crudely carved. The three Americans joined to listen, deliberately facing away from the rock wall.

"I'm getting that glow again," said Marianne.

"Where?" whispered Bagwell.

"Behind my left shoulder. Don't look."

"Is it a ghost? You're freaking me out," said Pike.

Suddenly Marianne pivoted around for a direct view. There was the old man, staring at her. She waved, then turned to Bagwell to point him out.

"Ray . . . ?"

By the time Bagwell figured out where to look, the figure was gone again. "Damn, nobody there. You sure about this?"

"Better than that. I recognize the guy."

Bagwell took a step backward. "You're kidding, right? From where?"

"Want to guess?"

"I'll pass."

"In the bakery this morning," she declared, with a touch of pride in her professional observing skills.

"Sweeping floors!" said Bagwell.

"Yup."

"Say, folks, rain's coming our way," noted Pike, pointing toward a wrack of clouds in the southwest. "We're going to get wet pretty soon."

"Let's move on, Ray," said Marianne, with an eye on the sky. She gestured dismissively at the endless line of stones still to be explored. The needle-in-a-haystack challenge posed by 1500 look-alike chunks of granite was beyond her.

"The stones here are just . . . stones. I'm not getting the Big Yes Feeling. I need a tart or something from *Boulangerie Pass-a-roo.*"

▼

It was late afternoon when the three Americans arrived back in Sarzeau. They huddled in their tiny Citroën, staring at Marianne's family bakery through raindrops on the windshield. A shower had passed over, wetting everything, but now the sun was breaking through heavy clouds, and the walls and cobblestone streets of the little tourist town were glistening.

"What time do they close?" asked Pike.

"Soon, I hope," said Marianne, using a sleeve to wipe fog off her window. "It's a sweatbox in here."

They watched and waited.

"What are we looking for, anyway?" wondered Pike after a while. He was getting antsy.

"Not sure," said Bagwell. "Marianne?"

"I'm not sure either. But that old man . . . I want to talk to him."

They watched and waited some more.

The church bells chimed six o'clock. The young woman they had seen at the bakery counter emerged from the store. She had a shopping bag under her arm as she walked away, apparently heading for the supermarket just around the corner. Pretty soon her husband followed, moving off across the street in the opposite direction.

Ten minutes went by, trying the Americans' patience. Then, at last, the old floor sweeper came out. He locked the door, turned, and ambled away up the street.

"That's him!" yelped Marianne. Before Bagwell or Pike could respond she was out the door, running after the guy.

"Dammit, Sarzeau," said Pike, starting the car.

"Hey, wait up," cried Marianne, waving both hands. The old man did not seem to hear her. Suddenly he disappeared into an alley. Marianne rushed to the corner. The old man was a block ahead of her. The Citroën came screeching up behind.

"Come on, Marianne," said Bagwell, leaning out the window, "we do this together."

The old man turned a corner and disappeared again. Marianne raced to catch up, ignoring Bagwell. The alley was too narrow for the Citroën, and it roared away.

After one long block she emerged onto a broad boulevard. There was no sign of the old man. She looked this way and that, trying to figure out where he went. Wait — *there!* — off to her right, another alley. She ran to see, and sure enough, the old man was sauntering calmly along, oblivious to her frantic pursuit. She slowed down, matching his pace, and followed discreetly behind.

At the end of the alley, the old man turned to his right. Thirty seconds later Marianne arrived at the same spot. Another boulevard, this one clogged with traffic. Her elusive target was gone again.

"Merde!" she griped, practicing her French.

She looked around. No more alleys. She was standing beside the *Hotel de Ville*, the town hall. Just beyond it, a wide expanse edged by little trees made space for a beautiful outdoor café. She strolled over and was disappointed to find it abandoned, its tables and chairs wet from the recent shower. The customers had all fled inside. She kicked a cobble in defeat, then jumped at a loud *Bang!* on the window behind her. She turned around, and there was the old man, sitting at a small table. He cupped a hand and motioned for her to join him.

The Citroën roared up just as she was opening the café door.

"Broomhandle!" yelled Bagwell.

She gave him an apologetic wave and stepped inside.

"Bonjour," said the old man. He indicated the empty seat at his little table. "Please, sit."

Marianne sat down. She noticed a beer in front of the old man, and a glass of red wine, already poured, for her.

"Hello," she said. "I don't speak French."

"Ça ne fait rien, I speak some English."

Marianne conjured an ironic smile and lifted her glass. "This is nice. You saw me, obviously."

"Obviously. I am very curious about you."

"And me you."

"Oui, I would have come forward before, but I thought it might be better without your minders. Who are they?"

"Just what you think. They look after me."

"Ahh, des gardes du corps . . . bodyguards."

"More or less."

"Government? Military? Spies?"

"I really can't discuss it."

"So, you have been recruited into an operation. I have heard of such things. A ridiculous fantasy to most, but adepts, rare and valuable, know better, yes?"

Marianne drew herself up. "How? How do you know?"

He smiled. "Family secret."

"Maybe I'm a distant cousin — I can see your aura. I sensed it out there in that rock garden."

"Color?"

"Greenish."

"Dans le milieu. That is proper. We are wary of outsiders."

"I'm here looking for my family, because I need to find something. Something to focus my . . . whatever it is I've got. My father is in a coma back in the states. I need to wake him up."

The old man thought about this for a while. Then he raised his glass and touched it against hers.

"À votre santé."

"Mud in your eye."

They both sipped their drinks. The old man thought some more.

"A coma, eh?" he said at last. "I am thinking it cannot be natural.

Someone has cast a spell."

"Good guess."

"Eh bien, if it were otherwise, your bodyguards would consult a doctor, not a witch."

Marianne bristled. "I'm no witch."

"Not yet, not yet."

"Whatever you think, I need help. I'm supposed to find a stone, but we're in Brittany . . . lot of stones here."

The old man nodded sympathetically. "Something you dreamed?"

"You got it."

He nodded again.

"I will tell you about myself. My name is Josse Rouvennec. 'Pasquillou' was the family name, as you supposed, but once upon a time a Mademoiselle Pasquillou fell in love, there was a marriage, and she became Madame Rouvennec. This was long ago, before emigration to America. I inherited the bakery, but I am old, and my son runs it with his wife. I just help them clean up."

"Unh-huh," said Marianne, trying to absorb the information.

"My powers are real, but weak. These abilities leap from one generation to another, skipping some, collecting themselves in others. My son is just a nice young man. For myself, it is all I can do to sense an aura now and again. You, however, I sensed the minute you approached our shop, like a light bulb."

"Green?"

"Vert et du bleu." He smiled. "How do you say? Teal."

"Okay. To find my stone . . . where? . . . how?"

"An adept's talisman must come from the family tradition. Those stones lined up in Carnac, they are not ours, you waste your time there."

"I figured."

The old man placed a small leather-bound notebook on the table and consulted it, turning pages, running a finger down the hand-written lines.

"You are a Rouvennec, and any Rouvennec must start here in Sarzeau, on the road to *Saint Gildas de Rhuys.*" He turned the notebook to show her a rough sketch.

"Where is that?"

"Just west of town. It is a menhir, it stands alone in a farmer's field, near *l'allée couverte*, a dolmen. Many generations who farm that land want to crack the stone and carry it away, but they do not dare. The stone has a power that tells them — *non, jamais!"*

Marianne looked lost.

"It is on every tourist map. Your bodyguards will know. But, listen to me — that is only the first step. You must wait there for a sign. A sign to direct you to your own *personal* stone. Be patient, wait, follow the sign."

"What's the sign? How will I spot it?"

"La foudre."

He made a jagged downward motion with his hand.

"Lightning?"

He shrugged a Gallic shrug.

"That doesn't sound good." Marianne pointed out the window. "The sun is shining."

"But you are here. You need a sign. Perhaps your spirit is strong enough to *demand* a sign."

"Not too sure about that."

He closed his notebook, drained his beer, and stood up.

"Take heart. I see the weather reports on television — the little shower today is a beginning. Thunderstorms are coming."

26

OFFICER OTIS made his case to Lieutenant Kazmarek, wrote up a tight report indicating probable cause, appeared before a county judge, and returned to the Progressive Business Park industrial motel with search warrant in hand. There he met with the building owner, a suspicious fellow named Bob Herman. The warrant seemed to satisfy the man, who used his master key to open the door to *Suite 019.*

Once inside, Otis hauled out a small digital camera and, without disturbing anything, took pictures of every item in the place. Herman, still suspicious, followed him around, ever watchful.

Once he had photo coverage of the whole interior, he went to work. First he stacked the mail into piles, separating the junk from the letters. Then he opened his notebook and set about reading and recording the brand names, model designations, and serial numbers of all the TV sets, DVD players, laptop computers, and bicycles.

Otis picked up the final bike and almost threw it over his head.

"Whoa, this one weighs nothing."

This piqued Herman's interest. He walked over to check it out.

"Let me."

He hefted the bike experimentally. "Nine, ten pounds all up. Looks like my client has money to spend."

"You ride?"

"It's that or golf. I hate golf."

"So this bike, what's the deal?"

"This, my friend, is a Trek Domane. Carbon frame, Shimano XTR components, Aeolus wheels . . ."

"Expensive?"

"Think Rolex watch. My God, it must have cost seven thousand bucks. At least."

Otis was astonished. "And it doesn't even have an engine."

He returned to the stack of mail, sorted through the letters looking for the Kiddie Karnival return address. There were two such envelopes, one postmarked two weeks ago, the other within the last few days.

"Your warrant doesn't say anything about opening my client's mail, officer," warned Herman.

"Don't worry."

Otis fired up his Maglite and placed the lens against one of the envelopes. He then examined the light pattern shining through to the other side. It wasn't hard to see the markings of a check. Peering closely, Otis determined the amount to be $650. And change.

"Now why," he mused aloud, "would anyone leave six hundred and fifty dollars lying around on the floor?"

Herman shrugged. "Maybe he's on vacation. Man who can afford a Trek Domane — well, sir, he might be over there in Hawaii, or hell, Dubai."

"Or maybe he slipped on a banana peel. When was the last time you saw the dude?"

"Hank Rogers? Never met him. We worked everything out on the phone. He sent in his deposit, and I left a key in the lock."

Otis' phone rang. He glanced at the screen and held up his hand.

"Just a sec, overseas call, gotta take it."

He strolled outside, pushed a finger into his free ear.

"Marianne? You again? Where's my postcard?"

Marianne's voice was tinny and distorted. "Hey, Otis. What's new?"

"I got a name for you — Hank Rogers. He's your climber. He has a portable wall that he trails around to carnivals. Now get this — when he isn't using it, he stores the thing right here in town, in a little warehouse."

"Get in that warehouse, bro!"

"Already done. I cited probable cause, got my warrant, I'm in there now. Guess what else I found?"

"Stolen goods?"

"Affirmative. Bulky stuff, treadmills, bikes, big TV sets."

"You the man."

"There's more. Yesterday some guy named Gawley called me. Said he runs a U-Haul franchise down in Jackson."

"My bud Wade. He's also a cop, like us."

"Well, he was trying to reach you. A U-Haul dealer in Sacramento has been calling around to other franchises, trying to find a missing truck."

Marianne was silent for a while considering the news. Finally she asked, "Think the dots connect?"

"Unh-huh. I think your climber rented a U-Haul to carry all this here loot, and ditched it."

He thought about his statement and amended it. "But look, the guy hasn't been around to cash his checks, so maybe he felt my hot breath and skipped town."

"What was the name again?"

"Hank Rogers."

"Home address?"

"This is it — where the carnival lady sends his checks."

"Get on that name, follow up, nail that guy."

"Hey, I been shagging my ass off. I should get a medal. You can take a flying follow-up when you come back. What are you up to anyway?"

"Waiting for a storm."

"Unh-huh, don't wait forever."

"Otis, you useless potato, run down that name . . ."

The conversation was interrupted by a burst of static on the line.

"Marianne?"

"Whoops," she came back, "I had to duck under an awning. It's raining again. Call you."

Otis' phone went dead.

▼

Morning in Placerville was evening in Sarzeau. Marianne had spent the day in the hotel, staring out the window hopefully, but not too optimistically, at clouds. She was restless. Late on, she volunteered to make a snack run to the nearby supermarket.

Her real purpose was the phone call to Otis. Now, absorbed by the latest news of her burglary case, she was walking back between the raindrops, lugging a bagful of grapes, a round of brie, a baguette, and bottles of sparkling water.

As Marianne turned toward the hotel, she paid no heed to a taxi pulling up on the *Place Richemont,* and completely failed to notice the oddly dressed woman who stepped out to scan her surroundings. Clicking away in her peculiar fashion, Firoz registered Marianne disappearing behind the church.

▼

After dark, when Bagwell, Pike, and Marianne were a block away having dinner at a French pizzeria, Firoz approached the desk at *Hotel Lesage.*

"Excuse me, sir, I am trying to contact my sister, a young woman. She uses the name 'Sarzeau,' like your beautiful town, and I am thinking she is registered here in your hotel, yes?"

The clerk eyed the woman, who was clearly not an American.

"We, ah . . . *on ne révèle pas les noms des clients.* You understand? No names of guests."

Firoz nodded.

"I see, and understand. You are very properly discreet."

Firoz knew, by the unsure way the clerk refused her request, that it must be so. The Sarzeau woman was here!

She returned to the street and made a telephone call.

"Dada Golay, sir, I have found the woman. She is staying in a hotel here in Sarzeau."

Pause.

"Yes, that is correct."

Pause.

"I have observed all day. They are three. One of the men is a soldier, a bodyguard."

Pause.

"I have engaged the driver as you suggested. I pay in euros, he is satisfied. I have described our targets, and he has discovered their car. If they move, we will follow. I look for the best opportunity."

Pause.

"Rely on me, sir."

27

MARIANNE awoke early next morning, still fighting jet lag. When the bells of Saint-Saturnin started ringing, she threw on a presentable blouse, added a sweater, grabbed a scarf she had bought yesterday, tied it over her hair, and crossed the street to attend mass. Her frequent contact with what she imagined was the spirit world had given her considerable respect for organized religion. One of few so inclined, she discovered, as she pushed open the church door and saw the rows of empty pews. Like any tourist, she was impressed by the vaulted roof, held aloft by tall pillars, and by the solid stone walls, now painted white. The solemn ambiance could not have been more at odds with the low ceiling and warm wood of Saint Patrick's back in Placerville, and it made her feel small. The elaborately carved details, the statuary, the stained glass, the sheer height of the ceiling, all bespoke the extraordinary devotion of bygone years, out of place in modern society. She prayed silently for success in her quest.

Then she joined her fellow travelers for breakfast in the *Hotel Lesage* café.

"What do you mean, bad weather?" Bagwell stared out the window at people hurrying past under umbrellas. A steady rain was splattering on the cobblestones, and it was driving Bagwell crazy.

Marianne finished her brioche and sipped at a tall glass of orange juice.

"I'm just going by what the old man said. We need to visit the menhir I told you about during a thunderstorm. I need a sign — lightning. I don't hear any thunder, do you?"

"No," he grunted.

Pike was optimistic. He seemed to know something about weather patterns. "We could get some boomers when the cold front pushes in. Thunderstorms often trail behind, just when a storm breaks up into showers. Our best chance will be late this afternoon."

Bagwell finished his *café au lait*. "All right. But what about your long-lost cousin, this man — what's the family name now? — Rouvennec? How do we know you're actually related? How do we know he is what he says he is?"

Marianne was irritated. *"We* don't . . . but *I* do."

"How? How is that?"

"I can see his aura. It's faint, but real, the sign of an adept. Now, he's the first to say his powers are weak, how they skip generations, and so on. But auras have colors, and as we were talking, his became bluer and bluer."

"Bluer?"

"It started out green. Blue means 'friend,' according to old lady Crowfoot, and that's what I sense. We can trust him."

Bagwell made a sour face. "Even though this is exactly how your father here talks, I don't actually trust anybody, but . . . fine . . . okay, we wait."

Just then the café door opened, and a man in a hooded anorak entered. He looked around, spotted the three Americans, and walked over to their table. He threw back his hood.

"Bonjour," he said.

"Monsieur Rouvennec!" said Marianne with a smile. "We were talking about you. These are my 'minders' — Major Bagwell, Captain Pike, meet Josse Rouvennec." She indicated her companions. They shook hands.

"Du café, monsieur?" suggested Bagwell.

"Ah, merci non. I am here with some news, *c'est tout."*

"What news?"

"I don't mean to trouble you . . . *mais* . . . I sense another aura. Not so good."

"Who is it?" asked Marianne. "I don't feel a thing."

"Someone who is not like us, not an adept." He leaned forward and held up a warning finger. *"Mam'selle,* you must act — soon, and with care."

"What's the problem?"

"Ah, it is this way. When I sense you, I see a pure spirit."

"Me? Pure?" She rolled her eyes.

"Clean is a better word. This other one is faint, but more to the red. You know what that means?"

"Trouble."

"Oui, I sense hostility, vengefulness, *le danger."*

"Oh boy."

"I must return to our store, my son is away in Paris. Here, I leave you with an example of something new we are trying for the American tourists. It is not McDonald's, but we do our best . . ."

He placed a paper bag on the table, touched his brow in a little salute, turned, and left. Marianne opened the bag. They all peered in. Three plump croissants were sitting there, still warm. Pike reached in, picked one up, took a bite.

"Mmm, bacon inside."

Bagwell did the same. "Damn, this is good. All right, Broomer, I changed my mind . . . we can trust him."

▼

The day wore on. After lunch the threesome migrated into the bar, nearly empty on a weekday afternoon. Bagwell was soon absorbed in a book on standing stones he picked up there. Marianne and Captain Pike were talking shop.

"So, the Glock — it's great, it's intimidating. But I like my little Beretta," said Pike.

"Really? Me too. My old department didn't have any standards worth a damn, so we picked whatever we wanted. What model?"

Pike produced the weapon from an ankle holster.

"PX4 Storm. nine-mill. 'The perfect storm'."

"I've got one just like it! Amazing. Of course, Ray wouldn't let me bring mine, but back home, I wear it all the time."

"Ever use it?"

"Yes. Last year I was in a fight. I'm no good with a gun, so I went through three clips, bang, bang, bang."

"You're kidding."

"I didn't hit a thing."

"Scared the dude, I'll bet."

"Yeah, it did."

"Now, I also carry a knife. You never know, close in, what could happen, so I've got this little job" — Pike unsheathed a Smith & Wesson military boot knife — "with the three-point-five inch blade. Concealed, out of the way, but you can tear up an opponent with one of these."

"I'd just cut my finger. No close-ups for me, except in the movies."

"Did you know," interrupted Bagwell, looking up from his guidebook, "that there are more than five thousand standing stones here in Brittany? Or, that no bodies have been found in most of the dolmens, which are thought to be tombs?"

Marianne and Pike both shook their heads.

"Or, that the stone cutters were probably immigrants from Spain, the so-called 'beaker people'?"

"News to me," said Marianne.

"Of course, this is just one opinion. Everything is still in dispute. Someday, DNA will tell the tale."

As the light of afternoon faded, Captain Pike brought out his Zombie Dice.

"Okay, Marianne, focus those powers and show me some brains."

She rolled, captured two brains, passed the dice.

"Hey, Ray, you want in on this?"

Bagwell's lip curled. He continued reading. Pike rolled, captured seven brains, then got himself shotgunned.

"It couldn't happen to a nicer zombie," declared Marianne, who went on to eke out her first victory.

Pike started another game. Shotguns again, this time accompanied by a clap of thunder.

"Hey!" said Marianne.

This was followed by a flash that lit the bar, then another.

Pike counted off the seconds. After fifteen, a low rumble growled through town.

"Five kliks," he said. "Three miles."

Marianne stood up and moved to the window. The evening sky was still blue behind broken clouds. After a while, another flash. Pike counted again.

"Three kliks. Closer."

"I didn't see any strike, just the sky lighting up," said Marianne.

"Heat lightning."

Bagwell closed his guidebook. "Showtime. The stone we're after is seven kliks down the road."

▼

Pike drove while Bagwell navigated from the map in his guidebook. *Rue de la Madeleine* out of Sarzeau, west on D780, *Route de Port Navalo*, then a roundabout and south on D198. Heavy rain alternated with the glow of sunset as they made their way through flat open countryside.

"Stop here," said Bagwell, pointing into a plowed field. "That's it, *l'allée couverte*, the 'covered walkway'."

Left untilled in the middle of the field was an overgrown pile of rocks, some standing, others laid on top, forming a crude passageway about fifteen meters long. The trio trudged across the wet ground, feet picking up mud from the rain.

"Now, the menhir we want is *près de l'allée* — near the walkway," said Bagwell, eyes still in his guidebook

Marianne glanced around. To the southwest she could see the top of a very tall menhir partially concealed by bushes and small trees crowding an inset corner of the field. It seemed to exert a magnetic pull.

"This way!" she cried and veered off toward it.

She rounded the bushy corner and stopped. There before her in lonely isolation was a huge egg-shaped boulder, at least twice her height, probably more. It was pale grey, splotched with moss and lichens, half as wide as tall. There was nothing else like it anywhere in view. She felt a commanding presence, as if the menhir were a guardian from some ancient age of the world, still on duty, frowning down upon her in severe judgment. She half expected to be asked for a password.

As she stood there admiring the granite block and wondering about her "sign," dark clouds rolled in under the twilit sky. A flash of light painted the landscape in high relief. A grumbling peal of thunder followed a few seconds later.

Pike and Bagwell, trailing behind, stopped in their tracks.

Crack! Boom!

Another flash, this time a jagged streak south of the field, and much closer.

"Marianne, you want to be careful here. We could all get fried if we move too close," cautioned Bagwell.

Marianne ignored him and walked toward the menhir. As she approached, the less imposing the stone seemed, and the more protective. A feeling of silent welcome washed over her.

"Marianne, your hair . . ." said Bagwell.

Marianne felt her scalp prickle. Her hair was lifting away from her head, standing on end in response to a powerful charge of static electricity.

"Too far, Marianne!" shouted Pike.

Marianne looked back at the pair. Both of them looked awfully uneasy. She grinned like a schoolgirl and continued up to the stone. She reached out and touched the rough granite, draining the static charge. Her hair fell back into place.

"How about a sign, big guy?" she said.

Suddenly, as if in response, the clouds burst, and rain came pelting down. Hail pellets bounced off the menhir and the Americans standing before it. Marianne's eyes went wide. She took a backward step.

Zzzapp! BLAMM!

A stroke of lightning sizzled the top of the menhir. The thunder was so instantaneous and loud it stunned Marianne and knocked her flat. Little rock chips bounced through the grass and bushes, sparkling like fireworks. Pike and Bagwell retreated ten meters.

"I'm okay, guys," said Marianne, staggering to her feet. "If that was a sign, I'm down with it."

She had been thinking that her sign, whatever it might be, would confer some newfound sense of power, but she felt no inward change.

BOOM . . . Boom . . . . . . boom . . .

"Hey, look," said Pike, pointing west. A series of lightning strikes blasted downward in a regular pattern, one after another, each one further away westward.

"What do you think of that?" asked Bagwell, staring in amazement.

Before Marianne could reply, the sequence replayed itself.

BOOM . . . Boom . . . . . . boom . . .

First a nearby lightning stroke, then a farther one, then a final one, off near the western horizon.

Pike counted down the interval between flash and bang. "Okay, that last one? That strike hit about six kliks west southwest from here."

Marianne was still shaking off the blast effects. She blinked.

"Wow."

She slapped at her jeans, dislodging some of the mud. "Just a wild guess, boys, but I think that little show was my sign."

"What have we got over that way?" muttered Bagwell. He thumbed an app to turn his smartphone into a flashlight and examined his guidebook.

"Aha! In Arzon, at just about the right distance, we have a very prominent dolmen in a national park. It's called *Le Cairn du Petit Mont d'Arzon.*"

"Better get over there," said Marianne. She returned to the menhir, placed both hands on its flank.

"Thanks, pal. Keep watching."

▼

It took the FULTAP expedition members a half hour to find their way into Arzon, a small seaside tourist village, and work their way through the narrow streets and byways to *Le Cairn du Petit Mont d'Arzon* on the coast. It was dark when they arrived. Pike stopped in the gravel parking lot at the end of the access lane. Bagwell read the sign at the gate.

"Le parc est fermé," he recited. "Closed."

"Then we won't be bothered," said Marianne.

Pike turned their car around and guided it onto a grassy turnout thirty meters back, far enough from the entrance to disguise their presence outside park hours.

They all got out. Here and there a star could be seen behind the still roiling clouds. Bagwell looked up at the sky and unfurled an umbrella.

"Not a good idea, Ray," said Marianne.

"No? Why not?"

"If this works, I'm likely to rev up the storm." She pointed upward. "That thing is a lightning magnet. You don't want to get hit."

Bagwell wrapped up his umbrella and threw it back into the car.

Pike scanned the area.

"No houses nearby, no lights, no crowd. It's almost full dark. Let's stay alert, shall we?" he said, shifting into special forces mode.

He handed his Beretta to Marianne. She checked the clip and passed it on to Bagwell.

"I don't think I should pack. You take it."

"I've got my revolver, what's wrong?"

"Nothing, but this is . . . I can't explain . . . a sacred thing. I should be clean before . . . before whatever it is."

"It's okay, I've got her six," said Pike, pulling an Uzi out of his duffel.

"All right then, here's the plan," said Bagwell, assuming authority. "You guys go in, I'll guard home plate. This is a national monument, not a farmer's field. If the *gendarmes* should appear with all of us in there after hours, we'll look just a tad too organized, and we'll wind up answering a lot of questions we'd rather avoid."

Pike nodded assent and rummaged around in his duffel some more. He pulled out a miniature night vision monocular. Then he yanked a small backpack free and threw it over his shoulders.

"Let's see that map again."

Bagwell held up his guidebook. Pike played the beam of a small flashlight over the open pages.

"Okay, looks like a couple of hundred meters through the woods, then an open field and the mound. Trails all around the thing. Main entrance on the northeast side, toward us. What is that concrete structure?"

"Nazis built a bunker right into the stones during the war. Destroyed one of the tombs. It's part of the tourist attraction," said Bagwell, skimming the text.

Pike handed Bagwell a tiny walkie-talkie, barely more than an earbud. He screwed an identical communicator into his own ear and pointed a finger at it.

"We'll talk."

He signaled Marianne, and they started down the lane.

"Here, this won't taint you." He handed her his flashlight, pulled another one out of a side pocket on his pants. "I'm guessing you'll need it."

They plodded along in silence, wiggled through the stile at the end of the parking lot, and entered a wide sandy trail hemmed in by tall bushes and scraggly trees. The evening was humid. Frogs were chirping in a hidden pond nearby.

On they marched. Suddenly the trees and bushes ended at a locked gate, with an open field beyond, and the Atlantic Ocean beyond that. Pike bent his knees and cupped his hands into a stirrup.

"Climb," he said.

Marianne placed a foot in his hands and heaved herself up and over. Pike legged it over without the slightest apparent effort.

"The burglar I'm tracking could climb right up walls. You'd give him some competition," she said.

"Unh-huh. Is that the cairn?" He pointed ahead, where the dark bulk of a terraced hillock stood.

"Hope so."

"It's big. Fifty meters at least. I had no idea. Imagine dragging all those rocks down here."

Indeed, the looming shape was a huge hill of stones piled in three layers by unknown ancient masons, each layer set back from the one beneath.

Here and there around the field other monstrous menhirs were standing or lying in the rough grass.

Pike pressed a finger to his ear. "Cheese? Reading me? We have the BFR in view," he muttered.

Back on the side of the road near their little Citroën, Bagwell heard Pike speak through his earbud walkie-talkie.

"Copy you," Bagwell replied. "Keep me advised."

Pike turned to Marianne. "So what are we doing here? What's the plan?"

"Wish I knew."

She started mumbling. Pike watched her eyes close, saw her body straighten, grow rigid.

"Hey, you okay? Talk to me."

She ignored him, continued to mumble.

"Marianne? What the fuck?"

"Shut up, I'm working. Trying to summon the weather."

"You're kidding."

"No, I'm not." She held out a hand. Raindrops spattered on her palm.

In another few seconds hail was bucketing down, bouncing off their heads, off the menhirs lying around, off the grass.

Pike pulled his boonie hat out of his backpack and jammed it down on his head.

"Jesus, Sarzeau. Is this you? You doing this?"

"Don't be a dope. I made a request."

"Well, looks like someone's giving you a big affirmative."

She started mumbling again.

Ssss! Whamm!

A dainty filament of lightning struck the face of the cairn. The flash turned the Americans' faces blue. The thunderclap jolted them both back a step.

Then Marianne was running for the entrance, a pair of tall stones standing upright, with another wide stone balanced across them, forming a gigantic gate.

"Come on, this is it! Gotta be!" she yelled.

When she reached the gate, she played the beam of her flashlight into a long stone tunnel running into the cairn. Unfortunately, the French National Monuments authorities had installed a door made of welded steel bars across the opening. She tugged at the knob, but it was locked, blocking her way.

Pike reluctantly joined her.

"This is it. Shit, I need to get in here."

She grabbed the bars and yanked on them, rattling the door against the stone opening.

"How do you know? You check the map?" Pike wasn't convinced. "Nothing really goes anywhere under this thing. Most of it is just a pile of rocks."

"I know, I know. And I did check. This is Dolmen 3, one of the tombs. It runs back in here quite a way, then dead ends. There's a chamber at the end."

"You sure? Why this and not one of the others?"

"You saw that lightning strike."

Pike nodded, pressed a finger to his ear again. "Cheese? News flash — Broomhandle has ID-ed our target," he whispered.

"Got it," said Bagwell, nervously pacing back and forth on the roadside. "Don't get in her way."

"Hooah," he muttered. He removed an item from his backpack, and affixed it to the latch on the gate.

"Stand back, and I'll show you how the pros pick locks."

He touched a pair of wires together. A fuse crackled. Marianne took a step backward. Pike yanked her around behind one of the standing stones.

Bang!

A small explosion blew the gate open, almost tore it off its hinges. It snapped around a hundred and eighty degrees and hit the wall with a loud *klank!*

"There you go, babe. Drive on." He pointed into the dark stone tunnel. Marianne took a cautious step inside.

"Wait here," she said.

"Fine by me," he replied, and stationed himself at one side of the entrance.

"If I'm not back in ten minutes, though, or whenever you get real antsy, come find me."

"Wilco."

"Be prepared for demons and goblins. Geez, this place gives me the creeps."

Marianne moved slowly into the tunnel, playing the beam of her little flashlight over the stones. The walls were a series of upright granite slabs, a couple of meters high. The ceiling was constructed of slabs as well, laid across the tops of the walls, but narrower, a meter and a half at most. Marianne instinctively turned herself sideways and hunched over as she inched forward.

"Broomhandle is entering D3," whispered Pike, finger to ear.

"Roger that," said Bagwell, checking his guidebook.

BOOM! BOOM!

Thunder from nearby lightning strokes reverberated through the rocks. Flashes of blue light reached into the passageway, illuminating the stones. Marianne could just make out faint carvings curling into strange patterns on some of them.

Five meters in she came to an alcove, the opening to a side chamber. She aimed her flashlight at the walls there. Engravings suggestive of axes or threshing tools stood out in the beam.

She moved on. A few meters further along, the tunnel opened into a large chamber. Marianne's flashlight revealed more axe images and what might be sheaves of wheat chiseled into the side walls. A tall triangular panel of granite was wedged into the back wall by skillfully laid courses of masonry. The interlocked stones were so cleverly fitted that no mortar was needed to hold them fast. Strange icons surrounding what looked like a wagon wheel with many spokes were cut into the panel surface. Or, thought Marianne, without any real knowledge, it was a picture of the sun, with its rays pointing to primitive signs of the zodiac she couldn't quite interpret.

Just to one side of the wheel was the incised image of a human hand, fingers splayed. A bygone king, or holy man, or artist, or maybe just a mischievous intruder had left his or her mark in the granite. It seemed to speak, to proclaim *I did this,* silently carrying the mystery of the human spirit to Marianne across a chasm of five thousand years.

All at once she knew what to do. She reached out and fitted her fingers into the image.

"Show me," she said aloud.

Zzzapp! KRAKK!

A tremendous bolt of lightning hit somewhere overhead. Rivulets of electrons swirled over the ceiling, danced down the face of the stone panel, lighting up the wheel, the enigmatic signs, the hand image. Marianne was catapulted backward. She hit the stone floor on her back, smacking her head. The power of the stroke knocked out her flashlight. She lay there for a moment, dazed, head spinning. Then she turned over and pulled herself into a kneeling position.

A chip of stone about the size and shape of an arrowhead was dislodged by the lightning and hurled across the chamber. It bounced off the far wall and skidded into a corner. In the darkness, it sparkled with the remains of the electric charge. She crawled across the floor, reached out and picked it up.

A shocking surge of electricity ran up her arm. She gasped. Her hand went numb. But she held on to the stone chip, held on tight.

Outside, Captain Pike saw the lightning bolt strike the cairn. The thunderclap staggered him. He peered into the tunnel.

"Marianne? You okay in there?"

She was slow to answer.

"Hey, Sarzeau, what's up?"

"I'm here. I'm good. I'm on my way to you," came her voice, small and tinny as it echoed off the stone-walled tunnel.

"Find anything?"

"Affirmative," said Marianne, sounding groggy. "I'll show you."

"Cheese?" whispered Pike. "Joy in France, Broomhandle has acquired the target."

"Get her out of there," said Bagwell.

Suddenly Pike straightened up and turned around to face the field in front of the gate.

"Uh, Cheese, listen up, we've got traffic," he whispered.

"What kind of traffic? *Gendarmes?*" asked Bagwell.

"Not sure. Nothing visual."

Pike bent his ear toward the trees. He thought he could hear a faint *clicking* noise. He readied his Uzi, brought his night vision monocular up to his eye, and scanned the area.

"I may be wrong," he said. "Could be insects."

But no, there it was again, stronger — *klik!* — *klik!* — *klik!*

Pike rescanned the area. This time he saw someone moving around the curving wall of the cairn, tiptoeing stealthily in his direction.

Klik! — *klik!* — *klik!*

The figure was only ten meters away. He called into the tomb.

"Marianne? Let's go, we're blown!"

He leveled the Uzi, placed a finger on the trigger.

"You there, stop where you are!" he commanded.

Klik! — *klik!* — *klik!*

A powerful beam of green laser light issued from the approaching figure. It swept across Pike's face, blinding him. He dropped his nightscope, fumbled with the Uzi. The figure rushed forward. Before Pike could get a shot off, the figure was behind him, and a knotted cord was closing around his neck.

Marianne heard the clicking, heard Pike's commands, and then scuffling and gurgling. She froze.

Klik! — *klik!* — *klik!*

Whoever was making that sound was now entering the tomb. Marianne herself wasn't far from the entrance. She edged backward, feeling along the wall with her fingers. Within a few steps her hand found the opening to the side chamber. She slipped inside.

Klik! — *klik!* — *klik!*

The sound was getting closer. Marianne bent down, scrubbed her hand on the invisible floor, came up with a half dozen pebbles. Leaning toward the sound and the opening of her little alcove, she flung the pebbles, one at a time, down the tunnel toward the main chamber. They clattered on the stone floor.

Klik! — *klik!* — *klik!*

A billow of air and the faintest whoosh of moving cloth told her that the mysterious figure had passed quickly by. Now's the time, she told herself. Gotta move. But she was terrified, rooted to the spot. She swallowed, gritted her teeth, and forced herself into the passageway, where she misjudged the width and crashed into the opposite wall.

Klik! — *klik!* — *klik!*

The figure turned at the new sound and was gliding back toward her. Some deadly peril loomed. Marianne gripped her new-found stone. It felt heavy. It felt warm. It seemed to her that it began to pulse with an electric charge. Her fingers were tingling. As swiftly as terror had overcome her, it vanished. A mysterious feeling of pride welled up. A sense of power formed. It lightened her heart, hardened her resolve.

"You — whoever you are — don't move!" she ordered, surprising herself with the emphatic authority of her own voice.

The figure stopped.

Klik! — klik! — klik!

"Stop that clicking!"

The figure fell silent.

Marianne turned and ran to the exit. She almost tripped over the prostrate form of Captain Pike just beyond the gate.

"What the hell — ?"

She bent down over him. Out here, the storm had abated. Clouds were parting. She could see — dimly.

"Pike! Captain! Oh, Jesus!"

She spotted his little night vision scope, picked it up, and used it to perform an examination. His neck was bruised black. His Adam's apple was crushed. She felt for a pulse. Nothing.

"Shit! Shit! Shit!"

The ugly sight made her sick to her stomach, but she was too scared to throw up. She removed the earbud walkie-talkie from his ear and jammed it into her own. She grabbed his Uzi and felt around the unfamiliar weapon for the bolt. She worked it back to load a round, accidentally ejecting a live cartridge in the process. Then she stood up and peered into the tunnel through the night vision scope.

There, halfway along, stood an immobile figure, swaying slightly. A thin athletic Middle Eastern woman. Firoz.

Even as she watched, Firoz' arms started twitching. She seemed to be emerging from the spell Marianne had cast, if spell it was.

Klik! — klik! — klik!

Marianne aimed the Uzi at her and started to squeeze the trigger. Then she thought better of the idea, turned around, and legged it out across the field, back toward the park exit.

"Mayday, Ray!" she yelled as she ran. "Mayday! Pike is down. Repeat, Pike is down!"

Bagwell had started to drift. He was leaning against the little Citroën when he heard Marianne's frantic cry of alarm. He snapped to attention.

"Say again?"

"Pike is dead! He's been strangled!"

"Leave him," he shouted. "Get your ass back here!"

He pulled his smartphone from a jacket pocket and stabbed a contact.

"Hello, hello — American TV & Appliance? Service Department, please. Product support. Got a stove on fire."

Pause.

"This is FULTAP. Tonight it's 'Cheese' to you. I'm in the wind."

Pause.

"My phone is already encrypted, for Christ's sake."

Pause.

"Okay, call me back."

He stared at his phone. After ten interminable seconds it rang.

"Cheese here."

Pause.

"You're checking? You better — we're on your manifest."

Pause.

"Right, hello yourself. Okay, then, mayday! We have a mission casualty. Ranger down, presumed deceased, this night, in Arzon. A-R-Z-O-N, Brittany. Alpha, Romeo, Zulu . . . French National Park on the Rhuys peninsula, *Le Cairn du Petit Mont d'Arzon.*"

Pause.

"This is not a drill. I am not telling you the sky is falling. I need a cleanup crew at this site, toot sweet. French authorities will be on the scene pretty soon. They will find gear and weapons. You may need to negotiate."

Pause.

"If you can, yes, bring some grease, diplomacy, paper, all of the above. You'll need it."

Pause.

"Understood, we are standing down. We were never there."

Bagwell tapped his phone to end the call.

Back in the park, Marianne hit the wire fence at the edge of the field. She threw her jacket over the little barbs on the top edge and rolled over with an adrenaline-filled burst of energy. Then she dodged through the trees to the access trail and sprinted along it as fast as she could go. Two hundred meters later, panting like a racehorse, she burst into the parking lot and discovered Bagwell sitting there in the Citroën, waiting for her. She jumped in beside him.

"Sure he's dead?"

"Shit oh God, yes. I'm sure."

"Had to ask. Find what you were looking for?"

She held up her little stone chip. "What now?"

"We jet out of town. Other people will clean up our mess."

Bagwell floored the accelerator and they raced away from the park.

Firoz emerged from the trees a few minutes later, apparently unruffled by the evening's events. She made a brief telephone call, and very soon a taxi arrived. She waved the driver down and casually slid into the passenger seat. The taxi motored away at a measured pace.

28

MARIANNE and Major Bagwell stood outside the freight terminal of *Aéroport Nantes Atlantique*, a hundred and ten kilometers southeast of Sarzeau, stoically enduring a light drizzle. They were about to leave France, but before boarding their own flight they were paying respects to their fallen comrade. They watched as Captain Pike's body, now enclosed in an aluminum coffin, was carefully placed on a baggage truck by a French ground crew and transported across the taxiway to a FedEx jet.

Bagwell looked at Marianne. She glanced back. Neither one spoke as the coffin was raised up to the cargo hold by a hydraulic lift. After it disappeared inside Bagwell made a little salute.

"Amen," said he.

Marianne took his arm and pulled him away.

"Come on, Ray, let's get out of here."

In the main terminal, the security lines wound around and around as people waited to catch flights to faraway destinations like Lisbon, Prague, and Morocco. Unfortunately, there were no direct flights to the States.

"Why can't we just head for Montreal, and change planes there?" asked Marianne, anxious to be gone.

"Our French security friends have had, what? A day and a half to think about us," said Bagwell. "So far, we're in the clear. If word gets to the wrong office, that could change. We can't chance a third country's passport control, just in case."

"Oh," said Marianne, mulling her naïve ignorance of espionage tradecraft. "Then why aren't we flying Uncle Sam?"

"Nothing going our way from *La Belle France*, and I don't want to cross back into Germany, same problem."

"Oh," again.

As the line moved forward, Marianne heard someone call her name. She and Bagwell both cringed. They swiveled around to check the source.

"Marianne!"

An old man was striding quickly toward them from across the concourse — Josse Rouvennec. He was waving energetically, puffing from the strain of rushing too fast for his long years.

He joined them in line, thrusting out his hands to shake theirs.

"Marianne, so happy to intercept. Major — ? You are almost gone, but I am here before it happens. I had to do much thinking to understand your travel plans. We are fortunate, no?"

"Monsieur Rouvennec," said Bagwell, in a cool tone.

Rouvennec registered his reserve. "Ah, I have heard something of your troubles, of a most unhappy death at the cairn in Arzon."

"Officially, we don't know what you're talking about," said Bagwell.

"What *are* you talking about?" asked Marianne.

"To express sorrow that your quest for a talisman should include a tragedy."

Marianne exhaled a weary *"Merci."*

"And yet, in all we do, it seems that the good mingles with the bad, the noble with the base. Is it not so?"

Bagwell stiffened. "I don't think we're ready for a lecture today, monsieur."

"And I do not provide one. I seek to know if against this bad thing, you can set a good thing to uplift the spirit."

Marianne reached into her bra and produced her little stone chip. Rouvennec's eyes lit up.

"So, you have done it. Take heart, then, and all will be well."

"Easy advice," said Marianne with a crooked grin.

"No, no, with this talisman your way to power is open before you."

"If you say so."

"All you need is the knowledge of our kind. The wisdom."

"Wouldn't that be nice . . ." she said.

"And, here, you shall have it."

Rouvennec reached into a pocket of his anorak and brought forth the little leather-bound notebook Marianne had seen him consult when they first met. He presented it to her with a little bow.

"Wait a minute," she protested, "this belongs to you, to the Rouvennecs, here in France."

"As I have mentioned before, my son is a good man, and I take pride in him. But he is powerless. I myself am weak. You, you are the vessel that truly holds the family heritage. This volume will sharpen your skills."

Bagwell lifted the book from Marianne's hands and glanced through it.

"He might be right, Marianne," he said, handing it back.

Marianne pulled the book tight to her chest.

"I will do my best to honor your trust," she said, trying for dignity.

Their position in line was inching toward the security scanners. Rouvennec took Marianne's hand and ceremoniously kissed it.

"Read. Study. Learn. There is deep matter within these covers."

"What about you?"

"I read and study, but I cannot put the words into action. That is for you."

She nodded, and planted a grateful kiss on the old man's cheek.

Rouvennec stepped away, blushing, as Marianne arrived at the scanner.

"If you get the chance someday, come and visit. September is best for a relaxing vacation."

"I just might," she said.

"Au 'voir!"

He tapped his brow and walked away.

Marianne stared out the window at the green country unrolling beneath their airplane on the short hop to Paris and Charles de Gaulle International Airport. A morose Bagwell, eyes closed, was either dozing or rethinking recent events.

They changed planes and were an hour into the long flight to San Francisco, cruising high above the Hebrides islands of northwest Scotland, when Marianne finally shook off her woes. She pulled Rouvennec's little notebook out of her bag and, for the first time, opened it up. She slowly turned the pages, noting little diagrams and symbols. Then she elbowed her traveling companion.

"Shit, Ray, it's all in French."

Bagwell roused himself from his continuing funk. He looked at the book, gave her an ironic grin. "You noticed."

"I can't read a word. This won't do me any good at all."

Bagwell took the book and leafed through it.

"Here you go, listen to this —"

> *Esprit puissant, garde-moi contre toute sorcière*
> *Qui essaie de me forcer à dormir!*
> *Je refuse de fermer les yeux*

En raison d'une mauvais sort.
Ce pouvoir je tiens jusqu'au ma mort!

"Okay, you got me, I give up. What the hell was that?" grumbled Marianne.

"It's a spell, I think. A useful one — a spell to ward off sleep. Here's a quick and dirty translation —"

Mighty spirit, shield me from any witch
Who would force me to sleep!
I refuse to close my eyes
For any evil spell.
This power I hold till death.

"Let me see that." Marianne took the book back and studied the text scrawled by the pen of some ancient member of her extended family.

"I guess it's okay in French, but the English is kind of plain. I could just say the same thing off the top of my head."

Bagwell issued a wan smile.

"Lend me the book for a little while. I'll have it translated, and I personally guarantee to improve the spells."

"And how will you do that?"

"FULTAP has many resources. And I was a modern languages major, with a Ph.D. in psychology. In another life I might have been a poet."

Marianne regarded him skeptically, waiting for the punchline.

"No joke," he added, with a glum shrug.

"You? Major FULTAP spooky spy? A poet?"

"Hard to believe, I guess," he said.

"Yes, it is. Okay ... suppose I lend you the book. Do I have your promise to get it back?"

"Absolutely."

"Cross your heart and hope to die?"

"If that's what it takes."

"No secret military bullshit that will let you weasel out?"

"None."

Feeling very uncertain, Marianne handed the book over.

"If I don't see this again, I will come after you. Spells and all."

"Got it."

A flight attendant rolled her cart down the aisle to their row.

"Du vin?" she inquired.

"S'il vous plaît," Bagwell replied.

The flight attendant placed two small bottles of Air France red on their trays. Bagwell cracked them open and filled two diminutive wine glasses.

"To staying awake."

They clicked plastic.

"And to our late Captain . . ."

Big sighs.

"Yeah, what a mess. Gotta jump past it."

29

"AND THE NAME of this park again?" asked the lieutenant.

"I think it was called 'The Cairn of the Little Mountain'," said Marianne.

She was seated in a windowless room somewhere on the grounds of Beale Air Force Base. She was groggy from sleeping in an airplane instead of a bed, and she was still roiling with inward guilt over the loss of Captain Pike.

Her questioner, a young lawyer with the U.S. Army Criminal Investigations Command, was flawlessly dressed in a crisp uniform, his pants perfectly creased, a tie neatly tucked into his blouse. He was leaning back against a desk, attempting to appear casual and friendly. A digital voice recorder was logging the interview, Marianne's third of the day.

"It's a French national park?"

"I believe so."

"And you were after a piece of stone. Minor vandalism, I guess. Is that right?"

"I was searching for a talisman with a connection to my family, as I think I've already told the other interrogators at least twice."

"And you did in fact deface a French national monument, did you not?"

"I didn't deface a thing. A stroke of lightning loosened up a small stone chip."

"You took it."

"I was in France to do exactly that. Someone must have explained FULTAP's mission. Major Bagwell, maybe?"

"I'm just trying to compare narratives."

He made a little note in a notebook and checked the digital recorder he had placed on the table to make sure it was running.

"Unh-huh. Where is Major Bagwell, anyway?" asked Marianne, rapidly tiring of the inquisition, which appeared to have hardly begun.

"He's being debriefed . . . elsewhere. Don't worry about him. We're here to find out what happened to you."

"I found my talisman, and Captain Pike is dead. That's my sad story."

"And your talisman is a rock, yes? An expensive one, it seems. What's this thing look like?"

"It's small, sort of triangular. It's a piece of granite, I guess, but I'm no geologist."

"Show me."

Marianne made an effort to compose herself. She shook her head. "Not a chance."

"I beg your pardon?"

"I'm not going to show it to you. It's mine, part of my family."

"We'll see about that. Meanwhile, why this particular, what is it, cairn, dolmen, little mountain?"

"Have you ever been to Brittany?"

"That's not an issue here today. Why this particular cairn? If it's granite, why not just drive on down to Yosemite? Why drag Army personnel all the way to France?"

"Five thousand years ago, people planted a lot of stones in Brittany. No one knows why . . . it's a mystery. My family probably did some of the work. I was advised by a distant cousin to check out a menhir that was still connected to the family."

"What kind of connection?"

"Uh, tradition? You've heard of that? Anyway, that particular stone pointed me to the mound, cairn, tomb, or whatever it once was in Arzon."

"Pointed? How pointed?"

"A line of lightning strikes."

"Really. What did you and Major Bagwell expect to gain by this expedition?"

"My father is the FULTAP unit's main asset — Sergeant Sarzo? — and he's in a coma. Major Bagwell thinks an adept put him there. I seem to have inherited some of Dad's unusual . . . abilities. We were hoping that with the right training and special items I might be able to wake him up."

"Correct me if I'm wrong. That did not work out."

"No, he's not here anymore."

"Pardon me, I know FULTAP is a lawfully authorized unit and all, looking into supernatural threats, but it's not clear to me it has ever accomplished anything. Comment?"

"Look, lieutenant, you have a job to do, but you're barking at the wrong girl. I've been involved for just about two weeks. I'm almost as ignorant as you are — and that's saying something."

The insult failed to ruffle the lieutenant.

"Let's press on," he said. "You have previously stated you did not witness Captain Pike's demise, but that you did see his attacker. Can you give me a description? Every detail counts."

"I was in the tomb under the cairn. Captain Pike was guarding the entrance. I heard some movement, some . . . uhh . . . sounds. Very scary. And then, whoever got him was in the tomb. She was making a weird clicking noise."

"She? You're sure it was female? You saw her clearly?"

"Oh yes. It's hard to explain. Very woo-woo. You ready for that?"

"Personally? I'm not a believer in witchcraft and magic spells. But I've got this recorder here, and it listens to anything."

"Okay, then. When I picked up the stone, I could feel my abilities come into focus. Maybe it was the incredible tension, but I *commanded* her to stop moving and stop that clicking noise."

"Commanded?"

"You would call it 'casting a spell,' I think. It worked — I was shocked. So I ran outside, grabbed Captain Pike's night vision scope and took a good look. I was surprised it was a woman. She was tall and thin, wearing funny silk pants and some sort of jacket or wrap. Her eyes weren't bright and shiny, like you usually see with infrared. She had a length of rope in her hand. Brown skin. Older than me."

"Just to nail it down, can you state a race? Ethnicity?"

"Not white, not black or Hispanic. Not American, that's for sure. She reminded me of one of those Indian actresses you see in the magazines, but not as pretty."

"Her clothing? A uniform?"

"No, just real strange."

"Now let's return to your stone. Since you found it while employed by the government, it belongs to Uncle Sam, not you. For the record, I need to have a good physical description, so hand it over."

Marianne's eyes narrowed. "Whatever you may think or believe doesn't matter," she informed him. "The stone saved my life — and it cost a good man his."

She felt a possessive fury boil up and overwhelm her. "It's mine, sealed in blood. I'm the keeper. If you don't agree, why don't you try to take it? Then I'll command *you.*"

The lieutenant was about to insist when the door opened and General Weaver appeared.

"I'll take over from here, Lieutenant," he announced.

The lieutenant snapped to attention.

"Yes sir, General, sir."

"You are dismissed."

"But sir, the CID investigates all non-combat deaths, and we've just begun in this case . . ."

"Stand down, Lieutenant. Dismissed."

"Just a few more questions . . ."

"Your interview is over. Get out of here."

"Yes sir."

The lieutenant turned bright red, saluted, and departed. General Weaver looked upon Marianne with fatherly sympathy.

"Sorry about the ordeal. I'm sure you and Ray knew what you were doing, and I'm just sorry it was a bad day for Captain Pike."

"Thank you, sir."

"But here's the thing. Until this whole mess is cleaned up, the folks I report to have told me to halt all operations."

"What? That's terrible. What about Dad?"

"Beale isn't really configured for serious trauma. He's been transferred to a state-of-the-art hospital where he will receive the very best care available."

"And that is . . . where?"

"Ah, well, I'm not at liberty to tell you that. We need to debrief him without prejudice when he wakes up."

"That's completely bogus. Where did you hide him?"

"Take comfort — he'll be in very good hands, and we hope that, eventually, he'll recover. No matter how long it takes."

"And Ray — ?"

"He's on administrative leave. The higher-ups have indicated some doubts about his judgment in the field. I'm sure, when the dust settles, we'll reconstitute the unit. But it may take some time — months, probably

— and we don't have the right to hold you in service involuntarily with nothing to do."

"I want my Dad."

"Someday, someday. Keep your chin up. But for now — go home. Go be a good police officer, as I know you can be."

Marianne sagged. "That woman who killed Captain Pike wanted to kill me too. What if she's still after me? I'm scared."

Weaver nodded understanding. "Look, what happened in France happened five thousand miles away. But I've put out the word, we'll be on her trail. I don't think you have to worry."

"Swear out a warrant, you mean?"

"Military version."

"Who's gonna serve it?"

"We've got people. And you've got your thing, your stone. You'll be okay."

He squeezed her arm affectionately, took her hand, and shook it.

"Drive on," he said.

Part FOUR

30

THE DAY was warm, the sun was bright, and Marianne was an off duty police officer, having just come from an explanatory meeting with Lieutenant Nina Kazmarek, her superior officer in the Placerville Police Department. As promised by Major Bagwell, her job was safe.

She strolled down Placerville's quaint Main Street, happy to be back in a California — not French — tourist town. The familiar territory eased her fears and put her into a suitably touristy frame of mind. When she reached Gold Country Gifts, she paused. The window display held a collection of necklaces in silver, gold, and turquoise. As the noon hour had arrived, the door was unlocked. She opened it and stepped inside.

"Mark Frey?"

The proprietor appeared from a back office and grinned.

"Well hello, there. Where's that cute uniform today?"

"Night duty this week. I'm not here on police business."

"That sounds promising. What can I do for you on this beautiful spring day?"

Marianne reached into her bag and brought forth her stone chip. She held it up for examination.

"I've got this rock, and I was wondering how I could get it attached to a necklace."

Frey took the stone and studied it. "This is just a chip of granite. I've got wonderful precious and semi-precious stones that would be a lot more attractive."

"It has sentimental value," she said.

"Of course," he nodded.

"Well? Do you know a jeweler or whatever, who could figure it out?"

He grinned again and pointed at his own chest.

"There's me. I'm a jeweler of sorts."

"Could you do it? It has to be perfect, no mistakes."

Frey examined the stone again. "What is it, an arrowhead?"

"A little piece of Brittany, that's all."

"Aha. We specialize in tourist tchotchkes. Okay, see this shallow depression near the narrow edge? I could drill here, and slip a chain through. How's that?"

"It won't shatter?"

"Not if I know the tools of my trade — and I do."

"Unh-huh."

"The big question is, silver chain? Links, or coils?"

"Uh, it has to be tough, unbreakable."

"In that case, how about a leather thong? Very stylish, like you see in the window there."

Indeed, the window was full of cleverly designed leather necklaces with stone and glass pendants.

"Okay. When could you do this?"

"Right now. My drill press is in the back." He stuck a thumb out.

"How much?"

He grinned mischievously. "Nothing, if you'll have dinner with me tonight."

Marianne winced. "Whoops, can't. Sorry, you seem nice, but look, we've been through this. I'm seeing someone. Steady boyfriend."

His face fell.

"Too bad. Still, what you're asking is practically nothing. Ten bucks."

"Let's go."

Marianne stood behind Frey, watching closely while he positioned the stone chip on the bed of his drill press and wound up the motor.

"Don't break it!" she chirped. She was very nervous.

"Trying hard not to."

Frey lowered a pair of safety glasses over his eyes, and brought the drill bit down on the stone. Very slowly and carefully he made a precise hole in Marianne's talisman. Watching, she clenched her fists, as tense as if a dentist was drilling her teeth without lidocaine.

"There!" He blew the dust away.

Marianne grabbed the stone and rubbed her fingers over the hole.

"Whew, had me worried there."

Frey threaded a black leather thong, complete with a silver clasp, through the hole. He strung the thing around her neck. She handed him a twenty dollar bill. He handed a ten back.

"So, you're sure of your boyfriend? Is he attractive?"

"Yes, very."

He smiled.

"Too bad. Everything on the up and up? No other women falling at his feet? Now, take me, I'm Old Faithful, what you see is what you get, no lies."

"Please," she said, squirming uncomfortably.

"I just want to understand the situation — because you're missing a big opportunity here. Dinner is completely out of the question?"

"'Fraid so."

"Sigh."

"But thanks for the necklace."

▼

Marianne hopped into her little blue Mini and headed on down to Applefield. She was planning to surprise Tom Wagstaff in his newspaper office, but then realized he was teaching up at Sacramento State. So she stopped in Ragtown at his mother's book shop instead.

"Oh my God, now *I* have seen a ghost!" exclaimed Lorraine, rushing out of her little office to wrap Marianne in a motherly embrace.

"Where have you been? Why the big mystery?"

"I guess I'm supposed to keep my mouth shut, but no one actually gave me an order. Last week I was — briefly — a secret agent."

"Like your dad."

Marianne fashioned a cynical grin. "Broomhandle, that's me."

Later during lunch at Ragtown's only eatery, the Fire in the Hole Café, Marianne found herself being grilled by her curious friend.

"What does the CIA want with someone like you? Or your dad?"

"It's not really the CIA, it's another group."

"Tom mentioned something called *Fulltap*."

"Yeah, FULTAP — the 'Full Spectrum Threat Assessment Program.' They specialize in psychic stuff. Dad, when he's awake, can sense people's intentions. They were hoping I could revive him, but I needed to up my game, so that's what I've been doing. In France."

"*France?*" Lorraine was incredulous.

"My family — you know all about that — Sarzeau and all. We went over there so I could get myself a talisman. According to old lady Crowfoot, if you get the right one, your powers expand."

"Good Lord, CIA, FULTAP, native witches. You are something."

"The plan came apart. Someone killed the soldier guarding me. A woman. She's still out there . . . somewhere . . . far away, it seems. Good for me, bad for justice. FULTAP has been mothballed pending an investigation."

Lorraine took note of her young friend's troubled mood. "Was this your plan? Your fault?"

"No, breaks of the game, I guess, but it makes me feel guilty. And, what's worse, Dad has disappeared."

"Where is he? Where'd they put him?"

"I don't know. The claim is, they want to debrief him when he wakes up without any influence from his daughter."

"Boy, the military — our tax dollars at work."

Marianne pushed her omelet aside. She made a wry face.

"I got my talisman, though."

"Let me see."

Marianne pulled the stone pendant out of her blouse. Lorraine reached out to touch.

"It's just a piece of granite."

"True. But it's a piece of sacred granite from a tomb in Brittany, very closely associated with my family. And also with the guy who got killed — if not for him, no stone, and I'd be dead myself."

"Good heavens. Is this over? Or are you off again when the bureaucrats get done with their crap?"

"Not sure. Probably off again. Sooner rather than later, I hope. Dad's still sleeping."

This news did not make Lorraine happy.

"What about your job? I thought you were a cop."

"*Am.* Am a cop. My lieutenant knows all about the charade FULTAP pulled. They told her. I'm still gainfully employed."

Lorraine turned to a bowl of strawberries, dispatching them slowly and thoughtfully.

"Have you seen Tom?" she asked at last.

"Not yet. He's teaching today."

Lorraine forked a final strawberry and delicately tucked it away.

"You just got back, you're hardly settled, but there's breaking news . . . you should probably hear it."

"Uh-oh. What now?"

"Kari Hamilton. Remember her?"

"How could I forget?"

"Gossip has it that she broke up with her boyfriend, some lawyer down in Folsom."

Marianne pushed a slice of cantaloupe around her plate. "And now she has her eyes on my guy, like you thought?"

"So it seems."

"Has Tom made a move?"

"They had dinner last night."

"Oh, shit."

"It's probably nothing."

"Come on, Lorraine. If you're worried, I'm worried."

"I'm not worried. Just a little bit concerned . . . slightly concerned."

"Then I'm not worried either."

Marianne knitted her brows together.

"That man is mine."

31

AS EVENING approached, Marianne put on her uniform, lapel radio all charged up, hair braided into a tight bun, loaded .40 caliber Glock 22 on her hip, little Beretta tucked into an ankle holster. This latter piece was a bit of a problem, since she didn't have DOJ permission to carry it on the job. One of these days, she promised herself, she would perfect the situation, but not tonight, first night back on patrol.

At the station, while she was fussing with her laptop, Desmond Otis strolled in, also relegated to night duty this month.

"Yo, Squeek, back from the dead?"

"Hi, Dez. Here I am. Any word on our rock-climbing burglar?"

"Nothing since we talked. Can't find a sheet on Hank Rogers."

"Any more incidents?"

"Not a one."

Marianne was checking her mail slot. Empty. She stuck a hand in to be sure.

"Damn, no mail for me. I guess the post office thinks I'm really dead."

"You expecting something?"

"Yes I am. Why?"

"What's it worth to you?"

"Come on, Dez, you've got that look. What's up?"

"You didn't get killed and go all the way to France for fucking french fries. So, tell me, what have you been doing over there?"

Marianne hesitated, then shrugged. She withdrew her necklace from concealment inside her blouse and dangled the rock pendant in front of her colleague.

"This."

Otis looked it over, brushed it with a finger.

"No way."

"Looks like an ordinary rock, right? But, nope — a lightning strike popped this from inside a five-thousand-year-old tomb."

"Just for you."

Marianne nodded emphatically.

"Just for me."

Otis reached into a duffel he was carrying. Out came a small package.

"All right, I been collecting your mail. I didn't know the Lieutenant was in on the deal, and I thought it might get placed into evidence or something."

Marianne took the package and opened it. Out fell a small leather-bound book, a note, and a computer flash drive. She read the note aloud:

> Broomhandle —
> Here's your translation. Done by computer, so it's rough, except for the spells. I had a hand in those.
> — Ray

"Broomhandle?" asked Otis, eyebrows arched.

"My secret agent ID."

"*Broooomhandle* . . ." Otis repeated, managing to inject satiric astonishment into the word.

Marianne blushed. "I know."

"You've got spells now? Jesus, Sarzeau, *spells?*"

"It's an old book, a family heirloom. Let's take a look."

She slipped the flash drive into a USB slot on her laptop and opened up the PDF file that appeared on the screen. She browsed through it, skimming the pages.

"Hey, slow down."

"You want a spell? Hang on, looking for something."

She continued skimming.

"Whoa, here we are."

Otis looked at the page on display.

"A love potion? Keep away from me, you sick chick."

Marianne studied the spell's details, which took the form of a little poem, with great interest:

> . . . three snips of ginseng . . .
> . . . honey, thick and sweet . . .
> . . . blood, red as wine . . .
> . . . drink, you'll ne'er be free . . .

Otis studied the poem as well. He snorted. "Kind of old-fashioned, you ask me." He thought for a while. "We can do better than that."

His head started popping left and right. He threw out his arms and spread his fingers, started putting down hip-hop moves. "Try this —"

Blood and honey, magic shit,
Hey, big guy, get into it.
Drink the crap that's in your glass;
Now, my man, I've got your ass.

Marianne slammed the lid of her laptop shut.

"I like the old one better," she said.

▼

Later that evening, after a routine patrol through town, she pulled into the Coffee Depot to brace herself for the long night ahead. With sixteen ounces of java in hand she studied the translation of her love potion recipe, checking the ingredients. Then she drove back into town and parked near the bell tower. The Nature Knows Best store was open until 8:00 PM, and she made it just under the wire, sprinting for the door as the clerk in charge was locking up.

"We're closing," he said.

"Hang on a sec. I only need a couple of items."

"And they are — ?"

"Ginseng and honey."

"We only sell the root itself, no powder. And we're out of clover, just alfalfa blossom today."

"Alfalfa? Isn't that for cows?"

"You might think so, but raw alfalfa honey has enzymes your body needs. It's a great throat soother, and antioxidants — well, forget orange juice."

"I just need a little bit, whatever you've got."

The clerk bagged up a ginseng root fragment and indicated the honey shelf. Marianne picked out an eight-ounce bottle of Beeline Organic Amber, paid in cash, and returned to her vehicle and a night patrolling the city streets.

Around nine o'clock she came across a juvenile with a spray can getting ready to tag Rafferty's Classic Auto Body. She turned into the parking lot, flipped on her code three lights, and hopped out to stop the minor crime in progress. But the juvenile was sprinting away before she could call a halt. Just as well, she thought. Stupid kids! But you never know, maybe a hint of gang activity. She made a mental note to mention the possibility in her report.

She toured the property, conducting a quick survey to be sure nothing more serious was amiss. She was reaching for the door handle of her patrol car, ready to move on, when a voice in her head spoke.

"Marianne, check your mirror," it said.

Marianne swiveled toward the driver's side rear-view mirror. A ghostly shadow was lurking there. It caused her to jump backward.

"It's you," she croaked, heart pounding.

"Welcome home. Found your talisman?"

"Yes, I did."

"Good, you're going to need it."

"You know something I don't, right?"

"Many things, many things. More important, I heard some news."

"About Dad?"

"Afraid not."

"Damn. Where is he? Where is FULTAP keeping him?"

"I don't know. This is about someone else."

"Tell me."

"Old Lady Crowfoot is dying."

"What? How do you know something like that?"

"I got a call."

"She phoned you up — hey, I'm dying."

"No telephones over here. Think distress signal. Don't try to figure it out, you'll never do it, just take my word."

"Where is she?"

"At home. Wasting away in her favorite chair."

"Oh my God. You — you have to do something!"

"I am doing something. I'm telling you all about it."

The shadowy image faded away.

Marianne stood there for a while, paralyzed by the news. Then she dug her smartphone out of a pocket and dialed 9-1-1.

"This is Officer Marianne Sarzeau, Placerville police. I just got a call reporting a woman dying down in Angels Camp."

Pause.

"Yes, it could be a hoax, but I know the woman. She's old, not very well."

Pause.

"All right, then, give me Calaveras Emergency Services."

Pause.

"Hello — Officer Marianne Sarzeau, I'm a cop up in Placerville. I have an emergency call referring to a woman, possibly at death's door, in Angels Camp. Can you dispatch an ambulance to her house?"

Pause.

"This is no joke, the name is Hannah Crowfoot. I know her, she's an elderly woman, could be sick, could be a heart attack."

Pause.

"Relation? I'm, uh, I'm her ... niece ... no, wait, she's my grandmother," she lied. "She needs help, and I'm on duty."

Pause.

"Yes, okay. Send the crew to 1399 Bush Street. I don't know what's wrong, bring all your gear, ready for anything. Call me when you get there."

Pause.

"Well, okay, I'll call the hospital. Mark Twain, got it, will do."

She put her phone away and, shaking like a leaf, got back into her vehicle and resumed her patrol.

Just after ten o'clock, the Placerville dispatcher directed her back to Main Street and suspicious activity outside the Hog Heaven Bar & Grille. By then she had calmed down and was ready for action. But when she arrived, Otis was already on the scene, wrangling a couple of rowdy drunks.

She leaned out the window.

"Yo, Dez, need a hand?"

"No, I'm just reasoning with these gentlemen here, and it looks like they now see things my way. Off the street and home soon. If not, when you swing by again, have at 'em."

"Later, then," said Marianne, and pulled away. She drove three blocks and parked behind the Buttercup Pantry. There she dug out her smartphone, checked her watch, and called Tom Wagstaff. She had already tried his line five times, and he had not picked up. But this time he did.

"Wagstaff here."

"Hello, Tom."

Marianne? That you? Where are you?"

"On patrol, in Placerville."

"You're back! Mom told me."

"Yeah, night duty for a while, but here I am. Why didn't you pick up before?"

"I'm still down here in the capital at State. Faculty dinner, all us journalist types trying to decide if our recent spy revelations make the leaker a hero or a villain."

"And the verdict?"

"He's news. We report it. Case closed."

Marianne didn't realize she was holding her breath until the words "faculty dinner" seemed to rule out a tryst with Ms. Kari Hamilton. She exhaled slowly.

"We could meet at my place, but I'm up all night rolling around the town, so . . . lunch tomorrow?"

"Sure. Where?"

"How about Rossi's, in Tarvolo?"

"Like the old days — see you then."

Marianne ended the call and embarked on a long meandering tour through the city's back streets. It proved to be a quiet night. Even the homeless camp on the eastern edge of town was orderly and subdued.

Back on Main Street, she checked her watch. Eleven o'clock. The Calaveras EMT team should have rescued old lady Crowfoot by now, so she stopped behind the Buttercup Pantry again. A 4-1-1 call produced the number for the Mark Twain Medical Center in San Andreas, and she dialed it up. After button-pressing her way past a telephone robot and explaining her inquiry to three different human operators, she found herself talking to a night nurse who actually knew what was going on.

"Ms. Crowfoot is out of the emergency room, she's been admitted, and she's sound asleep. She's stable, her chart looks normal."

"Have you talked to her? What did she say?"

"Well no, she hasn't spoken. She's exhausted."

"What happened? Heart attack? Stroke? I know she's not in the best of health."

"We don't have a diagnosis. The resident who saw her just wants to watch and wait. We'll know a lot more tomorrow, once she wakes up."

"But you think she'll be okay."

"She's not a young woman. She had been in that chair for a week or more and was dehydrated and filthy when we found her, but yes, we're pretty confident she's out of the woods."

"When can I see her?"

"Tomorrow afternoon. Come find me. Ask for Silvia Ramos, I'm on duty after three."

32

MARIANNE allowed herself four hours sleep following her shift and woke up groggy and disoriented around eleven in the morning.

She sat down in her little kitchenette with a strong cup of instant coffee and a day-old bagel. The PDF translation of her book of family lore was open on her laptop. She was re-checking the ingredients for a love potion, looking for details pertaining to blood. The news wasn't what she hoped.

"Eww, it has to be menstrual blood. I should have known."

Once before, while working down in Applefield, she had come across a similar requirement. It seemed as disgusting now as it had been then.

Dutifully following the recipe, she ground up the ginseng root, dropped it into a pan on her stove. She added some water and honey, let it simmer. Then she recovered a used tampon from the rubbish bin under her bathroom sink and, holding it daintily by its little string tail, dipped it into the amber liquid.

"Ugh."

She turned off the burner and let the mixture cool. Then she carefully decanted a small amount into a tiny travel-size plastic bottle she had picked up at the local pharmacy.

"There, Mr. Wagstaff. Take another look at me if you please."

▼

Rossi's Fine Italian Dining was the premier restaurant in Tarvolo, the plush gated community just outside Applefield. Marianne and Tom Wagstaff had many a meal there a year ago, and it felt like the right place for a happy reunion.

Marianne arrived early and chose a table just inside the huge plate glass window overlooking Tarvolo's exclusive golf club. She stood up for a big hug and kiss when Wagstaff showed up a few minutes later.

"Boy, it's good to see you, M," said he as they unglued, sat down, and sorted through their silverware.

"So how's the new job, Professor Wag?" she asked. She had been away for less than two weeks, but it seemed that everything in her life was starting over, including her relationship with Mr. W. She felt awkward and didn't quite know how to proceed. Wagstaff seemed to sense her uncertainty.

"Not too bad," he admitted. "I'm not really a professor, hardly a lecturer, but hey — a guy could get used to the life."

"No newspaper deadlines to worry about?"

He chuckled. "No, the kids have to do all the writing. What a great switch."

Marianne's conversational sallies were exhausted. She stuck her nose into her menu.

"What looks good today?"

"Uhh, I'm voting for the arugula salad and scampi. You?"

"I dunno. The primavera, probably. Should we have a glass of wine to celebrate my homecoming?"

"Geez, I can't — the paper needs my full attention this afternoon."

"Right, you're right. Iced tea, then."

The waiter sauntered over and took their orders, returned with cold beverages in tall glasses.

"You sound kind of stressed," said Marianne, edging around a sore subject. "I thought . . . with your new employee . . . things would be easing up."

"You mean Kari? Yeah, well they are. She's great at composing a page, but I've still got to come up with the copy."

"Unh-huh, of course."

"Do you know how boring it is to write about property tax increases?"

"Only what I hear from the pros." Marianne, eyes down, dove into her pasta.

"Hey, you okay?" he asked, taking note of her somber mood.

"I'm fine. It's good to be home."

"How's your dad? I know you were worried."

"He's somewhere, they won't tell me."

"Hmm, what did you call their little secret society, *Fulltap?*"

"FULTAP. Full Spectrum Need to Know Government Bullshit."

"Over there in France — did you find what you were after?"

Marianne withdrew her necklace from her blouse and showed off the modest granite chip hanging from the leather thong.

"A rock. That's it?"

"That's it."

"And it's supposed to do . . . what?"

"Heavy duty magic, I guess. Nothing so far, though."

"Let me know when you start cranking out spells."

"You'll be the first."

Wagstaff sat back and studied his lunch companion. Her face was drawn, her brow furrowed. She was trying to be cheerful, but he knew she wasn't.

"What's the problem? You're back safe and sound, we're here, the food is good . . ."

"No problem."

"Come on, you can't fool me."

"Hey, eat. This is lunch, not therapy."

"Oh ho — I get it, you are *jealous*. You're worried about Kari."

"As if — !" she blustered, coloring.

"Look, she's a good designer, knows her stuff, works hard."

"I hear she's also a good dinner partner."

"Oh that. You" — he shook a finger — "you've been talking to Mom again."

"Yeah, true. She's on my side."

"*I'm* on your side! Good God, M, this woman was in a relationship for five years, and he called it off. She needed some sympathy."

"How do you know who called it off? Maybe *she* did it with you in mind . . ."

Wagstaff reddened.

"What is this inquisition? Excuse me while I go see a man about a dog."

He stood up abruptly and headed for the men's room.

Marianne stared miserably at her plate for a long moment, then stealthily tugged the little potion-filled bottle from her handbag. She unscrewed the top and held it poised above Wagstaff's glass of iced tea:

> *Three snips of ginseng, horny root,*
> *That in the shape of man doth shoot;*
> *A tot of honey, thick and sweet,*
> *To kiss the lips when lovers meet.*
> *A drop of blood now, red as wine,*
> *So you'll be mine, and I'll be thine.*
> *Drink and know you'll ne'er be free;*
> *This is my will, so shall it be.*

She muttered the incantation with resolve, tilted the bottle, observed the thick liquid inside oozing toward the neck. A drop formed at the lip, bulged downward toward the glass of tea. But the bottle failed to tilt any further. Her hand was shaking. Try as she might, she couldn't make herself pour the potion out.

"Oh shit," she said and yanked the bottle away from its target. She smashed the cap on and stuffed the thing back in her bag.

A few minutes later Wagstaff returned. As he sat down he could not fail to notice red eyes and a runny nose.

"Hey, hey, babe, come on. This is not like you."

Marianne banished her wretched thoughts, told herself to be brave. She held up a trembling finger.

"My fault, not yours. I'm sorry," she sniffled. "You're right, I'm jealous. But I'll get over it. People should be free, you know? Go where their spirit takes them. So, okay, go. I understand. I'll be fine. Tough chick, remember?"

Wagstaff was dumbfounded.

"What is this? Broadway theater, all because I had dinner with Kari Hamilton? Shame on you."

"Yeah, on me."

He reached across the table and took her hand, squeezed it hard.

"Listen, M, you little dope. I don't give a damn about her. Well, not romantically, anyway. It's you. You're the one. Get that through your head, will you?"

She nodded weakly, dabbed at her eyes, blew her nose on her napkin.

"I'll make a note in my report."

33

SAN ANDREAS was fifty miles south of Placerville on curvy Route 49. Marianne, in her little Mini, made the trip in forty-five minutes. The high speeds seemed to clear her head, help her come to terms with Tom's declaration of loyalty. Just after three o'clock, she parked and entered Mark Twain Medical Center in search of Silvia Ramos and her new patient.

"Right this way," said the nurse, a trim woman in her forties. She led Marianne down a long hallway to a room with two beds. Only one of them was occupied, and in it lay Hannah Crowfoot. Her eyes were closed, her face was chalky white, but she was breathing comfortably. Her status was the business of an electronic medical monitor, informed by sensors glued to the old woman's arms and forehead. An IV drip was busy rehydrating her.

Marianne watched the little colored lines pulsing across the monitor screen.

"Have you talked to her?"

"Not yet. She's still sleeping it off. What an ordeal."

"You mean she's been out the whole time?"

"I just got back on duty, but yes, that's my understanding."

Marianne shivered. "She's in a coma, then . . . how bad?"

"It's not really a coma" — Nurse Ramos indicated one of the squiggly lines on the monitor — "see, her brain function is normal. She's asleep, just barely under, probably dreaming."

"Unh-huh. Ever see anyone else who just can't wake up?"

"No, to tell you the truth, I haven't."

"Well, I have."

"Really."

Marianne leaned close to Ms. Crowfoot. Under her closed lids, the old woman's eyes were moving back and forth.

"My dad."

Nurse Ramos frowned. She edged away from the visitor, obviously incubating doubts.

Marianne looked around, spotted a nearby chair, and sat down. She opened up her laptop.

"If you don't mind, I'll stand watch for a while. It looks like my aunt — um, grandmother — is kind of restless, and who knows? Maybe we'll get lucky."

"Oh, you know . . . hospital policy . . ."

Marianne put on a cheerful smile. "I'm a police officer. Don't worry, I know the drill."

"Well then, I'll be right down the hall. First nurse's station you come to. Give me a hoot if anything changes, and . . . don't touch anything."

"Right. Hands on the keyboard here."

Nurse Ramos was relieved. "We've got Wi-Fi if you're surfing. The password is "jumpingfrog.""

"Thanks."

Marianne watched Nurse Ramos move out of sight, then stood up, placed her laptop on the bedside table, laid one hand on Ms. Crowfoot's forehead, and gripped her little talisman with the other. She waited until it felt like the stone was causing her hand to tingle, then, looking carefully at the PDF document on her laptop screen, she slowly recited a passage she had found among the many spells written there:

> *I here command your mind shake free*
> *From ill-met sleep that captured thee.*
> *Wake you now with eyes made bright*
> *To face the day and shun the night.*
> *Bring wit and wisdom here and now;*
> *Let full awareness grace your brow.*

Marianne peered intently at Ms. Crowfoot, wondering how a few antique couplets, loosely rendered into English by Ray Bagwell, could ever produce a result. But after a while, the old woman's eyes slowly opened. They darted this way and that as she tried to make sense of her situation.

Marianne gasped.

"I'll be damned, it worked!"

"Where am I?" asked Ms. Crowfoot.

Marianne closed her laptop.

"In the hospital. You were asleep for a week."

"A week!"

"It wasn't natural."

"But you brought me back. Found your talisman, I take it."

"Yes, and a book of spells."

The old woman rubbed her eyes, blinked away the crust of sleep.

"I also know how it happened."

Marianne drew back. "Let me guess — kids."

"That's right. They came to my house with an old man, looking for you. Two girls and a boy, all three powerful adepts. They were shining like searchlights in my mind."

"So, how are you feeling?"

"I'm too out of touch to feel anything. A week! Good heavens, I must have been an awful mess."

"They cleaned you up."

"I should hope so. But look at me, look at this room!" She raised her arms and shook the wires and tubes. "How will I ever pay for it? I'd be better off dead."

"No you wouldn't. Here's another magic spell — Medicaid."

"It's humiliating. When can I leave?"

"Nurse Ramos will know."

"Go ask, will you? Lying here like this, I'm no good to anyone."

"Okay, but first . . ." Marianne paused for thought. "The spell worked. Amazing! Now I need to try it out on Dad. Will it work on him? That's tougher. He's been unconscious for weeks now."

Ms. Crowfoot dismissed the idea with a scornful wheeze. "If I were you, young lady, I wouldn't worry so much about Dad. Those kids weren't after me, but they *were* after you. They might come back."

Marianne shivered. "I know. Some woman killed a soldier who was looking out for me over there in France."

"Did she make a funny noise?"

"That's right! She clicked like a bat. How — ?"

"She was at my house too. Those kids! One of them tried to cast a confusion spell, but I'm a tough old bird. I remember everything. I could hear that woman clicking. I think she wanted to strangle me."

Marianne's hand flew to her own throat. She gulped. "One of those kids put me to sleep while I was looking for Dad. But I woke up on my own."

"Hmm. Lucky you, you're not as vulnerable as most of us. But your resistance isn't perfect. Don't trust it! If you want my advice on staying awake, get yourself some owl feathers."

"Owl feathers . . ."

"And eat a lot of almonds."

"Almonds . . ."

"They promote wakefulness."

"All right, you know a lot more about this than I do."

"That will help, but if you get in a fight, well, you'll need an ally." Ms. Crowfoot was becoming agitated. She wiggled around in her bed. "You'll need to conjure a *power spirit.*"

"Oh no, I already tried that. As you may remember — as you actually intended! — it almost killed me."

"Yes, that was a mistake. I didn't know you then. But conjure you must."

Marianne looked very doubtful. "I'll tell Nurse Ramos you're awake and feeling much better." She patted the old woman's arm and ducked out of the room.

At the nurse's station she passed on the good news. "Ms. Crowfoot woke up. She's full of beans."

"Well, isn't that something? We were wondering, but I didn't want to alarm you."

"Almost a miracle, huh?"

"You never know what will happen. People really are remarkable."

Marianne nodded full agreement.

On her way out of the building she passed by Ms. Crowfoot's room and stuck her head back in.

"So long now, take care of yourself," she said.

"Conjure!" commanded the old woman, exerting her authority. "You need a power spirit on your side "

Marianne wove her fingers together and wrung her hands. "I'll think about it."

She smiled uncertainly and departed. Ms. Crowfoot raised herself on one elbow and called after her.

"And, if you decide to conjure in fire . . . make it a *little* fire!"

34

THE WINTER had been wet and cold in Placerville, and spring was still in a half-hearted mood. Marianne was annoyed. She had to make three passes up and down Main Street before she could find a parking place not already occupied by tourists. Dodging the raindrops from an afternoon shower, she was forced to jog three blocks to Mark Frey's Gold Country Gifts, and she arrived pretty well soaked.

"Back again? In the rain? You must have missed me," said the ever-forward Mr. Frey.

Marianne let his unwelcome remark pass this time. She brushed her hair back and eyeballed the gifts and jewelry on display.

"Uh, I'm looking for something. Owl feathers. Got any?"

"One of my necklaces has little eagle feathers, but they're carved from basswood and painted. By genuine Native Americans, of course."

"Damn. I need some."

She looked around the shop again. The merchandise appeared to be well-crafted and pricey, but arranged indifferently. Sloppily, she thought. And, she also noticed, no other customer was taking the slightest interest, in spite of all the expensive cars from the Bay Area parked outside. It gave her an idea.

"Lot of outsiders in town this afternoon. How's business?" she asked.

The gambit hit home. Frey winced and waved a hand to ward off inner doubts.

"I'm maintaining. Rain drives away trade. Tomorrow the tourists will be streaming through my door."

"Or maybe not. Do you advertise online?"

Another blow.

"No, my stuff is upscale. An online presence just devalues everything."

"You sure about that?" Marianne swept an arm around to include the entire store. "Your displays — great looking things, but they don't add up."

Frey blinked. "What?"

"Your whaddaya call it — ambience. Each item making the others look good . . . making Gold Country Gifts look good. A little too disorganized for that, don't you think?"

"It's tasteful chaos. Customers love to discover little treasures tucked away here and there."

Marianne turned this way and that, giving the empty place an exaggerated once-over. "What customers?"

The shopkeeper froze. "I had no idea our police department was so business-minded."

"It's not. But it looks like you could use some help. Design help."

"Ouch."

"I happen to know someone who could make this place shine. New logo, get you on the web, maybe bring in a line of jewelry."

Frey started to protest further, then thought better of it. "Okay, I'll bite. Who is this guy? The steady boyfriend you mentioned?"

"Not a him, it's a her. Name is Kari Hamilton. I think she just might welcome a chance to burn off some of her amazing energy fixing up your store."

"She's a pro?"

"Oh yes. Works out of a studio down in Tarvolo."

He looked around his shop, seeing it with newly critical eyes.

"I've got money, you know. I own the building, I'm not about to declare bankruptcy or anything."

Marianne nodded politely and pivoted toward the door.

"She's not bad-looking, by the way — smoking hot, actually — although knowing you, that probably doesn't matter."

Frey was already reaching for his telephone as Marianne stepped onto the sidewalk.

"What's the name again?"

"Kari Hamilton. I know she'd love to meet you."

35

MARIANNE had a weakness for cats, although she didn't own one. Back in her trailer park days she used to feed an old tom. Today, hiking up the stairs to her new apartment, she was pleasantly surprised to discover a little black thing with a pink nose and white feet curled up on her porch. At her approach it stood up in alarm, vaulted onto the railing, and bolted away out of sight.

"Ohhh, wait, you're so cute."

The idea of taming the critter was irresistible. Marianne disappeared into her kitchen and was soon back outside with a bowl of chicken leftovers. She pursed her lips and whistled softly.

"Hey, little guy — gal — whatever you are. Come and get it."

In no time the cat reappeared around a corner of her building and warily crept up the stairs. Marianne held out the bowl of food for a sniff, then yanked it away. She gripped her talisman, idly attempting an experiment without any real hope of success.

"You want? Okay, you get — but first, bring me some owl feathers. Owl feathers, got that?" She smiled playfully. "One order of owl feathers, and make it snappy."

The cat eyed Marianne coolly, then turned and slinked back down the stairs.

She watched it go, then went inside, there to ponder the delicate matter of her romantic difficulties; whether she should call Tom, or wait for his call, or call Lorraine, or just sit tight. Guilt over her near breach of a lover's trust — that stupid love potion! — was nagging at her, and she didn't know how to shake it off. On the other hand, she was amused by her little matchmaking adventure with Mark Frey, so, after some reflection, she decided to just sit tight and see how things played out. Tom would have to call her.

She kicked off her shoes and sat down in her old second-hand easy chair to unwind. She was near to nodding off when she heard a peculiar *meow* coming from her porch.

She rose, opened the door, and discovered the remains of a small owl lying there, bruised and bloody. The little cat was sitting behind it, looking mighty proud of itself.

"Oh my God. Owl feathers . . ." said Marianne. Her skin prickled. The hairs on her neck rose. She reached back inside for the bowl of chicken leftovers and set it down before her benefactor.

"Here you go. Food, you earned it."

Marianne waited while the cat gulped down the snack, then reached out to get better acquainted. But the little animal was having none of that — it bolted away again.

"Damn, you are one skittish little beast."

Marianne returned to her kitchen. She plucked off half a dozen flight feathers and threw the rest of the carcass into the trash.

She was still thinking about Tom, but she also began to wonder about Ray Bagwell. Where was that guy? Recent experience — waking old lady Crowfoot, commanding the cat — told her she now had the chops to revive her father, but she still had to find him, and she thought Bagwell would want to know all about her new abilities.

She googled up a phone number and dialed. A robotic voice answered.

"Beale Air Force Base. Home of the 124th Reconnaissance Command. If you know the extension of the party you are calling, dial it now."

Unfortunately, Marianne did not know Bagwell's extension. She spent the next few minutes punching her way through a long multi-branching telephone tree.

While she was navigating she rummaged around in her pantry and found a can of almonds. She opened it and started snacking.

Finally, a live operator came on the line.

"I'm looking for Major Raymond Bagwell," said Marianne. "Can you dig him up for me?"

"I'll check, please hold."

After a long pause, a different voice spoke.

"American TV & Appliance. How can I help you?"

"You sell TVs at Beale?" Marianne was miffed by the ridiculous deception.

"Tell me how to direct your call, please."

"Uh, Ray Bagwell." She thought for a beat, then added, "FULTAP business," to make sure she sounded serious.

"He's doesn't seem to be picking up. Here's his voicemail . . ."

The line clicked and hummed. Then Bagwell's voice announced his regrettable inability to answer the phone. "Leave a message after the beep, and I'll try to return your call."

But after the beep yet another voice intoned a robotic apology. "We're sorry, but the voicemail box you have reached is full and cannot accept messages at this time. We're sorry, but the voicemail box you have reached is full and cannot accept messages at this time. We're sorry . . ."

Marianne ended the call just as she heard the wheels of a large SUV grating on the rough pavement below her flat. A moment later footsteps were bounding up the stairs. Then Tom Wagstaff was at her door. He threw it open and stepped inside, a paper shopping bag under each arm.

"Let's eat in tonight," he said, placing the bags on the kitchen counter.

Marianne ignored the groceries and pulled him close.

"Sorry, sorry, I'm *so* sorry, I was really stupid today," she said.

"That makes two of us, I guess," he replied with a wry grin.

"Oh? How's that?"

"Well, I could have strung you along. Now you know enough to take me for granted."

"But I never will," she declared, planting a big smooch.

Wagstaff dug around in the bags and came up with a can of spaghetti sauce, a box of linguini, and a nice bottle of Italian red wine.

"Pasta okay? I'll cook."

Marianne bounced up and down on the balls of her feet, thinking it over.

"I'm off duty tonight. How about Subway instead? I know a good one."

"What? Are you nuts?"

"In Marysville. I need to check out Beale. I need to flush Ray Bagwell out of hiding."

"The guy who was pointing a gun at you the last time I saw him?"

"The same. He's my only link to Dad."

36

A U.S. AIR STRIKE in Somalia, reported to have taken out as many as nine suspected Al-Shabab fighters, was in the news, reinvigorating the weary protesters at Beale. Code Red was on scene at the main gate, vying with the rival group Live And Let Live for marching space. Someone on a mobile phone claimed *Channel Four News* would arrive soon, but few were truly hopeful. Everyone seemed to understand that they were involved in a re-run, an evening of personal affirmation rather than effective political action.

Such was the mood as Marianne and Wagstaff drove up in his big yellow SUV. They parked in the dirt turnout fifty yards back from the barricades and walked forward.

For dramatic effect, Marianne decided to show up in her police uniform. This decision did not endear her to the demonstrators, and many a disapproving glance was cast in her direction.

She surveyed the participants, now milling around a ten-foot-high drone mockup slapped together with sticks and cardboard. It was standing in the middle of the road, tended by a couple of morose protesters.

"They're waiting for the TV crew, and then they're going to light it on fire," surmised Wagstaff.

Nathan Harris, the man who helped Marianne enter the base in what seemed like a lifetime ago, was in the crowd. He overheard Wagstaff's remark and strolled over.

"Like Burning Man," he said. "Only we're not too hopeful about TV coverage tonight."

"Hello, Nate. There's always YouTube," said Marianne, trying to be helpful.

Harris looked at her, his lip curling in contempt for the uniform. Then he smiled and stepped close to shake her hand.

"My God, it's you. Dressed as a cop, not a good idea in this crowd."

"I am a cop, didn't I tell you?"

"Nooo. Ever find whoever? Your dad, was it?"

"Not yet. You ever stage your civil disobedience act?"

Harris looked at the ground and toed an imaginary pebble. "Not yet. We saw what happened when they threw you out — nothing. Without public prosecution, we can't get traction."

"I think you should try it. I was over the line when they caught me. Who knows how it will turn out if there's enough of you on the march."

"Yeah, well, we're still working on the plan."

"Don't plan forever, dude."

She held up her fist. They bumped. She walked on, with Wagstaff trailing. The zaniness had him bewildered. He tugged at Marianne's elbow and pointed to one of the signs:

DRONICIDE IS GENOCIDE!

"Over the top, maybe?"

"Maybe a little bit."

Marianne came to a halt at the K-Rail barrier. She placed a hand on Wagstaff's chest.

"Okay, here we are. Wait for me, I'm going to cause a ruckus."

"Marianne — !"

"They aren't going to shoot anyone."

"How do you know?"

She hesitated.

"All right, plan B. Follow me forward, with your smartphone out as if recording everything I do. They sure as hell aren't going to shoot me on camera. Talk about YouTube!"

Wagstaff snorted, but he brought out his smartphone and got it ready for action.

Marianne looked around at the demonstrators. Her eyes fastened on one of the older women present. She was dancing around a small fire in fine form, except the music she was bopping to came through a set of earbuds, unheard by all the rest. She looked kind of crazy.

Marianne smiled. She jumped over the K-Rail, ran up to the chain link barrier, and yelled at the closest guard standing behind it.

"Hey, you, corporal! Come over here!"

"Step away from the fence, ma'am," he replied, striding toward her.

She hooked her fingers into the steel mesh and started to climb.

"Hey, hey, hey! Down, girl!"

She stopped, but did not descend. The guard raised his M-16 with the butt poised above her fingertips.

"Down, right now, or I will force you down."

Marianne withdrew one hand, grasped a piece of paper stuck in her duty belt, and pushed it through the fence. The guard let it drop to the ground.

"That's my phone number. My name is Marianne Sarzeau, I'm a cop in Placerville."

"This ain't Placerville."

"Whatever. I'm detailed to check on the demo. And there's a deranged woman out here. A mental. I'm worried she could incite to violence."

"What are you talking about?"

"Celestial agent *Broomhandle*. She claims to be working for an intelligence agency called FULTAP. And she knows who crashed your drones a couple of weeks back."

"What the fuck is *Fulltap*?" The sentry didn't believe a word she said, but he lowered his weapon.

"I have no idea. Broomhandle. FULTAP. And someone called Major Bagwell. She's going to *kill* him if he doesn't call her *immediately*."

By now, a young lieutenant took notice of the confrontation and hustled over.

"What's going on? You are trespassing on Air Force property, and I am within my authority to shoot you."

Marianne dropped off the fence and took a couple of steps backward, hands held high. The officer eyed Wagstaff, recording it all from ten feet away.

"Corporal?"

The corporal shook his head and pointed to the dancing demonstrator. "Celestial agent Broomhandle, out there, thinks she works for some agency called *Fulltap*. She's got the skinny on our drone crashes, according to the babe here."

"FULTAP. You said FULTAP?" asked the lieutenant.

"Yes sir."

Marianne repeated the keywords. "Broomhandle! FULTAP! Major Bagwell! Call the number on that piece of paper!"

The officer bent to pick up the fallen note. When he stood up, Marianne and Wagstaff had already slipped away among the demonstrators.

"That's it? That's your trick?" asked Wagstaff when they were out of sight.

"Best I can do. Let's hope Lieutenant Mindless back there is curious enough to check it all out. Then maybe Bagwell will hear about it and get in touch."

"Good luck with that," said Wagstaff.

"Mmm."

On their way back to Wagtaff's truck, a tall thin man in his middle years watched them from the edge of the crowd. As they passed, he detached himself from the protesters and moved quickly to follow.

"Excuse, please. Wait, wait."

Marianne and Wagstaff turned to see who was calling them.

"A thousand pardons for impeding you on your way, but I am looking for someone. You are police. Maybe you have seen him."

Wagstaff stepped forward to shield Marianne. "Sorry, we're not from around here. We don't know any of these people."

"Ahh, no, but miss, I heard you say 'Placerville'."

Marianne moved out from behind Wagstaff.

"Placerville, yes. Help you?"

The man held up a flyer with the crude picture of a face printed on it. The similarity between the picture and the older man was striking.

"This is my brother, Habib. He is missing, and the family wishes to find him."

Marianne took the flyer and examined it.

"Habib Rajput? That's him? That's the name?"

"Yes. I am Kahlil. He is young and restless. He has sometimes expressed his dislike of the American drones, so I thought, perhaps . . ."

"Sure, a demonstrator, why not? But why missing?"

"We do not know. A year ago he left San Jose, where the family lives. We had a letter from Placerville, but without a return address. He said he was off to join the circus."

"Join the circus. Habib Rajput. What kind of stunts does he do?" Marianne's curiosity was aroused.

"No stunts. Until not so long ago he was at peace, with a passion only for mountain climbing. Many trips to Yosemite. But he did take an interest in newspaper stories. Sometimes they made him angry."

"He became an activist." said Wagstaff.

"Yes, that's it. Activist."

"A Jihadist?" pressed Wagstaff.

"Wait a minute," said Marianne, interrupting. "You say he's a *climber?*"

"Very accomplished. Right up the cliffs of Yosemite. But, sadly . . . talent, skill, they do not make a career."

"A climber!" said Marianne. "Habib Rajput!"

"Yes."

"Thanks for the info, Mr., uh, Kahlil. May I keep this?" She pointed at the flyer.

"By all means. My telephone number is printed there. I am very much appreciating all your help."

"We're on it, we'll investigate, we'll let you know."

"Yes, yes, please, very good."

▼

Marianne was on the phone with Officer Otis before Wagstaff had driven them out of the parking lot.

"Dez? Marianne. You're on duty tonight, right?"

"Evening, Squeek. That I am. My presence on the streets has halted all crime in Hangtown."

"Good, you're bored."

"Oh yes."

"Listen — I may have a lead on our burglar."

"Oh no."

"Come on, get on your laptop. Run down this name — *Habib Rajput.* He lives somewhere in our little town and guess what? He's a climber."

"Jesus, Sarzeau, Where do you get this stuff?"

"I just ran into his brother. Our guy is missing in action, and the bro is worried."

"Oh man . . ."

"Otis, you lazy slug. Initials, H-R! Rogers, Rajput — same guy! It's our best lead yet. First name, Habib, H-A-B-I-B. Last name, Rajput, R-A-J-P-U-T, got that?"

"I'll call you back."

"You better."

Twenty minutes later, halfway down to Roseville, Marianne's mobile phone rang.

"Hey, Sarz. No joy on the suspect. His driver's license shows a San Jose address, over in the fucking Bay Area."

"Try county records for house ownership. Try Backgrounder-Pro, try . . . I dunno, everything you can think of."

Miles later, Wagstaff pulled over at a Subway restaurant in Roseville. He and Marianne were finishing their Flatizzas when her phone rang again. Officer Otis was on the line.

"Ho-ho, Sarzeau!" he cackled. "The department owes me another medal. This guy Rajput you're talking about? He rents, or maybe rented, a house at two-two-niner Billy Hill Drive."

"Bingo! How — ?"

"Took a while. I know a guy at one of the bill collection agencies. Rajput hasn't been paying his rent."

"You know bill collectors?"

"My careless youth still haunts me."

"I'm in Roseville. Thirty minutes. Meet you there."

37

229 BILLY HILL DRIVE was an undistinguished clapboard house halfway up a dead-end canyon a mile south of Placerville's Main Street. Officer Otis was waiting out front when Wagstaff and Marianne pulled up in his FJ Cruiser. The policeman eyed the yellow vehicle and its shaggy-haired driver.

"Some cop car. Who's your partner?"

"Professor Wagstaff."

Otis wiggled his eyebrows. "At least you're in uniform."

"Yeah, showing the flag at a drone demonstration."

"You can't be political wearing the cloth. Kazmarek will have a cow."

"She will never know. So, here we are. Let's go see what's what."

"I dunno. We don't have a warrant. We go in, we blow our chances in court."

Marianne bounded up a set of concrete steps and peered into a darkened window.

"You see any lights?"

"No."

"And the grass here — not cut, dandelions sprouting, might as well be a hayfield."

She turned on her Maglite and placed it against the window glass. The beam picked out a table and chairs. There was some kind of large poster on the far wall. Tired adhesives had failed, and it was drooping sadly.

"I claim abandoned property. We're good to enter, we're not violating anyone's rights."

"You better hope not."

"Come on. If this doesn't work, we'll just have to nail the bastard some other way."

She tried the door. Locked, of course. Otis bowed his head. Then he sucked in his breath and stepped up beside her.

"Fuck it, let me."

The door's upper half was a pane of glass. He smashed it with his elbow and reached through the hole to turn the knob.

"Bang. I love this shit."

They started inside. Wagstaff was down at the curb. He waved his arms.

"Hey, what about me?"

Marianne held up a cautionary hand. "Civilians will remain on the street and will not interfere with police business. This is a crime scene."

"You sound like you mean it."

"Better believe it, bub."

Inside, they shined their flashlights around. Marianne found a wall switch and flipped it. Nothing happened. The electricity had been turned off.

It appeared they were in a dining room. A plate of carrots was still on the table, shriveled up to little sticks. If anyone lived here, they had been gone for a while.

"Hello? Mr. Rajput?" she called out, to verify her assessment. Silence. Otis checked the kitchen, then moved on into the living room.

"Hey, Sarzeau, get in here."

He stood in the doorway, mouth agape, playing his flashlight beam over the strangest sight. Marianne joined him.

"Whaddaya got?"

Three large flat screen television sets were backed against the far wall. Fancy stereo receivers were piled up on expensive home theater speakers in front of them.

"Stolen goods. Same thing I found at the warehouse. But have a look at this . . ."

He tilted the flashlight downward, where it lit up a newspaper page on the floor. The main story was all about the crash at Beale. A plastic model airplane, half-melted, was crushed nose-down against a large photo of the incident. Red swaths of paint radiated away from the model and out across the room.

"Holy crap," she said.

In a corner was a little altar. Two Disney Princess figurines were standing on a cardboard box alongside a plastic statue of Rudolph the Red-Nosed Reindeer. Above them on a smaller box was a GI Joe action figure. His uniform had been burned away, and he had been dismembered — head here, an arm there, one leg missing. A garland of plastic flowers ringed the arrangement.

"Kids. They know how to get out there."

They climbed the stairs to check out the bedrooms. Bunk beds in one, a narrow cot in another. An *Iron Man* poster on one wall had a big red *X* splashed across it. *Star Wars* figurines were melted into a puddle on the floor.

Beside the narrow cot was a diorama made of Lego bricks. Three little minifigures were planted on the tiny buttons covering a grey plastic base. They were standing beside what looked to be a demolished airplane. A roofless room built on the same base contained a control panel and another minifigure with a little lever fastened on its head. Gloopy swatches of red and yellow paint decorated the construction.

"Geez, what a mess. Where's mom when you need her?"

In the bathroom, model airplane parts were stuck to the mirror with duct tape. Red lipstick circled each part. Words were scrawled below the parts:

Die Drones !

"Look at that," said Marianne.

Otis grunted. "I've seen enough. Meet you downstairs."

Marianne waited until he was gone, then she yanked her little stone talisman out of her blouse and held it tight. After a few seconds, her hand started to tingle.

"Hey, Mr. G. If you're cruising anywhere nearby, I could use some advice."

"You don't need my advice," whispered a virtual voice.

The mirror darkened, and suddenly her reflection was blurred and distorted by the presence of a shadowy figure. Marianne was so startled, she stumbled backwards and sat down on the toilet with a *thunk*.

"Whoa!" she croaked, "Got me again. Damn, I'm never ready."

"Didn't mean to scare you."

Marianne took a deep breath to calm down. She stood up. "Okay, two and two make four. I just found out a guy named Habib Rajput is an anti-drone activist. Now I'm in his house. It's abandoned. Turns out he's the burglar I've been tracking, and I think the kids who knocked out my father and old lady Crowfoot lived here with him. What do you know about this?"

"Not a thing."

"Great, big help. Any news from Dad? My good buddies in the Army won't let me see him.

"Not a word."

"I don't know what to do. I need Bagwell, and he's disappeared."

"Why are you asking me? This is witch's work."

"But I'm no witch, in case you forgot."

"You don't know what you are. Summon him! Isn't that what Crowfoot would tell you?"

"Yeah, she probably would."

"Well, then, Little Miss Modesty, it's up to you. Go with what you know."

"Hey, Squeek, who you talking to?"

Marianne whipped around to face Officer Otis, who had returned to witness her little séance.

"Jesus, Dez." Marianne covered her heart with a hand to ease the pounding.

"So, who?" He pointed to the mirror. "That your ghost in there?"

She peered into the mirror and nodded weakly. "Yeah. Gone now."

"Forget your shadow, visitor, whoever the hell he is, if anyone. I found something you should have a look at."

He led the way downstairs, through a side door, and into an attached garage. On the floor were a rowing machine and a couple of kayaks. Undoubtedly stolen. He aimed his flashlight at the opposite wall.

There before them was a large rectangular diagram or crude map, clumsily sketched in brightly colored chalk. It might be meant to represent the United States, but it was hard to be sure. Red circles had been scrawled at several points within the diagram. Little plastic bugs were stuck to the wall in their centers. If in fact it was a map, one of the circles marked the approximate location of Beale Air Force Base. A beat-up GI Joe doll was dangling upside down from a pushpin driven into the spot A rubbery praying mantis was glued to his head.

Marianne whistled.

38

PLACERVILLE on a May morning. Blue sky, warm weather, calm and quiet. Nevertheless, tourists on their way to Lake Tahoe and the Sierra were already crowding the sidewalks, looking for late breakfasts, early lunches, and foothill souvenirs.

Marianne managed to squeeze her Mini into a tight spot under the bell tower, got out, and surveyed the little square and Main Street stretching away eastward beyond it.

She waited until she was pretty sure no one she knew was within sight, then hauled out her little fragment of Brittany granite, clutched it tightly in her hand, and murmured an incantation.

"Ray, wherever you are, listen up! I need you in Placerville. Get down here. Right now, or forthwith, or whatever means *immediately*. Got that?"

She winced inwardly at the idea of attempting to summon the guy. It seemed so ridiculous.

She put away her stone and leaned against her car for a little while, eyeing the tourists. Her thoughts, bent on Major Bagwell at first, slowly drifted away to the night before with Tom. Their reunion had been frantic, prolonged, exhausting, and — ai yi yi — their new bed squeaked! The vivid memory made her smile. Feeling the glow (and the after effects of sleep deprivation), she strolled up the street at a leisurely pace, taking in the sunshine.

She had gone three blocks when a voice called out, "Broomhandle!"

She turned around, looking for the source.

"Over here, this way."

Jaywalking across the street was Ray Bagwell. He ignored the irritated drivers slamming on their brakes. He was smiling broadly.

"I'll be damned," she said.

When he caught up with her, he slowed and hesitated. "I've been looking for you," he said, spreading his arms. "And here you are!"

He tentatively held out a hand. Marianne shook it. "And I've been looking for you. Where the hell have you been?"

He gestured toward the rest of the world. "Away. Administrative leave is the term, I believe. But I got your message, if you can call it that. Quite a stunt you pulled up at Beale."

"Except it didn't work. So I *summoned* you!"

"You're not serious."

"Just now, with my rock, but I started the thought process last night."

"Really? God in Heaven. But then, I suppose that's what a good book of spells will do."

"Yeah, thanks for the translation. You don't need a formal spell for summoning, but — get this — I used one to wake up old lady Crowfoot."

"Did you!" He was impressed and pleased.

"That's not even the news of the day. Otis and I found the safe house your drone-crashing kids were using."

▼

The property at 229 Billy Hill Drive was now gaily cordoned off with a festival of yellow tape — *POLICE LINE DO NOT CROSS*. Marianne led Bagwell into the garage. By police order, electricity had been restored. She flipped switches and a bank of floodlights brought the odd diagram on the wall into view.

Bagwell sucked in his breath. "Well. Gotta have pictures of this."

He raised his smartphone and began taking photographs. Then he moved closer, fingering each of the plastic insects in turn.

"You're a cop. How do you read this?" he inquired rhetorically.

"Map of the U.S. — sort of — and a series of targets, right?"

He nodded thoughtfully. "And the doll pinned up here?"

"Mission accomplished at Beale."

"I think so too."

"The question," she said, "is . . . what next?"

He studied the chalk marks. "Looks like we've got four more objectives to worry about. At least. But this map — if it is a map — is so rough, it's hard to tell exactly where they are. Northeast, southwest, that much is obvious."

"These crazy circles — are they all Air Force bases?"

"Not sure. I'm not Air Force. I need to check a list."

"What a nightmare."

"Don't feel too bad. We're making progress."

"Not that much, it seems."

He regarded her speculatively, pursing his lips. "More than you think."

She gave him a doubtful look.

"I know where your father is."

Marianne recoiled. "I'm glad somebody does."

"I found him. It's what I came to tell you about."

Back outside they ran into Officer Otis, who had just arrived. "Who's your friend?" he asked, already guessing the answer.

"Dez, Major Bagwell. Ray, my partner, Officer Otis."

The two men nodded to each other.

"I hear the military is taking over the site. True?" asked Otis.

Bagwell coughed. "Well, yes, I suppose so. I can't tell you much, except the usual — national security. I've asked for a guard until our own team arrives."

"Unh-huh."

"You're the guard, yes?"

"Unh-huh, so I was told." Otis studied the Army man, then turned his attention to Marianne, standing uncomfortably beside him.

"So, Officer Sarzeau is dead, and it's Agent *Brooomhandle* again, off to save the world, am I right?"

Marianne nodded demurely.

"Should I tell the lieutenant?"

Bagwell coughed again. "Not necessary, she's been informed."

"Well shit, watch your ass, babe."

"Don't worry, officer," said Bagwell. "We won't kill her this time."

Marianne fisted Otis on the chest, and she and Bagwell drove away in the major's Cadillac Escalade.

Part FIVE

39

"OKAY, WHERE are we going?"

Bagwell and Marianne were rolling west down U.S. Route 50. The outer suburbs of Sacramento were closing in on either side. The Army man appeared to ignore her question.

"Hey-ho, time to tell me," she persisted. "I need to make a call, and Tom will want to know where the hell I'm off to this time."

Bagwell looked over at his passenger, showed her a crafty smile.

"Make your call first, then I'll tell you."

Marianne muttered a curse and lit up her smartphone. Bagwell lifted the device out of her hands and stuffed it into a pocket.

"Here, use mine, it's secure."

He handed her his own mobile phone. Marianne fumbled with the controls, dialed a number.

"My, aren't we being stealthy," she said, waiting for the ring.

"You never know," he replied, "so we don't screw around." He considered the situation, then added, "And we're not authorized. FULTAP is standing down, as you may have heard. We're volunteering our services on this little mission."

She nodded unhappily. After some mysterious electronic beeps and burps, she could hear a phone ringing.

"*County Courier.*"

"Tom! It's Marianne!"

"M, where are you?"

"On the highway. With Bagwell. We're on our way to find Dad."

"Where is he? Where are they keeping him?"

"I can't tell you." She shrugged. "Actually, I don't even know. Bagwell is keeping a big secret from his tattletale assistant."

Bagwell scowled at the accusation.

"This sounds like trouble," said Wagstaff. "When are you coming back?"

"I don't know that either. It depends. I've packed some stuff in my roll-around, just in case."

"So it's not just Dad you're after."

"No, probably not."

"Jesus Christ, babe. I don't like this."

"I know, I know. Not your lifestyle. Stay positive, and hands off Ms. Hamilton."

"Ha! Not to worry. She's up in Placerville, consulting with some gift shop. I think she kind of likes the owner."

Marianne suppressed a smirk. "Really? Good for her."

"Be safe, M."

"Yeah, I'll try. Take care of yourself while I'm gone — and fix that damn bed!"

She ended the call and dialed another number.

"Lorraine?"

"Marianne. How are you?"

"I'm okay, I'm fine. I'm on the road again, I thought you'd like to know."

"What now? You warned me, I guess. What weird off-the-wall quest is it this time?"

"Dad."

"You found him?"

"Major Bagwell did. We're on the way there now."

"Goodness, you and your spies."

"Then we're going to find the people who put him to sleep."

"Be careful, kiddo."

"I will. Tell Howard Turnbow, will you? Tell him his Golden Girl is gone, gone, gone."

"Be glad to." Lorraine paused, then coyly added, "As it happens, he asked me to dinner tonight."

"No way." Marianne was thunderstruck. "But, silly me, of course he did," she sputtered.

"Now, now, be kind to your elders. It seems we hit it off while mourning for you, back when you were dead."

"Tell him not to worry, no blood spilled at the radio station this trip."

"I'll let him know. Try not to spill any real blood, okay?"

"Roger that."

She closed the phone and dropped it into one of the cup holders.

"You done?" asked Bagwell.

She cranked out a sullen little nod.

"The answer to your question, then, is this — Travis Air Force Base, in Fairfield."

"Did Weaver come clean with you? He wouldn't tell me anything."

"The general is not involved. I did some detective work. You should be proud of me."

"Why Travis? How'd you figure that?"

"It was an obvious possibility. Not that far from FULTAP's temporary HQ, and they've got a big military hospital there."

"Weaver, what a bureaucratic toad."

"Go easy on him. He's refereeing a complicated ball game. It takes a lifetime to learn the rules."

"He's on our side? Who needs bad guys?"

Bagwell didn't bother to reply. They drove in silence for a few miles. In the middle of the capital they crossed the Sacramento River and joined Interstate 80, heading for the Bay Area.

After they passed the University of California campus in Davis, Bagwell adjusted his driving position and spoke up.

"Here's a question for you, the talented adept. In that book of yours, got any confusion spells? I can't remember."

"Oh great, you found Dad, but you have no idea how we're going to sneak in to see him."

"Very astute, officer."

"And you think I'm going to use magic powers?"

"One may hope."

"Dad ever do anything like that?"

"No."

Marianne exhaled through clenched teeth. What a half-assed operation they were embarked upon. "Well, what the hey? Let's have a look." She reached into her bag, removed a sheaf of papers, and began leafing through them.

"I printed the PDF you sent me. Got old man Rouvennec's damn book on paper, where it belongs."

It only took her a couple of minutes to be sure. "No, nothing like you're talking about."

"Maybe we won't need a spell, maybe you can just *command* a free pass," said Bagwell optimistically.

"That might work . . . if I'm really tense and all excited. But maybe not. Spells help adepts focus their thoughts."

"All right then, let's make one up."

"Oh sure . . . 'hey, hey, hey, take a look the other way'."

But Bagwell was intrigued by the possibility.

"It's got to be more poetic, don't you think? Try —"

> *Look away from your inspection,*
> *Here you see a mere reflection . . .*

"Yeah? That's it? Not much of a spell."

"It's just a start."

"It needs a sense of purpose, some kind of result."

Bagwell thought it over and added:

> *I'm a cloud just floating by*
> *Something something by your eye.*

"Pretty lame, you ask me."

They continued to work on the phrasing all the way into Vacaville. There Bagwell pulled off the Interstate and into a gas station. While Marianne browsed the food mart, Bagwell disappeared into the men's room toting his overnight bag. He emerged in full uniform with ribbons on his chest and oak leaves on his shoulders. Marianne was impressed.

"Look at you. Should I have worn my outfit?"

"No, cops are cops, and they make military people nervous. Who knows what some drunken non-com did in a local bar last night? But I'm in the club. When in Rome, etc."

"What about my piece?"

"Are you packing?"

She removed her Beretta from its little ankle holster.

"Stow it under the seat. They have metal detectors."

Five miles down the line in Fairfield, Bagwell directed the big black Cadillac onto the Air Base Parkway off-ramp. Three miles later, past the endless sprawl of houses, light industry, schools, and shops that had grown up around the base, they pulled into the Travis visitor center. Bagwell flashed his government ID and obtained a pass for his civilian companion. Then he reversed course, hooked a left to the David Grant Medical Center gate, where their identities were double-checked. The guard expressed mild curiosity about Marianne, but was reassured by Bagwell's description of her as a physical therapist, there to consult on a patient's wounds.

They were in.

Bagwell led the way through the huge medical complex to the Osterheim Trauma Center.

"Why here? He's not wounded or anything, is he?" asked Marianne, suddenly filled with dread.

"They're hiding him. Our whole operation is under review."

They approached the nurse at the desk, a young male captain. He looked at Major Bagwell, examined Marianne's papers, and refused entry.

"I'm sorry, I guess you've come a long way, but the patient is not receiving visitors."

Bagwell wiggled his eyebrows at Marianne, the signal to rev up her magical powers. She steadied herself, concentrated on the young man sitting at the counter, and bravely chanted a spell under her breath:

> *Look away from your inspection,*
> *Ignore what's just a dull reflection.*
> *Vague as clouds do I now seem,*
> *Floating past as in a dream.*

The nurse seemed puzzled.

"It's okay, we can go in. We're family," she said.

"Uh, no you can't," he replied. His expression hardened. "No visitors. No exceptions."

"On whose orders?" Bagwell inquired, fishing a pen and notepad from a jacket pocket.

"Doctor Mellencamp."

"Will that change? This is his daughter."

"Anything's possible. It might be a while, though. I understand the man is very sick."

Bagwell clicked his pen, made some notes.

Back outside, Marianne was sulking. "I don't think that spell was any good," she groused. "*Inspection . . . reflection*, what a steaming pile."

Bagwell laughed. "These are not the droids you're looking for? Come on, I loved *Star Wars* when I was a kid."

They drove out of the base and back into Fairfield, to the nearest FedEx Office, west of the Interstate on Oliver Road.

Inside, Bagwell hauled a laptop computer out of his briefcase and sat down at a workstation. Marianne was irritated by their unexplained detour and was instantly bored, but her interest picked up when Bagwell pulled his pen apart, revealing a USB plug.

"What the — it's a flash drive."

Bagwell grinned. "Also a camera. I took a few pictures."

He opened up a copy of Photoshop and began shuffling images, tweaking the color, the angle, the size.

"See, what we've got here is a photo of our uncooperative captain's badge. Look at that insignia, the barcode."

"Yeah . . ."

"And what we also have, over here, is my collection of superior ID badges." He jabbed his finger at the screen. "So, now I straighten out the photo I took — the good one — crop it to the important parts, brighten it up, saturate the color, size it to fit, glue the result onto my own card, and *voilà* — we have an ID that would fool the Chief of Staff."

"On the computer, maybe," she said.

"Right. Now we print."

He dumped the finished JPEG onto a different flash drive, called to the attendant, and requested a copy on heavy card stock. Cost, twelve dollars. He sliced the resulting print down to size with the store's paper cutter. For another five dollars the attendant laminated the print. Suddenly, it looked pretty official.

"Not bad. Will anyone buy it?"

"By itself? I think a letter of authorization would also be in order. I happen to have one on the drive here somewhere. Yes, type in a few changes, and here we go —"

> *To whom it may concern:*
>
> *The bearer, **Major Raymond Bagwell, U.S. Army, CIA, NSA,** is hereby granted Presidential authority to conduct an investigation pertaining to **Sergeant Emile Sarzo**, Patient, on directorate business without hindrance or inquiry. This operation is classified **Blue Haze Secret** and will go forward without acknowledgement.*
>
> *—Robert P. Foley*
> *Director of National Intelligence*

"Wow, that's telling it like it is."

Bagwell printed the letter on heavy paper.

"Now watch this . . ."

He fetched a metal document sealer from his briefcase, clamped it over the printed letter, and squeezed the handles.

"Look at the seal there, properly embossed. And that's a copy of the director's actual signature. At six hundred dots-per-inch, no one will question its authenticity."

▼

Back in the Osterheim Trauma Center, a different nurse was on duty when Bagwell and Marianne returned. The major presented his credentials. This time they were accepted without question, and the two were swiftly conducted into Sergeant Sarzo's hospital room.

There they discovered Doctor Mellencamp ordering staffers to disassemble the elaborate apparatus that kept Marianne's father alive.

"What's this all about?" Bagwell wanted to know.

"We have recently learned that the patient has signed documents, properly notarized, that refuse 'extraordinary measures' to prolong life beyond reasonable expectations. We're simply following the man's wishes," the good doctor explained.

"Oh no you're not," said Marianne. "You're not going to let my father die."

"Beg pardon?"

"I'll take over here, doctor," said Bagwell, showing his badge. "Leave him to me."

"I don't know, this is quite unusual, outside my experience really . . ."

"You're excused, doctor," said Bagwell.

The doctor motioned his staff away from the wires and tubes.

"Get out. I need to question this man," ordered Bagwell.

"He's comatose. This is ridiculous," said Doctor Mellencamp. "You're just going to cause worse harm."

"I'll be the judge, thank you. National security prevails over personal well-being in this matter."

"Where's your authorization for this nonsense?"

Bagwell showed him his letter. Doctor Mellencamp read it twice.

"As you wish," he said stiffly. "I am complying under the most extreme protest."

"Duly noted."

Doctor Mellencamp and his minions made their exit. Marianne advanced to Sergeant Sarzo's bedside.

"Oh my God, he looks so thin," she said.

"Scanner? Milo?" asked Bagwell of the inert form lying there. He got no reply.

Marianne took out her paper copy of Rouvennec's spell book, thumbed through to the right page, and, with one hand wrapped tightly around her little stone talisman, recited the *Waking* spell she used to revive old lady Crowfoot.

But nothing happened. Bagwell and Marianne stood by in silence for several minutes.

"Maybe this wasn't such a good idea. I hardly know what I'm doing," confessed Marianne.

"Read it again," Bagwell suggested.

"No, it worked on Crowfoot, it should work on Dad. Hang on, let me look in here." She thumbed through her book again.

"Whoa. What about this? I found a *Listening* spell."

"What are you waiting for?"

Marianne read the spell aloud:

> *Prepare your ears and listen well;*
> *Understand what I will tell.*
> *Free your mind from darkest thrall;*
> *Hear my voice when I now call . . .*

"Did you see that? I caught a little twitch there," said Bagwell.

Marianne tilted her head. "Maybe, I don't know . . ."

"Come on, he stirred. Now read the wake-up thing again," urged Bagwell.

"Give me a sec."

Marianne rummaged in her purse for her owl feathers, which she removed from a little plastic baggie and placed on the sleeping man's eyelids.

"What in the world?" wondered Bagwell.

"Crowfoot says owl feathers promote wakefulness. Owl feathers and almonds. Except, Dad can't chew right now, so screw the almonds."

"Getting very witchy on me, Sarzeau."

"Stop. I'm not a witch. Just — maybe, hopefully — an alarm clock."

Marianne clutched her talisman. Her hand began to tingle.

"The book has a couple of different *Waking* spells. I'll try the other one." She read from the book:

> *Hear my plea and hear my cries;*
> *Open lids that shield your eyes.*
> *Stir from sleep's too warm embrace;*
> *Let light of day shine on your face.*
> *Set your mind to favor reason;*
> *Now's the time, and now's the season!*

They waited again. For many long seconds, nothing. Marianne was in despair.

"I like that spell," said Bagwell, trying to cheer her up. "The original French was obscure, but it turned out well, I think, don't you?"

After what seemed like a very long time, they heard a faint groan. Then another. Then Sergeant Sarzo was twisting and turning on his bed, crying out, thrashing his arms and legs.

Marianne and Bagwell instinctively grabbed for his limbs and held him down.

"Dad! Dad! Wake up!"

Suddenly the thrashing stopped. The man seemed to relax. His eyes popped open and rolled around to check out the room.

"Where am I?" he inquired. "Some damn hospital, I guess."

Marianne let out a whoop. He turned to look at her.

"Who are you?"

"It's Marianne."

"Mary Ann . . ." He seemed puzzled.

"Your daughter."

He got himself up on one elbow, stared at her. Gradually the light of recognition shined through. "Of course. Daughter. Been a while."

He started to sit up, then fell back. He reached out and yanked the remaining tubes from his arm.

"Here, Milo, let me help," said Bagwell. He gripped the man's arm, placed a hand under his back. Thus supported, and moving very slowly,

Marianne's father sat up. He swiveled his legs to the floor and sat there for a while in some kind of daze. Then he leaned forward, lowered his head into his hands.

"I could feel you near, you know," he said. "Mary Ann . . . I could tell you were coming to get me."

"Can you stand up?" asked Bagwell.

"I think so."

"Then you probably should. I'm not sure my little ruse is going to work forever, and Doctor Mellencamp may be back with reinforcements."

"Okay. Give me a hand here."

Bagwell and Marianne each took an arm, and Sergeant Sarzo stood up.

"I wanted to wake up, you know. I knew I was asleep. I could see the door, but I couldn't find the handle."

"Until now," said Marianne.

"Until now. Until you did . . . whatever it was you did."

They shuffled him out of his hospital room and into a bathroom where he removed the catheter that had been installed back at Beale, chewing a knuckle to ease the pain. Then they continued along the adjoining corridor, moving away from the main hospital entrance. After a hundred feet they found another exit. The nurse at the desk, a dark-haired young woman, nodded politely as they left the building.

Marianne was starting to relax, but Bagwell peered back inside with nervous anxiety. "Keep walking, get out there in the parking lot, put some sheet metal between yourselves and the building. I'll get the car."

Bagwell took off at a quick pace. Marianne guided her father into the middle of the lot. There Sergeant Sarzo held up a hand.

"Let's stop."

"Okay." She loosened her grip on his arm. "Can you stand on your own?"

He nodded, wavered, and shot a hand out against the nearest car to steady himself. He coughed noisily. Gritting his teeth, he raised his arms to demonstrate his returning balance.

"See? I'm upright. Good as new."

Marianne noted the skinny legs under his flimsy hospital gown.

"Well, almost. It's been a month."

"That all? Seems like forever."

They looked at each other. Dad was small and thin, not much taller than Marianne. His dark brown eyes bored into her, trying to make sense of the grown-up daughter standing in front of him. Marianne withered under his inquisitive gaze. It made her feel oddly shy.

"So . . . when was the last time I saw you?" he asked.

"I was fifteen."

"And you wound up with Aunt Imogen."

"Yes. The Dairy Queen herself. I ran her store for a while."

"Now you're what, twenty-eight? And, good God, a cop."

"Twenty-nine, Dad. Thirty in August."

"I should know better, but distance blurs the details."

He thrust out a diffident hand.

"Maybe we ought to introduce ourselves after all these years. How do you do, officer?"

Marianne tentatively gripped his hand in hers.

"Very well, thanks. Nice to meet you at last." She bit her lip. "Sounds funny, huh? But that's what it feels like."

A horn sounded in the next parking lane. Bagwell was waving furiously from his big black SUV.

"Hey, over here. Let's go, gotta roll."

Bagwell ordered a Bacon Slamburger. Marianne ordered a Super Bird. Dad, newly outfitted in a baggy golf shirt and chinos, was eyeing the Bourbon Chicken Skillet, but settled for a Grand Slam, eggs scrambled. They were sitting in a Denny's Diner in the middle of Vacaville's Nut Tree complex, just off Interstate 505, drinking coffee and iced tea.

"Will you be all right, eating this stuff?" asked Marianne.

"I will take my chances. I'm starved," said Dad.

"Suit yourself. Men's room is over there around the corner, just in case." She pointed.

"Thank you, nurse."

Bagwell reached into his briefcase and pulled out several large photo enlargements.

"Look at these, Milo. Marianne discovered a map of sorts on the wall of the garage where your tormentors were holed up. See here — looks like

Beale, the crash site. And then we've got these other marks. Here's a close-up . . ."

Bagwell sorted through the pictures. He pointed out the little plastic insects stuck within each circle.

"What have we got? Eidetic symbols?"

"Or focus points. Identifiers, maybe. Tier two or three," mused the sergeant.

"There was all kinds of stuff like this. Airplane parts, Lego blocks, GI Joe dolls all cut up," said Marianne.

"Narrative constructs."

"Think so? Not intensifiers?" asked Bagwell.

"That would be the adult methodology. But these are children. Pre-visualization. It helps them project."

Marianne sipped her iced tea. She was beginning to feel left out.

"They manifested, you know. Three agents. Kids. All adept."

"You could see them?" Marianne was amazed.

"It was part of their rite. Interior avatars. Lucid barrier deployment. To wake up they said I had to come through a door, and they were standing in the way."

Bagwell whistled. "Powerful reification."

"Tectonic. We've never seen architecture like this before."

"I wonder who they are," mused Marianne.

"I even know their names."

"What?"

"They told me. I guess they thought I wouldn't remember. Two girls and a boy. The older girl, an adolescent, really, is called Yasmin. The boy is Rafiq. The younger girl is Zohra."

"They can't be here on their own. Who's running them?"

"Someone they call *Dada*. And they're all far away now. Beyond my sensory radius."

"A hundred kliks."

"At least."

Dinner arrived. They ate in silence for a while. Sergeant Sarzo wolfed down his eggs and then, looking ill, pushed the rest of his food away.

"Those other marks on the wall — they bother me," he said.

"Target ideation, you agree?" ventured Bagwell.

"Exactly. And that toy airplane they melted. In my sleep they bragged and bragged. Death to RPAs and those who fly them."

"What's an RPA?" asked Marianne.

"Remotely Piloted Aircraft. A drone," Bagwell explained.

"We have to get after them," said the sergeant. "Follow those marks, vague as they are, before General Weaver finds out I'm missing in action."

Bagwell stirred his coffee. "If we stay under the radar, go commercial, why not? I've got five credit cards we can use to bankroll the operation."

"We fly out, cruise the drone bases, maybe I'll pick up a tickle."

"I'll get a list. We can catch a plane out of Stockton."

Marianne snorted. "Listen to you two. You're kidding yourselves."

"Beg pardon?" said Bagwell, brought up short by her doubts.

"You won't get five miles. Doctor Melonhead is already on the hotline. The same guys who quizzed me are going to come running."

"We can dodge 'em."

"Don't be ridiculous. Us against the Armed Forces? We lose."

Sergeant Sarzo seemed to look at his daughter for the first time. "What's your alternative?" he asked.

"Your only shot is General Weasel. So he's a bureaucrat, so what? He cracked the FULTAP egg, let him put Humpty Dumpty back together again."

"I thought I might have mentioned how tricky military politics can be, especially with a death in peacetime," grumbled Bagwell.

"Look, here's Dad, exhibit A. I revived him using my abilities, powers, eidetic mojo, or whatever, when no one else could do it. That's what France was all about. The big general has got to be impressed."

"She's right, Ray," said Dad.

Bagwell put his photographs away. He sighed. "I know Weaver, I know the command structure he's up against. I know how weird our operation seems to most every officer in uniform. Don't underestimate his lack of enthusiasm."

But Marianne was undeterred. She leaned across the table.

"You want to fight? You need backup, support, resources. Whoever is behind this business is using adepts. My God, we even know their names. Now it's our turn."

40

AT SUNDOWN, a white Ford Fusion rental car turned off East Molloy Road and into the Rodax Industrial Park. It drove around behind the main buildings and parked in the lot. Darius Golay, old bones creaking, lifted himself from the driver's seat, removed his sunglasses, and opened the door for his passengers. Yasmin, Rafiq, and Zohra scrambled out of the back seat.

The evening was warm and humid. Cicadas were humming. Yasmin strolled around the lot weaving between other cars, stretching and twirling like a cheerleader. Rafiq stood on one foot, straining to catch fireflies. Zohra ran into the grass and turned cartwheels.

Golay flopped a sheet of copy paper onto the hood of the Fusion and studied the Google map fragment printed there. Firoz got out of the other side of the car, came around, and joined him.

"Dada Golay, sir, is this place as you believe?"

"Yes, Yasmin has already smelled the pilots. They are clustered in boxes on the base — here." He touched the map with his finger.

"I must accept your good word, Dada."

Golay chuckled. "Of course. You move so well I often forget. We will let the light fade, then go in. I am always amazed at the foolish Americans. Here we are in a public parking lot, open to anyone, and an enemy air base, flying missions of assassination, is right here in front of us. Unguarded!"

"We are blessed in our work, Dada."

"It is so, Firoz. If we have difficulties, you will feel Zohra summoning you. She is good at that. Otherwise, stay here, by the automobile. We are not assassins ourselves. Not yet."

"Yes, Dada. Should we eat first?"

"Ahh, by all means." He looked around. Parked nearby was an empty flatbed truck.

Golay waved his young charges to his side.

"Children, we are having a picnic."

"McDonalds? Remember, you promised," said Rafiq.

"McDonalds! McDonalds! McDonalds!" chanted Zohra.

Golay grimaced. "Did we promise, Firoz?"

Firoz suppressed a shy grin, dropped her eyes to the old man's shoes. "I could not refuse, Dada. They insisted."

Golay laughed and nodded toward the truck. "Well — here's our picnic bench."

Firoz produced a large box from the Fusion's trunk. Yasmin guided her to the truck. Golay spread a heavy blanket over the splintery wooden load bed, and they all sat.

"Are we drinking Pepsi or Coke?" he asked.

"Both!" cried the children.

Golay found he could not touch the vile industrial food from the McDonalds factory, but the kids loved it. They chattered away like ordinary school children while they peeled the aluminum foil wrapping off each new item, sharing everything.

It was getting dark. Nearby streetlights had all turned on, and insects and nighthawks were buzzing around them. Once the soda cans were empty, Golay rose, gathered up the blanket, and pointed toward the trees.

"Now, my dears, over there. Let us go and befuddle our enemies."

Golay led the way. In just a hundred feet the little group was walking beside the base boundary, a chain-link fence topped with rows of razor wire. They quickly reached a sharp angle in the fence line. Golay folded the blanket and threw it over the wire.

"Remember this place. When we come out, we come this way," he said.

They followed the boundary for another couple of hundred yards, moving through green stands of oak and maple trees, newly leafed out.

Then they were at the main gate. Golay walked boldly up to the kiosk.

"Hello, air base."

"Yes sir, what can I do for you this evening?" asked the noncom at the window.

"We are foreigners. English not so good. We want to sightsee your fort. Show my grandchildren here American strength." He curled an arm, and the three kids ran up and squeezed themselves together inside it. They put on winning smiles, but the guard was unmoved.

"I'm very sorry, sir, but this is an active base, and we don't offer tours."

Golay did his best to seem very disappointed at unexpected bad news. "Ahh, of course. Ha ha, I see what you mean. Sabotage is your worry."

"Yes sir, that it is, sir," said the noncom.

"And I understand. It is a good worry. Yasmin?"

Yasmin muttered her incantation, held up a hand, and the noncom guard slumped to the floor of his little kiosk, banging his head on the window frame on the way down. Golay and company marched past him and into the base.

▼

"Can you see where they are flying?" whispered Golay to his charges as they crouched behind what appeared to be a modified cargo container. The hour was late. After hiding behind buildings and sneaking between them, guided for half a mile through the base by Rafiq's uncanny sense of direction, they had arrived at a tight collection of steel boxes the size of house trailers. Each box was connected to overhead power lines. Air conditioners hummed on the roofs.

"They are hunting," said Zohra. "Hunting for people in stone houses on big hills."

"Afghanistan," said Rafiq. "Isn't that right, Yasmin?"

Yasmin nodded. Her eyes were wide — jackpot.

"It is a Reaper, Dada," continued Rafiq.

Golay's brows came together in righteous anger. "Yasmin, cause sleep. Rafiq, turn the drone. Zohra, tell Firoz we are coming."

"Yes, Dada," they choroused.

Twenty minutes later they were back at the boundary. Golay found their blanket, draped it over the barbed wire, and they all climbed out. First Yasmin, then Zohra, then Rafiq. Finally the old man struggled up the chain links. Rafiq leaned back across the top and helped him to safety.

Back at their car, Golay allowed some excitement to show.

"After such a hard day of work and travel we should all be in bed. Soon, soon we will be. But first, on the road here tonight, I noticed a decadent American shop. Who wants ice cream?"

The kids shouted. Firoz smiled.

41

MARIANNE, Bagwell, and Dad were cooling their heels in an empty office on the grounds of Beale Air Force Base. A security guard was standing watch just outside the door.

The trio had spent the night in a Marysville motel and appeared at the gate bright and early next morning. Sergeant Sarzo made a telephone call, and to the astonishment of the sentry on duty, an escort arrived in a Humvee and led the big Cadillac Escalade onto the base.

They had been waiting for half an hour when General Weaver finally showed up. "All right, son, you're relieved," he said to the guard, a nervous young man whose finger never strayed far from the trigger of his M-16.

"Sir?"

"I know these people."

"Yes sir."

The guard saluted and left his post.

Weaver opened the door and stood there gazing at Sergeant Sarzo.

"Well well, Agent Scanner, look at you. Wide awake."

"Morning, General."

"So it's true — Broomhandle, here, managed to bring you back."

Marianne showed off her little slice of granite. "With some help from a French dolmen and a book of spells my family gave me."

Weaver nodded approval, stepped forward, grasped Sergeant Sarzo's arm, and shook his hand vigorously.

"Good to see you on your feet again, sergeant."

"Thank you, sir."

"So, the way I hear it, you three were on the lam." He shook his head. "Doctor Mellencamp, what a drama queen. Now you've turned yourselves in. What changed your minds?"

"Success," said Bagwell, standing up. "Look here, we went off to France, and came back with the tools to revive Agent Scanner, our primary asset. In the process we have developed another asset, Agent Broomhandle. She has acquired a talisman, magnifying her already considerable talents. She has learned how to perform waking spells, thus

proving the efficacy of her little book, and I believe we will be able to discover more useful formulas in the future."

Sergeant Sarzo was more emphatic. "Better than that — I believe we will be able to find the perpetrators of this sabotage campaign, and negate their powers."

Weaver stuck his hands in his pockets and slowly toured the room, considering the claim. "On what basis?"

"My daughter located the safe house where these people were holed up. Three kids and their minders. We have a map, with targets."

"Show me."

Bagwell dug out his photographs and handed them over.

"You call this a map?" grunted Weaver, staring at the chalk marks.

"Yes, we do," said Bagwell. "There's a target back east — see, over here — plus three more in the southwest down near the bottom."

"Suppose you find them. Negate their powers? You, sergeant? That would be new. How would you do that?"

Sergeant Sarzo looked at his daughter. "Mary Ann is already far beyond me, and there's no upper limit. She's going to do it."

Marianne rocked back in her seat. "Oh sure I am. And how the hell, I'd like to know."

"Well?" asked Weaver.

"I'm going to train her," said Dad.

Weaver toured the room again, walking off his doubts. Then he opened a folder he was carrying under his arm and extracted a yellow telex message. "All right, I might be persuaded. Listen to this —"

> RPA lost over Afghanistan this day. Crashed within sight of American patrol. Eyes on the ground claim it appeared to be targeting our own personnel. Cause of loss resolved to stateside pilots asleep on duty.

"Fit the pattern?"

He handed the telex to Bagwell, who read it and passed it on.

"Where were the pilots?" asked Marianne.

"Air National Guard Base, Hancock Field, in Syracuse, New York."

Bagwell rattled his photographs. "That's got to be the eastern target we see on the map."

"What do you need from me?" asked Weaver, retrieving the telex.

"Everything you've got. FULTAP reinstated, logistical support, cooperation from the affected units," said Bagwell.

"Special forces?"

Marianne jumped in. "That didn't work too well last time."

Sergeant Sarzo echoed her sentiment. "We'll be better off sneaking around on our own. They're not using fire power, and these are our weapons . . ."

He touched his head and his heart.

42

EIGHTEEN HOURS later, the FULTAP team was cruising across the country in an executive jet with Air Force markings. It was small and fast, very much like the airplane that crashed bringing Bagwell and Sergeant Sarzo to Beale. The similarity made Marianne nervous.

Her watch said 2:00 AM, but she couldn't sleep. She passed the time alternately poring over her spell book, staring at the lights of American civilization sliding beneath the jet, and checking on her father, dozing two rows ahead of her.

At sunrise, the copilot emerged with coffee and sweet rolls. Marianne sipped and nibbled, composing her thoughts. Then she leaned across the aisle and tugged at Bagwell, pulling his attention away from last month's *Atlantic* magazine.

"Hey, Ray," she whispered.

"Mmm, what?"

"What's wrong with me?"

"Nothing. What's the problem?"

"My long-lost father has barely said a word. The best I could do was a cool handshake. Jesus, is he always like this?"

Bagwell studied his young companion.

"Not really. Have a look for yourself."

"He's asleep. Sitting at attention."

"No, no, inside." He touched his forehead.

"Meaning?"

"I know you can sense him. What color do you see?"

Marianne slumped back in her chair. She closed her eyes and let her mind relax. Very gradually an impression formed . . . a hazy aura centered on her father.

"Okay, blue. A friend . . . theoretically."

"And what color does he see in you?"

"Blue, of course."

"That's where you're wrong."

Marianne was stung. "How could that be?"

"I don't know the history between you two, but he senses a kind of greenish yellow."

"Veiled hostility, if old lady Crowfoot has it right," said Marianne, wincing.

Bagwell regarded her sympathetically. "Correct. Ask yourself — why is that?"

Marianne's eyes started clouding over. "I haven't seen the man since I was a kid. I guess I wanted him to stick around . . . with Mom and with me."

"He failed. You blame him. He senses that. And he blames himself."

"Ohhh, geez . . ."

Marianne stared out the window. The New York finger lakes were passing under the starboard wing. Early morning sunshine glinted off the water.

"How do you know any of this?"

"We talk. I've known him longer than you have."

She nodded miserably. "What should I do?"

Bagwell smoothed his thinning hair. He smiled helplessly.

"Turn blue."

▼

The airplane turned a hundred and eighty degrees to approach Rochester International Airport from the east. Marianne caught glimpses of Lake Ontario as they descended through broken clouds.

Once on the ground, Bagwell rented an SUV and drove them through the ring roads and shortcuts to the New York State Thruway, Interstate 90, heading for Syracuse, eighty-odd miles further east.

"We'll be on base at Hancock Field in ninety minutes," he said, checking his watch.

"Why didn't we just land in Syracuse?" Marianne wanted to know.

"Come on, girl, think. The last time your father and I landed anywhere near these kids we crashed, remember?" said Bagwell.

"Oh, right," mumbled Marianne, sleepily embarrassed by her failure to see the obvious, and not for the first time. "But I've got my rock. I'm ready."

"No you're not," said Dad. "Let me see that book of yours. We've got work to do."

Marianne handed it over. Her father skimmed through it, re-read several sections, chuckled over some of the poetic spells.

"Listen to this," he said:

> *A tot of honey, thick and sweet,*
> *To kiss the lips when lovers meet.*

"A love potion. Pretty frilly, these spells."

Bagwell blushed. "My fault. I did the translations."

"Hmm," grunted the sergeant. He turned around in his seat to eyeball his daughter.

"What about it? Got a fella?"

Now it was Marianne's turn to blush. "Yes, I do."

"Is he like us?"

She shrugged apologetically. "No, just a regular guy."

"Hmm. Does he know about you?"

"Some of it. He knows I can see a ghost."

He held up the book. "Did you try this stuff on him?"

"Almost. But then I didn't."

Her father nodded. "That's best, I suppose, if you're confident." His eyes drilled into hers. "Are you?"

"More or less. Most of the time."

"Unh-huh."

He studied the book some more.

"Tell me about this book, where you got it, the old man you met."

"Ever been to France?"

"Many times."

"To Sarzeau?"

"Never had that chance."

"So, you've never met Monsieur Rouvennec, or any of our relatives?"

"No. What's he like?"

"He's kind. He helped me get this" — she tapped the stone under her blouse. "He can sense people, sort of. A little bit. He sensed me. He decided I was the family inheritor. Pretty flattering."

"Rouvennec . . . in Sarzeau, France. *Sarzeau* . . . where our name comes from."

Uh-oh. Time for a small confession. "I didn't tell you, but I changed my name," she said.

"You did what?"

"Back to the French spelling, like the town — S-A-R-Z-E-A-U. And my first name, it's all one word now, M-A-R-I-A-N-N-E."

"I warned you about your grandfather."

"I know. I just like the tradition. I'm not going to turn into a witch or anything."

"We'll see about that. Marianne, is it?"

"Yeah. Over there they say, Mahr-*YANN*." She giggled self-consciously.

Her father suddenly turned around to face forward. He stared through the windshield, intent on something outside. After a moment of silent concentration, he spoke. "How far out, Ray?"

Bagwell glanced at the odometer. "Thirty miles, give or take. Got a signal?"

Sergeant Sarzo pointed down the road. "Just now. Lot of noise, but it's them. They're here."

He turned his attention back to Marianne's spell book, flipped through it, found the page he was looking for.

"All right, then, Mahr-*YANN* Sar-*ZOH*. We're going into combat. You will need to conjure up an ally."

"Oh no I won't. What kind of ally?"

He tapped a page. "Power spirit. Got the recipe right here."

"Not in fire. No way. I tried that and almost got myself killed."

"Water, then. Here's the bumf — we need lavender, wings of the monster that brings life to the dead, and, oh boy, urine."

"Urine? Mine, no doubt," said Marianne, lip curling.

"One of life's little perks," said Dad.

"Monster — life to the dead?" Bagwell scratched his head. "I was wondering about that wordage, so I checked the original French. The translation is accurate. What is it?"

"Yeah, what?" wondered Marianne.

"I do not know," said Dad.

None of them had the answer. They watched the countryside roll by. Marianne was impressed by the lush greenery of upstate New York. Well-tended farmers' fields shaded by tall trees were streaming by one after another, full of hay, red clover, cows, horses, and the occasional llama.

A few miles later, Bagwell handed Marianne his smartphone.

"Find me a Home Depot near our target."

Marianne tapped on the keyboard, got directions.

"South of the Thruway. Milton Ave, in someplace called Camillus." She handed the phone to her father.

He looked at the display. "Next exit. Go right and south."

After some twists and turns in unfamiliar territory, Bagwell pulled into the Home Depot parking lot.

The trio trudged across the asphalt to a glassed-in nursery, where Marianne and her father discovered the lavender plants. After some debate, they settled on a particularly aromatic specimen.

Bagwell had noticed a nearby Dollar Tree store as they arrived. Now he re-parked, and purchased a small travel-size bottle there.

"For a urine sample," he explained, handing it over.

"Oh great, can't wait," said Marianne.

Next stop, the Fayette Gardens Residence Hotel in downtown Syracuse.

"I booked us here to steer clear of the base until we're ready to make our move," said Bagwell.

Marianne looked around at the comfortable but otherwise unpromising establishment. "I'm hungry," she said.

"I believe there's a Denny's just up the road."

Marianne groaned. "Of course there is."

"Perfect for lunch."

At Denny's the threesome held a spirited discussion about monsters bringing life to the dead, and what that enigmatic magical ingredient might be. They failed to reach a conclusion.

On returning to their car they encountered an unattended pile of pet waste.

"Watch your step, team," admonished Bagwell.

"Don't they have cleanup laws here?" groused Marianne, wrinkling her nose.

At their approach, a cloud of flies rose from the mass. Marianne came to an abrupt halt.

"I know what the monster is," she declared.

Dad stopped and stared at her. "Tell us."

"Well, somewhere in school I learned basic forensics, how bugs get into corpses in a particular time sequence? Flies lay eggs on deteriorating flesh. The eggs are alive. So the monster bringing life to the dead is ... just a fly."

"And we just need a pair of wings," said Bagwell.

Dad crouched near the dogshit, hand cupped. Suddenly he swiped it over the pile, closing his fingers as he did so. He raised his fist in triumph.

"Winged monster," he said. "Got one."

"Good hunting, soldier," said Bagwell.

▼

Marianne was asleep in her clothes as soon as the latch clicked on her hotel room. Later on, at the dinner hour, she woke up to a knock on her door.

"Marianne?"

She sat up, swallowed, blinked away some of the sleepy seeds, and stretched. Her father was calling.

"Yeah? What?"

"Time."

She checked her watch.

"Time for what?"

Her eyes swiveled over to the bedside table, picked up the empty plastic bottle sitting there.

"Oh my God, I've been out for hours. Give me a minute."

When she opened the door Sergeant Sarzo entered cautiously, holding up a hotel-supplied ice bucket half-filled with warm water redolent of lavender. Marianne replied by showing him her plastic bottle, now half-filled with a pale yellow liquid.

"And the monster wings?" she asked.

"Already in here."

"Where are we doing this?"

"Ruckels Park, it's just down the street a block or two. Bring your book."

They strolled along Fayette Street, past a pizzeria, past a little corner delicatessen, past Dunkin' Donuts, past three different bars. The evening was warm. Ruckels Memorial Park was small and lush, a public garden hemmed in by slender young maple trees. They took a seat on one of the benches and waited for the other visitors, a couple of homeless people with shopping carts full of bottles and cans, to wander off.

"Are we sure those kids aren't hanging around here?"

"I sense them. They're miles away."

Once the park was empty, Sergeant Sarzo stood up, placed his ice bucket on the bench, and aimed a finger at his daughter.

"Your turn."

Marianne poured the urine she had collected into the water.

"Now, recite the spell. Let's see what you've got."

Marianne fumbled with her sheets of paper, thumbed through them until she found the correct incantation:

> *Flow ye spirit —*

"Wait a minute."

"What?"

"You can't just read anything. Focus first. Form an image." He pointed at her forehead. "In there."

Marianne rubbed her hands together. "I'm doing it. I'm imagining a wispy little guy. A *friendly* little guy."

"All right for now."

She picked up the bucket, sloshed the water around, put it back down, grasped her stone talisman, and read the magic words:

> *Flow ye spirit to my side;*
> *Perform my will as I shall guide.*
> *Think your purpose as my own;*
> *Obey the power of my stone!*

She lowered the book and peered into the bucket. Sergeant Sarzo moved beside her and did the same. The water surface remained calm.

Marianne waited a minute, then jiggled the bucket. "Hey, come on, boil and bubble, toil and trouble . . ."

"Don't joke."

She puffed her lips, exhaled, slapped the pages of her book against her hip. They waited some more in silence. A young woman dressed in a business suit drifted into the park, playing with her mobile phone. She barely glanced at the adepts and their oddball experiment.

After what seemed like eternity to Marianne, bubbles formed on the bottom of the bucket. They rose and gathered on the water surface. A thin vapor appeared above and spiraled upward in a ragged vortex.

"Ahhh!" said Marianne, startled by the apparition.

"Shh," said her father.

They watched as the gauzy column filled in. Vaguely arm-shaped appendages grew outward. Something like a head appeared on a half-formed body.

"Can you see it?" she whispered.

"I do see something. I think. It's hazy."

The vapor detached itself from its watery origin and floated out across the park, toward the young businesswoman.

"Uh-oh," whispered Marianne. "Think she can see it?"

"Command it," said Dad.

"Come back here, you. To my side, pronto!" hissed Marianne.

The vapor swirled around and floated back toward them. The young woman, now in the middle of a phone call, paid no heed.

"Now, touch my father."

The vapor floated right through him.

"Okay, enough," he said.

"Right. Back in the water, no argument."

The vapor centered itself on the bucket, and wound itself down into the water. Bubbles roiled the surface for a few seconds, then all was calm again. The young businesswoman ended her call with a smile and strolled away, off to a date or an evening with friends.

Marianne picked up the bucket of prepared water and turned toward her father.

"Hey, Dad, not bad, huh?"

"Yes, you conjured a demon."

She shrugged, affecting modesty.

"A pretty tame one."

"The best kind. I'm impressed. I couldn't do it. Not many can."

Marianne considered their little expedition together. It seemed like a good time to conjure the tricky spirit of human relations.

"Listen, Dad, I'd be lost without you. I know you think I'm not grateful, but I am. Do I wish you had been around when I was dragging my ass through high school? You bet I do. But we're family, we share these weird abilities, these things that set us apart."

He said nothing, but stared intently at her. It made her squirm.

"And, and . . . if you were never around, what the hell, I survived. I forgive you."

He continued to look at her, dark eyes seeming to penetrate to the bone.

"Hello . . . Earth calling Dad . . ."

"No, you don't," he allowed, finally.

"Don't? Don't what?"

"You don't forgive me. I wish you did, but you don't. I still sense your aura, somewhere between green and red."

"But I just . . . doesn't anything I said mean anything?"

"Part of you wants to forgive, but deeper down, you resist. You are one tough woman. I should have known that my daughter would grow up to be a real Sarzo, stubborn as the rest of us."

Tears started in Marianne's eyes. She wiped them away. "Fuck that shit," she said.

Sergeant Sarzo leaned forward and kissed his daughter lightly on the cheek.

"Drive on," he said.

▼

Over dinner, at the little pizzeria Sarzo & Sarzeau spotted near the park, the FULTAP team discussed strategy and tactics.

"Milo should stay here," said Bagwell, "out of range."

"I'll be fine," said Sergeant Sarzo.

"You are dangerously susceptible to these people. It's out of the question. I'll fly support on this one."

"What am I supposed to do?" asked Marianne.

"Put them to sleep, or curse them," said Dad.

"A curse, that would be terrific," said Bagwell. "But I don't remember anything like that in Rouvennec's book."

Marianne confirmed his doubts. "No curses, and I couldn't do it if there were. They haven't killed anyone. They're kids."

"Scary kids. Don't forget."

"Where are they?"

"North of us, near the base. Waiting for nightfall, probably. This is why I have to come along — pinpoint the enemy. I'm guessing they'll gravitate to the drone command posts, but who knows?"

Bagwell dropped his credit card on the bill. He checked his watch.

"Let's go see the man."

▼

"This has happened before?" asked Colonel Stuart Huff, the man in charge of the 274th Attack Wing, an active Air Force unit based at Hancock Field.

True to his word, General Weaver had smoothed their path, and the FULTAP team was escorted directly to Huff's office when they arrived on base.

"Yes, sir, at Beale, out in California," said Bagwell. "Two Global Hawks and a C-21 crashed there. Luckily for everyone, there were no fatalities."

The officer studied Bagwell's credentials. He handed them back with a skeptical growl. "FULTAP. Good God, until tonight, I never heard of it. And you say children crashed my RPA?"

"We've always thought an escalating jihadi campaign might produce a dirty bomb," said Bagwell. "Instead, that's right, they sent children."

"Not just any children," added Sergeant Sarzo. "These are adepts."

"And the reason my pilot and crew fell asleep on duty is the result of what, a *magic spell?*"

"Yes sir."

"That's hard to swallow."

"Understood, sir."

"And you two — what is your role in this?"

Bagwell motioned his companions to silence. "These are my assets. They too are adepts. Tonight we will either nail the saboteurs in the act or chase them away."

"How can you be sure they're here? Or that they penetrated our security in the first place?"

"They might not have. It's possible they operate from beyond the perimeter, but more probably they need to get close." Bagwell held his hands up, a few inches apart. "You know, square of the distance law."

"Spells obey the laws of physics?"

"Of course. It's just that some of the laws haven't been discovered yet."

"Will we win the Nobel prize?"

Bagwell's face grew long and grim.

"I suggest you alert your security people, and post them on the perimeter. Once we move, they'll move too."

43

DARIUS GOLAY parked his rental car in the Rodax Industrial Park for the second time in three days. After the first attack, he waited for ISI confirmation of the downed drone. It took more than a day and a half, but the news, when it arrived from Pakistan, was excellent. The children passed the long hours in their rundown motel watching cartoons on the Disney Channel and playing *Angry Birds* on Mark Frey's stolen iPad. Now it was time to strike again.

He and his charges waited until dusk before starting for the boundary fence at Hancock Field. As they ducked under the trees, Rafiq stopped short.

"Yasmin — listen."

Yasmin stopped too.

"What is it, children?" asked Golay, with a touch of irritation in his voice.

"The American adepts are here. Ahead of us, on the base."

Golay looked around for signs of trouble. "You're sure?"

"We're sure."

"I see them too, Dada," affirmed little Zohra.

Golay considered the situation.

"They have found us. Can they match your skills?"

Yasmin shook her head. "When I look, I see confusion. The old one sees us, nothing more. The young one is untried."

"This development may thwart our plans here. The security patrols will be alert. But all is not lost. Perhaps," mused Golay, "it would suit us to test ourselves. Learn something for another day."

Zohra nodded vigorously. "The young one is the policeman I put to sleep before. I will stop her."

▼

Soon the interlopers were stationed near the drone command posts, crouching behind a communications shelter. Perhaps the base security forces were on elevated alert, but if so, they had not appeared and clearly posed no challenge.

"Can you see the pilots, where they are?" asked Golay.

"Near the Pakistan border. They are flying over an American patrol," said Yasmin. She knotted her eyebrows in an angry frown. "It is hard to see — the American adepts are approaching. They confuse me."

"We must be quick. Rafiq, can you cause them to fire on the American soldiers?"

"I will tell them their friends are their enemies. They will believe me," vowed the boy.

"Dada, the American policeman. She is near," warned Zohra.

▼

Not far away to the west, the FULTAP team was gathered inside an open hangar, poised to advance on the drone command posts. Sergeant Sarzo peered around the nose of an old A-10 ground support aircraft that was parked there.

"Our targets are east, two hundred meters, down at the far end of those containers."

"I call it. Far as you go, Scanner," said Bagwell.

Marianne was chewing almonds. She passed the half-empty can to her father.

"Eat some nuts."

"What?"

"And hold onto a couple of these . . ."

She handed him a pair of owl feathers. He looked askance, waved them back and forth as a question.

Marianne grinned to acknowledge the peculiarity. "Dr. Crowfoot's prescription for wakefulness. You military guys need to hang out with the natives more."

She had taped an owl feather to each of a pair of bent-open paper clips. Now she replaced the turquoise studs in her ears with the makeshift earrings.

Bagwell smiled. "Some uniform."

"Where's that ice bucket?" said Marianne. "Time to conjure."

▼

Rafiq was deep in concentration, slowly gaining influence over one of the drone pilots. That man, who was busy flying a mission on the other side of the world, was himself not more than thirty feet away, hidden behind the steel walls of his cockpit container.

Suddenly a gauzy vapor floated around the corner of the comm shelter.

Zohra shrank back against Golay.

"Dada! A ghost!"

It seemed to reach out and place misty hands on Rafiq's head. He jerked around, losing his focus on the drone pilot.

"Ahh! Let go of me!" He crawled away on all fours.

Yasmin windmilled her arms through the vapor. The thing broke up into little cloudlets. They drifted away. Then the apparition re-formed and approached again. Zohra and Rafiq took up defensive positions near Yasmin, bravely shielding Golay.

Just then Marianne came into view. She was pointing at them and shouting commands to her diaphanous power spirit.

Yasmin stamped her foot. "Stop, you! Go away!"

Marianne kept coming.

Yasmin muttered her sleep incantation. All three children thrust out their hands.

Marianne stumbled and fell, unconscious before she hit the ground.

Golay led his charges toward the southeast corner of the base. They were all running, and the old man was puffing like a locomotive.

"Hurry, children, we must be gone before we are discovered by the Americans. Surely they know we are here by now."

They hit the fence line and ran along it. Golay found the blanket he had tossed onto base property earlier that evening. He threw it over the barbed wire just as an angry voice boomed out over a loud hailer.

"You there! Stop where you are!"

The headlights of a Humvee had found them. Golay shaded his eyes against the harsh glare as the security vehicle roared forward to cut off their escape.

"Be calm, children. It is no use running further."

44

MAJOR BAGWELL, Sergeant Sarzo, and a duty nurse were standing in a corner of the Hancock Field Joint Health and Wellness Center, where three beds constituted the urgent care unit. One of the beds was obscured by a nylon curtain.

"She's sleeping peacefully, but we can't keep her here. If she doesn't wake up soon, we need to transfer her to a facility that's equipped to deal with her . . . with her . . . uhh, injury," said the nurse.

Bagwell showed the nurse his credentials.

"This is FULTAP business. Give her a few more hours. On my authority."

"I'm against it, there could be damage."

"My problem."

The nurse gave them a frustrated *whatever* wave and walked away.

"What about it, Milo? Could you manage one of her spells?"

"Not a chance."

"Then we wait."

"Some more."

"And hope."

"Coffee?"

"No thanks. You go ahead."

"Later."

"This sucks."

"Tell me."

Suddenly the curtain surrounding the occupied bed was whisked aside by a trembling hand, revealing Marianne. She was sitting up with her legs dangling. She looked this way and that, trying to get her bearings. It took her a while to focus on her colleagues. When she finally did, she managed to wave a woozy greeting.

"Yo, boys. Morning? Afternoon?"

The two men rushed to her side.

"Easy now," said her father.

"Get this damn tube out of my arm and point me to the bathroom. I really, really, really have to pee."

Sergeant Sarzo delicately removed the IV drip. Marianne tore off the electrical monitors, stood up, and wobbled off to the toilet, hospital gown flapping.

"Parental opinion . . . she okay?" asked Bagwell.

Sergeant Sarzo considered his daughter. "She's headstrong. Impulsive, but resilient. Her powers don't extend to seeing very well, however. That seems to protect her from the worst our enemies can do . . . well, to some degree, anyway."

"Will she ever learn?"

"Always the hard way."

Bagwell jingled the coins in his pocket.

"Will she ever forgive you?"

Sergeant Sarzo threw his hands in the air. "Who knows? She's like her mother. That woman could carry a grudge that weighed a thousand pounds."

"And just wait until you tell her all about Aunt Imogen."

Sergeant Sarzo bristled. "Someday I may have to. Not today."

A few minutes later Marianne wobbled back.

"Where are my street rags? How long have I been out, anyway?"

Bagwell handed over a large plastic bag filled with items of clothing.

"Almost a day." He checked his watch. "Fifteen hours, I guess, all told."

"That all? Seems a lot longer." she said.

She took the bag of clothes, snapped the curtain shut for privacy. "What about our foreign friends?" she asked. "Did we nail them?"

Bagwell chuckled. "They were confronted by a security patrol at the base perimeter. They commandeered the Humvee somehow and drove right out through the gate."

"They put security to sleep?"

"Yes. It's a fiasco. Colonel Huff is very embarrassed. The man never did order up adequate security. Too skeptical about magic, it seems. Well, we won't be talking about magic anymore."

"They all got away?"

"Gone, hours ago. Out of range." said her father. "I don't sense them."

The curtain parted. Marianne was now dressed in her more familiar jeans, T, and flannel shirt.

"Then let's find them. Man, those kids gave me a hangover."

▼

An hour later they were on the other side of Hancock Field in the Military Courtesy Room of Syracuse Hancock International Airport.

"Our ride will be ready for travel in forty-five," announced Bagwell, ending a brief telephone call.

Marianne was anxiously parading back and forth in front of him.

"Give me your phone for a sec," she said, reaching.

He jerked his hand away. "Unh-unh, tell me why."

"Police business. I need to check in."

"No mention of where we are, no mention of where we're going."

"Of course not. Where *are* we going, by the way?"

"West. Details to follow your *brief* and *circumspect* telephone call."

"Yeah, yeah, I'm on board, gimme that thing."

She walked away across the lounge, dialing a number.

"Tom? It's me."

"M? How are you? Where are you? When you coming home?"

"I'm all right. Getting a lot of sleep — too much, actually. But I can't talk about any of it right now. How about you — everything okay out there?"

"I'm fine, all is cool. Are you safe?"

"Pretty safe."

"Being careful?"

"Trying hard. Beretta on my ankle."

"Jesus, stay out of gun fights."

"So far so good."

"That's not very comforting, you know. You're talking in riddles."

"Sorry, I'm not even supposed to be calling you. I told Bagwell I wanted to check in with the cops."

"Hey, that reminds me. Some guy named Otis — your partner in Placerville, right? — called me. He's trying to get in touch with you."

"Really? I'll call him."

"Get back here, M. All in one piece, okay? I'm worried about you, what you're getting into."

"Soon as possible. Promise," she vowed.

"Don't break it."

Marianne ended the call and dialed another.

"Officer Otis here."

"Hi, Dez, Tom said you wanted to talk to me."

A strange howling noise rippled across the secure connection.

"Sarzeau? That you? What the hell was that?"

"Secure line. I think it's some kind of satellite link. What's up?"

"That U-Haul dealer in Sacramento called your friend Wade Gawley again. And Gawley called me. This time he got some more information. The missing truck was rented by, guess who — your favorite wall-climbing jook, Haba-daba Ram-zo. Ring a bell?"

"Big gong."

"Okay, that's not all. Ram-zo put down his warehouse address, like I already found, and he gave the man a phone number."

"Hey, that's a break."

"Yeah, but it was for one of those pay-as-you-go deals. I checked, no way to trace any calls."

"You forget the company I keep. Give me the number."

Otis read off the number. Marianne closed up the phone and marched back to Bagwell, who was absorbed in the local newspaper. He was grateful that the Hancock Field security breach went unreported in its pages.

Marianne hooked a finger over the newspaper and tugged it away from his face. "Hey, Ray — here's something for you, my burglar's cell phone number. It's from one of those things you buy in the supermarket, untraceable, but I thought you might be interested."

Bagwell put down the paper. He was very interested.

▼

They were in the air for more than an hour before Bagwell let Marianne know their destination. "Davis-Monthan Air Force Base or Tucson International, depending on how you look at it."

He hauled out his photographs of the map Marianne found at 229 Billy Hill Drive and pointed to one of the chalk circles vaguely positioned in what might be read as the American southwest.

"Arizona?"

"Right. Fort Huachuca, down near Sierra Vista, is an Army RPA base, among other things. We need to take a look."

"Hey, Dad, sense anything there?" she prompted.

But Dad was napping.

"How long till we land?"

Bagwell checked his watch. "Three hours."

Marianne nodded absently, reclined her seat, and closed her own eyes.

A few minutes later Bagwell's secure telephone rang.

"Bagwell. What have you got?"

He listened to a long message and scribbled a note.

"Thanks, this is helpful. Track the man for me." He consulted his notebook. "Subject has an alias, Hank Rogers — spelling Romeo, Oscar, Golf . . . yes, that's right. Track that name too if you will."

Marianne woke up. "What is it?"

"Might be a lead. My sources at American TV & Appliance have some powerful tools. They did in fact trace a call that your man Rajput received on his throw-away phone. It was made from a line in the Department of Comparative Religion at UCLA, from the office assigned to a visiting professor from Pakistan, someone named Darius Golay. He's a Zoroastrian, here in America to teach his faith during the current school year."

"He's not a Muslim?"

"An Irani — from a family driven out of Iran when Islam took over, centuries ago."

"He believes in Allah, though, right?"

"Not at all. Zoroastrians have two gods, Ahura Mazda, the Lord of Light, the creator who embodies all that is good, and Ahriman, the god of evil. There's a constant battle between them."

"Who's winning?"

Bagwell's lips twisted into a sardonic smile. "Look around. So far, it's a draw, I guess. At best."

"And the kids?"

"Nothing known. But how about this? The man himself is missing. He hasn't been seen on campus in Westwood for six weeks. His classes have been canceled."

"Think he's running our magic show?"

"If I were a gambler, I'd like the odds."

45

DARIUS GOLAY, Firoz, and the three Pakistani children were packed into a subcompact Ford Fiesta, southbound in central New Mexico on Interstate 25. Golay had rented the car three hours previously, following a Southwest Airlines flight that deposited the group in Albuquerque.

"Dada," asked Zohra, wedged uncomfortably into the tiny backseat between Yasmin and Rafiq, "why are we driving in such a small car?"

"Because, my dear, we must be very careful with money."

"And why is that, Dada?" asked Rafiq, elbowing the younger girl. "I liked the big one much better."

"Because our friend Mr. Rajput did not succeed in delivering the funds he promised."

"But why? Why do we need any money at all?" pouted Zohra.

"Because this is America, silly," said Yasmin. "Money is everything here."

"Quite right, Yasmin," said Golay with approval. "The Americans worship their dollar. That is why they are weak."

Just south of Socorro they turned off the Interstate onto U.S. Highway 380, proceeding southeast through dry scrubland.

Golay pointed out the window. "There, off to the south, out in the desert — that is Trinity Site, where the Americans first tested their devil-bomb, long before you were born." His face colored with righteous anger. "With this bomb they have threatened the world to conform to their corrupt godless ways. Now our country has this bomb as well, and we can no longer be threatened."

"That's good, right, Dada?" asked Rafiq, just to confirm his own opinion.

"Of course it is, little brother," said Yasmin. "Nobody can threaten us now."

"But more important than the bomb," continued Golay, "we have you three!"

"Us three! We are the strongest!" said Rafiq.

"And possibly, in some corner of our miraculous country, we may have more like you. Here in New Mexico we will defeat the naïve pilots who are just learning to fly their monstrous drones. And we will cause great doubt and consternation among the unbelievers."

"Cause a lot of trouble," echoed Zohra.

Golay glanced at his gas gauge. "Yes, trouble. But before we do, to avoid trouble of our own, we need petrol. Yasmin?" He handed her a roadmap.

Yasmin unfolded the map and studied it. "Turn right when we come to road number 54. There's a town there called, um, Carrizozo. They will have fuel."

"I want ice cream," said Zohra.

"You shall have it, my dear," promised Golay.

46

THE EXECUTIVE JET carrying the FULTAP team to southern Arizona was less than a hundred miles from touchdown when Bagwell's secure telephone rang. He roused himself from the pages of *Time* magazine.

"Bagwell. Say what? When? Oh no. Shit and monkeys!"

He threw down his phone, vaulted from his comfy leather seat and hurried forward.

"You in there!"

He pounded on the flight deck door, closed and locked these days, even with patriotic secret agents on the passenger manifest.

The copilot cautiously cracked the door open. "What's up, Major?"

"We need a new flight plan. Our targets have revealed themselves, and they're not here, they're back in New Mexico."

"Where? Where do you want to go?"

"Albuquerque, I guess. Kirtland is probably safe. We don't dare come anywhere near Holloman, where we really want to go, because that's where they're undoubtedly heading."

"That's a problem?" asked the copilot.

"You bet it is. They crashed our airplane at Beale."

"All right. Let's see if we have fuel for a redirect. Take a seat, please, we'll let you know."

Bagwell shuffled back to his seat, rubbing his fuzzy head, lost in thought.

"What was that all about?" asked Sergeant Sarzo, waking from a long nap.

"Yeah, what on Earth?" chimed Marianne.

"American TV & Appliance strikes again. I asked them to track Mr. Rajput, and they have detected a credit card with his name on it buying gas in . . . Cardozo, Carrizo, Carrizolo . . . someplace like that. New Mexico, anyway."

"Holloman . . ." mused Sergeant Sarzo.

"Gotta be. Where the fuck is Carri-zippo?"

Marianne reached in the seatback pocket for a map. "Here it is," she reported. "Carrizozo. It's a little town north of Tularosa. Half way from

Albuquerque to Alamogordo. What's going on there?"

"Holloman Air Force Base is just outside Alamogordo," said Bagwell. "They run a training camp for RPA pilots. It's a drone control base."

"The kids and their handlers probably flew into Albuquerque and are driving down there," said Marianne.

"Your view, Milo?" asked Bagwell.

"Good guess."

Bagwell checked his watch again. "Damn. We won't arrive in Alamogordo until late. They're hours ahead of us."

The copilot emerged from the flight deck. "We don't really have fuel to double back to Albuquerque, but we can reach Las Cruces — that'll get you a lot closer to Alamogordo anyway. What do you say?"

Bagwell didn't have to think it over. "That's great. Let's go."

The copilot gave him a little salute and returned to the cockpit. The pitch of the engines changed, the nose tilted upward, and the airplane banked left, making a wide climbing turn eastward, back toward the Land of Enchantment.

▼

On the ground in Las Cruces, Marianne quizzed Bagwell about his travel plans.

"Want to hole up here, spend the night, or drive?" she asked.

"Drive. We should press our case."

So they did.

Alamogordo was seventy-five miles away to the northeast. While Bagwell drove on into the early evening, across the Rio Grande, through the arid hills, past the baked gypsum wasteland of White Sands, she consulted his secure telephone in search of a suitable motel.

"Got one. Days Inn, right in town, looks decent."

"Let's hope our targets aren't staying there," said Sergeant Sarzo.

"They seem to favor less-expensive establishments, if I'm not mistaken," said Bagwell. "I think they've got money trouble, or they never would have used that credit card."

"Think Rajput is traveling with them?" asked Marianne.

"I don't know. I'm starting to wonder about Mr. Rajput, what his role is — or was."

"I have never sensed this guy," said Sergeant Sarzo. "Just the five we know."

Marianne spread her fingers on the little screen for a close-up look at the map. "Here's some good news for you, Ray — found a Denny's right across the street."

"Thank God. I'm hungry."

A few miles farther on, near the outskirts of Alamogordo, the main gate of Holloman Air Force Base came into view. Sergeant Sarzo, who had been slouching in the front passenger seat of the FULTAP team's rented Dodge van, suddenly jerked upright.

"The five we know!" he exclaimed. "They're here."

47

COLONEL FRANCIS ISAACSON, commander of the 99th Training Wing, left his office and drove along Periphery Road to the Holloman control tower, the better to watch his student pilots' evening landing sequence. After a long day behind his desk, the colonel, a former Air Force pilot himself, liked to stretch his legs and savor the hint of action that the robotic aircraft represented.

The sun was already setting behind the San Andres mountains when the exercise concluded. There was a light breeze from the north, and Isaacson could see the nearest RPAs turning into the wind to land on Runway 34. At fifteen hundred feet, they were flying above the mountain shadow, and sunlight was glinting off their wings.

"How many we got?"

The flight controller pointed to the south. "Afternoon, sir. Three lined up. First in is a QF-86, then two Predators. There's another group due in just about an hour.

"Any problems?"

"No, sir. Well, we're talking students, so you never know for sure. But we're clean today."

"Glad to hear it."

Isaacson poured himself a cup of coffee and settled back to watch.

The QF-86, an antique jet from the Korean War era retrofitted for target practice, thundered in at 120 knots and touched down right on the big **III** zone marker. A few minutes later the first Predator drifted in and landed at 65 knots, so much slower it seemed to be suspended in midair.

A second Predator followed the first, but something about its trajectory alarmed Colonel Isaacson.

"He's not right. Not on the beam."

"No, sir, he's not. I'm on it."

The flight controller a made a frantic call to the student pilot. "Abort, abort! Predator abort!"

Colonel Isaacson was incredulous. "That damn thing is coming right at us."

"Yes, sir, working on it, sir."

Indeed, the Predator was descending toward the base, and it was lined up right on the tower, a quarter mile west of the runway.

"Sir, I think you should get yourself out of the tower, sir."

"Son of a bitch!" The colonel made for the elevator, then turned around and came back. Watching the Predator home in on him was fascinating.

▼

Bagwell slowed as the FULTAP van approached the base.

"Hey! Look at that!" Marianne pointed. A little metallic green Ford Fiesta was parked by the side of the road where the base fence angled in from the north to parallel the highway.

"It's them," said Sergeant Sarzo.

"Are you sure?"

"Pretty sure. Strong signal. Five entities, three-and-a-half are adept."

"Stop the car!" shouted Marianne.

Bagwell pulled over a hundred feet past the Fiesta.

"Let's get 'em," she said, sliding the rear door open.

"Hey, now, hang on, we're not prepared for an encounter here."

But Marianne was already out of the van. She skipped across the road, and was soon running along the fence line, moving out into the desert scrub, dodging creosote bushes.

"What are you doing?" called Bagwell, stumbling out of the driver's side. "Get back here — your spells don't work, remember?"

Marianne stopped, leaned down and freed up her little Beretta. She grinned at the two men now standing beside the van.

"Gonna try some real force," she yelled.

"Oh no you're not," said Sergeant Sarzo, starting after her.

Marianne was not far along when she spotted four people huddled near the fence. Three children and an old man. They were squatting down in the weeds with their attention focused on a trio of descending aircraft. She crouched low and eased herself toward them. As she was moving, the first aircraft in line, an older jet fighter, swooped overhead with a terrific roar and landed somewhere beyond a line of trees.

Marianne inched forward, drawing closer to the saboteurs, when a large drone flew overhead on final approach. Compared to the jet, it was moving at a snail's pace, gliding lazily downward.

Ahead of her, Rafiq suddenly lost all interest in the third incoming drone and turned toward the advancing policewoman.

"Dada! It is the American. She is here!"

Old man Golay rose from the spot where he was kneeling and peered toward Marianne.

"We must retreat, children. Come! We have been discovered."

"Hold it right where you are!" shouted Marianne, standing up with her Beretta trained on the little group.

▼

Colonel Isaacson cringed as the Predator zoomed toward the Holloman tower. The flight controller was yelling and cursing into his microphone. Then he gave up and dove under his desk.

Suddenly the drone's engine revved up, the wings tilted, and the machine flew by the tower's big picture windows with just a few feet to spare.

The flight controller crawled out from under his refuge and watched it climb into the evening sky. Pretty soon sunlight was glinting off the wings again.

"Get that thing on the ground, son," said Colonel Isaacson, marching to the elevator. "I want to talk to the pilot. That boy is about to find out what *debriefing* means."

▼

Sergeant Sarzo couldn't help noticing the old man and his gaggle of children hurrying away from the base perimeter. He paid them no mind, however. Instead he swerved back and forth through the chaparral until he came to his daughter, lying face down in the crusty sand. He checked her pulse. Strong and regular. With a weary sigh he tucked her Beretta into a pocket, reached out, and picked her up.

Bagwell was leaning against the van. He stood up straight when he spotted Sergeant Sarzo returning with a bulky burden in his arms, staggering under the weight.

"Oh, for Christ's sake! What now . . ."

He jogged across the highway and helped the man unload his unconscious daughter. Looping her arms over their shoulders, together they dragged Marianne's limp form the rest of the way to the van and laid her down in back. Sergeant Sarzo clicked her into a pair of seat belts and climbed into the passenger seat.

"Better find a hospital," he said.

Bagwell was stabbing a finger at the screen of his smartphone. "Or we introduce ourselves to the local wing-ding right away. That would be quicker."

Marianne's eyes popped open. She wriggled around in the grip of the seat belts.

"Hey! I'm okay. Un-fucking-hook me. Where's my gun?"

The two men swiveled around in their seats.

"Agent Broomhandle," said Bagwell. "We feared the worst."

48

IN THE CLEAR LIGHT of morning in the Tularosa Basin, the FULTAP team was driven along the Holloman flight line to a hangar whose wide doors were pushed apart just far enough to admit Colonel Isaacson's jeep. There they dismounted and squinted into the relative gloom. The colonel led them across the stadium-size interior to the Predator that almost greased him on the previous evening. The forward fairings had been removed, and maintenance specialists were going over the exposed innards with tools and diagnostic gadgets, searching for clues to its spectacular misbehavior.

"Here she is. Some kind of casualty has undoubtedly occurred, but we have yet to find the cause of the tracking error."

"What's on your suspect list?"

"Too complicated — who knows? K-band satellite comm unit? The GPS receiver? By the time anything gets mil-rated it's ten years out of date."

"I hear you," said Bagwell.

"I'm guessing it's a software bug. I hate those things."

"Mmm. The pilot — did he report sleeping, by any chance?"

"On duty?" The colonel was offended.

"It's possible. We've seen other instances."

"The pilot reported momentary confusion. But he recovered. His instructor landed this thing on the go-around."

"Glad to hear it."

Colonel Isaacson studied the blinking lights on one of the probes. "There's a lot going on in here, and it's a rat's nest of low bids," he concluded with a jaded shake of the head.

Bagwell eyed his companions. Sarzo & Sarzeau both scowled. They were not persuaded by the commander's assessment.

"There's nothing wrong with this aircraft, Colonel," said Bagwell, tapping one of the electronic components.

"You've got a different explanation?"

"We can't discuss the details. But our view is sabotage."

"Sabotage!?" exclaimed the colonel. He was astounded.

"Granted, here in America, far from the world's troubles, it's a long shot. Just in case, I'd beef up your perimeter defenses until further notice. Your student's confusion wasn't accidental."

"Sabotage — how is that possible?" The commander's tone made it obvious he could not imagine such a thing at Holloman.

Bagwell held up two fingers. His expression was grave. "Two words, Colonel — *electromagnetic pulse.* Looks like our adversaries have a novel technology that can strike from miles away. Think about it."

"You security people . . ." Colonel Isaacson let the thought hang.

▼

Not too many miles away, in a cheap motel, Darius Golay was on the internet, reading and responding to a news article that appeared on the *Islamabad Daily Register's* website. The many tragedies and disasters of the day in Pakistan's ninth largest city were spread across his laptop screen. The particular story that caught his eye was an account of spiritual healing among school children in the tribal areas of South Waziristan. The headline was unusual:

SCHOOLGIRL TAMES WILD GOATS

The story beneath, an enlightening, uplifting, and amusing piece on the healing of mountain goats by causing injured animals to fall asleep, was what attracted him. He was fully aware that the story, like the newspaper website itself, was a complete fabrication; nothing more than a means of communicating with the Inter-Services Intelligence apparatus.

His online comment read:

> *Here's to brave young girls. Perhaps they are tired after their exertions in the mountains. Shouldn't they return to their homes and the proper life of women?*
> *— Uncle Dari*

What he was really asking was more serious: he and his group were under surveillance; their activities were known to the unbelievers; and was it not time to abandon their mission?

Firoz appeared beside him.

"What is your will, Dada?"

"To do my duty. But I am concerned about the Americans. They are tracking us. We have not been able to elude them. So I am asking advice from our friends at home."

"Are their words wise?"

"I hope so. I hope they are wise enough to understand our predicament." He ran a hand through his white hair. "Perhaps it is time to fade away. We have already done much and learned much. There will be other times and other opportunities."

Firoz stiffened. "Dada, with respect, I am ashamed to hear you speak so. We must not abandon our work. I cannot believe that our superiors will allow it."

Golay looked hurt. "Firoz, ever the warrior."

He clicked the *reload* button on his web browser. A new comment now appeared beneath his own:

> *Uncle Dari betrays his adherence to the old ways and customs of our people. We must find our path in the modern world. I truly wish this young girl and her likeminded friends to continue in their humane work for the good of our sacred nation.*
> *— Aladdin123*

Golay read the comment and closed his laptop. He growled, stood up, and stalked about the room. "So it is ordered — we must continue. I am worried, Firoz. Little good can come of this foolhardy directive."

Firoz was undaunted. "You are right to worry, Dada. You are always right. But there is a solution to our problems. Those who pester us are few. We must go on the offensive. Lure the Americans into a trap. Eliminate them."

Golay halted mid-stride. He stared at the ceiling.

"Perhaps . . . perhaps you are right." He grinned, anticipating a new game with new rules. "We must make a plan. Then we shall see."

▼

On the other side of town, the FULTAP team was back in the Days Inn, and Bagwell was on the phone with American TV & Appliance.

"Say again?"

He scribbled a note in his notebook.

"Okay, got it. Have a good day." He ended the call.

Marianne was slouching on the little sofa in their "executive suite."

"So, those kids are sending an 'electromagnetic pulse'? Why lie? That guy, Isaacson, he's on our side."

Bagwell's mind was elsewhere. "Hmm? What?"

"Electromagnetic ... pulse." Marianne emphasized each word with undisguised disdain.

"Oh that. Well, who knows — if some scientist gets a grant and studies hard enough, maybe we'll find out that's what a spell amounts to."

"Are you kidding?"

"Sure that's not the case?" he contended with cynical authority.

Marianne gave him the flinty look of a very bored soldier.

"There's also this — Colonel Isaacson is a dunce. And the rule, my dear young adept, which I failed to follow, is — never show your cards."

"Not even to your friends?"

"Only your partners in crime. I made a mistake at Hancock."

He studied his notebook.

"Here's what we've got: Golay is an ISI operative. Firoz is an ISI hitter. Both of them have been in service for twenty years or more. First in India, then in Afghanistan, Yemen, and the U.K. Those kids — they're the mystery. They are not on anyone's radar. As far as TV & App knows, they are Muslim children with unusual abilities discovered by this man Golay. They arrived here via Canada on student visas, with Golay as their sponsor, based on his appointment to UCLA. Firoz is listed as their caregiver. How sweet."

"Whoever they are, they're trouble," said Sergeant Sarzo, opening a can of beer liberated from the refreshment center. "For the record, I am not sensing them. Looks like they've skipped town."

"And we have no idea where they are, much less what they're up to now," grumbled Marianne.

Bagwell re-examined his notes. "We have a list of probable targets. Not that many drone operations, remember."

"Right," she said. "That list will burn up a lot of jet fuel."

She rose from the couch and withdrew into the bathroom. At the mirror she dug around in her bag and held up the badge that once belonged to her cantankerous police chief. In the other hand she clasped her stone talisman. She tightened her grip on both objects.

"Hey you!" she hooted.

Nothing happened right away. As the seconds passed she backed away from the mirror, anticipating the shock of her virtual visitor's arrival.

When her image began to ripple, and her ghost bloomed into view, she gasped involuntarily.

"Ahh! I never get used to this."

"What's on your mind today, Agent Broomhandle?" said the voice in her mind.

"This case — these damn kids and their spells — we've lost them. What should we do?"

"How should I know?"

"Come on, you were the best cop I ever met. What about it?"

"Try being a cop yourself — I seem to remember you were sworn, although I often wonder why. Ask yourself — three children and an old man traveling together. Who would notice?"

Marianne was silent.

"Well, who?"

"Um, who? The person who would notice would be . . . um, wait . . . hotel clerks!"

"Don't give up that Placerville job, you might get good at it."

Marianne winced. "Yeah, I know, like you once told me — someday, far in the future."

"Is that all? May I go?"

"I don't think I could stop you. But I do have a question."

The ghostly image appeared to stifle a yawn.

"Shoot."

"How do I know this isn't all happening inside my head, some sort of weird schizophrenia or something?"

"Don't get skeptical on me, Miss Not-So-Normal. You've seen plenty of evidence."

"But it could all be something one part of my brain told another part, without me actually knowing . . . here in the middle, if you know what I mean."

"I don't."

Nor did she expect that he did. She was shy about her real question and wanted to ask it in a roundabout way.

"All right then, how about this: My dad sees auras. He can tell how others feel about him. For some reason, he knows that, deep down, I can't forgive him for leaving when I was a kid. How do I get over this hump? It's a big one."

"I don't worry about human frailties anymore."

"Lucky you."

"And I am not your father."

"Thank God, one's enough."

"Tell the man your troubles. I'm pretty sure he loves you. He'll listen."

"You sound like *Ask Abigail.*" she griped.

Her ghost did not reply. He was gone. Marianne swore under her breath, left the bathroom, and resumed her seat by the motel window.

"Ray, here's a thought."

Bagwell looked up from the photographic prints he was studying. "You know," he mused, rattling the glossies, "that diagram we've got is pretty crude. I can't pin down the next target."

"Forget the diagram. Five foreigners — an old man, a strange woman, and three little kids check into a motel. Who would notice?"

"Are you telling a joke?"

"Seriously, who would notice?"

Bagwell opened his mouth to object, then stopped himself. He raised a finger to grant her point, dropped the photos, and pressed a call button on his phone.

"American TV & Appliance," intoned a robotic voice. "How may I direct your call?"

"Customer service please."

Pause.

"FULTAP here. Need an assist on a shot, can do?"

Pause.

"Here's the drill — poll clerks at all motels in Alamogordo, New Mexico, and surrounding environs. See if anyone remembers checking in an old man and three kids, not citizens of our fair land."

Pause.

"Oh, and while you're at it, maybe see if the Rajput credit card pops up again."

Pause.

"I'll stand by."

He hung up.

"Still the cop, I guess, huh?" he mumbled, feeling stupid.

"Sometimes," said Marianne. "When I, uh, concentrate."

49

AN HOUR LATER the FULTAP team was at Motel 6 on the southern edge of the city, standing in a pair of adjoining guest rooms. Rooms that were paid for, as American TV & Appliance had quickly learned, with Habib Rajput's credit card. The place was a mess. Fast food wrappers and soft drink containers everywhere. Couch cushions thrown around. Chalk drawings on the walls.

Bagwell studied one of those drawings. It consisted of a pair of large boxes, each one almost square. Occupying the lower left-hand corner of the left-hand box was an X ringed by multiple chalk circles. An arrow shot across from the middle of the right-hand box to point at the mark.

"Looks like they're headed for Arizona," he said.

Marianne was checking photos of the Placerville diagram for comparison. "This map was made by the same people," she declared.

"Those kids," said Sergeant Sarzo.

"I sure wish they could draw better," said Bagwell. "It would make our job so much easier."

Marianne walked slowly around, peering at the tourist flyers, restaurant menus, and other pieces of paper scattered everywhere. She followed the casual discards into the other room. There, lying near the TV set, was a road map. She picked it up.

"Hey, guys . . ."

Marianne handed the map to Bagwell. He opened it to reveal the highways, byways, and population centers of the American Southwest. Sierra Vista, a small city near Arizona's Mexican border, had been boldly circled by a magic marker.

"Fort Huachuca is just west of Sierra Vista," he said, snapping a finger against the map. "Beep."

"Let's go," urged Marianne. They're driving, we're flying, we can beat them to the punch."

"Right, lemme call our ride."

Dad had other ideas.

"Not so fast, folks. To me, this doesn't smell good. These people are aware of us. How do we know they didn't drop this 'clue' on purpose?"

Bagwell idly kicked an empty soda can against the wall. "We don't."

"Worse, my daughter, Agent Broomhandle here, already got knocked cold three times. And that wisp she conjured didn't even curl the opposition's hair."

"What are you suggesting? We can't give up."

"Of course not. But we need to tune up the band."

"How's that?"

"We need some firepower to throw at those kids. First, to stop them. Then to put them out of business."

"A spell to negate their powers? There's nothing in the book, I looked," said Marianne.

"I looked too," said her father. "We'll have to make one up."

Bagwell flopped down in a chair. "We already tried that. Our efforts were not rewarded."

"So we try again. As I understand things, spells aren't magic in themselves. Their purpose is to focus the mind of an adept. Some real person once wrote the spells we've already got. We'll just be making another contribution to family lore."

"What are we looking for? What's the gist?" Bagwell was clearly hoping to dodge the task.

Sergeant Sarzo turned to his daughter. "You're up, Angel."

Marianne thought for a while. "Okay, it's like this. These things always invoke some kind of power, that's number one. Number two, we need to glue it to the speaker — me, I guess. And three, we need to announce the purpose."

Bagwell waggled his head back and forth, dismally trying to absorb the outline. "One, two, three," he grumped.

"That's about it."

Sergeant Sarzo looked at his watch. "While you're thinking, Marianne and I are going to find a shop that deals in witchcraft."

"We are?"

"We need datura blossoms."

"We do?"

"Your book explains how to conjure a demon in fire. You need to practice up before we get in another fight."

"Oh, no I don't."

Sergeant Sarzo regarded his daughter sternly. "Yes, you do. It's our only real chance to stop the enemy."

▼

After consulting the white pages, the yellow pages, Yahoo!, and Google Maps, they found a moldy little shop advertising witch's supplies. A sign above the door read:

Wiccan Wares

It was on the east side of town, an isolated cabin almost into the foothills. Marianne was nearly overpowered by the funky vibe emanating from the place. Small animal carcasses were hanging from the ceiling. Various biological objects of uncertain origin were pickling in jars on the shelves. Semi-precious stones and meteorite fragments were on display in tall glass cases. Feathers from half a dozen supernaturally important bird species were fastened to velvet-covered bulletin boards with pushpins. The odor was dank, hinting at marijuana. She forced herself to navigate through the jungle of oddities to the counter.

"Datura blossoms?" she asked the proprietor, a jovial older man, bearded, not quite obese. He pointed across the room.

On the far wall, among the other botanicals, were several baggies containing dried datura blossoms. Marianne selected one of them.

"Cat hair?" she asked.

"Hahaha, very funny," was the proprietor's response.

"What's funny?"

"Oh nothing. We don't have any eye of newt either, hahaha. That will be twenty bucks for the flowers, please."

Sergeant Sarzo paid the man.

"Are you looking for a talisman? I've got every kind you could think of, right over there in those drawers. My regular customers are unanimous in recommending their powers. On sale this week."

"We need to find a cat," said Marianne.

The proprietor angled his head and regarded his customers with a quizzical eye. He seemed to be gauging them, vaguely aware that the young woman and her father were . . . different.

"Well now, I see you're serious," he concluded. "You might try the Denny's downtown. Some animal lover working there throws out scraps now and then. That's where the feral cats hang out."

▼

Behind Denny's, the dumpster was full to overflowing, and the lid was tilted back, possibly left open by the alleged animal lover. Several cats were exploring the bags and boxes piled up there, digging for bits of food.

Marianne had a pair of scissors from her toilet kit. She advanced warily toward the open bin, ready to clip.

"Maybe they're eating the remains of our dinner last night," she said.

Sergeant Sarzo kept himself hidden behind her, then suddenly darted forward and seized one of the scrawny felines.

"Cut! Cut! Cut!" he said, wrestling with a blur of claws.

Marianne managed to snip a tuft of hair from the cat's tail. Dad dropped the animal, which scooted under the dumpster, yowling in outrage.

"Now blood," he said, giving his daughter a significant look.

"Menstrual blood, that's what you're talking about, right?"

"That's the tradition."

Marianne's mouth twisted in distaste. "Screw tradition — I think it's just another focus tool. The last time I tried anything like this, I skipped the blood part, and still almost got myself killed."

"But the recipe —"

"For your information — *Dad* — my period isn't due for another couple of weeks. Forget it."

"Okaaaay . . . "

▼

The Days Inn, where the FULTAP team was staying, backed onto open desert. The nearest building to the east, some sort of featureless concrete box, was at least two hundred yards away. At sunset, Sergeant Sarzo led Marianne out across the parking lot and into the scrub. After searching carefully, he located an isolated creosote bush. He kicked at the small plants sprouting nearby, scuffing them out of existence.

"Here we go — we can light this up without starting a brushfire."

He opened a bottle of hand sanitizer and poured it over the bush.

"What are you doing?" asked Marianne, not at all convinced that their little exercise was a good idea.

Sergeant Sarzo held up the empty bottle. "This stuff is seventy percent alcohol. Got your ingredients ready?"

She nodded glumly.

He held a lighted match to a glob of sanitizer hanging from one of the branches. After a few seconds the alcohol caught fire. Soon the entire bush was engulfed. In the fading evening light, the flames ballooned upward. A grave danger to Marianne's eyes.

She watched the bush consume its alcoholic tinder.

"Come on, do your stuff," urged Dad.

Marianne dutifully removed a plastic bag from a pocket on her hoodie, dug out a pinch of ground-up datura blossom, and tossed it into the bush.

Foom!

The fire doubled in size. She picked out a few strands of cat hair and threw them in as well.

Hiss!

The flames leaped up to her chest.

"Say the words," ordered Dad.

Marianne clutched her stone talisman and opened her spell book with trembling fingers. Her voice shook as she read aloud:

> *From searing flame bring forth the beast,*
> *The creature that on foes shall feast.*
> *Behold his fangs and claws and eyes,*
> *The spirit that my burning buys.*
> *Now manifest at my command;*
> *For witch's work, you're my right hand!*

Father and daughter watched the fire. At first, they saw nothing but a burning bush. After a minute or so, however, Marianne thought she could detect hot spots in the flame — a pair of otherworldly eyes regarding her. She shivered.

"See that?"

"See what?"

"Eyes! Something is looking at us."

"In the fire?"

"Where else?"

Suddenly the fire blazed up above Marianne's head. The eyes rose within the flames, taking their place in something like an incandescent head. Crude arms bulged outward. Sparkling claws formed. The fiery apparition flailed this way and that, a supernatural predator eager for prey.

Sergeant Sarzo, full of curiosity, stepped forward as Marianne backed away. The strange being watched her move. Legs appeared. It stepped out of the bush and lumbered toward her. With each step, small fires broke out under its feet.

"Do you see it?" asked Marianne.

"I see a blur in the air," he replied. "A smoky blur."

Marianne kept backing away. The power spirit took a swing at her. Red-hot claws singed her hoodie.

"Come to meeeee . . ." rasped a smoky voice.

She panicked and ran — but after just a couple of strides she tripped over a pincushion cactus, came down hard, and somersaulted into a sagebrush plant. The power spirit advanced upon her prostrate form, claws at the ready.

"Get back! Keep away from me!" she howled. "Stop where you are, I *command* you!"

But the apparition kept coming. It bent down over her.

"You are for meeeee . . ." it gloated.

"Dad!" pleaded Marianne.

Sergeant Sarzo couldn't really see everything that was happening. But his daughter's terror jerked him into action. He ripped off the light jacket he was wearing to ward off the evening chill and threw it over the burning bush, smothering the fire.

The apparition disappeared. All the little fires it set on the desert floor vanished along with it. Sergeant Sarzo pulled his jacket off the bush, releasing a cloud of black smoke into the evening air.

"You okay?" He held out a hand. She grasped it. He yanked her upright.

"Holy crap," she said.

"What was that thing?" he wanted to know.

"A power spirit, I'm guessing. Once it manifested I had absolutely no authority, no control."

"I thought you did this before. That's what you told me."

"Once. Last year. I was tricked into it, remember?"

"Same result?"

"Pretty much."

"That's odd. Your aura is strong. You just need practice."

"Ouch. Not until I pull all these cactus needles out of my hide."

Sergeant Sarzo slapped at his still-smoldering jacket, knocking sparks out of the burn holes.

She smiled. "Thanks for saving my ass."

"You're welcome." He paused, then added, "Anything for my only daughter."

Marianne took this as a conversational opening.

"Look, Dad, I'm having a hard time with you," she said, teasing a thorn out of her sleeve. "Why is that? Why can't I let bygones be bygones?"

He studied his ruined jacket, then turned his dark eyes on her. "I don't really know. It's partly my fault, I suppose."

"My fault is your fault?"

He pondered the matter while staring at the darkening sky. "Stars are coming out. Jupiter over there in the Twins. Mars in Virgo." He pointed at the planets.

"Yes? And?"

He looked at his daughter, looked away again. "I probably should tell you about Aunt Imogen."

Marianne colored. "Something I don't know? About you and her? You and her and Mom? I've collected plenty of hints."

"Now we're getting somewhere," said he, with an ironic nod.

"Where? Where are we getting?" she demanded.

"See — you're as hot as your demon. I understand. But you know, Gen couldn't have children, or didn't want them, anyway. Probably both. And I wanted . . . I wanted — you."

This was news to Marianne. She thought about the meaning. "So, you and Aunt Gen . . ."

"Gen introduced me to her sister. I didn't exactly cheat on your mother — rest her soul — with some floozy I met later."

"So, first you hooked up with Aunt Gen. But then you married Mom. And, *you bastard*, you didn't stop seeing your old girlfriend."

"No, I didn't. That's where you've got me. Guilty as charged."

"Boy oh boy . . ." Marianne paced an angry circle around a yucca plant.

"When was the last time you saw your aunt?" asked the sergeant.

"Just after I started cop school. She sold her Dairy Queen and moved away."

"Yes, to Macon, Georgia."

Marianne stopped pacing. "Wait a minute — are you telling me . . . you *still* see her?"

"As often as possible. FULTAP keeps me on the road a lot of the time."

"Jesus Christ Almighty! You live together!"

"No, we don't. Imogen is an independent woman. She owns an Arby's franchise, has a nice house, does well for herself."

"I bet."

"You should pay a visit. She'd love to see you. She loves you."

"Oh fuck. Tell me — it can't get worse — was all this going on back when I was, like, a teenager living in her house?"

"Never there. Remember her DQ Conventions in Reno?"

"Shit, I knew it. I knew something was up. Okay, here comes the big question — ready?"

"Fire away."

"Were you ever in love with Mom?"

"It's hard to explain how your heart works. But the short answer is, yes, always."

Marianne removed the last of the cactus needles from her clothes and dusted herself off.

"I'm cold. Let's get inside before I die of exposure," she said.

Sergeant Sarzo stretched an arm toward their motel.

"After you, Angel."

Part SIX

50

OFFICER OTIS was often bored with the routine demands of Placerville police work. Today was no exception. In the early morning hours he arrested a woman so drunk that she couldn't find her way home. Later on he stopped a red light runner on Main Street. After lunch he drowned a cook fire in the squalid homeless camp at the east end of town. At four o'clock he took a bewildered old man who was raving about the evils of tourism off the streets. After depositing the fellow in the Marshall Medical Center on a 5150 hold, he found himself at loose ends. He started to think about Marianne's U-Haul truck, the one with the picture of a spider on the side.

If that truck was still missing, as Wade Gawley's recent call had indicated, and if it had been used in a series of burglaries, as now seemed likely, maybe it had been abandoned. And if it had been abandoned, where would a guilty burglar abandon the damn thing?

"In a parking lot!" he said aloud.

But that didn't help much. Otis was perfectly well aware that parking lots in the nearby foothill towns and malls numbered in the hundreds. A needle in a haystack situation.

With that gloomy assessment his speculations fizzled out, so he drove to the Coffee Depot and ordered up an Americano at the drive-through window. While he was waiting for it, he thought some more. If a U-Haul truck was left in a commercial parking lot, hidden in plain sight among a sea of customers' cars, after a while store management might notice, and they might become annoyed. Most of those lots had signs threatening to tow vehicles not parked for shopping purposes.

His drink arrived. "Here you are, sir," said the attendant.

"The truck was towed!" Otis exclaimed.

"I'm sure," said the attendant. "You have a nice day."

Otis grabbed the cup, backed his patrol car around the building, and parked beside the attendant's old Honda. There he consulted his smartphone and his laptop. Pretty soon, with the help of Google Maps and the police department records clerk, he had compiled a list of towing companies serving the foothills.

A dozen phone calls later, Otis thought he had his truck. The office manager at Wrangler Towing Services in nearby Shingle Springs seemed to remember bringing in a U-Haul truck with their big rig. Their storage yard was a large one, she couldn't leave the office, and she didn't know if it was still impounded.

Otis flipped on his code three lights. He whipped his black & white cruiser across Main Street, bringing traffic to a screeching halt, turned west onto U.S. Route 50, and sped downhill toward Shingle Springs.

Wrangler Towing was located on Durock Road, just off the highway at the edge of town. In addition to impounded vehicles, the company rented out storage space for idle motorhomes and trailers. The office manager opened the gate for him.

"Be my guest," she said. "I'll be at my desk if you need anything."

Otis found himself in a maze, with his view blocked by tall white slabs of recreational metal and fiberglass in every direction. He wandered around and between the collected RVs. Here and there he came across an impounded automobile. It took him fifteen minutes and many missteps to scour the yard. But finally, wedged in between enormous fifth-wheelers with pull-out bedrooms the size of hotel suites, he spotted a U-Haul truck. As he edged around it, the supergraphic decal came into view — and there was Marianne's yellowish spider, boldly splashed across the cargo box. The illustration was six feet high. It showed a monstrous animal with eight long legs, and sure enough, on its slender abdomen was a perfect smiley face. *Theridion grallator,* looking big enough to attack a city.

"Happy fucking Godzilla," he said.

The truck was filthy. In addition to the accumulation of dust and bird droppings, the sides were covered with mud.

He checked the driver's door. Locked. He checked the cargo door. Locked as well.

He looked underneath. More mud, and a tangle of vegetation stuck to the suspension.

He took a dozen photos of the vehicle, from every angle he could think of. Then he wrote down the registration, a California plate.

"Got the keys, by any chance? I'd like to check the paperwork," he told the office manager.

"Sorry, that one came in like you see it. Carl, our tow guy, opened it up with a slim jim to release the brakes, of course. We don't want to cause any damage. But then we locked it up. There were no papers, or we'd have them on file," she said, giving her hair a little flip.

"Let's open her back up. Do a double check. This vehicle was involved in a crime."

"Well, you wonder about things, don't you? A U-Haul truck? Who would leave that sitting around? But I can't authorize a break-in."

"I'll need a warrant."

She nodded sympathetically.

"You'll need a warrant."

Otis did his best to contain his temper. "Okay, I'll get one. But listen here, under no circumstances will anyone else tamper with this truck, understand? Placerville police business."

"All right," she gulped. "Please take it off our hands. Legally. We don't store vehicles for free, you know." She started scribbling on a notepad.

"And if anyone approaches you about it, you are to call my department right away, got it?"

He wrote the telephone number on her pad.

She tore off the sheet and stuck it on her reminder board with a little magnet.

"Got it."

51

ON THE FULTAP JET, outbound from Holloman, Bagwell was
ending a telephone call.

"That was General Weaver," he said. "I briefed him, he blessed our
trajectory."

Marianne pulled her eyes away from the rugged southwest landscape
thirty thousand feet below the airplane. "Is he actually on board, or did
you just out-talk him?"

Bagwell registered a thin smile. "You can't out-talk Vernon. He's got his
doubts. He's giving us some rope."

"More rope, you mean," said she, with grim resignation.

"Yup. More. A few feet."

Bagwell punched buttons on his phone, making another call, this one to
Fort Huachuca.

"Ramirez here. Speak to me."

"Colonel? Major Bagwell, FULTAP, on our way to you. Whatcha got
down there?"

"Who did you say? *Fulltap?*"

"That's right, we're tasked to investigate and interdict a sabotage
operation. I'm following up a call from General Weaver. You heard from
him, yes?"

"Uh, Weaver . . . my exec took the call. What the hell is *Fulltap?*"

"We're a special IC unit constituted under joint authority of the DNI
and MI. Someone should have briefed you."

"Hang on, I have some notes here . . . okay, FULTAP it is. You say
sabotage?"

"That's right, sir. It qualifies as an ongoing terror attack. Small group,
localized, but we have reason to believe they are headed for you."

"Well, damn."

"My question this morning is — have you had any casualties in your
drone operations?"

"Someone's after my drones?"

"Yes, sir."

The colonel laughed. "We run border patrol support, as you no doubt
know. Yesterday, one of my pilots briefly lost his concentration, I guess

you'd call it."

Bagwell leaned forward in his seat. "And the result?"

"This is the good part. He was driving a Reaper. It lost fifteen thousand feet of altitude, buzzed a coyote and a couple of dozen illegals, scared them the hell out of some tunnel they were excavating, and sent them running back to *MEH-hee-co.*"

"The pilot recovered?"

"Oh yes, he's fine."

"Take that man off duty, Colonel. He may well have experienced the effects of a *directed electromagnetic pulse.* Have a doctor check him out, just as if he suffered a concussion."

"Are you kidding? I'm thinking of writing up a commendation. Adding his little maneuver into our regular flight ops."

Bagwell groaned unhappily. "As you think best, Colonel. But put some guards around your flight teams. Watch your perimeter. The group I'm trying to stop has a range weapon."

Sergeant Sarzo was listening to Bagwell's side of the call. "Another partial score for the bad guys," he surmised. "I think they have to get close for full effect."

"So they haven't wiggled through the fence?" asked Marianne.

"Not yet, anyway."

The copilot emerged from the flight deck with doughnuts and coffee. "Descent into Davis-Monthan in one half-hour," he said.

After an interlude for snacks, Bagwell stood up and arched his back. He reseated himself, dug through his briefcase, and, looking very ill at ease, brought out a sheet of paper.

"Listen up, you two. I spent some time with your book and cobbled some spells together."

"What kind of spells?"

"The one you asked for, primarily — negating magical powers."

Marianne took the paper and read the incantation scrawled there.

"Not bad — on paper. Who knows if it will work?"

"Let me see," said Sergeant Sarzo.

Bagwell pulled another sheet out of his case and handed it over.

"You'll notice I also put together alternate spells for sleeping and conjuring."

The two adepts studied his little poems.

"I'll be damned, flowery, but they look okay," said the sergeant, allowing himself to express cautious approval. "Like they were written by some old-time master."

"They were. Parts, anyway. A lot of the spells in that book repeat a bunch of standard phrases. I just followed the pattern. Let's hope they fool the bad guys."

"We don't want to fool anyone. We want them to work."

"Right, you're right, that's the important thing."

Marianne wasn't listening. She was already curled up in her seat, memorizing.

52

THE RITEWAY INN, situated in the northwest corner of Sierra Vista, was a charmless blockhouse catering to Fort Huachuca contractors, unsuccessful salesmen, and the occasional immigrant of doubtful status. Darius Golay and his little group of saboteurs were holed up there. Despite their proximity to Fort Huachuca and Libby Army Airfield, the old man had no plans for further attacks. Instead, he was on the internet, trading messages on *The Islamabad Daily Register's* website.

The latest comment on girls and their goats disturbed him:

> *Some have doubted the work of our brave goatherds. Inshallah, if God wills it, even children can restore the health of animals. Such is our heritage — to work tirelessly, sacrificing personal comfort, and thus to bring blessings upon our great nation.*
> *— Aladdin123*

"Ahh! This Aladdin fellow knows *nothing!* He is an idiot who steps in mud when he thinks it is sand." Golay's fingers pounded the keyboard of his little laptop. He wrote:

> *But wise women wear the veil, cook for their husbands, and do not venture into the marketplace unattended.*
> *— Uncle Dari*

A minute later Aladdin123's answer appeared:

> *It is not enough to cook. A wife must be faithful, otherwise she is of no value.*

Golay slammed the lid of his computer shut. He stood and roved around the tiny room, waving his arms and growling.

"Now we are threatened! We, the faithful servants! The ones with ideas! The ones with initiative! The ones in harm's way!"

Firoz hurried from her games with the children and took his arm.

"Dada, be calm. Surely we have both been in worse difficulties."

Golay clenched his fists.

"Yes, we must do our best. First, our pursuers. We must dispose of them. Then the drones. It must be as ISI wishes. We cannot fail. But not here. Here, on the border, the guards are too many. The children cannot put them all to sleep."

▼

After a late night arrival following a long drive south from Tucson, the FULTAP team was waking up in the cushy Hampton Inn across town.

Marianne was dressed by seven. She knocked on Bagwell's door.

"Yeah?" came a hoarse croak.

"Ray, I'm off to confession. I need the car."

"Where?"

"Saint Andrew the Apostle, it's way over near the base. Give me the keys, I'll be back before you eat your waffle."

The door opened. Bagwell was tucking his shirt into his pants. He dangled the keys.

"Have you thought about this? Sense anyone?"

"Yes and no. I'll be careful."

"Don't fuck around over there. And don't tell the priest anything he doesn't need to know."

"Mum's the word."

▼

Saint Andrew's, the only Catholic church in the city, was a huge stucco box looking more like a factory than a cathedral. It was located in a northwest neighborhood, not far from the Riteway Inn and Golay's supernatural saboteurs.

Rafiq climbed onto Yasmin's bed and jumped up and down.

"Yaz, it's her! The American! She is not far away."

Yasmin's eye popped open. "Stop jumping, Rafi!" She stared at the ceiling, stuck fingers into her eyes to clear away the sandman's work. "Yes, I feel her too."

They ran down the hall to Golay's room and pounded on his door.

"Dada! Dada! The American is near!"

Golay shook off his nightmares, eased his arthritic old frame out of bed, and shuffled across the room. He opened the door.

"What? It is very early."

"Dada! The American policewoman!"

They were pointing. Golay craned his neck and looked up and down the hallway, half expecting to see Marianne marching toward them.

"Wake Firoz. We must act."

▼

Marianne parked the FULTAP van in front of the massive Church of Saint Andrew the Apostle. Relieving the building's unimaginative design was a rounded steeple on the corner, vaguely echoing the Spanish missions of another age. A ceramic tile façade enclosed the arched entryway.

Inside, the walls were white. A fine wooden ceiling devoid of visible support ran the length of the interior. Statues of saints were standing watch in niches along each side. Chandeliers of silvery metal hung from the rafters. Lights on their curling arms and dozens more embedded in the ceiling gave the place a luminous ambience, quite unlike the warm dark wood of her own church in Placerville or the cold stonework of the chapel in Sarzeau.

She had to ask where the confession booth was located. Once inside, with the door shut, she knelt at the screen and crossed herself.

"Forgive me, Father, for I have sinned. My last confession was, let's see here, six months ago . . . or maybe more . . . make it eight months."

"You can always be reconciled with God. Are you truly sorry for your sins?" asked a soft voice in a faintly Hispanic accent.

"Yes I am. Since then I . . . uh . . . I have had unclean thoughts, I have taken the Lord's name in vain" — she paused, then blurted — "and I'm wondering if it's a sin or something if I use my magical powers."

This abrupt departure from the standard list of ordinary peccadilloes resulted in a long silence. Then the voice said, "Tell me about your powers."

"Ready for weirdness? I think I'm what you call an adept. For the past couple of years I've been seeing a ghost in the mirror. Not all the time — he comes and goes. Now I find out, if I relax, I can see other adepts' auras. And, this is the part that bothers me — it looks like I can cast spells."

"Really? You're serious?"

"Very."

"This is . . . unusual," said the voice, obviously wrestling with something beyond priestly expertise.

"You ever hear of anyone else like me?"

"Only in fairy tales. Pardon me, but have you sought medical advice?"

"Ha. You mean, see a shrink? No."

"Counseling is often very helpful. I think you should consider it."

"Yeah, you're skeptical. Who wouldn't be? But counseling? You're it,

Father. So . . . let's say what I'm telling you is true. For argument's sake, okay? The question is — can I cast a spell without, you know, committing a mortal sin?"

"What kind of spell would that be?"

"Things from a book I inherited. Waking people up, kids out of line mostly, keeping awake myself, negating evil powers, stuff like that."

She couldn't bring herself to mention the conjuring of power spirits.

"I'm not sure what to tell you. No servant of the Church knows anything about *actual spells*. Just remember the basics — all good things come from Almighty God. If He has conferred powers upon you, whatever they might be, then He must have a reason, and you must use them in His name, for good purposes only. Do you understand?"

"I think so. Stay on the good side."

"That's right. If you take my advice, as someone who would be your friend, then don't use your special abilities any more than you have to. They sound dangerous."

"Roger that."

"For your venial sins, ten Hail Marys. Now . . . through the ministry of the Church, may God give you pardon and peace, and I absolve you from your sins in the name of the Father, and of the Son, and of the Holy Spirit."

"Amen."

▼

It was still early when Marianne left the church. On her way back to the Hampton Inn she got to thinking about power spirits and was reconsidering the possible value of mixing some of her blood into a conjuring attempt. The Safeway on East Fry Boulevard was open, so she parked and entered. The store was immense, and practically empty. She wandered the aisles, looking for pharmaceutical supplies, hoping to find an employee to point her in the right direction.

▼

Meanwhile, the saboteurs were slouching in their little Ford Fiesta in front of the Riteway Inn, waiting for a sign. Suddenly Yasmin pounded the front seats, alerting the adults that the American policewoman was on the move. Golay turned the key and they motored slowly through a series of back streets, working their way toward the center of the city.

"Where now?" asked Golay.

"She was moving. Now she has stopped. We are getting closer."

The Fiesta turned onto East Fry Boulevard. As they passed the Safeway, Yasmin began bouncing up and down.

"Here! She is here! In this store, right here!"

Golay hit the brakes and turned into the parking lot.

"Now, take care," said he. "This American adept may be able to sense us. Calm yourselves, no frantic thoughts. Let your minds float free — and then . . ."

"Yes, Dada."

"I will station myself near the entrance. When Yasmin puts her to sleep, I will carry her to the car, and we can finish our task elsewhere. Firoz?"

"Understood, Dada. It is a good plan."

▼

Marianne didn't see another customer in the store, but she did encounter a young employee stocking the detergent shelves.

"Excuse me — I'm looking for one of those diabetic blood sugar things. You know, prick your finger, do a test?"

English was not the man's first language, and it took him a few seconds to decode Marianne's request. She was about to repeat it when he pointed toward the rear of the store.

"*Pasillo veinte* — aisle twenty — *caso está cerrado. Hable con el farmacéutico.*"

"Twenty? *Gracias.*"

Marianne hiked the length of the housewares aisle, rounded a corner, and not having had any breakfast, was instantly distracted by the pastry displays near the deli counter. She thought briefly about buying something for FULTAP team snacks, then decided against the idea.

She passed a display of pay-as-you-go cell phones, and that stopped her. She couldn't resist the chance to reconnect with her personal life, so she picked up the cheapest one, paid at the customer service counter, and dialed a number.

"*County Courier.* This is Wagstaff."

"Hi, Tom."

"Yo, M — ! I've been worrying about you. Where the hell are you now?"

"I'm not supposed to reveal that secret classified information to civilians. Uh, think Mexican food. Somewhere like that."

"Arizona?"

"Can't say yes, can't say no."

"Oh babe, you are terrible."

"How are things at the paper?"

"Tomorrow's issue is printing as we speak."

"And how's your, um, assistant these days, Ms. Hamilton?"

"Yeah, well, you'll like this — she and that guy from Placerville are weekending up in Tahoe City. I think he owns a shop up there."

"Nice to hear some good news for a change. We're still on the hunt, tracking bad guys. Well, naughty kids, anyway."

"Are you safe?"

"More or less."

"Listen here — if you get killed, I will never forgive you."

"But I'll be dead, so you won't have to."

"Except, you might come back as a ghost to haunt me."

"I'll come back soon, I promise. Alive and warm-blooded, how's that?"

"Can't wait."

Firoz followed Yasmin into the store. While the young teenager checked the aisles for their target, she happened to pass by the pet supply section.

Klik! — klik! — klik!

There, hanging from a display hook, a nylon dog leash attracted her attention.

Klik! — klik! — klik!

Although not in the plan, she picked it up and tested its strength by snapping it taut between her hands. She murmured satisfaction — now she had herself a makeshift garrotte.

Klik! — klik! — klik!

Her peculiar sonar system told her that the store was almost completely free of customers at this early hour. *Inshallah,* why not finish the job right here in the store?

▼

Marianne wandered past the collection of cheap electronic goods, turned a corner, and discovered that aisle twenty, with its pharmacy and beauty aids, was far away on the other side of the vast supermarket. She started toward her goal without a care, humming a little tune. Gradually she became aware of a reddish sensation in the back of her mind.

"Whoa, what's that about?"

She slowed and adopted the tactic of peeking down each aisle before crossing. Not a soul was in sight. But at aisle fifteen she spotted a slender teenage girl coming toward her. She was wearing a head scarf, proper Muslim attire. Marianne was shocked to see her. Already the girl's right hand was rising, palm out. Yasmin? That's what Dad had called one of his tormentors.

Marianne planted her feet, raised her own hand, and muttered a formula especially prepared by Bagwell for a moment like this:

> *Mighty hand, hold up thy shield;*
> *May my awareness never yield*
> *To those who wish to close my eyes*
> *And claim my wit as their own prize.*
> *Harmful spells cast all awry;*
> *This is my power, so say I . . .*

Yasmin marched forward, muttering in Urdu. She thrust out her hand emphatically as she closed the distance between them.

"You American witch — you sleep now!"

The girl's spell hit Marianne like a fist and made her dizzy. She rocked back on her heels, but did not lose consciousness. Yasmin stopped ten feet away and stared in disbelief. She raised both hands and tried her sleep spell again. Marianne felt a wave of confusion pass through her, but it quickly evaporated. She folded her arms.

"You better scoot, kid," she said, "before I put *you* to sleep."

But Yasmin stood her ground. She gesticulated wildly, muttering all the while.

Marianne took a wary step toward her. Yasmin took a step back. Marianne took another step. Yasmin backed away again.

"You know, you're awfully young to be spying on people. Who're you working for? The old man — is he your grandfather?"

The color disappeared from Yasmin's face. She took another step backward.

By now the two were standing at mid-aisle in the seemingly empty store. Marianne was about to reach out and grab her adversary when she registered an odd sound:

Klik! — *klik!* — *klik!*

She turned around. There was Firoz, the woman who killed Captain Pike, tiptoeing toward her with a nylon dog leash held tightly between her hands. A couple more steps and she would have Marianne's neck in a noose.

"You!" exclaimed Marianne, heart suddenly thumping, adrenaline rushing. She reached into her blouse and gripped her stone talisman. It tingled in her hand.

"Stop where you are!" she ordered. "I *command* you!"

Firoz stopped. Her hands dropped to her side. The dog leash went slack.

Marianne bent down and yanked her little Beretta out of its ankle holster. She raised the gun toward Firoz.

"All right, you fucker, listen up —"

> *Close thine eyes and nod thy head;*
> *Make thy way to some soft bed.*
> *Find a dream as if a boat;*
> *Climb aboard, and downstream float.*
> *Sleep now take thee far away,*
> *Far from where my power holds sway!*

Firoz' eyes rolled up in her head, and she slumped to the floor. Bagwell to the rescue again.

"Nooo!" screeched Yasmin. She brushed by Marianne, kneeled beside Firoz, and cradled the older woman in her arms.

▼

Marianne moved off to find the personal products in aisle twenty, where, in consultation with the pharmacist on duty, she selected a small blood glucose tester equipped with a sharp little lancet.

"By the way," she said, affecting the indifference of a busy shopper, "just now as I was walking by, I noticed a woman lying on the floor in aisle fifteen or so. I think she must have fainted. Maybe you should call someone."

53

IN LATE SPRING, grass in the California foothills was already turning a golden brown. But on this grey morning in Placerville the streets were wet. Officer Otis was forced to use windshield wipers on the way to collect his search warrant for the spidery U-Haul truck in Shingle Springs. He was thankful that the late storm would reduce the number of dangerous campfires, picnic fires, cigarette fires, model rocket fires, and what-the-fuck fires he would have to deal with in the coming summer heat.

He was hoping for a minimum of bureaucratic bullshit at the courthouse, but was forced to cool his heels while the clerk checked his authorization. A long hour went by, relieved only by a nasty cup of burned coffee from a dispenser in the hallway, before he had warrant in hand.

He arrived at Wrangler Towing Services just as the office opened up. The previously uncooperative office manager was flipping switches on her office machinery as Otis walked in and presented his papers.

She glanced at the order, reached into a desk drawer, and brought out a slim jim. "Now that you're right with the judge, let's have us a look in that truck," she said.

Otis followed her through the RV maze and watched while she expertly inserted the slim jim down between the glass and metal of the U-Haul's cab door and popped it open.

Otis climbed inside. There was nothing in the glove compartment, but fishing around turned up the rental contract, jammed under the passenger seat. Crumpled and dirty, but otherwise intact. The renter's name was Hank Rogers, with an address at the business park Otis had already searched.

"Looks like we found your truck, Squeek," he said to his absent partner.

The only other item of the slightest interest was a toy dragon made out of Lego bricks that was hanging by a string from the rear-view mirror.

At the rear of the vehicle Otis fingered the padlock on the door latch. "What about the cargo box here?"

"Hold on," said the office manager and marched away to her office.

Otis walked around the truck while he waited for her return. He was struck again by the dried mud and plant material clinging to the grill, the sides, the wheels, the undercarriage.

The office manager was soon back with a heavy-duty pair of bolt cutters. She placed the jaws around the padlock and — *snap!* — cut the shackle in two.

"You're good at that," observed Otis.

"Done it before," she replied.

Otis had a look inside. The interior was empty except for a fancy child's rocking horse lashed to one of the tie downs.

"Aww, how cute is that?" he grunted.

54

DINNER AT DENNY'S . . . again. The pleasures of orange and magenta décor. The comfort of vinyl upholstery. Another Slamburger, another Super Bird, another Grand Slam Breakfast. Hot tea, iced tea, herbal tea. Marianne longed for a beer, but it was not on the menu.

"I don't sense them," said Sergeant Sarzo.

"I might have scared them off," said Marianne through a mouthful of coleslaw. She was starting to get used to the food, a fact of government travel that didn't bother her as much as she thought it should.

"There's an Army base right next door," she continued. "That clicking woman is bad news. We should have called in the troops."

Bagwell disagreed. "And have them all take a nap? Or, better yet, shoot the walls off a supermarket?"

His phone was on the table, optimistically placed for a call from American TV & Appliance. He was ordering an apple crisp for dessert when it buzzed. He answered without excusing himself.

"FULTAP, Bagwell here. Unh-huh. Right. Everywhere. Right. A progression. Right. Three instances. Right. Thanks for the eyes on our target. What? Oh, sure, hang on." He handed the phone to Marianne. "Officer Otis wants to talk to you."

Marianne was mildly surprised. "Hey, Dez, how did you get this number?"

"I worked a deal with Kazmarek, who had a different number that got me to another number that got me to this half-assed fake-o company that got me to you."

"The deal?"

"Overtime again. I will die rich from fatigue."

"What's on your mind?"

"Your truck. I found it. Papers show our mysterious Hank Rogers as the renter."

"Fantastic. Where was it?"

"Towed from a Safeway lot in Cameron Park, wound up impounded down in Shingle Springs."

"Nice sleuthing, buddy."

"No other useful evidence on board, I gotta say, just the rental ticket. But here's the thing — it's covered with mud, it's got plants, reeds or something, stuck all over it."

"Don't let anyone touch that truck until I get back. Don't let anyone claim it. Make sure the company calls you on the slightest hint someone else is interested."

"Hey, ease up, officer. I already told 'em."

"Take care, Dez."

"You too, Squeek."

She put the phone back on the table. Bagwell tapped his fingers on it. His apple crisp was forgotten.

"Before you discussed your high crimes and misdemeanors with Officer Otis there, the diligent technicians at TV & App were reporting three uses of Habib Rajput's credit card. First here in Sierra Vista, to rent one of those CruiseAmerica camper rigs. Another in Tucson for gas and, uh, ice cream. Then a cheap motel in Wickenburg." He dragged a fork across his placemat. "Does this northerly pattern suggest a destination to anyone?"

Sergeant Sarzo downed the last of his Grand Slam. "Vegas," he said.

"It would be nice to arrive first, yes?" Bagwell lifted his phone. "Let's see where our ride can take us."

"Hang on a sec," said the sergeant, leaning forward in their uncomfortable little booth

"What now? Let's get this over with."

"Marianne resisted the sleep spell, commanded that bitch with the dog leash, and sent her to dreamland, too. But she's not ready to take on the whole team."

"Broomer? What do you say?" demanded Bagwell.

"Well, yeah, it's tricky conjuring in fire, tuning the fire, and we haven't even tried my blood tester thing."

"What thing is that?"

Marianne reached into her bag and showed him her blood glucose tester. "It's the reason I stopped into that supermarket."

Bagwell ripped the packaging away, removed the cap exposing a tiny lancet. He poised a finger speculatively near the very sharp tip. "You're diabetic?"

"God, no. I didn't want to use blood, and especially not the sort of blood mentioned in my book — too dangerous. Believe me, I know. But this thing comes with a neat little way to prick a finger."

Bagwell was irked. "We'll be a day late and a dollar short again."

"Our girl put up a good defense," said Dad. "That's progress, but it won't stop them. We need an offense. The book there shows us how, we've just got to learn the drill."

▼

The snowy flanks of the Huachuca mountains were glowing in the twilight of a late spring evening as Sergeant Sarzo led his daughter into the vacant lot near their motel. There was a chill in the high country air.

"Watch out for snakes," he said.

Marianne skipped nervously through the chaparral, dodging thorns, eyeing the ground underneath each bush.

After a hundred yards or so Sergeant Sarzo came to a halt and produced a can of Sterno from a lightweight backpack.

"Okay, far enough. Let's try this." He pried the top off the container and touched a match. An almost invisible blue flame appeared. He placed the thing on a patch of open ground.

"That's not going to keep us very warm," said Marianne.

"No, it's small. That's the whole idea. With luck it will produce a small spirit."

"Do I feel lucky?" she wondered.

"You're going to win the lottery all over again. Got your stuff?"

She held up the little plastic baggie containing a mixture of shredded datura blossoms and cat hair.

"How about you? Got a candle snuffer, just in case?"

Sergeant Sarzo pulled a square of quilted cloth out of his backpack.

"Where'd you find that?"

"Under the bouquet in the motel lobby. They won't miss it."

She nodded uncertainly, inhaled, fidgeted timidly, told herself to get a move on, and finally, with a spasmodic jerk, sprinkled a few flower crumbs and cat hairs over the fire.

Sizzle!

The blue flame turned bright yellow and flickered upward. She jumped back.

"Come on, Angel, you can do this."

"Right . . . yup . . . here we go," she muttered. She unfolded a piece of paper and read off her conjuring spell in a shaky voice.

Whoosh!

The fire spiraled up and became a miniature tornado. Marianne stared at it warily, seemingly hypnotized by the spectacle.

"Okay — now blood — gotta try it," urged her father.

She shook off her doubts, popped the cover off the tiny lancet on her glucose tester, pricked her finger, and shook a droplet of blood into the flames.

Vuuurp!

Blazing eyes and arms erupted. Flaming claws sprang out. The apparition inflated until it towered over Marianne.

"You see this?" she asked in a quavering voice.

"I do, kind of. I see a column of sparks," said her father. "Amazing — must be your blood. Now read the commands."

"Which one do you want?"

"Try anything. Quick, before we lose this guy."

Marianne flipped the sheet of paper over and read another spell, raising her voice into what she hoped was a commanding tone:

> *Flaming spirit burning hot,*
> *To be my slave, this is your lot.*
> *Search my soul to see my thinking,*
> *Then rise up and do my bidding.*
> *Be thou now my witch's torch;*
> *Those who wrong me, thrash and scorch!*

The power spirit writhed and wriggled. Its eyes sparkled. Electrical arcs shot from its claws. It advanced upon Marianne with apparently murderous intent, then stopped. Offering the faint suggestion of a courteous salute, the incandescent creature bent forward and bowed before her.

"I know your desire and shall fulfill it," declared a smoky voice.

With that the monster turned and flew at Sergeant Sarzo. The man threw up his arms and tottered backwards, stumbling into a creosote bush. He lost his balance and crashed to the ground.

"Dad!" yelled Marianne.

She kicked at the can of Sterno, flipping it end over end. The whirling flame flickered, almost went out, but the power spirit remained. It floated over the bush and descended upon her father, who dug in his heels and thrust backward, propelling himself into a prickly poppy. The spines bit and stung. He groaned. The power spirit raked his face with its fiery claws. He howled.

"Dad! Dad! Oh my God, Dad!" Marianne screamed and rushed toward him. She tore at the power spirit, which ignored her.

"You! Spirit! Stop! I forgive him!

The thing hesitated, then resumed its attack. Sergeant Sarzo's shirt was now ablaze.

"Listen! I forgive my father — leave him alone!"

The power spirit raised itself from its victim and turned to regard its master.

"Let me punish the faithless wretch."

"No! That's all in the past!"

"Are you sure?"

"Yes, I'm sure. Get off him!"

"So you forgive him? Well and truly?"

"Well and truly! I truly do! Go away! Go! Depart! *Be fucking gone!"*

Fiery shoulders composed a shrug.

"I hear and obey."

The apparition's glowing body parts shrank into the Sterno container. *Poof!*

The erratic flame vanished in an explosion of sparks and embers.

Marianne fell on her father and slapped at his shirt to quench the fire.

"Dad! Are you okay? Oh, God, look at me!"

Dad cracked an eye open.

"Angel . . ."

His eyebrows were singed. Patches of skin were burned crimson. Marianne cradled his head in her hands and kissed his cheek.

"I forgive you, Dad. I forgive you, I forgive you."

He tried to smile and winced instead.

"I know," he croaked. "Your aura is blue now."

She buried her own face in the ashes of his shirt and held him tight.

55

JUST AFTER NOON the next day, the FULTAP team flew into the airport in Laughlin, Nevada, where American TV & Appliance had arranged for a Cadillac Escalade to be waiting.

In keeping with Bagwell's insistence on undistinguished fare, and allowing for Marianne's objections to yet another Denny's, they lunched at an enormous IHOP beside the Colorado River.

"Sense anyone?" asked Bagwell.

Sergeant Sarzo's face was covered with medicinal cream. The flesh underneath was blistered. It pained him to speak.

"Nothing," he managed to get out.

After pancakes and crepes, Bagwell pointed them north toward Las Vegas, seventy-five miles away. Now that they were down from the high country of southern Arizona, the day had turned hot. The big SUV's air conditioner was humming.

▼

Bagwell had arranged for rooms at the Bellagio. Dad still didn't sense the presence of their adversaries, and Marianne had never been to Las Vegas before, so she took his hand, and the two of them passed the afternoon touring the Strip. The theatrical opulence of the Bellagio, with its art collection, marble floors, and high-tech fountains had both of them agog. They were even more impressed by the faux Italian décor of the Venetian Hotel. There, while Dad stopped off for a beer at the B&B pub, she wandered the halls. The costumed buskers in St. Mark's square had a crowd hanging on every word. The singing gondolier was in fine voice, apparently unaware that his boat was floating through an impossible canal on the hotel's second floor.

After dinner Marianne led her teammates through the Bellagio's gaudy casino. The racer lights, whirling slot machines, and busy blackjack tables all stirred her curiosity.

"Got any good luck spells, Ray? I didn't find any in my book."

"You want to stay away from the slots, Agent Broomhandle, everything's rigged for the house," said Bagwell.

"Gambling is addictive," added Dad, being fatherly.

"Come on, help me out here. I'm a chick from the sticks. I want to live a little."

Bagwell sat down at one of the nearby bar tables. He thought for a while.

"Okay, um, um —"

> *Bags of money come to me,*
> *Wealth be mine completely free.*

"Oh crap, that won't work. I need inspiration, not a joke."

Bagwell thought some more:

> *Fortune rough and fortune bold,*
> *Multiply the wealth I hold.*
> *Make my luck run fast and rich;*
> *Serve the power of this witch.*

"I dunno, that's pretty crude," groused Marianne. "And I'm not sure I like the 'witch' part."

Bagwell threw up his hands. "Best I can do. If you decide to try it out, and you win anything, which I doubt, cut me in for a percentage — I should get paid for writing, like any author."

"Sure thing, boss."

Marianne strolled away through the rows of slots, murmuring Bagwell's little spell. As she passed a video machine featuring characters from *Star Wars*, a prickly feeling made her stop. The hairs on her arms rose. This particular *Droid Hunt* seemed to be radiating the prospect of especially good luck.

She inserted a silver dollar coin and pulled the handle. The video reels whirled. The first one to stop showed a Tie fighter on the payline. The second one showed another Tie fighter. The third reel stopped, teetered, inched down a bit, then back up on a third Tie fighter — *jackpot!*

"Woo-hoo."

She inserted another silver dollar, and pulled the handle again. This time she drew two laser swords and a combat droid helmet. No payout.

On the third try she wound up with three Princess Leias. Lights flashed. A siren whooped. Bagwell ambled over, sipping a martini.

"How much so far?" he asked.

Marianne studied the video display. "Fifty bucks?"

"Jesus."

Marianne inserted another dollar, pulled the handle again. This time she was treated to three Obi-Wans on the payline. Another winner. The machine went off like Big City fireworks on the Fourth of July.

Bagwell was very impressed. "That's another fifty," he noted, as the rollup jingled the total. "You go, girl."

Marianne looked around. A small crowd was gathering to watch her work; everyone loves a winner.

She pulled again and won again. Oohs and ahhs when the lights flashed. Shouts of encouragement.

The ease of beating the odds and the attention she was attracting made her cringe. Her buoyant mood evaporated. She gritted her teeth and hit a button, causing the accumulated payout to splash out of the hopper and into her bag. She fished around, collected a pile of coins, and handed them to Bagwell.

"Your share, Ray. Thanks for the words."

She walked away to a chorus of groans from the spectators. Bagwell hurried after her.

"Where are you going? Don't leave now, it's classic, you're on a roll. All that stuff about house rigging? Looks like we re-rigged the place."

She stopped, folded her arms to hug herself, and stared bleakly at the flashing lights. She pursed her lips, sifting through her feelings.

"Sorry. The spells, the good luck, the power — wow! — it's like a belt of tequila. But, you know what . . . I don't want to be a witch."

She made a little finger wave and trudged off to the elevators and the solitude of her room.

56

IN THE MIDDLE of the night, Sergeant Sarzo's eyes popped wide open. He scrambled out of bed, jumped into his clothes, and picked up the phone.

"Morning, Angel — we've got company. Early start. Up and at 'em."

Then he stepped into the hallway and rapped on Bagwell's door.

"Ray, wake up in there. Red alert, DEFCON 1."

Bagwell opened up. He was wearing a hotel bathrobe. "Got a signal?"

"Five-by-five. Can't be more than twenty kliks, max. They're here."

"Direction?"

"Don't have that. We need to move around to get a fix."

A sleepy Marianne appeared. She looked at her watch. "God, it's oh-dark-hundred. What's going on?"

"The bad guys have arrived in town."

Indeed, just then a CruiseAmerica camper van was slowly nosing along Las Vegas Boulevard. After some confusion and backtracking, it turned into the KOA campground behind the Circus Circus hotel. The driver, an old man with a funny accent, roused a dozing attendant, paid a fee, and found a spot for the night.

All the restaurants and cafés at the Bellagio were closed, so the FULTAP team hiked across the Strip to the Paris Hotel, where they grabbed coffee and pastries before setting out on patrol.

Bagwell directed the team's SUV through the intersection at Flamingo Boulevard and up onto northbound Interstate 15. In the hours before dawn traffic was nonexistent.

Sergeant Sarzo thought he detected something as they passed Circus Circus, but wasn't sure.

"Everyone's asleep. That makes it harder," he said.

In North Las Vegas they dropped down the Cheyenne Avenue off-ramp and headed east.

"Where are we going?" rasped Marianne, feeling woolly-headed and not bothering to pretend any different.

"Nellis," said Dad. His usual laconic manner was made worse by his lingering burns.

"No drones there, we know that," explained Bagwell. "But down in Sierra Vista our saboteurs were lying in wait. And they tried to trap us — well, trap you, anyway. Big change in tactics. I'm somewhat concerned they'll change tactics again. Maybe they'll be after piloted aircraft now."

"Did the job on us," said Dad.

"I'll say," nodded Bagwell. "We need to check."

"Fine. Wake me up when the action starts." Marianne closed her eyes and nestled down in the back seat.

Bagwell drove on for a few blocks, glancing at Marianne now and then in his rearview mirror.

"What have we got, Milo? Agent Broomhandle in the back seat there, or just Mademoiselle Sarzeau? Will she hold up? Do her job?"

Dad turned to gaze at his sleeping daughter.

"Doesn't love our work, but she's willing. Got some juice. More wattage than Hoover Dam, if she ever figures it out. Problem is, she shines like the moon. If I sense her, those damn kids do too. We have to be careful how close we get, or we'll scare them off."

"What about shielding?"

"Sleep helps, of course. A lead box might work, or heavy concrete."

"Lead box . . . great."

Bagwell parked where Cheyenne Avenue ended at the southwest corner of a military runway. He reached back over the seat and nudged Marianne.

"Hey, wake up. Put on your magic hat."

"Huh? Where are we now?" she yawned.

"Nellis Air Force Base. Sense anything?"

"Nope. I can't even see straight." She rubbed her eyes.

"How about you, Milo?"

"Faint signal. Back in town, probably. Stronger there."

"Damn."

Bagwell killed the engine and leaned back in his seat. "Okay," he decided, "we're here, so let's see what develops. What happened to those bear claws?"

Marianne tossed a cellophane-wrapped pastry into Bagwell's lap. He tore it open and scarfed it down.

After ten minutes went by in silence, Bagwell started fidgeting. "What's on the radar, you two?"

"No change," reported Sergeant Sarzo.

"Sun's coming up," said Marianne, squinting into dawn light.

Bagwell grumbled unintelligibly, started the engine, and backed the Escalade around. They motored north onto Las Vegas Boulevard and cruised past the air base's main gate. Bagwell made a 180-degree turn at Beesley Drive and parked.

"What now? Anything?"

"Nada," said Sergeant Sarzo.

"Nothing at all?"

"They haven't moved."

"Shouldn't you alert the base commander or something?" asked Marianne.

"No point unless we have to go in, and I don't see that. In case you didn't know, there are two Air Force bases in southern Nevada, Broomhandle. No drones at this one, but the opposition might not be so well informed."

"You mean we're on a snipe hunt." Marianne yawned again. "Great, thanks for the wake up call."

"Creech, Ray. Creech," said Sergeant Sarzo.

"We'll get there. Better to sign off here first, though, right? Closer, lives at stake, due diligence and all?"

"That's how General Weaver would have us do it."

"Right. Check all the boxes."

"Well, I'm seeing zip. Let's call this one checked."

"Roger that," said Marianne.

▼

Creech Air Force Base, Las Vegas' other Air Force installation and a major drone operator, was actually fifty miles northwest of Sin City across the highway from Indian Springs, a tiny desert community far from the bright lights.

It took the FULTAP team an hour and a half to get there, slowed by Marianne's insistence on an actual breakfast, which they consumed in the

Brass Ring Casino & Wedding Chapel on their way into the raw desert.

"Not bad," said Bagwell.

"Might as well be Denny's," retorted Marianne. "Would you like fries with your wedding?" She aimed her fork at a sign over the door:

First Time Around, Second Time Around, Any Time Around, We're Always Around.

"What a heart-warming slogan," she opined.

Bagwell sipped his coffee. "You are one bitchy witch today, Broomer."

"I'm tired. I miss Tom, and Lorraine, my friends, and my work." She raised a finger. "And . . . I am not a witch. Remember?"

"Let's call it a temporary assignment."

Sergeant Sarzo looked from one to the other and, when it appeared that the grouchy exchange wasn't going to escalate, finished his ham and eggs in silence.

▼

The FULTAP team rolled into Indian Springs on U.S. Route 95 and cruised slowly past the length of Creech Air Force Base where it abutted the north side of the highway.

"It's amazing," growled Bagwell. "The runway can't be more than a quarter of a mile from the road here. And look, you've got a trailer park, completely public, tucked right into the base itself. Drive in there, get even closer."

"Not the best way to avoid sabotage," said Sergeant Sarzo.

"God, no. Sense anything?"

"Faint. The opposition is miles away."

"Right. Waiting till dusk, probably."

"We can't hang around here, Ray. Those kids will pick us up long before we see them," cautioned the sergeant.

Bagwell turned the Escalade around and backtracked into the main settlement of Indian Springs on McFarland Avenue.

The desert community consisted of rundown ranch houses on lots full of junk and double-wide trailers up on cinder blocks. A few luxury homes occupied lonely strips of asphalt where foolhardy development projects had stalled out. Here and there scraggly trees testified to the blessings of an aquifer percolating just below the dusty surface.

Much of the town acreage was given over to storage yards filled with under-utilized semitrailers, road graders, concrete mixers, and power line repair trucks. Although no more than a thousand souls called this little corner of the desert home, these works of modern man sprawled across eighteen square miles.

A network of streets climbed gradually from the highway into the outlying foothills of the Spring mountain range. Towering above the sandy knobs and gullies loomed Mount Charleston, highest point in southern Nevada. Snow shimmered on its northern slopes.

Bagwell worked the Escalade southward for a few blocks, vectored west on Raleigh Lane, then south again on Sky Road.

"What are we doing?" asked Marianne.

"Take it easy — patience is a virtue. See anything, Milo?"

"Not yet. Keep driving, who knows?"

At the far end of Sky Road they happened upon an abandoned mining operation that had once scraped large quantities of gypsum out of the nearby bluffs. Among the derelict buildings left standing was a warehouse with concrete walls and ceiling thick enough to stop a bomb.

"Here we go," said Bagwell.

He turned onto the property. As they came around the warehouse a number of forty-foot cargo containers revealed themselves. Long after the mine failed, someone was still using the area to store empty shipping containers, far, far from the nearest port of call.

Bagwell parked. The two men got out of the SUV and conferred.

"We could put her in there."

"The windows are all blown out."

"Or shielded by the concrete walls, inside one of these containers."

"We can't be sure that will work."

"We can test the arrangement. Put Broomhandle in there, and you and I will drive back down to Creech and see if you still sense her."

Marianne joined the pair. "Wait just a minute. I am *not* going to crawl inside some damn box full of spiders and snakes."

"Line of duty, Angel," said Dad He walked over to the nearest container and tried the latch. Rusty hinges protested loudly, but it opened right up. He switched on a small flashlight, beckoned Marianne to follow, and stepped inside. A puff of stale air greeted them. She sniffed at the musty odor.

"Jesus Christ, what's that in the corner?" She grabbed her father's flashlight and aimed it into the far end of the container. A cobweb glistened. She advanced cautiously for a closer look. A shriveled-up spider husk showed how barren the steel interior actually was.

"I don't have anything to sit on," she complained.

Anticipating the problem, Bagwell was already rolling a large wooden cable reel into the container. He tipped it sideways. "Your throne, *mam'selle.*"

Sergeant Sarzo checked his watch. "Now look, Angel, we're going back into town and see what I can see. With luck, you'll be invisible. So hold the fort, and we'll be back in a jiff with snacks and drinks."

"Bring a snake-bite kit."

While they were gone, Marianne opened her pocket mirror and placed it on the wooden reel beside her. She removed Chief Ibañez' police badge from her bag. Then she tugged her stone pendant out of her blouse. Clutching her talismans tightly, one in each hand, she appealed to her ghost for advice.

"Hey you, Mr. G!" she cried.

She waited for several minutes and tried several times, but her virtual visitor did not appear in the mirror.

"Well, shit."

Twenty minutes went by with Marianne sitting in darkness. She made a point of scanning her surroundings every few seconds with her father's flashlight, expecting rats and rattlers to attack. But all was calm.

Then the latch clicked, hinges groaned, the container door opened, and Bagwell and her father were back.

Sergeant Sarzo handed her a tall cup of coffee, a bag of chips, and a turkey sandwich wrapped in plastic.

"Chow time."

She eyed the drink. "It's hot in here. Where's my beer?"

"No alcohol today, young lady," said Bagwell. "We have to be combat sharp."

"So, how did your little experiment go?"

"You're not here," said Dad. "Well, that's not completely true. I do get a vague impression, as if you're fifty miles away." He spread his arms to indicate the container and the surrounding mine buildings. "If this fooled me, it will fool those kids."

"So now we wait," said Bagwell. "Worried about spiders? Don't — now we're the spiders."

The two men joined Marianne sitting on her wooden reel and proceeded to down their food.

"While we were out I made a call to the Creech base commander," said Bagwell, munching potato chips. "He's going to double up guards and patrols."

Marianne snorted. "You fed him the *electromagnetic pulse* line, I bet."

Bagwell waggled a hand to admit the lie. "We'd be derelict not to warn him, although it just puts more people in danger, since the real battle will be up to us."

"Up to us," muttered Marianne uncomfortably. "If you mean me — conjuring! — well, I'm as big a threat to our health and safety as those kids."

"Got to chance it," said Dad. "Here's some stuff from the mini-mart. Better work on those spells and commands."

He handed her a little bag.

"Think small," he said.

"What's this?" Marianne pulled out several small items, including three cheap camping headlights. She strapped one to her forehead, opened her book, and began to review magical instructions by the light of Dad's little gift.

"So far, the kids only try to penetrate a base after dark," said Bagwell, putting on a headlight of his own. He opened his briefcase and held up one of the photos of the diagram found at 229 Billy Hill Drive. He tapped the chalk circle in the lower left corner. "And look — this is the only spot left on their 'map'."

"Your point?"

"We fended them off their previous targets. We're onto them, they're reacting. Cat and mouse. If their leader has any brains, he knows this can't go on forever. I think this is their final target. We need to nail them before they fade away and take themselves off to God knows where."

"But before we do that, I need to poke around outside," said Marianne.

"You can't —" began Dad, then stopped, warned by her tart expression. "Oh, all right, stay on this side of the warehouse, please."

Marianne found a secluded niche behind a shed, pulled down her pants, and relieved herself. Then she hiked around the gravel yard without the slightest regard for concealment. From one side of the concrete warehouse she had a view of Creech, far below on the desert floor. The base was situated in a dry lake bed, she realized, deriving its long and level runways from the flat expanse. As she gazed north through hazy air, she could just make out an airplane taking off. One of the drones, she supposed. It rose steadily to the west, then turned and flew back toward Indian Springs. By the time it passed overhead it was already a tiny silhouette. She could just barely hear the buzz of the propeller as it went out of sight.

"Good purpose, good purpose," she murmured, recalling the admonition of her priestly confessor back in Arizona.

"Who am I kidding? Drones are drones." She stared into the empty sky, then slapped her hands together. "Screw them. I don't give a damn. It's the pilots and people like us I need to worry about."

57

GOLAY and his group motored slowly away from Las Vegas in their CruiseAmerica motorhome, heading northwest.

"Where are we?" demanded the old man.

"We are in the American desert, Dada," said Rafiq, looking up from the map he was studying. "Road number 95."

"But where? Where is Indian Springs?"

"Not far, Dada. Next town. Next town for sure."

Golay nodded uncertainly and tightened his grip on the steering wheel. He wasn't much of a driver, and the bulky recreational vehicle made him nervous. Worse, the late afternoon sun was shining directly in his eyes. He slowed another five miles an hour below the speed limit. Cars were honking and passing in angry haste.

When he motored right by the Indian Springs Casino, Yasmin, kneeling between the front seats, started yelling.

"We're here! We're here!"

Zohra chimed in. "Stop, Dada. I'm hungry."

Golay shook his head to concede his mistake, drove on for a mile, found a paved crossover, turned back, and nosed into the Indian Springs RV Park, located hard by Creech Air Force Base.

Like the town itself across the highway, the park was located above an underground aquifer. Gnarly cottonwood trees grew everywhere, giving the impression of a desert oasis.

At the park office, Golay paid with Rajput's credit card and was told to pick any open camping spot he liked. Rafiq knew what to do. He ran across the grass and concrete to the cinder block wall that separated the tourist operation from the air base. He bounced up and down on a concrete pad there.

"Over here, over here!" he shouted.

With guidance from Rafiq and Yasmin, and with many little adjustments, Golay succeeded in maneuvering the still-unfamiliar rental RV into place. Firoz helped him hook up the water and electrical lines.

In the restaurant attached to the nearby casino, a disgusted Golay watched the three children gobble down detestable hamburgers and french fries, slaking their thirst with Coca-Colas.

"The meat is not *halal,*" he said, wrinkling his nose.

"It is a sacrifice we make for our country," returned Firoz, always patriotic.

Golay noticed the *Enjoy Wi-Fi Here* sign above the restaurant's cash register. He removed his laptop from its carrier bag and opened it up.

"What's the bad news from Islamabad today?" he muttered.

The *Islamabad Daily Register*'s website was still featuring the goatherd story. Golay scrolled down to the most recent comment:

> *After heroic labors with their goats, these girls deserve a great reward. Inshallah, they shall have it when they return through the northern pass.*
> — *Aladdin123*

He closed the laptop, reached across the table, and squeezed Firoz' hand.

"This is the final test of our mission. The service has called us home."

"No doubt further plans will be made," offered Firoz, "after our success with the stupid Americans."

They stepped outside. Zohra was licking a two-scoop ice cream cone. Yasmin nibbled on a chocolate bar.

"What do you see, children? Where are our American shadows, the ones who pursue us?"

Rafiq opened his arms and slowly turned himself through 360 degrees.

"They are not here, Dada."

Yasmin marched back and forth under the trees. "The woman is far away, but I do sense her. Her shape is faint."

"She's not faint, Yasmin. I see her. She's not far away," countered Zohra. "She's a policeman, and I put her to sleep."

"Don't be silly, Zoh," said Yasmin. "If she was anywhere near I would see her before you, you're just a kid."

"Am not," pouted Zohra. "I'm a secret agent."

Golay gestured helplessly at the world. "Now, girls. Which way?"

Yasmin thought it over, then pointed southeast. "Las Vegas, where we stayed."

"No, she's here," insisted Zohra. "I will put her to sleep again!"

"Shut up, little monster," said Yasmin. She handed Zohra the uneaten half of her chocolate bar.

"Rafi? What do you say?"

The boy looked around. He closed his eyes and stood very still for a minute or more.

"Yasmin is right. Far away. Beyond the hills. We are safe."

"Good," said Golay, rubbing his hands. He glanced through the trees to the west, where the sun had just set. "Let us prepare for the night's work."

▼

Sergeant Sarzo opened the cargo container door a crack, slipped outside, and walked slowly across the defunct mine's gravel yard for a view of the air base. Twilight was descending on southern Nevada. The sky was turning purple, and the desert landscape was already in deep shadow. While he watched, the base's runway lights blinked on, a triangular necklace of luminous blue beads stretching across the dry lake for a mile and a half in three directions. He stood watch for a few minutes, gathering paranormal intelligence data. Then he returned to his companions.

"They're here. In the RV park, just like we thought."

Bagwell checked the loads in his revolver.

"Ready, Broomer? Got your gun? Got your lucky charms? Memorized your lines?"

Marianne yawned, stood up from her wooden seat, nodded affirmatively.

"When they show up, I will say *boo.*"

"Come on, Marianne — serious business here."

"I'll use my scary voice."

▼

Rafiq held the door of the CruiseAmerica RV wide open while Golay and Firoz guided a folding aluminum ladder through it. They placed the thing against the concrete wall bordering the air base, returned to the RV and carried out an identical second ladder.

With help from all three children, the two guardians managed to erect the first ladder at a location on the wall behind the RV, concealed from the rest of the park. They climbed up and unfolded the second one on the air base side of the wall. Then the entire group climbed up, over, and down.

"The pilots, where are they?" asked Golay.

"Over there," said Yasmin. She pointed toward a row of administration buildings. "Way over. You can't see them from here."

Suddenly a jeep appeared from around the corner. Its headlights lit up the five saboteurs. The driver accelerated toward them. Unintelligible warnings blared from a public address speaker mounted on the front fender.

"Yasmin! Zohra!" yelled Rafiq.

The three children crowded protectively in front of Golay and Firoz. The jeep slowed as it approached. Dire warnings were repeated. The airman in the passenger seat was raising his assault rifle. The three children held up their right hands and chanted their jinx together. Instantly the driver slumped behind the wheel. The passenger pitched forward and fell out of the open vehicle, dropping his weapon. The saboteurs scattered as the jeep continued past them and — *krunch!* — smashed into the barrier wall.

Firoz pulled the driver out of his seat and laid him on the ground. Golay inspected the damage. It was light — nothing more than a bent fender.

"Let's go, children. Jeep ride!" said Golay, sliding behind the wheel. The group piled in beside and behind him. Golay wrestled with the manual transmission, backed around, found the wrong forward gear, and headed slowly out toward the flight line with the jeep bucking and heaving like a wild horse.

▼

Bagwell had the FULTAP SUV racing through the back streets of Indian Springs at three times the speed limit.

"Jesus, Ray. If I was in uniform, I'd pull you over," said Marianne, gripping the armrests of her seat with white knuckles.

"Got to move fast. Now we're out in the open, those kids are going to sense us, and guess there's a trap. Let's spring it first."

The Escalade roared into the Indian Springs RV park and, directed by Sergeant Sarzo's unusual sensory abilities, stopped behind the saboteurs' CruiseAmerica RV.

While the two men searched the RV, Marianne ran around the far side.

"Look here, ladder on the wall," she shouted.

Her companions came running.

"Whoof, they're already over the line," said Bagwell. He opened his phone and made a call.

"Yo, Creech, FULTAP here, on the hunt. Our twenty is the base perimeter at the RV park. The saboteurs have penetrated your security. Need a pick-up, pronto."

The team climbed over the wall and discovered the unconscious security patrol. Marianne whistled.

"Evidence," said Bagwell.

The two men dragged the sleeping forms to the wall and propped them into a sitting position. Marianne bent down over them.

"What's your call? Shall I go to work?"

"Please do," said Dad.

"Unh-huh," affirmed Bagwell. "Let's repair the damage."

Marianne grasped her stony talisman, waited for her hand to tingle, then chanted her *Waking* spell. After a minute or so both men began to stir. Their eyes opened. The change in circumstance startled them, made them twitch.

"What happened? Where's our ride?"

Marianne put a hand on each man's chest. "Shh. Calm down, you're okay, you're going to be fine. Help is on the way."

"Combat casualties," mumbled Bagwell. "Thank God for survivable wounds."

"Luckily, they're not adept," said Dad, "so the kids' spell doesn't dig deep, doesn't last."

The security men felt around for their hats and sidearms, moving robotically, like confused sleepwalkers.

Bagwell was staring at Marianne. Seeing her in action caused him to remember something. He dug fingers into a jacket pocket.

"Here, Broomer. Another spell." He handed Marianne a slip of paper.

"What on Earth?"

"Banishment for your power spirit. Just in case . . . you know . . . if he gets out of hand again."

"Oh, man . . . "

"Probably won't have to use it. I was bored waiting around all day, and I thought, why not write something?"

At that moment the requested security patrol roared up in a Humvee.

"Stay here, Milo. Any further, and you're in harm's way. Those damn kids'll knock you out for a year."

"Hooah," said Dad, accepting the inevitable.

Marianne gave her father a quick squeeze. "Wear those owl feathers I gave you." She reached into her bag and hauled out her little can of nuts. She shook a handful into his palm. "And eat these things."

"If you feel the bad guys coming at you, don't wait for us, shag out of here in the Escalade," ordered Bagwell.

"Drive on," said Dad, with a wry smile.

Marianne and Bagwell swung aboard the Humvee.

"Where to?"

"You tell me — wherever the flight crews are operating your RPAs."

"GCS is out along the flight line. Hold tight."

The Humvee bolted forward, turned sharply around a hangar, and moved out along the taxiway beside Runway 26.

▼

Yasmin warned Golay that they were near their targets, so he parked the jeep beside a shed, and the group edged forward on foot.

"Where are the steel boxes the pilots use?" he muttered.

Unknown to the saboteurs, Ground Control Stations at Creech were all inside a long featureless hangar-like building.

"We need to get inside, Dada," said Rafiq.

Golay led the way to the main entrance, a pair of glass panels with flowering yuccas planted on either side. A guard was visible behind a counter. Yasmin and Rafiq were conferring about the best tactic to put the man to sleep when Zohra piped up.

"The lady policeman is here. A soldier is with her. They are coming."

Golay spun around. "What? Are you sure, Zohra?"

"She is coming, and, and — she is *mad* at us."

Golay craned his neck to see what she might be talking about. There! Coming along the taxiway, a military truck of some sort.

"Yaz? Rafi? What's going on here?"

"Ahh, it is true, Dada. Now I sense her," said Yasmin.

"Dada, you and Firoz should hide," said Rafiq. "We will put her to sleep. We will put all our enemies to sleep."

Golay pulled Firoz into the shadows.

"They may have found us, but they will not stop us! Get ready, Firoz, we must fight."

▼

The Creech security Humvee moved cautiously forward.

"Wait, stop, far enough," ordered Bagwell. "We can't just ride to the rescue. We'll spook the bad guys."

The Humvee stopped.

"Lights out, soldier."

The driver killed his headlights.

"Come on, Ray, bail out," said Marianne, jumping to the ground.

Bagwell cautiously followed. He drew his revolver. "Got a fix?"

Marianne stood still. She looked at the blue lights outlining the runway, trying to relax. "Mmm, not sure. When I don't stress too hard, sometimes the radar works. I'm tracking two auras, I think. Maybe more. Hostile." She hooked her do-it-yourself owl feather danglers into her ear lobes.

"Watch your ass."

She started toward the GCS building and suddenly found herself face to face with three Middle Eastern children who came forth from around the corner. Two girls and a boy. The same ones who knocked her unconscious at Hancock Field. All three angrily thrust out their right hands and began to chant.

Marianne was staggered by the force of their combined wills as if hit by a fist. She felt a wave of confusion lap against her mind. She tried to mouth her *Waking* spell, and found she couldn't remember the damn thing. She turned and ran.

Once around the corner of the building she slowed a little, trying to clear her head, searching for a hiding place to recover. After a hundred yards bounding along the concrete like a terrified rabbit, she saw an airport sweeper truck parked on the taxiway beside a jeep. She crouched down between the huge cylindrical broom and the jeep's rear wheels.

"What? What? What was it?" she mumbled, racking her brain to recall her defensive incantation. She could hear small feet slapping on the pavement, running toward her. Finally some words slid into place. Not the original spell from her book, just some doggerel Bagwell wrote. It would have to do. She slipped a hand under her blouse and grabbed her stone talisman. At its touch, a jolt of mysterious energy coursed through her fingers and shot up her arm, melting her fear.

She stood up straight, and there were the three children, skidding to a stop in front of her. She reeled off the couplets:

> *To those who wish me fast asleep*
> *With body sprawling in a heap,*
> *Try your best and do your worst;*
> *Those who curse are themselves cursed.*
> *You cannot stun me, little fools;*
> *Stand against me, see who rules!*

All three clapped hands over their ears, grinding their teeth in pain. Rafiq recovered first.

"Go to sleep!" he shouted.

"No thanks. I'm not tired," Marianne replied. "Instead, I'm going to show you a magic trick. Watch this!"

Marianne reached into her bag and produced a small BIC cigarette lighter, purchased earlier in the day by her father. She flicked the knob.

Zip!

A tiny flame appeared. She held it up before her adversaries. She dug a pinch of crushed datura and cat hair out of a small plastic bag and sprinkled it over the fire.

Crackle!

The flame licked upward. She showed them her blood glucose tester, waved it back and forth dramatically, and pricked a finger. She let them see the drop of blood forming on her fingertip, then shook it over the flame.

Flash!

Instantly the fire whirled into an angry vortex. The children stared with wide eyes.

"Now, here's a little poem — "

> *Rise, bright spirit from the flame;*
> *Join me here, and be thou tame.*
> *Obedience is what I ask;*
> *To work my will is now your task.*
> *Cast my foes into the dark!*
> *Burn away their witch's spark!*

Fiery wings emerged from the vortex. A head formed. Burning eyes appeared. Now a small monster, the size and shape of a hawk, was perched on Marianne's BIC lighter. No cryptic voice addressed her respectfully, but an angry cry pierced her skull:

"*Krrrrr* . . ."

The three children shrank back in terror.

The flaming spirit flapped its fiery wings and flew at them. Red hot claws gripped Zohra's hair. The uncanny thing twisted and tugged, throwing Zohra to the ground. She screamed.

Rafiq bolted. The spirit brushed his shirt, igniting it. The boy fell to the ground and thrashed around, desperately trying to put the fire out. The spirit descended upon him and sank its glowing claws into his head. He wailed in agony.

Yasmin, however, did not run. She marched forward with hands raised to grab and strangle.

"Evil witch! You die!"

Marianne backed away and unholstered her Beretta.

"Sorry, kid, not tonight."

Before Yasmin could reach her, and before Marianne felt threatened enough to pull the trigger, the spirit's claws were grappling with the girl's head scarf, setting it alight. Yasmin tried to beat the fire out, but couldn't do it. She ran back and forth with her head burning like a torch, windmilling her arms, shrieking uncontrollably.

The spirit then turned and dove toward Marianne.

"Enough, be gone!" she commanded.

"*Krrrrr* . . ."

The spirit flapped up in the air, flew in a circle, dove again. Marianne ducked and dodged.

"All right, you!" She voiced a final spell, Bagwell's afterthought:

> *Spirit hot and spirit bold,*
> *Your hour is past; you're growing old.*
> *Return now to the other side.*
> *Be thou gone and there abide!*

The spirit lifted high into the air and exploded like a skyrocket. Little sparks floated down around Marianne and the moaning and groaning children.

Three jeeps drove up. Security teams jumped out and advanced with weapons at the ready. All the fires sputtered out. Yasmin pulled her companions to their feet. They huddled together in the glare of the headlights, eyes vacant, clothes in rags, hair singed, faces burned.

"These your saboteurs? These *kids?*" asked the airman in charge.

Marianne nodded. She stuffed her Beretta back into its ankle holster.

"Where's the gimmick?"

"What?"

"The thing they use to generate the electromagnetic pulse we heard about."

Marianne rolled her eyes.

"Oh, well . . . fuck that. I think it blew up."

▼

Bagwell watched the whole thing from the taxiway. He couldn't quite see the power spirit itself, just a blur, but the fires that erupted and engulfed the screaming children looked real enough. He was hypnotized by the tumultuous sight.

Firoz was hiding behind an aircraft pushback tractor. She noticed that Bagwell's attention was riveted on Marianne. She circled around the empty Humvee and advanced stealthily upon the Army major.

Klik! — klik! — klik!

Bagwell failed to notice Firoz' strange navigation technique for what it was — an advertisement of impending doom.

Klik! — klik! — klik!

Firoz pulled her knotted garrotte from her silk robe and held it taut between her hands.

Klik! — klik! — klik!

She closed the distance, reached out to snare Bagwell.

Marianne was still chatting with the security forces, now busy taking the bewildered children into custody, when movement on the taxiway caught her eye.

"Ray! Ray! On your six!"

Firoz' garrotte came down over Bagwell's face. Bagwell's gun hand thrust upward at the same instant. Firoz yanked hard, but Bagwell had the barrel of his revolver in between the garrotte and his throat.

Marianne was sprinting in his direction. She stopped when she saw the plump and balding FULTAP officer reach back with his free hand, grab Firoz' arm, and throw her bodily across his back.

Whuff!

Firoz came down heavily on the concrete with the wind knocked out of her sails. She wheezed noisily until she caught her breath, then scrambled to her feet and melted into the night.

Marianne rushed to Bagwell's side. He was bent over, with hands on knees, breathing hard.

"Ray, oh my God, you all right?"

Bagwell was peering into the shadows, looking for his assailant.

"Yeah, fine. I'm fine."

"That was some move, man."

He brushed himself off.

"What? You think I just write poetry?"

Darius Golay was hiding among the service vehicles and fuel barrels on the taxiway. As events unfolded he clenched his fists. When his young charges were felled by balls of fire, his face grew dark with rage.

At the same time Bagwell was repelling Firoz' attack, the old man saw red and green wing lights blinking on the far end of the runway, heard the whine of a turboprop engine and the buzz of a propeller. An evil drone, he realized, preparing for takeoff.

He turned away from the children and the security forces massing to corral them and jogged purposefully out toward the runway. On the way he passed a confused Firoz.

"Dada!" she reached out to take his arm, but he shook free and continued onto the asphalt strip.

The turboprop whined urgently, the propeller revved up, a headlight bloomed on the undercarriage, and the drone, an MQ-9 Reaper, began its takeoff run.

Golay marched on toward it, waving his arms and hurling curses.

Klik! — klik! — klik!

Firoz hustled after him. She grabbed at his shirt. He shook free again.

"We shall not fail."

"No, Dada, never. But now we must escape. Come with me."

"When our work is done, Firoz. Only then."

He continued marching toward the drone, shaking a fist. The aircraft was now moving toward him at high speed. Firoz was frantic. Just before the drone reached them she managed to get both hands on the old man's back and shove him to the ground. The Reaper sped by.

Wham!

The nose wheel caught Firoz in the chest, smashing her ribs.

Slice!

The propeller on the tail took her head off.

Marianne and Bagwell heard the ghastly explosion of blood and bone and turned toward the runway. The Reaper's nose wheel was bent back under the fuselage. The sensor package was scraping the asphalt, raising sparks. The thing slewed around and headed right for them.

"Heads up!" shouted Marianne.

Everyone standing nearby ran for cover.

Ka-blaamm!

The Reaper smacked into the security Humvee, caromed off, and plowed into the fuel barrels. Aluminum parts flew every which way. The barrels spewed A-1 jet fuel. Hot engine fragments made contact.

Foof!

A conflagration erupted. Marianne, Bagwell, the security crew, and the captured children all retreated from the ferocious heat wave that blew outward like a solid wall.

▼

Half an hour later Creech fire crews had reduced the blaze to smoldering embers. The security forces dispersed, carrying the frazzled children away. Sergeant Sarzo arrived in the FULTAP Escalade. He worked his way through the cleanup detail to Marianne, who was staring at the wreckage. He placed his hands on her shoulders and studied her for evidence of psychic damage.

"You okay? I could feel the force of those spells all the way across the base."

"I think so. Numb . . . a little numb, maybe."

"But, you got 'em," he said, suddenly beaming with pride. He executed a crisp salute.

She returned it with an awkward salute of her own. "Yup, we did."

"So, tell me. What did it look like?"

"The spirit? Like a big bird. It had wings and claws. Brrr."

"What about the old man and that strange . . . woman?"

Marianne pointed toward the runway. "She was hit by the drone that crashed. She's in pieces." She circled her arm aimlessly. "No one has seen the old guy since."

Bagwell had his eyes on the departing security forces. "How about those burns? Will the kids heal?"

Marianne glanced at her father. His own burns had faded quickly. A little too quickly, she thought, for purely natural injuries.

"I think they'll be okay."

"Will they recover their powers?"

"Good question."

58

TOM WAGSTAFF was sitting in his mother's book store in Ragtown, California, morosely sipping a latte. Lorraine, equally glum, busied herself with the pastry selection, the newly-arrived-fiction table, and her pile of unopened mail.

"When was the last time you heard from her?" she inquired.

"A few days. She wouldn't tell me where she was. I tried calling the number she was using, but it's out of service. I think the Army took her real phone."

"Secret agent games," sniffed Lorraine, tossing unread advertising flyers into the trash.

"I just hope she's okay," said Tom.

"Me too. That girl, honestly — the stress! — she owes us bigtime."

A shapely young woman in police attire came through the front door, just in time to overhear Lorraine's remark.

"I owe you guys bigtime," she said.

The Wagstaffs let out simultaneous shrieks of joy and jumped out of their chairs.

"Marianne!"

The three friends grabbed each other in a tenacious group hug. Tom picked Marianne up and whirled her around the store. Then he held her face in trembling hands and planted a big kiss.

"M — *mmmm* — am I glad to see you!" he exclaimed.

"Same here," said Marianne, straightening her collar.

When they all calmed down, Lorraine brewed a macchiato for the prodigal policewoman.

"Double shot and a drop of milk, right?"

"Thanks."

"So . . . tell us everything."

"I can't. Don't want to either. Very hairy, boring, scary, you name it, and it's all classified information."

"Come on, spill. How's your dad?"

"He's okay. Recovering from burns received in the line of duty."

"And *where* is he?"

Marianne checked her watch. "What time is it? Uh, by now, Virginia, probably. Him, Ray Bagwell, and General Weaver, the whole FULTAP team. Langley. Debriefing CIA brass."

"Good Lord."

"Hey, you two, don't look so gloomy. I'm back. Back on the job, looking for criminals, arresting violators."

"At least tell us this — did you stop the sleepers?"

"Yeah, we did."

"How?"

Marianne toyed with her coffee. "You really want to know? Don't laugh — magic spells."

"You're kidding."

"Think fake-o Shakespeare couplets, like you read in college."

The two Wagstaffs exchanged looks. Marianne registered their doubts with a weary smile.

"Yeah, who knew?" she said.

"These spells — anyone get hurt?"

After some thought, Marianne decided they should have a better idea of her adventures after all.

"One of the adults in the gang was killed when she was hit by a drone taking off."

This revelation produced long faces. Neither Wagstaff had ever seen a dead person, and both hoped they never would.

"You saw this? Saw the body?"

Marianne nodded sadly.

"And it's not over. Dez Otis and I are still working on a burglary that's tied into the whole thing."

▼

Later that day, Officer Otis led Marianne into the maze of RVs in the Wrangler Towing impound down in Shingle Springs.

"Now where the hell was it?" he muttered, lost as soon as they entered the gate.

But after a couple of false leads and some backtracking, they came around a fifth-wheeler, and there it was — Habib Rajput's U-Haul truck.

"Tah-dah. Fucking spider and everything."

"Christ, what a mess," she said when she saw all the dried mud. "When I saw this thing go by on the night of the burglary, it was spotless."

She walked around the vehicle, noting, as Otis had before her, the weeds stuck to the bumper. She peered into the cab, opened the cargo door and surveyed the interior, bare except for the child's rocking horse.

"Shit, I'll bet Rajput meant this for Zohra."

"Who's Zohra?"

"One of the kids I was after."

"Unh-huh." Otis had no idea what she was talking about and decided not to ask.

Marianne peered at the rear axle. More mud, more weeds. She then got down on hands and knees and crawled underneath the thing.

"Hey, found something."

She backed out and stood up. She was holding a snarl of fence wire with a broken fencepost dangling from it. "Your take?" she asked.

Otis considered the possibilities.

"Well, shit, it could be that this truck here was out in the tulies collecting all this greenery. On some ranch, I guess, where it crashed through a fence."

"A pretty muddy ranch. A lot of those weeds look like cattails to me."

"Water. Down near some lake, most likely."

"And what would a U-Haul truck be hauling out there?"

"Yeah . . . . . . what?"

"On my little trip, we noticed that Rajput's credit card was paying the bills. But the man himself never turned up."

Otis nodded, slowly coming to a grim conclusion.

"Foul play, huh? Murder. Body dump. I'll buy that. But, hey, Sarz, offed by children?"

"There were adults along. One of them was a professional assassin. She killed a soldier who was watching out for me."

"Problem is, we're in big open country. How many ranches? How many miles of lakeshore?"

Marianne threw up her hands.

"Yeah. We're screwed."

▼

That night Marianne was sitting on the edge of her new bed in Placerville. Tom Wagstaff was already under the covers beside her. She wiggled around, testing.

"Squeaks are gone."

"I tightened the bolts, wedged a board that wasn't milled just exactly right," he said. "Come on, hop in."

"Wait a minute." She stood up. "I'm going to find a mirror and talk to my ghost. I know that sounds weird."

"Dressed like that?"

Marianne was stark naked. She giggled, snatched a bathrobe off a hook, and wrapped it around herself. Then she leaned over Wagstaff and bestowed a lingering promissory kiss.

"Don't wait up."

"Ha ha ha," he said.

She lifted Chief Ibañez' police badge from her bag and marched into the bathroom. Holding it aloft in a tight grip, she performed her oddly brash, but sometimes effective summons.

"Yo, Chief! Mr. G! Got a minute? I have questions."

Nothing stirred in the mirror. Just her own face staring back. She noted a hint of healthy color from her outdoor exertions. She judged she was a tad leaner in spite of all that Denny's food. She was also thinking that the lines of her brow and cheeks had sharpened up, giving her appearance some maturity. She was congratulating herself on the new look when her image began to blur. Ripples formed in the reflection and resolved into a spooky silhouette.

"What's on your mind tonight?"

"Thanks for showing up. It's not always this easy."

"I wanted to give you a pat on the back. Nice work, officer."

"You know about the kids?"

"And the spells. Word gets around."

"The spirits are bragging."

"That they are. They seem to like you."

"Oh, man — *like* me?!"

"Respect you."

"They damn well better. So listen, here's the thing — the burglary I've been working on has turned into a murder case. At least, I think so. Looks like the perps used a U-Haul truck to dump the body. We've got weeds and mud and some fencing stuck to the vehicle."

"One of the reservoirs."

"Yeah, we think so too. But which one? And even if we had the name, these things are huge, with miles of shoreline."

"I thought you were a cop. How many times do I have to say — think like one."

"I'm trying."

"Not hard enough."

Marianne heard a footstep. She turned. Wagstaff was standing in the doorway behind her.

"Mind if I watch?"

She turned back to the mirror. Her shadowy visitor had disappeared.

"Sorry, he's gone. And, damn, he was no help at all."

Later in bed, in the middle of making love, she rolled over and sat bolt upright. Wagstaff groaned.

"Oh my God. We've got a broken fence. A broken fence near a lake. What was behind that fence?"

Wagstaff scratched his head and sat up.

"Is this a rhetorical question?"

"Cattle," she declared, shaking her head. "I'm so slow! The answer is cattle . . . or horses. Animals, anyway. A broken fence means animals roaming free, getting on the road, causing trouble."

Wagstaff's mind was still focused on other things.

"Your point, officer?"

"If farm animals got out of control, someone might have noticed and complained. If I call around, one law enforcement department or another might have a report on file, and they will know where that fence was broken."

"That's terrific. Good deduction. Great stuff. Come back to bed."

Wagstaff eased himself back under the covers. Marianne flopped down beside him and, exhausted by solving her problem, was sound asleep in an instant.

▼

Next morning Officer Otis and Marianne sat together at a desk in the Placerville police department, drinking coffee and making phone calls. After an hour trying, Otis got a hit.

"The Golden Fleece ranch? Say where?"

Pause.

"Upper Bar Lake, unh-huh, outside Tarvolo. Spell that for me, please."

He grabbed a pencil and started scribbling.

"Tarvolo, with a V, Amador County, Upper Bar Lake."

Marianne, busy on her own call, offered hasty thanks to someone else and hung up.

"Got a lead?"

"That was Amador County Deputy Sheriff Al Burns. A few weeks ago some fisherman ran into a herd of alpacas all over the road near the southern arm of Upper Bar Lake, down beyond Tarvolo, wherever the hell that is. Burns personally went out there to help corral them."

"Tri-Town. My old stomping grounds. Upper Bar Lake — I've been there."

"Well then, you drive."

▼

Roads leading down to the undeveloped southern shore of Upper Bar Lake were few and far between. Marianne drove Otis' slick Taurus Interceptor along Copper King Road out of Applefield, past her radio station, through Tarvolo, past the reservoir's marina, past the main gate of the Golden Fleece ranch. A couple of miles later she turned onto the Old Stage Highway, paralleling the lake. Once upon a time it had been a major artery conducting miners into the hinterlands. Now it was rarely used, and after a hundred yards the pavement gave out. The cops continued slowly downhill along the gravel track. They were a long way from cell phone service, so Otis was studying a paper topographic map.

"Give it another quarter mile or so, look for a service road to the right. 3N41, I think it is," he said, eyeing the small print.

Marianne made the turn. 3N41 was poorly maintained and barely qualified as an actual road. Bushy oak savanna alternated with ragged stands of conifers along the narrow lane. They noticed fencing as they neared the lake. When the lake itself came into view they also noticed a small herd of fluffy alpacas grazing behind the fence. Evidently the adjoining land belonged to the Golden Fleece operation.

Marianne parked. The two police officers got out of the car and walked around, surveying the area for evidence of a break in the fence line.

"Over here, Dez," shouted Marianne. She was standing beside a post that was smooth and upright, not as weatherbeaten as others nearby. The galvanized staples fastening the wire were still shiny. Deep ruts, possibly made by a U-Haul truck, led away into a knot of sticky monkey flowers and manzanita bushes.

Otis wrinkled his nose. "I don't smell anything."

"Been a while," said Marianne. "You ready?"

"As I'll ever be."

Neither one of them wanted to move past the fence, dreading what they would find. Otis held up the wire so Marianne could duck under.

"Heh, you first, Squeek."

They trudged along the ruts until they were in among the bushes. There Otis spotted the faded remains of a plaid shirt. Then a belt and a pair of running shoes came into view. Bones were showing.

"Oh, shit," said Marianne, covering her mouth. "Coyotes have been here."

Otis hauled out his camera and began snapping pictures.

"Crime solved?"

"We'll need teeth for an ID, but I bet this is Rajput. Our burglar, what's left of him."

59

SPRING turned into summer. The days lengthened, the foothill creeks dried up, hillside grass turned golden brown, and Placerville got hot. Marianne was thankful for night shifts.

On the summer solstice she drove up to Gold Bug Park, patrolling there to make sure the annual sunset party didn't spawn too many fires or drunks. Most of the revelers had congregated on the hilltop in front of the city water tank for the best view. Marianne hiked up to show the uniform and was amused to spot Mark Frey and Kari Hamilton there, holding hands. They waved. She waved back.

At dawn she pulled into her apartment complex, checked her mail, and discovered a note from Major Bagwell:

> *Broomer —*
> *Our MI briefing dazzled the brass. General W. at his bureaucratic best. Spectrum is now Full again, off to can't-tell-you-where. Don't forget those spells I wrote, just in case we call up the reserves next trip. Google Golay for latest news.*
> *— Ray*

Marianne was intrigued by the reference. She revved up her aging laptop, opened a browser, and performed a web search. The third response contained the information she was looking for:

PROFESSOR CHARGED IN CREDIT CARD FRAUD

A visiting professor at UCLA was apprehended trying to cross the Canadian border in Blaine, Washington, yesterday. Darius Golay, a citizen of Pakistan, is charged with fraudulent use of a stolen credit card. He allegedly racked up big bills for motels, meals, and motorhomes while touring the country to research American culture. He faces a sentence of two-to-five years if convicted in federal court.

Meanwhile, U.S. Immigration officials have learned from police in Placerville, California, that the proper owner of the credit card is deceased. Foul play is suspected. If Professor Golay is implicated, further charges may be brought.

▼

The month of July brought tourist hordes and police work drudgery. Car alarms, car accidents, car thefts. Domestic disputes, public drunks, heroin shooters, domestic disputes, parking tickets, shoplifters, crazy people, domestic disputes, and more domestic disputes.

The only point of interest was watching Desmond Otis work on his career. Just after the Fourth he interviewed for a detective position down in Folsom. A week later Marianne thought he was gone, with a better salary and better hours.

"I can drive to Kings games from there," he said.

But then, just after the official job offer came through, he decided to stay in Placerville.

"Housing is tight in the valley. Nothing to do with you, Squeek, don't flatter yourself."

▼

In August Marianne received the usual birthday greetings from her distant father — a postcard:

Happy birthday, Angel —
Ray and I are in the wind again. Spiritual allies @ home this trip.
Imogen sends her love.
— Dad
(p.s., seen the latest battle front bulletin?)

Like all of Sergeant Sarzo's mail, it was postmarked APO 31905, Fort Benning, Georgia. The picture was a close-up of decorative ceramic pots. Marianne surmised that the ambiguous image was deliberately chosen to hint at Dad's actual location. Holland, or Poland, or — good Lord — China, she thought. He was somewhere far away, doing something dangerous, for sure. Before she joined the FULTAP team, espionage was just a page she turned in a magazine while waiting for a haircut. Then, for a little while, it all became real. Now, months later, memories were fading, and her days on the road seemed like an overly vivid dream.

Marianne scanned the postcard several times, and wondered about the "battle front bulletin," whatever the hell that was.

On the off-chance that the local news vendors were lazy, she stopped into the Smoke & Firewater to check out last week's papers. No luck. They had already been recycled, so she motored down to Ragtown to dish the dirt with Lorraine Wagstaff.

Marianne's refusal to reveal her role with FULTAP to Tom and his mother had lasted one week. In the end they threatened bodily harm if she didn't come clean. At last she gave in and, swearing them both to uttermost secrecy, laid out the details.

Lorraine now spent a good part of her leisure time surfing the web for information about spies, counterspies, terrorists, and psychic surveillance. As a result of her new enthusiasm, she was ready with hot news when Marianne walked in the door of the Book Nook.

"Look what I found, kiddo," she said, pointing to one of her computers while she expertly whipped up espresso.

Marianne examined the screen. Lorraine's browser was aimed at the *Washington Post* website. The item in question, which she had disinterred from the back pages with a dozen mouse clicks, was already a week old:

SPY SWAP IN VIENNA

Michael Barazad is on his way home. This American citizen, a U.S. embassy attaché, languished behind bars in a Pakistani jail for three years following an automobile accident in Islamabad. When his car was stopped and searched, he was accused of bribery, money laundering, and assault. His arrest triggered a diplomatic earthquake, further unbalancing already shaky relations between two nominal allies. His jailers screamed espionage. The State Department denied it. Now it appears that he may have been working for the CIA after all.

Yesterday in Vienna, American personnel turned over three young Pakistani children in exchange for Barazad. Why these children were in American custody, how they got there, where they were found, are unanswered questions.

"Will they be back?" asked Lorraine, imagining a vengeful attack on Marianne at some future date.

"Maybe they learned a lesson. I sure did, and . . ." Marianne stopped in mid-thought. "Whoops — what's that hanging around your neck?"

Lorraine blushed to the roots of her grey hair.

"This?"

She fingered the pendant dangling from a braided gold necklace; a silver swan with its neck bent in a graceful curve and wings outspread. Small diamonds sparkled on every feature.

"It's extravagant, but Howard noticed I had my eye on it and insisted."

"Howard *Turnbow* bought you that?!"

"Mmm. While we were in Reno."

"You were in *Reno* together?!" Marianne was stunned.

"Don't look so shocked. We're both widows, you know. Well, he's a widow-*er*, anyway. So what if we're not twentysomethings? We had fun."

A week later Marianne was buying groceries for a picnic. She had a date with Tom to pan for gold down on the middle fork of the Stanislaus River. He had been upgrading his gasoline-powered suction dredge and was eager to try it out. Since the launch site wasn't far from Angels Camp, she was also buying a care package for Hannah Crowfoot. The old Native woman had yet to fully recover from her ordeal at the hands of the Pakistanis, and Marianne thought she could use some TLC.

At the checkstand, a headline in the *Mountain-Democrat* newspaper made her scowl. She added a copy to her purchase:

DRONE ATTACK KILLS 12 IN YEMEN

The White House has announced another battle in the war on terror, this one fought with militiamen belonging to the rebel Ansar Al-Sharia organization on the Arabian peninsula. Twelve suspected foes of the present regime in Yemen were arranging an ambush north of the capital when a Hellfire missile from a Reaper UAV (unmanned aerial vehicle) struck their Land Rover. Four bystanders, including a mother and young infant, were among the fatalities.

Ansar representatives have disputed the U.S. account. They claim the dead tribesmen were family members on their way to a wedding in Sana'a.

Marianne winced when she read the article. She turned the page, looking for something a little less downbeat, like fires and earthquakes, and discovered another drone story:

BEALE PROTESTERS ARRESTED FOR TRESPASS

Twenty-four members of the activist group Live and Let Live were arrested in Marysville yesterday as they entered Beale Air Force Base, raised protest flags, and marched en masse along residential streets, chanting anti-drone slogans.

Nathan Harris, the group's spokesperson, vowed to fight the arrest in court as a violation of his constitutional right of free speech and his right to petition for redress of grievances.

Beale officials have admitted that their eastern perimeter is not as well-fenced as other parts of the base. They indicate changes will be made to prevent further incursions.

They also noted that Beale is not home to any armed drones. Beale reconnaissance squadrons fly RQ-4 Global Hawk and U-2 Dragon Lady intelligence-gathering aircraft only.

Sources interviewed for this story believe charges will be dismissed in order to avoid the unfavorable publicity of a court trial.

60

SEPTEMBER found Marianne pulling night shifts again. Tom Wagstaff was tied up designing a new journalism course at Sacramento State while also struggling to publish his weekly newspaper. The two lovers hardly ever saw each other.

One morning on a day off, Marianne drove up the hill to Saint Patrick's Catholic Church. She tramped around the grounds for a while, then bucked herself up and, trying to be casual, stepped into the rectory. There she was glad to see Sister Bianca, someone she knew, holding down the reception desk.

"Morning, sister."

Sister Bianca smiled a vague smile of greeting that sharpened into genuine pleasure when she recognized her infrequent visitor.

"Mary Ann, the ghost girl!" she said. "How are things on the other side these days?"

"Okay, I hope. There's no post office, you know, no email, and I haven't heard anything from the horse's mouth for ages, so I'm just guessing. Eternal, though, right? Always there, just out of reach."

"Yes, where are the heavenly cell phones? No doubt the Almighty has His reasons. What's on your mind this morning?"

"Is there a priest around? I'd like some advice. It's not confessional, just, I dunno, some help."

"Early mass is over, and Father Dirksen has gone down to Lodi this morning."

"Here's the thing," said Marianne, plunging in. "I'm seeing this guy, Tom. For a while now. I think he's going to make a move, and I don't know what to do."

"What do you mean?"

"Well, he's a teacher, a journalist, a desk jockey, and I'm a rootin'-tootin' cowgirl. I don't know if it's going to work."

"I'm sure you know *I* can't offer any advice. Maybe if you were looking for the right kind of dishwashing soap, but life choices? Sorry, dear."

Marianne wasn't giving up.

"Suppose — hypothetically, then — that I had this boyfriend, and things are going to happen, what do you think?"

"Does this hypothetical person have a job lined up in L.A., and you'd rather move to Idaho?"

"No, nothing like that."

"That simplifies matters. Does he love you?"

"Pretty sure."

"Do you love him?"

"Hypothetically . . . that would be the problem."

"No, no, I'm sure Father Dirksen would agree — that's the solution."

Marianne expelled a huge sigh of relief.

"You already knew the answer," said Sister Bianca.

"Probably . . . it's good to hear it out loud."

She thanked the nun, squeezed her hand, and skipped away on lighter feet.

▼

Tom Wagstaff finished his academic designs. He put the latest *County Courier* to bed. He suggested dinner to his main squeeze. She checked her schedule and accepted.

They motored down to Rossi's Fine Italian Dining in Wagstaff's big yellow Toyota. It was a fair evening with twilight lingering under a pale sky. They were shown to seats on the patio overlooking the Tarvolo golf course, where they ordered glasses of red wine.

"Cheers, M," said Wagstaff.

"À votre santé."

They sipped their wine in a comfortable silence that slowly became awkward.

"Hey, look — a coyote." He pointed toward the 18th fairway where, indeed, a blond doglike creature was loping across the course.

"Let's go for a walk. Might see a deer out there."

Wagstaff reached over and pulled Marianne upright. They strolled onto the grass, holding hands, walking quietly. He guided them to a stand of conifers on a little knoll.

"Sent the latest edition of the *Courier* to the printers," he said.

"Unh-huh."

"It's pretty good. Exposé of that mini-mall proposal smack on Ragtown's designated park land."

She chuckled. "Howard will be pissed."

"Yes he will."

Wagstaff pulled a folded-up slice of newspaper out of his pocket.

"That it? That the article?"

"No, just some back pages stuff."

He unfolded the clipping with theatrical flare and showed her the headline:

SARZEAU & WAGSTAFF TO WED

"Holy crap — tell me you didn't print that!"

"Of course not . . . next week, I hope."

He got down on one knee, as tradition demanded, and presented her with a diamond ring in a little velvet box.

"Marry me?"

Marianne frowned.

"Listen, Tom. Full disclosure. These days I see auras. A couple of months back I learned how to command spirits. I mix potions, I cast spells. Sometimes I see a ghost in the mirror."

"So what?"

She bent forward and kissed him.

"So, you *know* what. The answer you're looking for. But — whoooo — are you sure about this?"

"You bet I am. What's the problem?"

"Well, think what you're getting into . . ."

She airily waved a hand.

" . . . I'm a witch."

▲   ▲   ▲